# Tangled PATHS

## TANGLED IN TIME BOOK 2

### CAROLINE CORVIN

First published in 2022 by Grenwyvern Publishing

Auckland, New Zealand



Cover design © 2023 Covers By Jules

www.carolinecorvin.com

# Content Warning



TO WRITE ROMANCE is to write about life in all its beauty and ugliness, joy and sadness. In my work, you will encounter all of these, therefore parts of Tangled Paths may be confronting, or triggering for some readers.

If you are concerned that this story may include sensitive topics for you, I encourage you to visit my website www.carolinecorvin.com and check out the content warning. Please, take care of yourself first when deciding if this book is right for you.

XO Caroline

Invasion

# Calum

Helmand Province, Afghanistan – November, 2012

Dust prickled at his eyes, crusted around his nostrils and penetrated his throat, despite the grimy bandana wound tight for protection. The taste of red dirt sat silt-like on his tongue, its acrid smell inescapable.

At least he was in the lead vehicle, not like the poor bastards behind. They bore the full brunt of the dust stream kicked up by the hurtling sand-coloured Husky, its armoured nose set on course for the base. Inside the convoy, the human cargo also had its sights set on the destination, every man and woman fantasising about showers and a meal, thankful that their training mission with the local Afghan troops was complete.

On all sides, the view was the same: golden-hued hills, their jagged edges stark against a harsh blue sky. He had seen many barren landscapes, even had a soft spot for some of them—the rocky upper reaches of the Cuillins on Skye, the emptiness of Glencoe. His homeland had its share of emptiness. But nothing like this. No touch of heather to relieve the endless beige, no brave sprouts of tussock springing between the rocky outcrops.

He hadn't predicted how much he'd miss the water either, until he'd arrived in this landlocked country, trapped with no possibility of escape to a sparkling seafront to soothe the mind. And all of this magnified by the heat, oppressive and unrelenting.

Raised in Scotland, you only considered rain and snow bad weather if you chose the wrong clothing. Here there was no clothing that could ward off the daily assault of the sun. Even tossing off all your clothes and running around naked would only result in sunburn in unpleasant places and a visit from the army shrink. Each morning he'd wake up to see not a single cloud in the sky, not a hint of rain, and think "Another fucking sunny day." His mates at home, toiling in grey British weather, would consider that a cause for envy. How wrong they'd be.

Calum glanced at his driver, a feisty young Welsh woman whose delight in barrelling down the rough roads sparkled in her eyes, the only part of her visible above her own protective fabric mask. He'd found out that Erin Davies and he shared a common passion for the outdoors. They'd filled many a long dusty ride reminiscing about home. So while he used thoughts of Scottish mountains and lochs as an escape from the reality of this hell-hole, he knew Davies was, in her mind, walking the hills of Wales. Or perhaps belting around its back roads, given her love of wrangling vehicles. He liked riding shotgun with her. She was a handy medic and a capable driver, but that dry sense of humour set her apart from the others.

"Not too hard on your arse there?" she yelled over the clatter of the vehicle as they juddered across a particularly rocky patch and he grabbed at the dash to steady himself.

"You testing my limits, Davies?"

"Nah, I know you're a tough old bugger."

He laughed. Old? He knew only a couple of years separated them in age, but in terms of time here, yes, he was old. Three years to her six months. Three bloody long years. He had no regrets about joining the army. In fact, he loved the life. But lately he'd become nostalgic for home, perusing other assignments, even going so far as considering his resignation. He was growing old—and sentimental, too.

And the incident last year no doubt had something to do with it. Despite his training and experience, he'd been ill-prepared for that day. Not physically. Not mentally while it was happening. And certainly not for the aftermath. No one told you how to erase those images from your mind. Memories of that day, almost nine months back, would always haunt him.

———

The patrol was making a careful sweep through an abandoned village. They had a band of ragtag but brutally effective rebels on the run. All along their escape route, villagers fled for the safety of the mountains, not wishing to encounter the rebels, and even fearful of the pursuing British soldiers. Calum and his patrol traced their way through empty streets, the weight of their heavy combat gear cruel under the searing noonday sun.

"Poor bastards," he'd thought, seeing the scattered possessions in the houses, on the streets, all left behind in the inhabitants' decision to put their lives ahead of their meagre belongings. The smell of decay permeated the air, rising in waves from the debris underfoot.

A stick-thin donkey, ribs standing out like fence railings, bleated in a plaintive voice. It lifted its head slightly as they passed, the fly-encrusted eyes imploring them to stop. Lying on the roadside, discarded as of no use to the fleeing inhabitants, it had one grotesquely distorted leg, obviously broken. He made a note to ask one guy to come back and put the thing out of its misery when they'd finished their reconnaissance.

The team moved on past this only sign of life, their disciplined movements quick yet hushed, ears straining for any sound of humans.

Coming to an abrupt halt, with a raised hand, he silently signalled Foster, the man beside him, to do the same. There was a sound. Not his imagination. It was a baby. The distinctive squawk of a very young baby. Then it stopped, choked off.

Foster gestured at a house down a narrow side street, a battered iron door blocking the entrance. Calum nodded in agreement and the two men set off, their stealthy footsteps light as dancers, with little sound betraying their approach.

Before they could reach the door, it burst open, and an Afghan man toppled out into the street, falling in an untidy heap almost at Foster's feet. Seeing the pair of guns trained on him, he stretched out his hands, palms upwards, the gesture suggesting he posed no threat. A frightened torrent of words cascaded from his mouth.

Calum inwardly cursed himself for his lack of ability in the language. He'd relied heavily on the local interpreters and now regretted it. The speed at which the man spoke meant there was no way he could piece together his meaning. He appeared unarmed, not the enemy, but their training told them to assume nothing. They were fighting a war where rebel fighters were indiscernible from the locals. To assume anything invited death.

A flicker of movement in the doorway drew Calum's eyes. There was someone else hidden in the gloom of the house. He swivelled his gun in that direction, leaving Foster to cover the man at his feet. A second person appeared, roughly thrust out into the sunlight. The woman, her eyes wide with fear, cradled the source of the sound. In her arms, the tiny baby wailed more loudly, both its voice and slitted eyes protesting the bright light. The man behind her was barely visible. One arm wrapped tightly around her neck, trapping her head against his chest. In that hand, he clasped a knife pressed to the side of her throat. His other arm pointed a gun.

Calum knew the sour taste that swamped his mouth. Fear. He swallowed it down. There was no room for that today. People said that in moments like that, time stood still. But not for him. It was over in seconds. The staccato of gunfire, a thud as the wounded Foster sprawled on the ground, the screaming woman, the crying baby, the kneeling man pleading. And amongst that cacophony, he'd acted.

He stopped, forcing himself to put away thoughts of that day, as he'd put aside the medal he'd earned for his actions. In this job, it was best not to revisit those memories. While he felt pride that he'd saved four lives that day—Foster, a woman, a child, the father—you never really recovered from taking a life. Not at close range like that. Not even if it was one of the bad guys. Much better to resume his reveries of home.

Through the late afternoon haze, he could faintly make out a rocky path etched into the side of the rugged hills to the left of the road. It reminded him of one of his favourite hiking spots. In his mind, he returned to relive a late summer trek up Beinn Alligin, imagining its steep winding route and the vista from the top where you were king of the world with the sea and islands laid out beneath you. He'd definitely head up there when his next home leave came through. Only a month more to go.

"Shit!" Davies wrestled the vehicle hard to the left.

Something had spooked a mob of goats, and they tumbled from between high rocky outcrops to their right, sprawling across the road in front of the vehicle. She could have mowed them down without the bulky military transport even missing a beat, shaking off their shaggy bodies like feathers. But for a moment the instincts of a Welsh country girl overruled all her army driver training, as she tried to avoid them. The knobbled wheels tracked off the graded road surface, kicking up bigger plumes of fine, dusty desert sand.

The explosion came without warning, tossing the seven-ton vehicle as if it weighed nothing, its four occupants flung about like rag dolls. It barrel-rolled a few times and came to rest, rocking lightly back and forth with a creaking sound. Gunfire rang out and the convoy's machine guns swiftly chattered in reply.

It was a freak injury, they told him later. The gear stick rammed into Calum's thigh, pinning him there, finding an artery. He only remembered the blood: the metallic taste in his mouth, its cloying odour, the rhythmic pulse in his body and the delicate flow across the skin of his leg exposed by the shredded army fatigues. But strangely, there was no pain. The look on Davies' face as she loomed over him told him it was bad.

"I hope they get the bastards."

His last conscious thought. Then blissful oblivion descended upon him as he accepted, more calmly than he'd ever imagined, that he was going to die. He'd rehearsed dying in his head. Saying goodbye to the world, the people that mattered, Mam, his friends. But just as today's journey hadn't gone to plan, so today's dying had thrown out the script, his mind ad-libbing, abandoning the practised lines.

He was on a mountain top, somewhere in the north. He could see the sun setting over the western isles, a fiery red. Red sky at night, shepherd's delight. He turned to his companion. At least he wouldn't die alone. And then confusion overtook him. He was unsure why thoughts of death permeated this evening here on Beinn Alligin, when simply looking at her made him feel so alive, swept up in a rush of elation that she was there, beside him.

A tangle of wild, dark hair framed her heart-shaped face, giving her an untamed appearance. Eyes the colour of whisky, large and thick-lashed, met his, and he read desire written there. Her generous mouth held the hint of a smile. Accepting the invitation of her full lips, he leaned forward to kiss them, losing himself in the taste of her, inhaling the smell of her, like the heather, sweet and woody.

She drew back, smiled down at him from beneath a wayward spiral of hair. Just above one dark arched eyebrow, he caught the gleam of a scar, a jagged zig-zag. It relieved the almost perfect symmetry of her face. He smiled to himself, thinking there was perfection in this imperfection.

There was a brief flicker of a question. Who was this woman who'd unexpectedly invaded his mind? The face of a stranger, her name eluded him, but her hand tracing the shape of his compliant body as it moulded itself to hers, was the knowing touch of a lover. Calum clasped her to him, anchoring himself in the moment, as powerful emotions forced their way to the surface. He gently drew her down to lie by his side.

"It'll be ok," she said. "Lie still." She rolled over to blanket him, the weight of her comforting as she pinned him beneath her, the rocky ground nudging sharply into his back.

———

A stab of pain in his leg jarred him away from the sensations, a moan swelling up from deep in his gut. Later, he was unsure if the wave of distress that overwhelmed him was the sudden awareness of his injury or the pain of being dragged from her embrace. He struggled against it, longing to return to her, but they wouldn't let him.

The face looking down at him now was familiar. Davies, her eyes clouded with concern, the small dark brows knotted, and her voice commanding.

"Lie still Mac. We've got this, but you need to lie still." He realised the immense pressure on his leg was from the full force of her diminutive body pressing down on it. His head swam.

"Stay with me. Stay with me, Mac." He didn't want to stay. He had somewhere else to be, someone to be with.

Urgent voices and running heavy-booted feet approached. Davies drew back as others crowded him. He could feel the decisiveness in their deft movements. Davies' small hand reached for his, clasping it in reassurance, cementing him in the here and now.

Today was a rehearsal. Dying was for another day.

Part 1 – Here

CHAPTER 1

Conscripted

# *Sarah*

Wellington, New Zealand – July, 2007

SARAH DUMPED THE LARGE awkward box at the top of the staircase and slumped beside it. She brushed back a rogue strand of dark hair, escaped from her practical ponytail. Below her, Mel teetered up the stairs, dwarfed by another massive box. Sarah hadn't seen her closest friend for three months and now, on the first day of her Wellington holiday, they were spending it as unpaid labour.

"What's wrong with this picture?" she asked. "Tell me again why your sister, who has an unlimited budget to pay a moving company, has the two of us lugging boxes on her behalf?" Claire was such a piece of work. She had no shame in manipulating people to do her bidding.

"I know, I know." Mel grumpily launched her burden onto the landing, turning to perch on the top step next to her. "She said it's because she didn't want the packers handling all her personal stuff. Seems she heard horror stories about pervy removal men going through ladies' undies."

"Hmm, well I can't believe any one woman owns this much underwear."

"No, not underwear in these. She's bringing that. No, she's given us her entire evening wear wardrobe to transport in these boxes. But that has its benefits."

"You reckon? And what would those be?"

"Follow me," Mel said mysteriously as she wrangled one box into her arms and headed towards a bedroom.

They navigated around Claire and Jonathan's substantial bed, which, despite its magnitude, appeared tiny in the space. Beyond that, a closed door suggested an adjoining room.

"Now," said Mel, pushing it open, "what Claire calls her walk-in wardrobe is what the rest of us call a spare bedroom."

Sarah followed her into the room, seeing three walls lined with well-stocked shelves of shoes, banks of drawers, and poles crowded with coat hangers. The fourth was the backdrop for a dressing table featuring an enormous mirror framed by Hollywood lights. Floor-length dresses in silk and lace already adorned some hangers. Mel placed the enormous box down with a thud, clawed open the top, and from the depths produced a similar gown, this one in a startling magenta. The satin made an expensive rustle and shards of light bounced off its narrow diamante straps as she shook it free of its clear plastic cloak. A faint smell of perfume, Claire's signature expensive perfume, wafted up, intermingling with the pungent remnants of dry-cleaning chemicals.

"The benefit is we choose whatever we like from all of these to wear to the party on Saturday."

"It's that formal? We need a gown?"

"Oh yes. Claire and Jonathan are desperate to launch themselves back into the social scene with a bang. I mean, one would need to celebrate after the hardship of six months living in a two thousand square metre apartment in the city."

"Yes, it must have been simply dreadful." Sarah smirked at the sarcasm they reserved for Mel's sister and her husband.

For most people, the Khandallah mansion they were sitting in would have been perfectly adequate as it was when they'd bought it. But Claire and Jonathan weren't most people, insisting they couldn't possibly live in the house as it was. It might be the right address, but they considered it uninhabitable until the completion of an entire makeover. Now it was done, and they were eager to show it off to all their friends.

Sarah was unsure whether the party coinciding with her two-week stay in Wellington with Mel was a good thing or not. She had never been to one of their soirees before and was curious. But she had met some of their friends over the years and none had impressed her. These people were uniformly snobbish, their money and their power within the country's economic elite giving them a sense of entitlement and an air of disdain for more ordinary mortals such as Sarah. Simply opening her mouth would be enough to repel them, let alone if she confessed to her current employment as a dairy farm worker. Even if it was on a large and productive family farm. Even if it was a conscious choice she'd made to return home, leaving behind the life she really wanted to salvage her father's.

"I know some of the guests won't be our sort of people…" Mel had seen the battle between the competing voices in Sarah's head written on her face.

"*Some* of the guests?" She couldn't hide her scepticism.

"OK. Most of them. But it will be a chance to dress up, eat great food, drink expensive champagne—and they've got a band, so there'll be dancing in the ballroom."

"All right. You convinced me with promises of champagne."

"So, help me unpack this box. Then there are another four filled with evening clothes to come up. After which, we are going to play dress-ups."

By the time they had finished unpacking, Sarah counted at least thirty gowns in a rainbow of colours, each jostling for attention amongst her equally beautiful neighbours. Who even owned that many evening gowns? She knew Claire was loaded, but this seemed excessive, even for her.

An hour later, after they'd helped each other in and out of nearly half of the selection, the shortlisted gowns hung separated from the others, projecting an almost palpable pride at being chosen ahead of the competition.

"What do you think? The gold or the red?" Sarah asked.

"Definitely the red. It's your colour. And you'll make a splash amongst that conservative lot. They usually turn up in twenty different shades of black. Claire's kaleidoscopic wardrobe is a rarity amongst her friends."

"How about you?"

"I'm thinking of the green. Not a colour I'd usually go for, but I love the cut."

"You know we're going to freeze our arses off in these dresses at this time of year?"

"Nah, Claire will have the central heating cranked up to the maximum. Not to mention all the hot air blowing around with that many oversized egos gathered in one place."

Sarah laughed. "You're not doing anything to reassure me I'll even enjoy this party."

"Oh, I guarantee you will. How long is it since we've been to a party together?"

"Too long."

"Right before we bundle up these beauties, one more thing I *must* show you. Come and look in here."

She beckoned Sarah over to a large, mirrored sliding door.

"Take a look at that," Mel said, pushing it across with a flourish to reveal yet another wardrobe space. Inside was only one item, a coat unlike any

Sarah had ever seen. It was fur, of an intense black, constructed from rows of silky pelts, evenly coloured and lush in texture, combined with such skill, that it was impossible to see evidence of a seam joining them. While captivating in its beauty, the coat was also repulsive. She shuddered at the thought of all those small animals' lives sacrificed for this rich woman's vanity.

It wasn't the killing of them. After all, she herself was a pragmatic farmer's daughter who had no illusions about where meat and leather came from. But she'd seen the photos of those poor wee animals, living their brief lives in overcrowded cages and horrendous conditions. No, to call it farming gave the rest of them a bad name.

"Ugh," she said. "Why does it not surprise me that Claire's turned a blind eye to the anti-fur movement? And where on earth is she ever going to wear it? It's not as if you get Siberian temperatures here."

"I know. I don't even ask questions like that anymore. I've given up trying with Claire. She's definitely gone over to the dark side. Sometimes I can't believe we grew up in the same family."

Melanie and Claire were born ordinary Kiwi girls, into a middle class family, their mother a teacher and father an accountant. But Claire had tossed all of her down-to-earth upbringing aside the moment she'd set eyes on Jonathan Blackwood. After a whirlwind courtship and eight years of marriage, Claire Blackwood was indistinguishable from the other capital city society wives, burying her humble past deep down where there was no chance of it surfacing to tarnish her carefully curated life.

"Animal ethics aside, even the cost of a coat like that seems obscene."

Sarah turned her back on the fur and focused on the red ball gown, holding it against her as she studied her reflection in a mirror. Yes, the colour suited her, showing off the faint tan she wore year round from her outdoor work, and contrasting with her dark hair—although she'd need Mel's help to tame that into a suitably elegant style.

The thought of the party gave her a warm surge of excitement. It would be a welcome reprieve from the monotonous sameness that overlaid her life lately. And a chance to have fun with this person standing next to her.

Mel, her best friend and confidante, was not only her physical opposite, with her pixie blond hair, and eyes grey like a Wellington sky, but so different in many other ways. Mel was quiet and nurturing, making her the perfect person for welcoming five-year-old students into school. Sarah was loud and confident, and more likely to challenge the kids to a wrestling match. But placed as roommates in the university hall of residence back in that first year, an unlikely friendship had blossomed. Mel had seen her through seven years of the best and worst times of her life.

"Right, grab that dress and let's get out of here," Sarah said. "Before your sister arrives and finds another job for us to do."

"And you need to get back to work on that proposal. I'll throw together some dinner while you work on your future."

Mel was such a gem. She knew without saying that Sarah was nervous about tomorrow's meeting. Three years ago, the university wanted to welcome her with open arms. A keen mind, a top scholar, all the qualities they demanded in prospective doctoral students. But that was before her world fell apart, catapulting her back to life in a rural backwater. And taking the edge off her confidence, leaving her with unfamiliar feelings of doubt in her ability to cut it with the best in academia. She wrapped an arm around her friend's shoulders and tried to summon that confidence now.

"Thanks hun, I appreciate it. Of course, it's also safer that way. You know me too well to let me loose in your kitchen." Mel smiled, having witnessed many of Sarah's history of culinary failures. "And yes, a couple of hours and I'll be ready for whatever Professor Jermaine plans to throw at me."

"Happy to do anything I can to help, my nerdy little friend. After all, to have you back in Welly would be amazing—same as the old days."

'Nerd' was an apt description. She *was* a nerd, loving nothing better than to bury her head in a dusty old history tome, keeping company with ancient Romans, sometimes to the neglect of real live modern people. But it was only when Mel said the word that it sounded like an endearment rather than an insult. New Zealanders on the whole valued practical knowledge above cerebral pursuits, regarding scholars with suspicion. Fortunately, her earthy rural upbringing allowed her to have one foot in both worlds. But it was the academia she'd been forced to abandon three years ago that beckoned her back now. All she had to do was overcome the unexpected shadow of imposter syndrome that lurked at her shoulder, attempting to sow seeds of doubt in her mind. She must show her old supervisor that she still had what it took.

"It's already good to be back, and maybe next time it will be to stay," Sarah said, closing the massive front door of the mansion behind them with a thud.

Dodging the raindrops, they plunged into the shelter of Mel's ancient wagon. It was embarrassingly tired, definitely not cool, and a stark contrast to Claire's Bentley convertible that had nosed into the driveway beside them. Mel edged the car into the tree-lined street while Sarah tossed a cheerful wave at Claire. Her sharp blonde bob framed a face filled with dismay as she realised her conscripted workers were making their escape.

## CHAPTER 2

# Party Girls

## Sarah

Wellington, New Zealand – July, 2007

THE YOUNG WAITER WAS careful not to waste a single drop as he filled her glass. The eye-wateringly expensive champagne flowed freely and there was no chance of it running out at this party. As Sarah waited, there was a prickling on the back of her neck and the vague sensation of being watched. She turned and met the intense stare of a man who was casually leaning against the door to the deck. He was in conversation with another, but appeared to be paying little attention, his sharp blue eyes fixed firmly on her. He was the epitome of casual elegance: a tan sports coat, white linen shirt, and dark tailored pants. Although conservative, his attire suggested a streak of non-conformity, standing out as he did from the other black-suited bowtie wearing males in the room.

"Oh god, Richard Norton," Mel hissed in her ear. "Don't make eye contact. You don't want him coming over here."

But it was too late. She had made eye contact and she could see the attractive, dark-haired man brushing off the person he'd been conversing with as he prepared to thread his way through the throng of people.

"Why?" She couldn't detect any hint of menace about him.

"Let's just say he's someone you'd rather not know. I'll fill you in later. Oh my god, he's coming our way."

There was a note of panic in Mel's voice, disproportionate to the amiable expression of the approaching man. The crowd parted before him, like fawning minor nobility making way at the approach of the king.

Within moments, Richard Norton was standing beside her, not quite in her personal space but far too close to be comfortable, given Mel's aversion to the man. And too close to ignore without appearing rude.

"Sir?" The young man at the bar acknowledged his presence.

"Whisky," he said. "No ice. Neat."

No 'please'—merely a terse request. It sounded like Richard Norton made sure the wait staff knew their place.

He turned to her, extending a large slender hand, with immaculately groomed nails, and a wide platinum wedding band. Now, at this range, she could see he was older than his boyish smile suggested, much older than her, in fact. At least forty, but damn if he wasn't good-looking.

She'd always brushed off the admiring glances and occasional advances of older men. There was something weird about hooking up with a man who was already dating before you were born. Which was odd once she thought about it, because she'd struggled to find anyone suitable amongst those of a more appropriate age. She'd gone out with some guys her own age who'd proved immature to the point of embarrassment. It was surprising to find how little they'd learned in the same twenty-six years she'd spent on this earth. There'd been others who lacked ambition and offered only prospects of a dull future within their tiny constricted worlds. It occurred to her that a dalliance with a more worldly older man might be an intriguing new experience.

"I'm Richard. We haven't met before, have we?" His voice was silky smooth, and radiated warmth, in distinct contrast to those glacial eyes.

"No," she spluttered. His rapid approach and Mel's warning had squashed her normal confidence. But she bounced back quickly. "Sarah," she said, meeting his gaze.

She stretched out her own hand, resplendent with the long red artificial nails that Mel had insisted were necessary, placing it in his chilly grasp. She shivered at his touch. It was cool, like his eyes.

"Hello Richard," Mel said, her tone wary. Most unlike Mel, whose naïve innocence generally led her to think the best of people. Sarah was on full alert. But the man didn't seem to notice, or if he did, wasn't the least bit deterred.

"Melanie," he said. "Haven't seen you for a while. Of course, with Claire and Jonathan not entertaining while the house renovations were going on. But here we are then, back to the usual social whirl. So is the lovely Sarah a friend of yours?" He spoke to Mel, but he had his eyes firmly fixed on Sarah.

"Yes, we went to uni together," Mel said.

"Oh, so what did you study, Sarah? A teacher like Melanie?"

"No, I did an MA, majored in history and a minor in classics," she replied with a smile, her confidence returned.

She was proud of her achievements. First Class Honours, even though they'd counted for naught since then. Her daily companions, the dairy cows with their soft muzzles and long lashes, demanded little and weren't the best conversationalists. And in provincial New Zealand, there weren't too many people who relished an in-depth conversation on the death throes of the Roman Empire. No one else who, as a small child, had fallen in love with the tale of Boadicea, developing an obsession with all things Roman Britain. But tonight, to say it out loud was satisfying, a definitive step towards reclaiming the person she'd been, who she wanted to be again. Yesterday's meeting with Professor Jermaine gave her hope that the three-year nightmare was almost over. He'd promised nothing yet, but he'd not rejected her proposal either.

Richard chuckled. "Why am I not surprised? A beautiful girl like you can always go where the whim takes you, not restricted to career-minded subjects. Flashing one of those smiles alone could convince any man to keep you in style."

She blanched a little at his flattery. She'd not traded on her looks, always preferring to rely on her intellect. And she had no ambition to become a kept woman. No, she would never consider relinquishing her independence for that.

But before she could fire a shot back at him, the band struck up a tune and couples immediately flooded the dance floor. Sarah had never been in a house like this before, where there was an actual ballroom. She hadn't known such houses existed in New Zealand.

"Dance with me, Sarah," he said.

It wasn't a question. Even though he spoke politely, it had the air of a command. Her instincts told her to refuse, but still unnerved by the surroundings, she couldn't think how to decline without causing a fuss. She took his hand and followed him to join the whirling group of dancers.

Sarah was an accomplished dancer, thanks to her dad. He was of the generation that grew up with weekly dances at the local War Memorial Hall. In fact, that's where he'd met her mother. And so while by day her father stomped around the farm in clunky gumboots, on a dance floor he glided, his feet sure, his arm propelling his partner skilfully, effortlessly navigating the traffic of other couples. At their country school they'd learned all the old-fashioned dances: waltz, foxtrot and the Gay Gordons. But it was Dad who'd taken on the task of polishing his daughters' education in this area, so they could account themselves adequately at the annual Young Farmers Club Ball, the Western Rugby Club Cabaret and the Wakefield Hall Society's winter fundraising dances.

Richard was equally skilled, but unlike the partners she'd danced with before, held her unnervingly close, far too familiar for someone who she'd only just met. She was acutely conscious of the weight of his hand on her back, firm and assertive. And of the attractive male smell of him, overlaid with a woody fragrance.

"You aren't from Wellington are you," he purred in her ear. He was tall, and although she was too, she felt tiny in his overwhelming presence. "This is a small town. I'm sure I'd have seen you before."

"No," she said, deciding to meet his forthright manner in the same way. "I was at university here, but I'm from Wakefield. A little place in Taranaki. I went back there after I graduated."

"Yes, I should have guessed. You have that provincial drawl."

She flashed him a look of reproach. Exactly what she'd expected from one of the snobs who circulated in these waters. He caught her meaning and backtracked immediately.

"Oh no, I didn't mean to imply anything negative by that. It was merely an observation. To be honest, it's quite refreshing in this world where everyone thinks that a faux-Oxbridge accent is some badge of honour."

His own accent was neutral. Definitely not a country hick, but not possessing the overly English-sounding affectations of most of the people in the room.

"Nice save," she said. "I'll forgive you—for now."

Even clasped close to him, she knew he had a smirk on his face, delighted that she'd not hesitated to call him on it.

"Tell me, how does a beautiful, educated woman like you exist somewhere like that without totally losing your mind from boredom? Surely the local yokels aren't up to discussing the fall of the Roman Empire or quoting Greek philosophers to you?"

She met his eyes this time. This man's questions were not the usual type of first dance patter. He raised one eyebrow as if waiting for her to challenge this statement as well, then continued.

"My favourite–if you get a good wife, you'll be happy; if you get a bad one, you'll become a philosopher." His eyes twinkled with mischief. "I love Socrates," he said. "The man had a sense of humour."

"Once made equal to man, woman becomes his superior," she flung back at him. "Also Socrates, and on that one, I don't think he was joking."

He laughed. It was a warm, friendly sound, and she relaxed a little in his arms. In fact, she was enjoying the sensation of whirling around the floor with such a capable partner. She loved to dance, and it took her back to happy times. Her father and mother, still so in love after thirty years of marriage, in perfect time, eyes locked, and a youthful aura about them as they danced as they'd done in their courting days. She and her two sisters, coupled with some of the local lads, earnest young men, their lives already wedded to the family farms, joining the older couples of the district in an annual celebration of rural life. Good times, long gone now.

She was disappointed at being pulled from this reverie when the music tapered off and Richard led her off the dance floor. He guided her with a firm arm around her waist, not back to the corner where Mel waited with a questioning expression, but through the doors onto the deck. He plucked two glasses of champagne from the tray of a passing server and handed one to her. She took a sip, enjoying the ping of the tiny bubbles bursting and the sweet foamy fragrance that tantalised her nose.

Outside, the air was cool, and despite the glaring honour guard of elaborate patio heaters, she shivered a little. It was after all the middle of winter and the particular ballgown of Claire's that she'd selected, while flattering her figure, left her shoulders bare. Its deep plunging neckline was far more suited to summer, and she could feel her nipples standing upright in protest at the cold. She didn't dare look down to check whether this fact was as obvious to others as it was to her. Maybe it was, because at that moment, with one deft move, Richard slipped off his jacket, cloaking her with it.

"Is that better?" he asked with a smile.

"Yes, thank you," she said, quietly pleased at his attentiveness. Quite the gentleman.

"Well, I hope you don't mind, but I wanted to have some time with you all to myself."

"I don't mind, but perhaps your wife will," she said, meeting his eyes directly.

"Oh, I can guarantee she won't. She's two hundred miles and five years away from caring about what I get up to."

Sarah frowned, confused at his response.

"We are *divorced*," he said, "a fact for which we are both equally grateful."

"So why the wedding ring?"

He shrugged, his face nonchalant. "The same reason many single women choose to keep a ring on their finger—a reasonably effective means of deflecting unwanted attention. Most of the time."

"Oh," she said. "I've heard some see it as a challenge. Be careful. It might actually make you a target."

She felt a warm sense of satisfaction at eliciting an approving burst of laughter from him.

Although he had to be in his forties, he was an attractive man. She'd taken the opportunity to scrutinise him discreetly as they danced, taking in the strong features softened by a mouth that turned up at the corners even when relaxed, as if suppressing a smile. And of course those arresting blue eyes. With his jacket off, she could see the hint of a well-honed body under the expensive-looking shirt. She imagined that his physical appeal, coupled with the money and power wielded by the men in this social circle, ensured he was an obvious target for aspiring social-climbers, hoping to snare themselves the perfect husband.

Sarah had disliked the men she'd encountered on the past brief occasions where her social life intersected with that of Claire and Jonathan. They were a pompous bunch, puffed up with their own self-importance and a desperate need to be admired. She decided that from his dress alone, it might be worth giving Richard a little more of her time. Attired with a casual elegance, unlike the other men, it suggested he didn't fit the mould. It could be a hint that he was different in other ways. She was curious. He must have sensed the questions that were tumbling in her head.

"Shall I give you the short version so we can put that behind us?" he said. "I married Victoria when I was twenty-two, fresh out of university. Christchurch born and bred like me. Her father was in banking, my boss. He wanted a bright and ambitious match for his daughter, and someone to work their way up in the firm. I was that bright, ambitious young man, offered a jumpstart on my career, and a wife whose connections could catapult me several rungs up the social ladder."

*Unbelievable.* That was practically an arranged marriage. Marrying for money and position. What a repellent notion.

"Don't judge me too harshly. It wasn't quite as awful as it sounds."

She knew the disdain in her mind had overflowed onto her face.

"Victoria was—is—a great girl. Attractive, personable, and although we were pretty much thrust into marriage by circumstances, we were friends and I think we loved each other a little. But it's no basis for a marriage. We grew up, grew apart, but stayed together in name only. Because of our two beautiful daughters. And because I couldn't have put Victoria through the shame her father would have heaped on her for a failed marriage. Finally, when the old bastard died, we were no longer trapped in the web he'd woven. We decided it was time to take back control of our lives."

"So, how old are your children?" she asked, in her mind picturing little dark-haired girls in frilly dresses, with the same blue eyes as their father.

"Hannah's nineteen, first year law at Otago University. Chelsea's sixteen, boarding at Nga Tawa. Not far up the road, so we catch up often."

*Oh my god, nineteen and sixteen.* While she'd decided his age wasn't something that stood in the way of her flirting with Richard, mention of those girls uncomfortably close to her own age put things in a different light.

"But we've talked far too much about me. Tell me about you. The long version."

And so she did. He'd been so open about himself, to a surprising degree, considering they'd met thirty minutes ago. That, and the fact he was easy to talk to, by turns smiling and encouraging, serious and sympathetic, invited Sarah to let her guard down. No doubt aided by multiple glasses of champagne, she let Richard into her life. The country girl, the youngest of three. The teenager who'd escaped her rural backwater, driven by her passion for the past, to immerse herself in five years at university. And now her current life, managing the family farm, milking cows, raising calves.

She could see disbelief in his eyes. That was to be expected. Dressed like this, her expensive gown was far removed from the rough work shirts and jeans, the gumboots and overalls that made up her workday wardrobe. Even she found it difficult to believe her own transformation. She only omitted telling him one thing, and she was thankful he didn't think to ask, even though she'd sensed the question on his lips. She avoided the reason she'd gone back to the farm, making no mention of the accident that had taken her mother's life and derailed her own. That was one step too far with someone new.

Twice she glimpsed Mel shooting concerned looks her way. The first time she smiled and waved back, communicating that she was enjoying Richard's company and didn't need rescuing. Mel returned a hesitant smile. The second time, she experienced a twinge of guilt at having left her friend amid a party where, although she knew many of the guests, she was unlikely to be enjoying the company.

"Richard, I think Melanie might need me for something." She looked to where Mel's beckoning eyes met hers from the doorway.

"Best you go then, although I say that with reluctance. To make up for abandoning me, promise you'll save me a dance?"

He held her to that promise, later weaving his way purposefully through the now drunken crowd as the band leader announced their last set. This time, she willingly stepped into the circle of his arms and relaxed into the rhythm of the music. This time his embrace was familiar and comfortable, tempered by what she had learned about him since that first dance. He wasn't quite the ogre Mel had painted him to be. She'd already told her so. But Mel's reaction had still been wary. Sarah reassured herself with the thought he had claimed this dance, not simply because she was a pretty young woman in a glamorous dress. She hoped that, now he understood a little about the person inside it, Richard was intrigued to know more.

When the last notes of the final slow dance trailed off, he gently leaned in, tilted her head upwards and kissed her cheek. It was a gentlemanly kiss, not beyond the bounds of what might be acceptable from someone she'd only just met, but enough to convey the promise of something more should she wish. As she bid him goodnight, there was a small unexpected pang of regret that the party was over.

---

Mel resumed her interrogation the moment they were in the back of the taxi. It wasn't far from upmarket Khandallah to Mel's grungy Newtown flat, but it was far enough for her to extract all the details she needed to know about Sarah's evening.

"So, tell me, you and Richard seemed pretty cosy there at the end?"

"Yeah, I suppose so," Sarah mused, feeling an unexpected dreamy happiness at the thought. "He's not what I expected. Based on your reaction to him, I was prepared for him to be a real jerk. But he was nice, easy to talk to." She turned to Mel, curious. "Why don't you like him?"

"Oh, it's not that there's really anything *wrong* with him. He's not the snob that some of those guys are, less so even than Jonathan. I mean, he doesn't have to impress anyone. He's at the top of the food chain. But to be honest, I've always found him intimidating. He's so bloody direct. And when he looks at you with those eyes, it's like you're a mouse and he's a hawk about to grab you and rip your guts out."

"That's a little dramatic." Sarah laughed at her friend's unusual discomfort. "But I know what you mean about those eyes. It's like he can see right inside you. He's so perceptive. And he doesn't have any filter on the questions he asks. God, after half an hour talking and a couple of dances, he probably knows as much about me as some of my friends."

"Not this one." Mel's laugh was wicked. "There are things I know about you... Well, I'm sure you *wouldn't* tell Richard all of them. Like that night you drank an entire bottle of Malibu and I found you slumped over the toilet begging for someone to put you out of your misery."

"Yeah, not my finest moment. You always drag that one up. In my defence, I was only nineteen. I think I may have learned a few things since then."

"I'm not sure you've learned enough to handle someone like Richard. After all, he's got twenty years' experience on you."

"Yes, there is that. I've never dated anyone that much older. Doing the maths, I think it's closer to fifteen years, but that's still quite the age gap."

"Oh, so we're talking about dates now, are we?"

Sarah, feeling the blush creep up her cheeks, was glad that the darkness in the cab masked her face. Richard had intimated that she'd be hearing from him again soon, but she wasn't ready to admit to Mel how much he'd captivated her.

"Oh, well, why not?" She tried to keep her tone light. "Wouldn't hurt to have him spend a bit of that money on me."

"To be honest, as long as I didn't have to face those eyes, I wouldn't mind the rest of him on me, either. I've seen him climbing out of the pool at Claire's beach house. By God, he might be over forty, but he's got the body of a twenty-year-old."

Sarah choked with laughter. "You don't change, do you? I can always rely on you to spot any guy with a good body within fifty paces."

"Yep, and I know how you appreciate the sensitivity of my radar."

They pulled off their shoes at the bottom of the steep stairs that led to the crumbling Victorian villa. Melanie's flat was on the ground floor. Once it had been her flat too, back in their last year of uni. Now employed as a teacher, Mel had no reason to live in such a semi-derelict abode, except for a sentimental attachment to those days. Sarah could see the attraction. All the stories that house could tell. And if her efforts of the last few days paid off, next year the two of them would be together again. Mel hadn't bothered to fill her old room with another flatmate. It sat waiting for her to move back in as if she'd never left.

As she made her way up the poorly-lit and rickety wooden stairs, Sarah struggled to maintain a careful focus on placing her feet. Her mind was churning, replaying the conversation with Richard and feeding her suggestive images of the body that Mel assured her lay underneath the stylish clothes. Once you'd met Richard Norton, he was not a man you could easily forget.

## CHAPTER 3

# Bright Light of Day

## Sarah

Wellington, New Zealand – July, 2007

THERE WAS AN UNEVEN thump as the courier's sneakered feet bounded up the stairs. The heavy panting as he paused on the porch was audible even above the faint whistle of wind that was an ubiquitous presence in this city.

Sarah swung the door open to see his one hand poised mid-air, ready to knock. The other clasped a riotous bunch of flowers. She had a fairly good idea of where they'd come from. Even after a couple of hours in his company, she was certain this was Richard's style.

"Ash," she said with a smile, recognising the familiar face. "You're still doing this run?"

Like many other Indian students she'd studied with, Ash had somehow held down almost full-time work in a family business while still meeting the demands of university.

"Only the weekend stuff now. Help my brother out when he needs me. No way I'd work my day job around the courier run." She remembered he'd been doing accounting. His day job would be busy. "Got a surprise when I saw your name on this."

He handed her a small card addressed in neat even writing and passed the enormous bouquet into her embrace.

"Yeah, I'm here for two weeks, spending some time with Mel during the school holidays." Seeing him glance behind her, looking for Melanie, she said, "She's still in bed. Too much party last night."

He nodded with a smile. "Always a party girl. She hasn't changed."

"No," said Sarah. "But she's out of practice. What she drank last night wouldn't have even touched the sides back then."

"So—a flash bouquet," he said. "Looks like the party might have gone well for you, too. A new admirer there?"

She blushed, surprising herself that she should colour so easily at the suggestion. After all, it wasn't as if this was a stranger she was talking to. This was Ash, who'd moved in similar uni social circles back then. But something about the thought of Richard, his obvious interest in her, sent an unexpected and subtly awkward rush of pleasure.

"Looks like I have."

"Well, it seems he's keen. And I would bet on him being rich. That particular florist—who isn't even open on a Sunday, and a bunch of flowers nearly as big as you are—well, let's just say the only way he'd pull that off is with a bit of money to sweeten the deal."

"So, it should impress me?"

"Definitely. You're the only girl in Wellington getting a delivery like that today. Well, I'd better get on with it. Sooner I finish, the sooner I have my weekend back. Good seeing you, Sarah."

"Good to see you too, Ash."

"Say hi to Mel for me when she eventually surfaces."

As she laid the flowers down, where they almost covered the entire dining table, the shuffling of slippered feet announced Melanie's approach.

Looking bedraggled, panda-eyed with smears of mascara, wild hair sticking out like a blonde porcupine, she squinted into the sunlight that flooded the kitchen.

"Who was that?" she mumbled, while filling a tumbler with water.

"Ash. With a delivery for me."

"Holy shit, that's some delivery."

Mel's eyes were wide now, mouth fallen open in shock, as she registered the flowers on the table, an explosion of colour where intense red and orange gerberas jostled for attention beside giant sunflowers. The florist's artful hands had somehow tamed this gaudy profusion into a stylish arrangement.

It was quite the most stunning bouquet Sarah had ever seen. Interspersed with the extroverts of the flower world, delicate freesias provided a sweet spring fragrance, even though it would be months before the season came to this part of the country.

"Richard, of course," she said, pursing her lips in disapproval. "Open the card. What does it say?"

For some inexplicable reason, Mel's urgent curiosity annoyed her a little. She would have preferred to read Richard's card without her friend eyeballing it. But they'd been through too much together for her to begin hiding things now.

She opened the heavy cream envelope and read off the card. There was a message written in a meticulous hand that she presumed to be his. He didn't seem the type of person who'd possess an untidy scrawl like her own.

*Good morning, beautiful Sarah. Yesterday was an extraor-
dinary day, only because we met. I've been a little presump-*

*tuous. Booked a table at Silver tonight. Pick you up at 7? Call
me. Hoping you'll say yes. R.*

His number was below.

"Well, *you* obviously created an impression. You must go, if only to be treated to dinner at Silver. Tables there are scarce as hen's teeth."

In a country as small as this, most people knew of Christian Silver, a New Zealand-born celebrity chef. Having tired of jet-setting around the world cooking exquisite food for the mega-wealthy, he had returned to his hometown a year ago to raise his family. And to open a restaurant that was the go-to dining place for anyone who was somebody. It seemed Richard Norton fell into that category.

"You know, I think I'd have said yes to seeing him again, anyway. I know you don't like him, but there is something strangely fascinating about the man. And we kind of clicked."

"It's not that I don't like him. He's certainly charming. But I feel like he's analysing my every word. You know me, I'm no good under pressure. I know you don't take crap from anyone. But I still wonder if it's wise to get mixed up with Richard."

Sarah smiled. "Oh, I don't know about that," she said. "He tried it on a few times last night. Testing me out. A few attempts to provoke me to see what I might say. I think I held my own. And obviously, I didn't put him off."

"He didn't get where he is by being easily deterred. You know he's the power behind the throne at Crombie Norton?"

Crombie Norton was the biggest fish in the country's small pond of merchant banks. Some thought them brilliant, with their daring takeovers of large overseas companies held up as an example of Kiwis batting above their average. Others considered them well-dressed thieves. The machinations of the company were fascinating, even to people like Sarah, who usually paid scant attention to the workings of the financial world.

"Really? I thought it was old Paul Crombie. He's the one you see on TV all the time. It seems the Reserve Bank Governor hardly takes a breath without some reporter shoving a microphone in front of Paul for an opinion."

There was something about the old devil, his wry commentary, and the way he outfoxed even the most astute interviewer that gave him an uncanny likeability. Sarah's father found him entertaining, chuckling to himself as Paul Crombie, wielding his acerbic wit, sliced and diced some young news reporter.

"Oh, no—Paul has his eyes on retirement in a few years. A chance to enjoy his millions. There's no doubt that Richard's running the place. That's why Jonathan loves to lord it up that Richard sees them socially. Likes the others to think they are such great mates. He's such a brown-noser, that brother-in-law of mine." Mel did little to hide her dislike of Jonathan, publicly maintaining a polite tolerance out of deference to her sister's choice, but privately slagging him off whenever she had a listening ear. "No, Sarah, I think there's no doubt you've captured the eye of one of the most powerful men in the country."

That was a further clue why Mel was so jittery around Richard. She'd always been a bit intimidated by people in authority. Whereas her sister Claire saw them as a meal ticket, Mel was more like her parents, a little insecure around the upper classes. But Sarah had been raised in the ilk of her father, to believe that it was actions that defined people, not money or a flash car, or a posh accent. She could still hear his words as he'd left her at the door of her university hostel. "Don't let anyone put you down, love. You're as good as any of them here."

"I suppose I have," she said, "if those flowers are anything to go by."

"So, are you going to call him? I mean—dinner at Silver. I think even I'd say yes to that invitation. They say the food is amazing."

"Perhaps I will." Sarah knew she would. "But not yet. Even if I decide to go, I don't want to come across as too eager. I'd prefer him to think I had to take time over my decision."

"Good plan. Keep him guessing."

"Come on then, you. Get dressed. We'll go for brunch. I'll think it through over some food and call him when we get back."

Mel screwed up her face. Her usually pale skin was a deathly white, with a sickly greenish undertone.

"Ugh, not sure I can stomach anything more than a bit of toast."

"We both know there's nothing like a good fry up for fixing a hangover. It's exactly what you need."

"Easy for you to say when you're not the one with the hangover."

Mel reluctantly headed for the shower, grumbling at the unfairness of it all.

She was right. All that champagne should have ruined Sarah's Sunday. But unlike her friend, headache free, and with an intriguing dinner invitation, the day was looking bright.

Four hours later, Sarah deemed enough time had passed. She slipped casually into the bedroom, her phone tucked in a pocket, unable to bear Mel's scrutiny as she made the call. In the privacy of her room, nervousness surfaced. It took her three attempts to punch in the number correctly, and her hand shook a little as she hit the final green button. Richard answered in that same smooth voice, like caramel, thick and enticing.

"Sarah! I was starting to think my efforts had been in vain. Unless, of course, you're phoning to decline the invitation?" He imbued the comment with a distinct air of resigned disappointment, as if he'd practised its delivery to maximum effect.

"No, not at all. I'd love to come. I hear Silver is pretty special."

She'd practised her acceptance over and over in her head, wanting to convey the right touch of enthusiasm, not letting the heady feeling and the circling butterflies in her stomach spill over into her voice and make her appear desperate to see him. But enough that Richard Norton knew she was interested.

"It is special," he said. "A special place to take a special woman." He let that remark settle for a moment. Meanwhile, the butterflies' lazy circling erupted in a frenzied clamour, and she forced herself to take a slow deep breath, hoping to dampen their wild flight. "So, I'll pick you up about quarter to seven?"

"Yes, I'm looking forward to it." The words came out in a normal tone, despite her feeling anything but normal.

"Me too," he said.

She marvelled that even those two words set the butterflies off on another wild dance. Despite her misgivings, and Mel's less than enthusiastic opinion, she genuinely wanted to spend time with Richard Norton. He was clever, fun to talk to, undeniably attractive, and definitely interested in her. Admitting that to herself triggered a warm, tingling euphoria that infused her body. Life had been dull for too long.

In fact, there'd really been no one since Justin. Another casualty of her return to the farm. He'd been an accounting student like Ash. Snared himself a great job with a big Wellington firm straight out of uni. And they'd been good together, rolling along on a trajectory that might have led to something permanent. But naively believing they could make things work long distance, she'd unwittingly trashed her only serious relationship and her academic career in one decisive moment. Here was an opportunity to put those regrets behind her, start again with someone new, and see where it led.

She stepped back into the lounge, unable to suppress a small smile. Mel looked up from a magazine and her eyes widened.

"Oh my god, you sneaky cow, you did it didn't you?"

"Yes, I did. And now for the second time in two days, I think I need the help of my personal stylist. What shall I wear?"

# Sarah

Wellington, New Zealand – July, 2007

ONLY YEARS OF PRACTICE at navigating these precarious stairs prevented Sarah from tumbling the last few steps before reaching the steadiness of Richard's outstretched hand. She'd rushed down to meet him, the result of an inexplicable need to avoid him meeting her at the door. For some strange reason, perhaps Mel's unflattering opinion of him, she was reluctant to have the three of them together until she was sure of where she stood with this man. And so she'd dashed out the door before that could occur, tossing Mel a hurried farewell, wobbling her way towards him in the unaccustomed high heels.

The shiny Jaguar crouched low, straddling the kerb. There was little room for any car to park on this narrow winding hillside street, let alone a huge sedan. He stepped forward, meeting her with a chaste kiss on the cheek.

Smartly dressed, in a variation of the previous night's sports coat and linen shirt, the lack of a tie rendered his conservative attire more casual. And he smelled good, an intoxicating fragrance, both sweet and masculine at the same time. No doubt it was an expensive male perfume, its undertone of spiciness reminiscent of her father's favourite Old Spice, but with a more sophisticated note. She was acutely aware of his hand placed firmly against her lower back as he guided her to the other side of the car, opened the door for her and steadied her as she folded into the seat, its leather soft and new-smelling.

She couldn't prevent her mouth falling open in shock as the roar of Led Zeppelin poured from the speakers, drowning out the throaty rumble of the car's massive engine. This car, this man—well, she would have expected something classical. Richard grinned at her, his delight at her surprise written in his sparkling eyes, as he nudged the volume up a further notch.

"Misspent youth," he said, raising his voice over the wall of sound. "Loud music and drugs. Well, mainly the loud music. But you know, everyone admits to smoking a bit of weed. Unlike some of them, I'm unable to swear I never inhaled."

Her mind delivered up an image of a younger Richard, at some outdoor festival, joint in hand and swaying to the music.

"Yeah, I can see you as a shirtless long-haired Robert Plant look-alike," she said

"Oh god, no. Poor Robert, I always thought he was rather too scrawny to be strutting around the stage like that."

He was right. Even fully-clothed, Richard's physique was obviously far from scrawny. She deftly turned the conversation back to the music, not wanting to dwell on this new picture her brain had conjured. A half-clad

Richard, muscled and sexy in a set of low-slung jeans. She almost blushed thinking about it.

"Yeah, not such an attractive man," she agreed. "But he sure is a musical genius. And I love this song—'Kashmir'. I always thought it didn't get the airplay it deserved. Like the shy girl sitting in the corner, while your gorgeous sister laps up all the attention."

"Well, I doubt that was ever you, but a good analogy," he said with a smile. He was right, she'd never been one to shy away from being noticed. "So, you know your Led Zeppelin," he said. "Hardly meet anyone of your age who's even heard of them. Oh, they can recognise 'Stairway to Heaven' but nothing more."

"Yeah, I love this stuff," she said. "Led Zep, The Who, the Stones. I sometimes think I was born in the wrong place and the wrong time. What I'd give to have seen Led Zeppelin in concert."

"Me too. A few years too young for that." He caught her double-take. "Really. I'm not *that* old. I'm forty-three. I was only sixteen when they split up."

"Oh," she said, feeling stupid. She quickly tried to gloss over her poor mathematics. "So tell me, who have you seen live?"

She was envious as Richard filled the journey with anecdotes of concerts long past. He'd been there in the thick of a crowd, immersed in the music, while she was still a toddler watching *Playschool* on the telly. It was a sobering reminder. He wasn't only older than her, but a lot older, and she was quite unsure how that made her feel.

***

Christian Silver had chosen an unusual location for his elegant fine-dining restaurant, nestled amongst the nineteenth century working-class homes of the Aro Valley. With its glossy white weatherboards and window frames outlined in black, Silver stood boldly amongst its neighbours, whose peeling paint and rust-pocked roofs alluded to the damp and mould that lived within.

"Give it five years and these won't be student flats," said Richard. "Christian's chosen well. Soon his young professional clientele will live next door in their villa do-ups."

Richard was right. Even now there was the odd house that looked as if it had evaded the risk of imminent demolition, with replacement boards, stripped paint and new-looking roof evidence of the creeping gentrification of the suburb.

At the entrance to the restaurant, a striking woman stepped forward to meet them, her dark hair swept up in a sleek roll, her skin a flawless gold. There was recognition in her lively brown eyes as Richard leaned forward, kissing her lightly on each cheek in a European-style greeting.

"Richard, so good to see you." She spoke in heavily accented English, possibly Italian. "And you too, my darling." She turned to Sarah and embraced her warmly. "Any friend of Richard's is a friend of ours."

Now Sarah knew how Richard had arranged a table at the last minute where they certainly would have turned away others.

"Sarah, let me introduce Giulia Silver. Christian is the magician in the kitchen, but Giulia is the heart of this place."

"Oh, Richard, you flatter me too much." She giggled, an incongruous child-like sound from that languid mouth and sensuous lips.

"Giulia, this is Sarah. She's visiting, so I couldn't let her leave without eating at the best restaurant this city has ever seen."

Giulia beamed at him, accepting this praise with a modest nod. She led them to a table in the bay window, where flickering candlelight bounced off sparkling crystal and genuine silver cutlery.

He fussed over her, arranging her into her seat, beckoning the staff at the slightest glimmer of her need for something, and guided her through the menu. Sarah hadn't appreciated how beguiling it was to have a man attend to her every whim with such charm and grace. She had not expected to enjoy his attentiveness so much or that she would feel so special.

The unobtrusive wait staff delivered entrée dishes that resembled miniature works of art. Richard leaned across, a delicate piece of paua ravioli balanced on his fork.

"You must try this," he said. "It's their signature dish."

There was something sensual in the gesture, an intimacy as their eyes met above the proffered food. As she parted her lips, he gently placed the tiny parcel in her mouth.

She closed her eyes, savouring the faint tang of the sea, delicious with a hint of lemon and subtle herbs in the stray droplet of creamy sauce that she licked off her lips. The taste brought memories flooding back. Her father, rounding them all up for a trip to the coast when the rhythm of the tides coincided with an opportune break in farm routines. Armed with knives, they'd scrambled over exposed reef, hunting the elusive shellfish. There were jubilant squeals at discovering the knobbly grey curved shells, then setting to prising them loose from their rocky hiding places with dangerous thrusts of their blunt weapons.

"Mmmm, you are right, that is so good," she said, opening her eyes again to see him watching her closely, his approval of her enjoyment mixed with a glimmer of something else. Her stomach lurched a little, recognising the same small surge of desire that was also tying her in knots. She steered the conversation to the food, hoping to take her mind off the uncomfortable but exciting sensation.

"It's a new take on paua for me. But delicious."

"So you're a fan of the Kiwi paua fritter?" he asked.

"Sort of. But none of the chippies make them like my mum's. No beating those." She smiled at the thought of her mother, furiously twirling the hand mincer, grinding the tough black shellfish into a grey sludge that, despite its unappetising appearance, she would magically turn into the traditional New Zealand delicacy. But the memory was bittersweet.

Another of all the little things you remembered. The ones you missed the most. "However, I think that ravioli might even top those," she said.

"You want to swap?" he offered, fork poised over the plate that he hadn't yet sampled himself.

"No, no," she insisted, picking up her own cutlery as she prepared to attack the intriguing pea and mint lamington that sat in front of her while trying to push aside the sad thoughts of her mother that had trickled through.

---

As the staff cleared the rubble of the first course and melted away into the background, Richard reached across the table, taking her hand. Turning it over, he examined the palm, brushing it with the lightest touch of his thumb. She shivered at the intimacy of that touch.

"You know you are a contradiction, Sarah. How is it that a woman who milks cows and tends a farm has hands as soft and lovely as this?"

Turning it back over, he lifted it to his lips, his soft kiss sending another thrill like an electric current that lit her up inside.

"Just because I moved away from the city doesn't mean I've gone feral. It is possible to find a good manicure even in the backblocks."

He laughed. "You are so far removed from being feral. There's a wildness about you, but it's mesmerising rather than off-putting. I still can't understand why you're there."

Sarah hesitated for a moment, mulling over whether she should tell him. She didn't willingly share her entire story with people, not until she knew them well. It was more than she could bear to face the pitying looks of strangers. Revealing the tragedy that had rocked her world was only possible with people who genuinely cared. She hardly knew this man, but for some reason she already sensed he did care, reading a sincerity in his eyes that invited her to confide in him.

"It wasn't a choice I expected to make, but three years ago my life changed. That day I'd had my thesis accepted. Mel and I were having a few drinks at the flat to celebrate. And the phone rang." Her voice thinned, and her breath caught in her throat. No matter how much time passed, uttering those words was painful. "My sister, telling me that mum was dead."

She blinked furiously, in a vain attempt to push back unexpected tears. It was as raw as if it had happened yesterday, but she rarely let others see that. He squeezed her hand in reassurance, his face kind, and it gave her the strength to go on.

"Our farm—it's on a road to the mountain. A tourist road. There was an American couple in a campervan. They'd pulled off into a picnic area. When they went back out onto the road, from habit, they drove on the wrong side. Mum was heading into town in her little Fiat. Met them head on, on a blind corner. She didn't stand a chance."

The tears were sliding down her cheeks now. This was so not her. On that day, she'd done all her crying for her mother and then put it behind her. To be the strong one. The one who held her family together while they grieved. She stood, preparing to flee to the bathroom, to find a quiet space where she might push back this flood of emotion.

"Excuse me Richard, I think I need..."

He rose and in one fluid movement, gathered her into his arms and pressed her face to his chest. He kissed her hair, his breath soft as he whispered words of sympathy. There was an unexpected safety there in his arms, as if he could put a barrier between her and her sorrow, that even after all this time was closer to the surface than she knew. Her tears soaked the white linen of his shirt, but he didn't seem to mind. When she eventually collected herself, he picked up a napkin, dabbing at her tear-streaked face, his movements tender.

"I'm sorry, I shouldn't have asked," he said.

"No, no, I chose to tell you. I didn't have to. But I wanted to." She'd admitted it out loud now. For some inexplicable reason, she trusted him with personal things, private things. "Not sure why it hit me hard today," she said, as he eased her back into the chair, his lingering hand on her shoulder a comforting touch. As he faced her again across the table, she saw not only sympathy in his eyes, but empathy, understanding.

"It does that," he said. "Grief. Even though it's been a long time, some days my mother's death blindsides me, too. Not as sudden as your loss—it was cancer. But it affects me the same. So I understand it. I don't think anyone truly gets over losing their mother."

A smiling young woman bearing two plates interrupted the moment, placing the magazine-worthy main course before them. They slipped back into a happier mood, murmuring thanks while admiring the cuisine.

"I enjoy it, you know, the farm," she said in between mouthfuls. "Although I'm not sure for how much longer I can keep it up. Or even need to. Dad's got things under control. He hired a good sharemilker. And what you said the other night, about the locals. You're absolutely right. I certainly don't see myself as a farmer's wife. For sure, there's plenty of challenge in it. You can't afford to be a slouch and expect to run a farm successfully these days. But I don't want to spend my life discussing milk fat percentages and grazing rotations."

"So no one special amongst the eligible rural bachelors to tempt a change of heart?" he teased.

"No. Absolutely not. I've dated a few. Nice guys, good men. But I have nothing in common with them—except that I could run their farm as well as they can."

"I bet you could. Or anything else you care to try your hand at." She sensed it wasn't idle flattery. There was a distinct touch of admiration in his voice. "So, what are your plans? When you leave the farm?"

"Well, I definitely want to travel. To exciting places. You know what their idea of travel is back home? A week in the Gold Coast once the cows have dried off. Or the more adventurous might take the kids to Disneyland."

"And you said that you've been up at the university this week. What's that about?"

"I'm working on winning back the doctoral spot they offered me three years ago. I met my old Masters supervisor on Friday and we're going for coffee later this week. He was almost as gutted as I was when things went pear-shaped, so he's rapt that I might be back. He doesn't have the final say, but if the offer comes, I'll take it."

"You should," he said. "Doctor Sarah Mitchell has a nice ring to it."

She'd never said it out loud herself, but hearing him speak the words, she had to agree. And it was more than just the title. A doctorate, even from a New Zealand university, would open doors to all kinds of possibilities—an academic, a museum position, a researcher.

"Yeah, I think so," she said. "Unfortunately, it won't start until next year. And I don't think I can survive another spring on the farm. Not when they don't need me."

"So, what will you do? In the immediate future?"

"Most likely I will grab the chance to go overseas. I've plenty saved up. Nothing much to spend money on living in Wakefield. And it's about time I stopped living my life vicariously. All those years studying European history and I have yet to go there. There's only so much you can learn from a book or a photograph."

"Why don't I take you?" he said, a little smile playing around his lips. It broadened as he saw the look of incredulity on her face. "I'm going to Rome in September," he said. "Business trip. Come with me. I'd love to be your tour guide in the 'Eternal City'. It's one of my favourite places. Especially that time of the year. The summer is unbearable, but the autumn is perfect. Isn't it Giulia?" He glanced up at their hostess, who had reappeared to top up the wine. An almost viscous, dark plum liquid swirled into the glass.

"Ah, Roma," she said, her voice wistful. "My home. I miss it. And yes, autumn is beautiful there. You should go, Sarah. I'd be there in a heartbeat.

Except that Christian would never forgive me for leaving him with all this," she said, waving her hand at the busy room of diners. "The things we sacrifice for love, huh?" She tossed Richard a wink and headed to the next table.

It caught Sarah off guard—not only Richard's offer, but also that she was seriously considering accepting it on the spot. She pulled herself back just in time, the voice in her head admonishing her: *Whoa there, girl, what are you thinking? You've known him for twenty-four hours and you're ready to pack your bags and go halfway around the world with him!*

"No hurry to decide." He spoke as if reading her mind. "It's not for a few months. But the offer's serious. If you're able to leave the farm, and you think you could bear my company for a few weeks, well, I can promise you a special holiday. And as many ruins as you care to visit. I don't pretend to be a scholar of history to rival you, but I've always been interested in that part of the world. The cradle of western civilisation, as they say."

Richard's offer provided an interesting backdrop to the rest of their evening. Once he'd said it, somehow they crossed a line, from feeling their way around each other like you did on a first date, to a comfortable, simple conversation you might have with someone you knew well enough to go on holiday with.

"Home to Mel's? Or a drink at my place?" he said as they left the restaurant, with Giulia's warm farewell and recommendations of things not to be missed in Rome, trailing behind them. "I'm flying to Sydney for two weeks on Tuesday. So please, indulge me with a little more of your time tonight. You'll be gone when I arrive back."

Curious to see where he lived, and also admitting that spending more time with him was an attractive thought, she accepted.

"Yes, it's not late. I'd love to come for a drink."

She expected they'd head for a mansion in Khandallah like Claire's. Instead, he turned the car towards the waterfront. They drove up to an enormous set of bland metal doors in the side of a weathered red brick dockside warehouse. He touched a remote, and the doors swung inwards, revealing an expanse of car parks, some of them occupied. In one corner, a white Lamborghini and its scarlet Ferrari cousin hugged the ground. She knew little about cars, but she suspected these two might even make Richard's Jag look cheap.

A mirrored lift took them silently to the top floor, its doors sliding open to reveal a vast open plan apartment worthy of House and Garden. The aesthetic was New York loft, exposed old brickwork contrasting with crisp white walls that soared high above. A network of pipes and electrical conduits unashamedly crisscrossed the ceiling, a reminder of the utilitarian features that sat behind the glowing banks of lights and the gleaming industrial kitchen. It a was stunning apartment, but unashamedly masculine. There was no evidence of a woman's hand within these walls.

The wall facing the harbour was completely glass, revealing the lights of the working port bouncing off the water. Out in the inky blackness of the sea, Sarah could see the day's last brave interisland ferry inching out past the protection of the heads, preparing to cross the treacherous waters of Cook Strait.

He flipped open the doors of a stylish modern drinks cabinet.

"Name your poison," he said, waving his hand at the glittering lineup of spirits.

"Brandy please." It had been her mother's favourite.

He poured a generous measure into the bulbous stemmed glass, handed it to her, and she inhaled the sweet smell that wafted from within. He deliberated over a row of whisky bottles before selecting one to splash into a crystal tumbler for himself.

The windows were like a magnet, drawing them over to stand in companionable silence. They watched the busy port vehicles scurrying back and forth, and the container cranes like prehistoric monsters, their box-like prey suspended from their jaws.

"You know, you're the first woman to share this view with me," he said.

"Moved in last week, did you?" she said flippantly.

"No. About a year ago. I'm not the playboy you seem to think I am."

"I find that hard to believe. That you saved all your charm especially for me."

"Believe it," he said. "There's not a single person I've been the least bit interested in letting across the doorstep. I've found it best to be choosy, otherwise getting rid of them gets complicated."

"Then why me? Why am I here? Did you think I'd be easy to get rid of if I became a problem?"

He laughed. "Quite the opposite. I can't imagine making you do anything you didn't want to do."

He put his glass down and reached for hers, placing it on a low table, but his eyes, now serious, never left hers. She swallowed nervously, as he placed one hand lightly on her waist, while the other traced the line of her cheek.

"So, why are *you* here?" he said. "I'll tell you why. I can't deny the obvious physical attraction. My god, last night when you walked into that room. It wasn't only that memorable red dress showing off your every curve." He grinned a little, his voice now throaty as one hand trailed downwards, resting ever so gently on the open neck of her shirt. She shivered at the touch, her body wanting it to continue on its path.

"Sarah." He said her name, almost a whisper on his lips. "I knew from the moment I saw you that there was more than that. And I was right. You're smart, and you're not afraid to tell it like it is. I find those qualities undeniably sexy."

"It sounds a lot like how I'd describe you," she said. "I like men who don't play games. Who are honest about what they want."

"Is this the time to tell you, then, what I really want?"

She blanched a little, took a gulp of air, while trying to decode the undercurrent in his words and the message in those blue eyes. They sparked with interest, but she detected a hint of something calculating behind them. As if he was weighing up how far he might go. This was moving too fast. She was still unsure about so many things. For a start, she didn't do first-date sex. Not that a romp between the sheets wasn't a tempting proposition. And she sensed it would take very little to nudge the night in that direction.

No, it was way too soon to leap into something with Richard, even if he wanted more than to bed her. For a start, there was his age to consider. Not to mention his complicated family situation, with daughters who certainly might resent someone close to their age in their father's life.

And then there was the vast gap between her world and his. He hadn't seen the real Sarah yet. Swathed in Claire's fancy ball gown or dressed in smart clothes for dinner, this was a different version of herself. He might find the everyday Sarah Mitchell far less impressive. However, he was the first man in a long time who had captured her attention. She didn't want to blow it by being too coy.

"The look on your face," he laughed when she didn't reply. He leaned forward, pressing a reassuring kiss on her forehead. "It's OK. I haven't lured you here to try to persuade you to leap into bed with me on a first date, tempting as that is." She tried not to let relief show, although she thought he couldn't help but notice her body relax a little. "No, what I really want is for you to spend a bit of time with me. Meeting at that stupid party, I think you have some ideas about me that aren't wholly accurate."

He led her to take a seat beside him on the huge leather couch.

"So tell me, Richard, what do I need to know about you?" Retrieving her brandy, she sipped at it, curious at what he might say.

"Well, apart from the obvious age gap, you and I are not so different. What you see here," he said, waving his hand at the decor, "this is all window dressing. I'm basically an ordinary guy from humble beginnings who's done OK for himself."

She thought of his strategic marriage. He'd not climbed to where he was now solely on his own merits. Like a mind reader who sensed her objections the moment they appeared, he went on.

"I'll admit I clawed my way up, but for me, it was the only option. The child of a single mother in conservative Christchurch. Back then—well, I was never going anywhere unless I grabbed all the opportunities that came my way."

"Your mother must have been a brave woman."

"Yes, it wasn't the done thing to have a baby on your own. My grandparents pressured her to give me up for adoption. But she stood her ground, even though it meant they refused to have anything more to do with her—or with me. Without their backing, it was a very brave decision. My father never showed. Never stepped up and took any responsibility for me. But we did OK without any of them."

"So it wasn't all bad."

"Oh no, I had a good childhood. Not a lot of material things, but enough. I did ordinary things with ordinary kids. Running wild through the neighbourhood. Fishing in a stream. Haring round on a rumpty old secondhand chopper bicycle with a flag. A simple life. I told you—we're not that different."

By the end of the evening, his revelations had eased some of her doubts. He was right. To her surprise, they did have a lot in common, and the conversation had flowed long after the time she should have asked him to take her home. She suspected Mel would wait up for her, anticipating a post-mortem of the evening. Arriving at the bottom of the steep stairs, a light in the window above confirmed her friend was doing exactly that.

Ignoring the possibility of surveillance, Richard tilted her face upwards, his first kiss light and playful, as if teasing her mouth into life. He tasted of whisky, like the pleasant smokiness of a winter fire, warm with promise.

Her body answered his touch with a flush of desire, and she parted her lips willingly, inviting his tongue, wanting to take him into her. He accepted her invitation, exploring her mouth with increasing fervour. The pressure of his body against hers rendered her clothing a flimsy barrier between the flame of desire radiating from him and the blooming heat of her own skin.

When he pulled away, she almost gasped out, "No!" not wanting it to end. A satisfied smile slid across his face, a sudden pleasure that he'd evoked this response.

"Tomorrow," he said. The promise of what that might bring hung heavy in the air between them.

"Tomorrow," she said, suspecting even then that they had taken the first steps down the path of no return.

## CHAPTER 5

Gold

# Sarah

Wellington, New Zealand – July, 2007

MEL HAD DUPED THEM. She'd turned in early, deeming it wise after the previous night's overindulgence, simply leaving a welcoming light to guide her friend up the treacherous stairs. But finding Mel already asleep had only delayed the inevitable. She lay in wait at the dining table the next morning, coffee in hand. She may as well have had the questions prepared on a list, ready to fire them at Sarah when she emerged from the bedroom.

"OK, you know the drill. Straight to the important stuff."

"No, I didn't sleep with him." No surprises there. Mel understood she was no prude, but also knew she'd never been one to pounce on opportunities for casual sex. Sometimes she wished she was different. She could have livened up her life with a few steamy one-night stands. But she'd always needed some connection to trust someone else with that level of intimacy.

"Yes, it was a lovely evening." No surprises there either. Dinner at Silver was always going to be a treat.

"Yes, I'm going to see him again. Tonight, in fact. He's off to Sydney tomorrow."

This was where Mel's expression altered. Whether it was because she expected to be proven right, that Sarah would back off once she saw Richard outside the buzz of the party, or that her best friend was bailing on her for the second night in a row; Mel's disappointment rippled across her face for a moment before she composed herself again. Sarah swallowed down her guilt. She didn't want to decline Richard's offer, as she had no idea when she'd see him again otherwise. And then there was the question of that parting kiss.

"You don't mind, do you?"

"Of course I don't. You deserve a little fun, even if it is with Richard." Relief washed over her. Mel was such an amazing friend. "With a distinct lack of action in my own love life, I'm happy to do what I can to help yours. As long as you don't skimp on sharing the details. So start from the beginning. I want to hear all about Silver."

They passed the day in comfortable girly pastimes: lunch in a quirky Cuba street cafe, investigating the secondhand stores for treasures, a whirl through pop-up shops where earnest young designers displayed their wares, and finally to their favourite old world department store, Kirkcaldie and Staines. While Sarah had told herself she didn't need to do anything but be herself to impress Richard, it took little convincing to splash out on some new clothes for their date. In Kirks, Mel nodded approvingly as the shop assistant gushed about what a perfect cut the new jeans were, and insisted the silky gold top was the perfect colour on her.

Later, standing in Mel's bathroom, she had to agree that the girl in the mirror reflected a balance between casual and elegant that she hoped would be perfect for a movie and dinner.

"He's here." Mel's head appeared around the edge of the door. Despite her reservations, even she sounded a little excited. "Be good," she called after Sarah, who ventured down the stairs more quickly this time due to her choice of marginally less precarious shoes. "And if you can't be good, be careful." Her voice drifted on the breeze, down to where Richard stood, poised to open the car door.

"Did she really just say what I think she said?"

"Ah yes, she did. That's Mel for you. Always trying to mother me."

"Don't wait up," he called to Mel, giving her a cheerful wave. "Might save you coming home to an interrogation later," he said with a grin as he ushered Sarah into the car.

"Oh, I doubt that. She's extremely patient, is our Mel. She'll still expect me to tell all in the morning."

He took her to a film festival movie that she'd mentioned the night before, and then they wandered along Courtenay Place in search of food. The wind whipped along the street, a brush of polar chill in the air, and she was glad of her bulky wool coat and the warm, safe feeling of his hand clasped over hers.

They ate tacos and drank margaritas in a tiny cafe with formica tables and the many faces of Frida Kahlo observing them while he talked of a holiday to Mexico. More places he'd been, things he'd done that emphasised the age divide between them, the life he'd lived before she'd even begun to live her own. And then there was the world he inhabited, so at odds with her own, mixing with people whose wealth and influence made the headlines daily. But she buried the doubts even deeper. This man intrigued her, and she wasn't about to let old-fashioned notions of what was age-appropriate or unwritten rules about class boundaries stop her from seeing where this might lead.

It went without saying that they'd go back to his place.

He poured them both a glass of red wine.

"Otago Pinot Noir," he said, handing it to her. The musty smell, hinting of the mushrooms she'd picked in the farm paddocks, floated up from the black depths. He looped an arm around her waist and they stood comfortable in each other's presence. No need for conversation. Below, the tireless port workers scuttled back and forth, the faint beeping of vehicles muffled by the sound of Pink Floyd drifting from the sound system.

"We stand up here spying on them—but can they see us?" she asked.

"No," he said, "a flick of that switch over there and the glass is opaque. Which is handy at times like this."

He turned her to face him, and still cautious, as if unsure of her welcome, leaned in slowly, his lips seeking hers. The kiss wasn't unexpected, but the immediate overwhelming surge of desire that once again flooded her body caught her off guard.

He responded to her obvious need, with another, this time even more slow and languorous, the spicy taste of the wine on his tongue. He broke away, trailing kisses on her hair, her neck, his hand clasping her to him. His breath was a tantalising tickle on her throat. His voice dropped low, its huskiness echoing the emotions he triggered in her.

"You know last night, when I said what I really wanted was for you to know me better?"

"Yes," she gasped, her voice swamped by the sensation of him, tasting her skin now, his tongue light on the bare shoulder he'd exposed.

"Well, I wasn't totally honest. That's not all I want." He raised his head to meet her gaze. From the expression in those blue eyes, dark now, the dilated pupils conveying his arousal, she anticipated his next words. "What

I really want is to take you through that door over there..." He nodded towards the bedroom. "And see what happens on the other side."

"And do you always get what you want, Richard?" She couldn't help the teasing smile that slid onto her face.

"Usually."

He placed his glass down, relieved her of her own, and stepped back into her, his hand gentle on her cheek, his lips warm and sensuous, finding hers again. Instinctively she relaxed against him, letting her body mould to his, her breasts crushed against that broad chest, her hips melded against him, where she could feel the hardness of his desire.

"I think you might want it too," he said, as his hand slid along her thigh.

"There's no might about it."

Her breath was coming in sharp gasps now. She was desperate to touch him skin to skin, to shed the layers of clothing between them, to seek the source of that heat. Earlier, she'd told herself that she was not going to sleep with him. That attracted to him as she was, it was still too soon to be leaping into bed with Richard. That no matter how much he plied her with his charm, she would stay strong.

But that was before. Now, confronted with her burning need for him, she cast those thoughts aside, like a leaf on the Wellington wind, and they twined together, moving as one in a slow sensuous dance towards what inevitably lay beyond the door.

As his frantic hands deftly unbuttoned her shirt, casting it into a golden puddle on the floor, Sarah wondered how this might play out. Most of the men she'd bedded were of a similar age to her, often lacking sufficient knowledge to light her up completely, but making up for it with youthful enthusiasm and vigour. Feeling his haste, she wondered if a man of Richard's generation might view sex as a self-centred 'wham bam thank you mam', fulfilling his needs while leaving her unsatisfied. Or maybe he would bring with him the lacklustre lovemaking of his admittedly passionless marriage.

However, as his hands and mouth moved with exquisite delicacy, exploring each newly revealed part of her body, as he unwrapped her like a precious gift, she knew that neither was true. Richard brought a similar thoughtful finesse to making love as he did to other parts of his life—the sophisticated clothes, the stylish house, the elegant car, even the expensive cotton sheets she lay on, oozing that intoxicating newly-washed smell. Now, sprawled across his huge bed, it was her turn to feel inexperienced, as he took her body to places it had never been before and she abandoned all thought, allowing her own hands and mouth to respond as they instinctively sought to bring him pleasure too.

She let her legs fall open in invitation, knowing from the smell of her own wetness that she was ready. Keeping one hand firmly occupied between her thighs, with the other, he reached for a bedside cabinet, rummaging around for a few moments, before both came to an abrupt halt in their work.

"Shit," he muttered to himself. "Wait a minute," he said, tumbling from the bed in one smooth movement. He padded to the adjoining bathroom, followed by the sound of drawers banging, a cupboard slamming, and another curse. While he thumped around, she stretched back, mulling over the evening.

She'd accepted last night's dinner invitation out of curiosity, but now, on reflection, it was always going to lead here. Richard Norton was a compelling man. It wasn't simply the beautiful proportions of his body that now stood framed in the doorway, completely at ease with her obvious scrutiny. God, Mel was right. That was not what she'd imagined an unclothed forty-year-old to look like. But no, she decided that in Richard she'd met her equal, and she liked it. However, at this moment, his awkward expression was quite at odds with all she'd seen and learned about him in the past two days. He shot her an embarrassed grin.

"One small problem—seems I'm all out of an important item."

"Give me one minute," she said, sure there were condoms in her handbag. As she strolled out to the lounge, she could feel the heat of his admiring eyes on her nakedness, and the resulting surge of excitement hastened her search.

It surprised her that such a good looking, self-assured man was unprepared. He certainly wouldn't lack willing sexual partners. With a small feeling of relief, she decided that perhaps he'd been truthful—he hadn't entertained women here. She wasn't merely another in a string of conquests. Either that or he was a blatant liar and there'd been so many that he'd used up his stash of protection...

She returned, waving the gold metallic strip at him.

"One advantage of us younger women, we come prepared." She tossed it to him and he caught it deftly in one hand, tore one off and placed the remaining two on the bedside cabinet.

"Keep them handy. We might need them," he said with a knowing grin. "Now, where were we?"

***

The alarm jolted her from sleep. Her first dishevelled thoughts surfaced, her mind attempting to comprehend where she was. The ceiling above was stark, an unembellished white, clean and crisp. Not the familiar tongue-and-groove of her bedroom in the farmhouse. Not the peeling, mould-speckled paint of her old room at Mel's. But the warm body that now rolled over to drape across hers was familiar. After all, she'd exchanged sleep for the opportunity to explore every inch of it during the night.

"I should have set it for earlier." His breath tickled her neck, and his arm snaked its way to lie across her stomach. "Would have given us some more time to play."

"Oh, I'm up for a quick game, if that's all we've time for."

He groaned and rolled away. "Don't tempt me. God, if I didn't absolutely have to make this trip, I wouldn't hesitate." He swung his feet onto the floor, rising to stand in one fluid movement. Her eyes couldn't help but be drawn to him. The muscled legs, the nicely sculpted abs, and those little valleys below his hips still tantalisingly visible as he pulled on boxer shorts.

"I thought being the boss you could do what you like."

"Only to a point. We've created a monster in this company, Paul and I. It's formidable, but without either of us there to control it, it would get away on us and we'd never pull it back."

"Mel said Paul's going to retire."

"Yes, that's right. Perhaps in a year or so. Two at the most. And then it's all on me. I envy him, already on his exit path. Me, I'm stuck with it a while longer, unfortunately. It's had its tentacles around my life for fifteen years, but one of these days I'm going to cut myself loose, too."

"You don't think you'll miss it?"

"I would have once. I thrived on it. It's a game where the stakes are high, and winning is extra sweet. But the thrill has gone. Time to step aside and let the young bucks have their day."

For the first time since she'd met him, she saw a glimpse of Richard's age on his face. Talk of the company brought forth a weariness that she couldn't simply attribute to the fact they'd had little sleep. She empathised with him at that moment. He was trapped in Crombie Norton, just as she had been trapped on the farm. To an outsider, it looked like Richard had it all. But now she'd seen that it came with a price.

"Enough about that anyway. I need to leap into the shower. There's room for two..."

The shadow lifted, and his face relaxed, that playful smile and one raised eyebrow enticing her from between the sheets to take him up on the offer.

"I thought you were short on time?"

"On second thoughts, we don't need much."

CHAPTER 6

Long Distance

# Sarah

Wellington, New Zealand – July, 2007

SARAH TOLD HERSELF THAT she *wasn't* waiting for him to call from Sydney, but every day she was. Her impulsive plunge into physical intimacy with Richard disturbed her. She never slept with men she'd just met, had always reined in any inclination towards recklessness—until now.

So the daily phone calls, the gradual getting to know each other as people, albeit with a thousand miles between them, brought reassurance. She genuinely liked Richard and had a growing sense that she could talk to him about anything. It would have disappointed her to have the memory of making love to such an attractively packaged man tarnished by him turning out to be a jerk.

At first, still in Wellington on her holiday, she'd tried to hide the calls from Mel. But it had been difficult, as the nightly conversations grew longer. In the end, deciding it was rather pointless trying to be secretive, she confessed to her friend: there was more to her and Richard than an exquisite dinner and one night of great sex. Mel needed to get used to the idea. Confronted with the truth, she was still a little in awe that Sarah had entered into a relationship with the formidable Richard, and blatantly unsure as to the wisdom of the whole affair.

"But you hardly know him."

"That's why we talk each day. I'm getting to know him. That's the whole point."

"You sure must be finding out everything. God, you were on that phone an hour last night. Chewing through your minutes for the month. It will cost you a fortune."

"Money well spent." And it was.

She'd worked with Mel to juggle their final outings together around Richard's calls as the nightly routine became compulsive. Her friend still didn't get it, but then she wasn't privy to their conversations, didn't understand the hidden depths of the man who was revealing himself slowly but surely, night after night, while encouraging her to do the same.

He filled in details of his childhood, a simple but reasonably happy one, running wild in a low-income suburban neighbourhood that he made sound rather idyllic. Despite the absence of a father, his mother had worked hard to provide for her son.

"My Mum loved fashion," he said. "She was so stylish. Seeing photos of her from the 60s and 70s, she looked like a model. Always wore the latest designs. Not bought though, copied from pages of magazines, all sewn herself. If things had been different, she could have been a fashion designer, I think. With me on the scene, she had to settle for working as a machinist in a clothing factory. But she loved it so much, she'd come home at nights and sew some more. Other women paid her to create things for them. I was always lulled to sleep by the hum of her machine."

"Wow, I envy people who can sew. I'm hopeless," Sarah admitted. "Mum tried to teach all of us. She was pretty good herself. Came in handy with three daughters to outfit. Even made us gowns for the school balls. But I was a lost cause. Vivienne and Katrina inherited her sewing and cooking genes. I think I got more from dad, the farm stuff came more naturally."

He took the opening, making a gentle query. "Tell me more about her," he said. "Your mother. What was she like?"

"To people outside the family—practical, organised, very straightforward."

He laughed. "You may not have got her skills with homemaking stuff, but I think the straightforward came through loud and strong."

"Yeah, I suppose it did," Sarah agreed. "But underneath that brisk exterior, she was actually the softer one of our parents. If there was something we really wanted to do, but needed to talk our parents around to it, or if we were in trouble, we went to Mum. She'd always listen, never belittle your ideas or how you were feeling. She was a beautiful, warm person."

"I think you got a lot more from her than you might realise," he said.

<hr>

Once back home on the farm, talking to Richard each evening was the highlight of Sarah's day. Winter was a dull routine of feeding out hay, rotating the herd across their grazing, and monitoring the pregnant girls due to deliver their calves early. With the grind of short gruelling days and long chilly nights, she needed something to lift her spirits.

And talking to him did exactly that. She discovered underneath the careful, rather serious image he projected to the world, he could be funny, even to the point of silliness. It was an unexpected dimension to his personality.

"Favourite movie?" he asked. They'd been comparing their favourites of all sorts of things and it was his turn to choose the topic. "I bet it's *Gladiator*."

"Nope," she said. "Historians don't make the best critics for historical movies. It's *Titanic*."

"What! What is that, if not historical?"

"It's a romance, silly. Trust a man not to notice there was more to it than a story about a boat. "Anyway, I just loved it." She could hear him chuckling to himself. "OK, your turn," she said. "I'm thinking *Wall Street*."

"No, too obvious," he said. "I'll give you a clue." And he launched into lines from *Lord of the Rings* with the most authentic imitation of Gollum she'd ever heard. "It came to me, my own, my love... my ... precioussss."

The sheer ridiculousness of hearing ugly, wizened Gollum's voice coming from handsome Richard's mouth sent Sarah into uncontrollable fits of laughter, coughing and almost choking with the craziness of it. She rolled around on the bed, shaking so hard she dropped the phone.

Hearing the uproar brought her father's tap on the door. "You OK in there, love?"

"Yes, Dad, I'm OK," she managed to gasp, before the laughter overtook her again.

"Sarah? Are you there?" She could hear Richard's voice echoing down the line as she retrieved the phone from where it had skidded across the floor.

"OK, don't do that to me again," she said. "That was just too silly for words"

"If you say so, my precioussss," he said, setting her off once more.

His ability to do entertaining impressions wasn't the only surprise phone conversation Richard had in store for her. One evening, after a day where particularly nasty weather had barrelled down off the mountain, she lay on the bed, exhausted. Her last job of the day, hauling hay, had left her with stray prickly strands inside her bra, grimy clothes and aching muscles. She even lacked the energy to shower. As she answered the call, she was pleased he couldn't see her.

"Hi there. How was your day?" His voice washed over her, calm and soft despite the echo on the line. It soothed away the aches of the day.

"OK, I suppose. Bloody hard work, to be honest. Helped Dad with some fencing and then chased the cows that had broken it down back to where they should be. A hot shower is calling me."

That caused the conversation to veer off in a new direction, Richard abandoning talk of the minutiae of their separate days. His low, husky description of how much he'd like to join her in that shower, what he longed to do to her, where he wanted to touch her, sparked her own desire and she found her hand wandering in that same direction.

Only two doors stood between her bedroom and the lounge where her father shouted at the telly, urging on the horse he'd favoured with his bet. She was thankful that the blaring voice of the racing commentator and her father's whoop of jubilation drowned out her own panting to reach the finish line.

Richard sounded pleased with himself, that even at such a distance, he evoked this response in her. That he'd even tried it, let alone succeeded, still left her slightly aghast. It seemed each day she was learning new and surprising things about him. And about herself.

CHAPTER 7

Farm Girl

# Sarah

Wakefield, New Zealand – August, 2007

SARAH SWUNG THE SET of heavy stainless steel cups with ease, settling them on cow number 137's engorged udder, and watched streams of creamy milk issue from the soft teats. She could see the cow visibly relax as the milking machine released the pressure on her undercarriage.

Sarah stood in the circular pit, monitoring the flow on the dials above her head. She was almost superfluous in the shed these days. One of the great Kiwi innovations, the rotary cowshed had been common in Taranaki for years. Her father had been an early-adopter, always keen on new technology to make the farm run efficiently. It meant that, at least in this early part of the season, with only part of their large herd coming into milk, it was possible to manage the twice-daily chore single-handed. So Sarah happily skipped the morning shift to gain an extra sleep in, but would often join their sharemilker, Jason, in the afternoons.

A familiar woollen beanie appeared over the side of the pit, her father's weathered face beneath it, sporting a broad grin. It was good to see him smile. In those grim days after her mother's death, she had thought never to see that smile again.

Always an easygoing, wisecracking and exuberant man, no one would have predicted that grief would have sent Noel Mitchell into the depths of depression for a year. Suicides were not uncommon in the rural community, usually because of money woes and the ravages of a fickle climate placing farmers under intolerable pressure. In Noel's case, it was the cruel way fate had ripped away the love of his life. Sarah and her two older sisters feared that having lost their mother, despair could also snatch their father from them. But he'd pulled through and while he would never be the same man they'd grown up with, he had learned to live with the gaping hole in his life and to appreciate the glimmers of his beloved Ellen in his children and grandchildren.

"Sarah," he called down from above, yelling above the rhythmic clattering of the machinery. "There's a bloke here to see you."

"OK, on my way. You alright finishing up here Jason?"

"Yeah, no worries," her workmate called back. His smile said what they both knew, that he could manage without her. Sarah knew it was partly because she was the boss's daughter, but also because he saw she loved the work that Jason tolerated her presence in the shed.

Sarah was curious about who this 'bloke' was. She'd already had one male visitor today. Kevin, a farm sales rep, had been on the phone that morning, badgering her about some new feed supplement. She'd begrudgingly agreed that he could call in for a cup of tea and give her the rundown. She was perfectly capable of reading about the latest advances and making her own decision, but humoured Kevin only because she'd known him for years.

"Have a heart," her father teased, as she'd complained about it over lunch. "You know the boy's always fancied you. Don't brush him off as if he doesn't have a chance. Let him have a little hope."

"Well, he doesn't have a chance. He's wasting my time and his, if he thinks making cow-eyes at me over a cup of tea and some brochures is going to change that."

Kevin was the kind but bland son of a neighbouring farmer, who, realising his boy lacked the skills to be groomed for the farm's succession plan, had pushed him into a job with the local rural supply company. They'd been at school together. As Sarah gloomily trudged down the metal track to the house, she thought about how Kevin was exactly the type of suitor that Richard had assumed awaited her in Wakefield. And it sounded like there was one on the doorstep right now.

In contrast to her sour mood, Jock, their young farm dog, danced around her in gleeful anticipation. He'd fulfilled his final task of the day, accompanying Jason on the quad bike to the far-flung grazing, and then noisily encouraging the cows along the race and into the yards. Like all dogs, a creature of habit, he now expected dinner would be forthcoming. While he performed his farm duties adequately, Jock was too young to have benefited from her mother's training. The dogs had been Ellen's responsibility, working with their herding instinct to mould them into valuable canine farm staff, at the same time as learning how to be well-mannered members of the family.

Noel had always bleated about her over-indulgence. Most farmers left them kennelled when not working, but the Mitchell's dogs had always lounged on the verandahs and played with the kids. Sometimes, when they weren't too smelly, Ellen had allowed them to sneak inside and sleep by the fire. However, Jock, only a pup when Ellen died, lacked the benefit of her firm training, and had absolutely no concept of acceptable behaviour. The moment he sighted the visitor standing on the deck, he abandoned his happy dance, turning into a guided missile, streaking down the path and jumping the gate to fling himself joyfully at the man waiting there.

This was no farm supplies rep. At first she did a double-take, not believing her eyes, but no, they were functioning perfectly. The person almost bowled over by the airborne bundle of enthusiasm was Richard.

She'd talked to him last night as usual and he'd given no hint that he was even back in New Zealand, making only vague noises about having finished the work and that he'd be home soon. And now here he was waiting at the gate. The grin on his face suggested he was very pleased with his deception.

And because of it, he was about to see the real Sarah, clad in overalls and gumboots. Luckily, there were no cow shit splatters on her today. The girls had kindly spared her that indignity. Although a quick sniff confirmed she still bore the inescapable tang of it, the cloying odour overwhelming the routine spritz of perfume she applied each morning.

"Jock," she bellowed in vain. "Jock! *Come here.*" But the dog, forgetting he had ears, was prancing on his hind legs, his paws printing a muddy abstract pattern on Richard's jeans.

"Oh god, Richard, I'm so sorry. Jock, you little shit, *come here now!*" But Jock took no notice, Richard's laughter only encouraging him further.

"It's OK," he said. "I love dogs." Jock flung a carefree glance her way as if to say, "Yeah, it's OK. He loves dogs."

"Yeah, but he's filthy. Jock, you are a *naughty* boy." The dog, having delivered his welcome, ignored her reprimand and raced off into the hedge, appearing with a ball.

"No, Jock, you've had your fun for the day. Come in Richard, you'll be safe from him in the house." Seemingly undeterred by her state of dress, he turned his back on the dog's pleading eyes and caught her in his arms. With the one kiss, suddenly the tedium of the day's work fell away.

"Well, when Dad said there was a bloke waiting for me, I didn't expect to see you. You never mentioned it on the phone."

"Yeah, probably should have given you a bit of warning," he said with a grin, as they made their way into the huge farmhouse kitchen, shutting the ebullient Jock outside. "But I wanted to surprise you."

"You sure did that. As you can see," she said, striking a model's pose in her rough work clothes.

He pulled her in against him, ignoring the dirt. "God, it's good to see you. No phone call–not even one of those phone calls," he said, with a knowing look while his hand slid over her bum seeking the gap between her thighs, "is a substitute for getting my hands on this." His other hand unzipped the overalls, and navigated the layers to find bare breasts. Standing there in the kitchen, she stopped herself from suggesting he make good on his promises on the phone. After all, Noel might appear at any moment. "Even in your farmer's uniform, you're beautiful. But the other guests at the lodge will think it a little odd if you arrive at dinner like that," he said, breaking into a smile.

"The lodge?" The tourist lodge perched high on the mountain was the gem in the crown of local attractions.

"I'm staying there. Had to fly up for a meeting in New Plymouth this morning and decided why not mix pleasure with business? So, put on something pretty, and..." He threw her a suggestive look. "Pack an overnight bag."

He tossed out that last casual remark and waited for a reaction. She returned a smile, damped down the desire to rip his clothes off right there, and separated from him with a playful push. She padded down the hallway in her woollen gumboot socks. Any man who could see her looking like this and still want to bed her had to be a keeper.

"Don't hurry," he called after her. "Jock here will keep me company." The dog, having nosed the door open, had snuck in, and was now laying by his feet.

In the end, it wasn't Jock who occupied Richard while she cleaned up. She had just discarded the last layers of work clothes into the laundry basket, and stood poised to step into the shower, when the clomping of gumboot clad feet echoed on the wooden verandah. She knew those footsteps. Her father. It seemed curiosity had got the better of him, and he'd decided to find out more about the man who'd come to see his daughter.

This was not how she'd planned to introduce Richard to Noel. Her father was a down-to-earth man of the land. He had no time for 'Queen Street farmers' as he disparagingly referred to the corporate types who'd been buying up farms all over the country, edging out the families who'd worked the land for generations. In fact, he was generally suspicious of anyone with money, assuming they'd most likely acquired it by dubious means. And she certainly regretted not mentioning Richard to him sooner. She could so easily have smoothed the way a little, using a lifetime of knowledge about her father to reveal Richard's existence in the most flattering light.

She cursed her stupidity. Of course Noel would come to investigate the strange man who'd turned up asking for her. Now Richard must face her father on his own. Knowing Dad's little quirks, she was confident she could have managed the encounter to their advantage, presenting Richard to him in ways that would encourage his approval. But it was too late. All she could do was shower, dress, pack quickly—and hope Richard did nothing to tarnish his image in Noel's eyes.

When she emerged, to her surprise, laughter and the tones of friendly male conversation drifted down the hallway.

"One of my mates," she heard Richard saying, "has a very nice two-year-old filly. Goes back to Danehill on the sire's side, and the dam was a group one winner. I was with him at Karaka when he bought her. Got her for a song. Seems the Chinese had spent all their money for the day. The trainer says she's going to be a cracker."

It was Richard's voice, but he'd dropped into the idiom of the typical Kiwi male. Chameleon-like, he had changed his colours to fit the company, leaving no hint of the smooth corporate operator.

"Nice bloodlines there," her father replied. "You'll have to let me know when she's racing. Sounds like it would be worth throwing a couple of bob on her."

She decided it was safe to push the door open.

"Hello love." Her father turned to greet her as she ventured into the kitchen. Two half-consumed beers sat on the table between them. "Your young man here's been giving me some good tips on the gee-gees."

Richard smiled at her across her father's head, and she couldn't help but smile too. *Her young man.* But while Richard appeared happy and relaxed, there was something in her father's eyes that worried her. On the surface, it seemed that in thirty minutes of conversation, Richard had secured a large tick of approval. But Noel still couldn't hide his uncertain expression when, a short while later, Richard whisked his only unmarried daughter away on a date. In the wing mirror Sarah glimpsed him standing on the verandah, following their progress down the bumpy gravel driveway, hands plunged deep in his pockets and his face thoughtful.

"Well, I think that went well," Richard said, as they clattered along the metalled farm track towards the road. "Once he got over the shock of finding that you'd left me sitting in the kitchen drinking his beer. Why didn't you tell him about us?"

"I was going to," she said, "except I wasn't exactly expecting there to be a deadline by which I needed to. That's what happens when you turn up unannounced."

"So you'd rather I hadn't come then..." She knew he was teasing.

"Don't be so bloody stupid. Of course I'm glad you're here. And I don't mind surprises, except this one may have a few repercussions. Don't worry, he'll get over it."

"Well, I thought I did a reasonable job of getting on side with him."

"Yeah, it sounded like things were going OK when I arrived. What on earth did you talk to him about? I would have thought you had nothing in common."

"Your dad's a good guy. I like him. And we had plenty in common."

"Yes, well, you struck the right chord talking about racing. He's addicted to it. The racing channel seems to run 24/7 on that TV of his."

"Yeah, and we talked a bit of rugby. I mean, I'm not a huge fan, but it always pays to keep up with the latest. Can't really go wrong with that as a topic anywhere in New Zealand." He was right. Whether you loved the national game or not, you'd have to be a hermit to not know a little about it. And talk of rugby definitely oiled the wheels in most social situations. "But you should give him more credit," said Richard. "He's a knowledgeable chap. Farmers like him have to be pretty astute businessmen these days. We had quite an in-depth conversation about the dairy payout and the state of the rural economy."

"Oh, that was perfect. He loves having a moan about that to anyone who will listen."

"And at first, when he was looking at me suspiciously, I remembered you saying he admired Paul. Once he found out I work with him, he decided I must be OK. Used my 'get out of jail' card to smooth the way." Sarah didn't have the heart to tell him that knowing Paul was most likely only the equivalent of a one-day leave pass. It would take more than a bit of name-dropping to earn her father's acceptance.

"Thank you for making an effort with him," she said, resting her hand on his lap. "While I don't need his approval for what I do in my life, it helps. He's had more than his share of problems these past years. I try not to be one of them."

"I don't think there's much chance of that. He adores you." He eased the car to a halt at the farm entranceway, leaned across and kissed her gently. "And so do I," he murmured in her ear before securing his hands on the wheel and manoeuvring the big vehicle onto the road. She sat beside him, her heart racing. This day was full of surprises.

C HAPTER 8

Alpine Escape

## *Sarah*

Egmont National Park, New Zealand – August, 2007

THEY ZIPPED ALONG THE narrow winding road, the hired Range Rover oblivious to the steady uphill climb as they passed through the gates of the National Park. The farmland was now usurped by native bush that filtered the late afternoon sunlight. Richard handled the vehicle with relaxed confidence and skill, although it wasn't sufficient to calm her. Since her mother's accident, Sarah had become a nervous passenger. Subconscious fear lurked in her mind, her body involuntarily tensing whenever in a vehicle on the open road. Richard glanced across and, noticing how she braced herself at each turn, slowed down.

"I'm sorry. Too fast for you? I'll ease off," he said, approaching the next tight bend with greater caution.

"No, no, I'm OK," she said. "It's not your driving. Honestly, I'm like this whoever's behind the wheel. Too many memories, especially on this road."

"I saw," he said, his voice gentle, as he eased back even further on the throttle, the huge engine no longer a throaty rumble but a soft thrum. "The cross further back. For your mum?"

In the time before, she'd seen those roadside crosses and wondered about the stories behind them, each one a sad reminder of a life snuffed out, a family destroyed. She'd never imagined that it would be her family devastated by a needless death. That it would be her stopping by a cross to lay flowers. To read the name she loved, Ellen Mitchell, inscribed in callous black lettering, evidence that it wasn't all a bad dream.

"Yes," she said. "It's not easy seeing it there, having to pass it all the time. But if it saves another life, reminds people to take their time, to be careful on this road, then it's worth it."

"You're the image of her," he said. "The photo on the hall table," he added in reply to her inquiring look.

"I love that photo. It was at a dance before they were married. You can see where it was heading even then."

In the photograph, seventeen-year-old Ellen looked directly at the camera, her dark hair splaying over her shoulders, a bold smile as she raised a glass to the photographer. Noel, seated next to her, might have been channelling Elvis, with his hair short at the back, the long, heavy quiff at the front swept up with hair cream, although an unruly corkscrew flopped low over one brow. But it was obvious he wasn't posing for the photo. With his eyes fixed on her, the smile betrayed he was already besotted with the woman by his side.

"The start of a great love story," he said, and she couldn't help but read in his glance a hint of the same look as in her father's eyes in that picture.

"Yes," she said softly, "it was."

They passed through a stone gateway with the words 'Egmont National Park' picked out in brass letters. Now officially on the lower slopes of the mountain, they climbed more steeply, the road crowded by dense vegetation, and increasing numbers of tall trees reaching their spindly fingers overhead, tips connecting. The musty smell of the bush permeated the car, the air thick with dampness. They drove without speaking, the hush of the world outside inviting their own silence.

On the last leg of the ascent, where the road became almost a single lane, the vegetation was lower, revealing the peak looming before them. At this altitude, relentless rainfall stunted the growth of the bush. Twisted goblin forest, the gnarled branches heavy with velvet moss and beards of lichen, surrounded them on three sides. The trees' tortured limbs held a strange beauty, like something out of an enchanted wood.

Up ahead was the perfectly formed cone of the sleeping volcano, its outline sharp as a cardboard cut-out against a cloudless sky. Despite her living most of her life in the shadow of this mountain, the sight of it always made her catch her breath.

"Been to the top?" he asked.

"Only once. That was enough. The summit track is easy enough, but the last few hundred metres..." She shuddered at the thought of the sheer drops, the fear she'd conquered to stand on the top of that mountain. "Well, it's scary steep, makes you feel like you're falling even if you're not."

"Perhaps I'll give it a miss then."

"I'm happy to guide you on any other track but that one. Been over most of them many times."

"So, you are an outdoorsy girl."

"I have to confess it wasn't my original motivation. My sister Katrina belonged to the tramping club. And I fancied one of the boys in the club. By attaching myself to Kat, I could hang out with him. Which also meant traipsing all over the mountain most weekends. I lost interest in the boy, but never lost my love of being up here."

Around one last tight turn they emerged into a clearing, where the replica Swiss-styled lodge snuggled into a blanket of bush, a small near empty car park out front, and lights inside glowing with a warm welcome.

The air in the lodge car park was cool, but as they stepped inside the huge double doors, warmth enveloped them, overlaid with the smoky breath of a massive open fire. That fire burned night and day, whatever the season, as winter steadfastly maintained a year round grip on this alpine area.

Sarah looked up into a familiar face, not unexpected with the lodge staffed by locals, a few living in, the others commuting each day from the town below.

"Sarah! Haven't seen you for a while. How are you?" Anna Murray, lodge manager, had been in the same class as her oldest sister Vivienne. "And how's Vivi? Busy with the kids, I imagine."

"Yeah, you said it. But I suppose it's to be expected if you forget to do the maths. Five under five. What was she thinking?" In six years, Vivienne had gone from just married to almost continuously pregnant, further complicated by a set of twins. Her unruly brood was much loved by the family, but exhausting. None of them understood how she survived. Sarah had vowed that although she was fairly certain that kids would feature in her life one day, she was equally certain she didn't need a whole tribe. One or two were more than enough—unless you were Vivienne Mitchell.

Anna laughed. "Yeah, rather her than me." Then, switching back into her role as hostess, she turned her attention to Richard, informing him that the table would be ready whenever they wished. As it was early, she suggested they leave their luggage for a porter to deal with and start at the bar.

As Richard wandered through ahead of her, Sarah glanced back at Anna to see a smirk on her face. She gave Sarah a thumbs-up signal and dropped her professional demeanour to mouth "He's hot!" Sarah grinned back, and couldn't help but agree as she looked at his slim waist and tight butt as he headed for the sofa.

Being recognised as a Wakefield local had its advantages. Anna ensured the perfect table in front of a massive picture window. Outside in the floodlit bush, delicate fern fronds swayed. Illuminated from beneath, they looked like ruffled lace cuffs on an antique gown. Droplets of moisture clung to hanging threads of moss, creating sparkling strands of diamonds. And above them, the snow-covered peak was lit against the twilight sky, reflecting the newly risen moon.

The dinner wasn't quite up to Silver's standards, but it was good. She had a sense of pride that her little province, far from the latest trends, could still deliver a refined dining experience. The wine and the conversation flowed easily, as it had on their daily phone calls.

"I want to know everything about you," he said. "You, your family, growing up in this place. Tell me more." And so she did. There was so much to tell of a happy childhood, a firm but loving upbringing, and a down-to-earth life dictated by the rhythms of the farm.

"I still can't believe you just turned up like that," she said, when reminded of just how down-to-earth she'd been when he'd surprised her earlier. "And there's me, all sweaty and smelling like cow shit, bellowing like a fishwife at the bloody dog."

"The look on your face was priceless. I should have filmed it. Just imagine the voiceover." His eyes danced with glee as he launched into his best Attenborough imitation, keeping a perfectly straight face while she dissolved into giggles. "Here we see a particularly rare species, the Sarah Mitchell, captured in its natural habitat, displaying its winter plumage of khaki overalls. But wait—listen a moment—is that its rarely heard mating call?"

"I wasn't exactly dressed to attract a mate."

"You'd attract me no matter what you were wearing," he said, with a suggestive sweep of his eyes across her deep v-neckline.

"Well, you couldn't have seen me in anything worse."

"Seriously though," he said. "I'm in awe of you. The way you can stand in two worlds and be completely at ease in both of them. I envy that."

"I guess I'm lucky. The country grounds me and the city energises me. I just go with it."

"It's a special quality."

"Doesn't seem that way to me. It's just about fitting in."

"It's special, believe me. I can't do it," he said, "—be more than one person. I've worked so hard at being this one for such a long time, I can't see beyond it. Don't know if I can be anything else."

"If you could be something else, what would you want to be?"

"Definitely far removed from this: corporate raider, deal maker, hard-nosed businessman." There was a bitterness there in those words, as if they were insults rather than achievements. "From the outside, it looks glamorous, fulfilling. But it's not. Sometimes I hate the person I've become—I've *had to* become—to make the company what it is. When I partnered with Paul, there was an agreement that we would do whatever it took, and I haven't let him down. But it's come at a cost."

The tinge of sadness in his voice spurred her to reach for him and offer reassurance. Placing her hand over his, she could feel the tension even in his fingertips.

"It's not too late," she said. "There's still time to make a different choice."

"Choice," he said. "That's the real gold. The freedom to choose. When I was younger, I thought money would give me that. It hasn't. OK, I can choose the car I want, the house I live in, where I want to go on holiday. Money gives you those kinds of choices. All my adult life, I told myself that I was choosing what I wanted. But looking back, I've never been free to choose. First in my twenties, my choices were made to satisfy Victoria's father. He put a lot of faith in me, gave me huge opportunities. But along with that came huge responsibilities. I couldn't let him down. I needed to prove I really could do the job, that I had what it took, not just that I was sitting there because I was his son-in-law."

"Tough position to be in," she said. He nodded and went on.

"And then there was Victoria and the kids. I told myself I was doing it for them, being the successful moneymaker, keeping her in the same lifestyle in which she was raised and giving the girls the same."

"Better than you had."

"Yes," he said. "But you see, I was wrong. I didn't understand that kids don't need flashy clothes and the latest toys. They just need people who love them. And a wife needs a husband who is there, not someone who is never home because he's too busy making money. Believe me, Victoria deserved a medal for putting up with life with me." He gave her a rueful smile, and she could see the pain of regret there. He hadn't loved Victoria, but he had cared about her in his own way.

"So what do *you* need?" she said gently. "And why aren't you going for it?"

"Right this moment, what I need is you," he said simply. "And I am going for it. That's why I'm here."

The intensity in his gaze overwhelmed her. She had to look away. Never before in her life had someone made her feel like she was essential to their very existence as he had in this moment. And right there she realised that this thing between them also came with the weight of choices. She felt the possibilities, that this was a huge opportunity to grow into something very special, but also came with a huge responsibility: to not break his heart.

Being local, she'd never stayed here. Swinging open the door to their room revealed a Swiss-themed decor that could have easily descended into kitsch. But obviously the lodge owners hadn't skimped on design expertise in these rooms.

The suite was simple and elegant. A preponderance of wood on walls and ceilings added warmth to the space, but one completely glassed wall prevented it from being overbearing. As in the restaurant, it faced an area of discreetly floodlit bush where tiny insects ducked and dived, hypnotised by the lights.

On a large coffee table, tiny scented candles floated in a bowl, their dancing flames reflected in the water, releasing an earthy, fresh smell that brought the greenness inside. In front of the window was an enormous bath, its sleek inviting curves adding a luxurious touch.

"Oh wow, that's amazing," she said. "I want to try that out. To have a bubble bath looking out on the bush. And you can pour me a glass of wine to drink while you wash my back."

"Save that thought for later," he said, tossing his jacket on the bed. "You might need it when I've finished with you."

A discreet knock interrupted that suggestion as a bottle of champagne arrived.

Sarah looked at Richard quizzically. "A celebration?"

"Hopefully," he said, but his face gave away nothing. "Take a guess."

Her easy familiarity with him dissipated in a flash, replaced by an unexpected twinge of nervousness, reminded that she didn't yet know him well enough to predict his moves or motives.

"No, I'm hopeless at that game. Too lacking in imagination. Just come out with it."

"Well," he said, his eyes fixed firmly on her, as if not allowing her to escape, "there's a question I need an answer for. An important question." She swallowed audibly, and he stared at her, his face serious. Then a smile broke through. "I want to know if you're going to come to Rome with me."

Sarah let out her breath, chiding herself for the ridiculous thoughts that had been dashing through her brain. For a moment there, she had genuinely thought he might be about to abandon all common sense and ask her to marry him. Of course it happened in books and movies. And it possibly did happen occasionally in real life. But not with someone like Richard. He was far more carefree than she'd have guessed at their first meeting, but surely he wasn't the sort of person who would leap into huge, life-changing decisions on a whim. Which was fortunate, as nor was she.

"Come on, Sarah, take pity on this bottle, languishing there unopened. And this poor man, dangling on your words." He was all playfulness now, the cutest boyish expression on his face. She was sure few people would think of Richard Norton and 'cute' in the same sentence.

"All right then, yes, I'll come to Rome."

With a flourish he whisked the bottle from its icy nest, and in moments she was cradling a tulip-shaped glass of sweetly effervescent bubbles. Their cheerful pops mirrored her own bright bubbly feelings of excitement. An alluring city with this alluring man. How lucky she was.

"I'll ask my PA to sort the airfares. And somewhere beautiful to stay. I know the perfect place. However," he said, placing his own glass on the table, "that can wait till morning. Other things can't." His hands were gentle, taking the champagne from her and drawing her in against him. Despite the warmth of the room, she shivered at the touch, and the words whispered in her ear. "I'm about to make good on my promises to you over the phone."

Her last thought before succumbing to the raw need that overtook her was that in four weeks, they'd be doing this every night.

---

"Sarah, is this an OK time to talk?" She hadn't anticipated calls this early in the morning, when they'd only just finished the hearty room service breakfast. She glanced across to see Richard still engrossed in his own phone call and said, "Sure," as she stepped onto the balcony.

Professor Jermaine. She'd not expected to hear from him yet. Maybe the academic committee had fast-tracked her proposal. A leap of hope accompanied that thought. Hope that he'd backed her, convincing them she was what the history department needed and they should grab her now.

"Professor, I wasn't expecting to hear from you so soon." Projecting a calm voice was difficult when excitement danced in her bones.

"No, no," he said. "I realise we're a way off from finalising plans for next year, but something's come up, and I thought of you straight away." Not the proposal then, but another opportunity. And she was the person he thought of first. "One of our junior lecturers in the post-grad diploma programme has had an unfortunate accident. Broke her leg in a football match. She's going to be off for weeks and, as you know, this is a busy time of the semester."

He was about to offer her a job, and her heart leapt in a thrill of anticipation.

"Oh, that sounds wonderful," she said. "Tell me more."

He rattled through details of the two course papers she'd be covering. "Of course I'll email more so you can see exactly what you'd be signing up for. That address I have for you is OK?"

"Yes, yes, send it through. I'm not at home right now, but I'll get onto it today."

"Right, well, I'm pleased to hear it. Not only would you be helping me out of a sticky situation, but getting you into the department will certainly tip the odds in your favour when the committee makes their decision. As you know, a couple of them are a little reluctant to take on candidates whose area of interest is outside the New Zealand context. But I'm sure if they get to know you, they'll see what I see. So, here's your opportunity to win them over."

"Thank you so much, Professor. I'm so grateful."

"Gerald," he said. "Please, call me Gerald. After all, we're going to be work colleagues."

She slipped back inside, where Richard was still in conversation with Gwen, his PA. He called her his lifeline for the way she smoothed his complicated life into a manageable form, and it seemed from the intense look on his face that she'd have her work cut out for her today.

Flopping onto the bed, Sarah lay back with her eyes closed, savouring the sense of elation washing over her. They wanted her. This was her chance.

There was a bounce as Richard arrived beside her, and his lips pressed against her upturned mouth, where a smug smile had taken up residence.

"All done," he said. "Booked and paid for. We are off to Rome." The smile evaporated, and she opened her eyes to see his furrowed brows. "What?" he said. "Don't tell me you've changed your mind."

She pasted the smile back on her face. She couldn't let him know that the happy flip-flops in her stomach had reversed direction, replaced with a sick feeling at the choice that now faced her. Follow her heart and follow Richard? That meant giving the university the brushoff, self-sabotaging her chance to leapfrog the other candidates, triggering inevitable comments about her lack of commitment. And risk the loss of the PhD spot she'd longed for.

Or take the job and send Richard off to Rome alone? And risk the loss of the best thing that had happened to her in a long time. Whatever her decision, either way, she was screwed.

CHAPTER 9

Road to Rome

# Sarah

Changi Airport, Singapore – September, 2007

SARAH SKIPPED ALONG THE travelator with glee. Fuelled by childish delight, a burst of energy surged through her at the odd sensation of the moving path beneath her feet, as well as the reprieve from the confines of the plane. The flight was the longest she'd ever endured. Her limited previous travel experience comprised three shopping jaunts to Australia's eastern seaboard cities. She and Mel had spent more money than they should in Melbourne's boutiques, delighted in quirky designer shops in inner-city Sydney and indulged in a factory shopping spree in a multi-acre Gold Coast mall with interludes at theme parks and the casino. Her only truly exotic holiday was a friend's wedding in tropical Fiji.

To her surprise, she didn't feel too bad after the first eleven-hour hop to Singapore, no doubt buoyed by the comfort of business class. The businessman himself trailed behind her, wrangling both of their carry-on luggage with the practised hand of a well-seasoned traveller. Her own bright pink floral case looked frivolous perched on top of Richard's subdued black Samsonite, but he didn't appear the least self-conscious, dragging it along behind him.

She hopped off the moving path at one gap and stood waiting for him. He shot her an indulgent grin. He'd displayed a good-natured tolerance of her gushes of excitement as she examined the accoutrements of travelling in the business class compartment—the bag of high-end toiletries, comfy slippers, a soft blanket. Even now, he appeared to be totally at ease with the woman-child persona that had overtaken her from the moment they stepped onto the air bridge in Auckland. It was unexpected, since he was basically conservative in nature and not prone to open exuberance, although behind closed doors, his youthful playfulness matched her own. And he was relaxed at her public displays of affection, like now when she stood barring his way, face tilted up expectantly.

"You shall not pass—unless you kiss me."

He obliged with a laugh and the requested kiss, then taking her hand, steered her past the rows of duty-free shops so unlike any she'd seen in the terminals of Australasia and the Pacific. Apart from the travelators and the travellers themselves, Changi Airport resembled a massive upmarket shopping mall. Shop windows glowed with alluring gold jewellery, bold and unashamedly flashy. Others bore the discreet logos of designers whose names were legendary, most too exclusive to have a presence in little old New Zealand. She dallied in front of one, curious to see if it lived up to the enticing ads in the women's magazines she read at the hairdressers, like *Vogue* and *Harper's Bazaar*.

"Later," he said. "I promise to let you wander in the shops before the next leg. After all, we've ten hours to kill. Let's go to the hotel, get some sleep." He'd made sure that Gwen's booking instructions had allowed them a brief layover on the way, so her first experience of long-haul flights wasn't too arduous.

"Or not sleep…" she said with a suggestive smile. This was the longest she'd had him all to herself, and it was intoxicating. She was looking forward to making the most of this holiday, hoping to dispel all her pent up need for him after a month of forced separation—he in Wellington doing whatever merchant bankers did; she on the farm lending a welcome hand with the busy spring chores, raising calves and doing the odd milking. Once in the air, she'd tossed around the idea of suggesting they join the infamous mile-high-club, but rejected it as crass. But she wasn't about to let the opportunity of this hotel bed go to waste.

On the flight, Sarah had decided that apart from his obvious good looks, Richard's old-fashioned attentiveness added to the attraction. So often he anticipated her needs, fussing over her to ensure she was comfortable, almost making the cabin crew redundant. He made her feel special, like the only woman in the universe.

Although it was hard to look past the outward package. Somewhere across the vastness of Australia, she'd been studying the contours of his face, appreciating how beautiful he was, relaxed in a gentle doze in the seat next to her, when she'd looked up to catch the discreet admiring glance of the flight attendant. They had locked eyes for a moment; the woman offering an embarrassed smile. Sarah had smiled back, feeling smug and wishing she could say it out loud: "It's OK, you can admire him all you want, because I know when he wakes up it's me he'll be interested in."

And it was only him that she wanted, quite badly. These recurrent overwhelming surges of lust took her by surprise. She had a healthy sexual appetite, had experienced a strong physical attraction to men before—but not to the point of impatience to get up against the wall with them in the first convenient corner. Like now.

The airport hotel room was small but well-appointed, with all the comforts you needed for a short layover between flights. And the most important item—a large comfortable bed. Richard had barely dropped their bags onto the luggage rack when she grabbed him by the front of his Lacoste polo shirt, making it clear that he should remove it.

"I think I'm going to need a holiday to recover from the holiday," he said, flinging it off before setting to remove hers.

She trailed her hand down the line of hairs on his bare chest, sliding her hand into the waistband of his jeans. "Start as we mean to continue, I say."

---

Afterwards she was exhausted, partly from the vigorous workout they'd just shared, but also the effects of broken sleep. They'd taken off right on midnight and flown through the night. But even with the cabin lights dimmed, and swathed in a mohair blanket, she'd slept fitfully, too wired with excitement to relax fully into the comfortable reclining seat. Feeling languid, she now drifted into a pleasant post-coital sleep.

When she awoke, she checked the clock, and was pleased to see she'd grabbed five solid hours. Climbing out of bed carefully so as not to wake Richard, whose rhythmic breathing suggested he was still well under, she headed for the bathroom.

The pressurised drops from the shower head pinged against her skin, like a million tiny fingers massaging her body. She swathed generous handfuls of a coconut body wash, removing the grimy sweat of the flight, and of their lovemaking, but not scrubbing too hard, reluctant to expunge the smell of Richard from her skin. She wanted to hold on to that small whiff of him, as if driven by some primal need to bear his scent, marking her as his property.

Here she was, in an airport hotel, en route to Europe. This was what she'd traded a more certain future for by declining Gerald's job offer. Tossed away an opportunity to get her foot in the door of the history department and dazzle those narrow-minded bastards. She knew her area of expertise wasn't sexy enough for them. No, they preferred people who wanted to delve into the more recent past. Some of it you could hardly call history when there were living, breathing people who had existed through it. Perhaps saying no had been her unconscious way of giving them a very large middle finger.

She may well live to regret it in two months' time when they handed out the few sought after spots in the doctoral programme. She'd agonised over how to break the news to Gerald. Could she still even call him that? Or would he expect her to revert to 'Professor Jermaine' until such time as she came to her senses? The tense conversation when she'd phoned him suggested he held out little hope of that. He'd told her she'd lost her mind. Even now, replaying that conversation in her head made her feel physically sick, yet she knew her mind had been very much present in her choice to come.

Two things had consciously swayed her decision. The first, a desperate need to do something different. She was famous for being decisive, but looking back, she knew that most of those decisions had been to do the expected 'right' thing. The youngest in her family, but she'd always been the responsible one, making grown-up choices, being the adult. She'd had enough of that.

And the second—well, he was asleep in the room next door, snoring softly. Drawn to Richard from the moment those eyes had first met hers, despite all Mel's warnings and her own niggling doubts about where this might all lead, she had still chosen him. It was a crazy, irresponsible thing to do, run off overseas with him. She hadn't told a soul what she'd given up to do this, not even him. And right now, she was unspeakably happy as she dropped the voluminous towel on the floor and slipped back into bed, wrapping herself around him, never wanting to let go.

They flew much of the next fifteen hours in darkness, but sleep evaded her. Cocooned in the generous seat, she grabbed snippets, lulled by the steady drone of the jet engines. But every so often, even in her sleep, awareness of a change in tone brought her back to wakefulness, stirred not only by the altered sound, but the sensation of the huge plane wheeling off in a different direction as the pilots tweaked the flight path.

The first time she raised the blind she looked down on a vast blackness, punctuated by a strip of fairy lights, like decorations on a Christmas tree. She flicked the screen in front of her to view the map, the blinking on-screen plane showing they were over the inky blackness of the Indian Ocean. To the right, the massive Indian sub-continent was also shrouded in darkness except for the trail of light along the endless coastal highway marking its perimeter.

Later, as the plane banked sharply, she saw they were circling an immense city, a glorious blaze of light extending far out into the night. "Oh my god, that's beautiful." She was careful to keep her voice hushed so as not to wake their slumbering neighbours.

"Karachi," Richard said. "Believe me, this is the best place to see it from. Went there once, a hellhole. Hot and dirty. Couldn't wait to leave."

Two hours later, the burgeoning dawn caught up with them. She paused on her way back from the bathroom and peered out onto what the flight map told her was the Arabian Sea. The flickering flames dotted here and there intrigued her, the flares of oil rigs pumping the earth's riches from the depths of the sea to fuel the energy hungry world. It reminded her of the lyrics to 'Beautiful Day' and from then on she couldn't chase the song out of her mind, dozing some more with it circling in her brain. It seemed rather appropriate. This was going to be a beautiful day—in Rome with Richard.

The pleasant voices of the cabin crew interrupted her last grab at sleep as they set about gently awakening their charges before delivering breakfast. Even in the comfort of business class, she was tired and smelly to an extent no amount of complimentary toiletries could fix. She longed for a proper shower at the hotel and a large comfortable bed with Richard in it.

---

As the airport train sped towards Roma Terminii, Sarah pressed her nose to the glass of the carriage, scanning the skyline for any telltale silhouette of an ancient structure. But to her disappointment, she might have been in any city in the world. Outside, a trail of ugly walls and broken-down corrugated fences whizzed by. The layers of graffiti at least gave some hint that she wasn't in Wellington now, with scrawls of Italian framed in spray paint art, none of it the least bit attractive.

As they'd made their way through immigration, the excitement of actually being in Rome kept her exhaustion at bay, but now it was creeping across her again, aided by the rhythmic swaying of the Leonardo Express that connected Fiumicino airport to the city. Richard had suggested the train over a cab, figuring that the interminable stop-start of navigating Rome's congested traffic at rush hour would not make for the most comfortable start to their day. She moved to lay her head on his shoulder, knowing the feeling of jet lag for the first time.

At the station, Richard navigated the platform with the air of a well-seasoned traveller, and they joined a small queue at the taxi rank. While waiting for a cab, the drifting smell of sewage assaulted her nostrils, and she wrinkled her nose in distaste.

"Get used to it," he said. "The charming fragrance of most European cities, and all of them in Asia."

"God," she said in disgust, "You think they'd have made more progress, given they've had a few thousand years to sort it." The ancient Romans had been engineers ahead of their time. It seemed their modern counterparts were not.

She was grateful when the next taxi inching forward in the line was theirs. But, as Richard had warned, a taxi ride in Rome was akin to being sucked into a game of 'Grand Theft Auto'. They hurtled through the main streets at breakneck speed, plunged into massive multi-lane roundabouts that lacked any lane markings, and then dived off into a maze of tiny side streets. The driver frequently swerved around pedestrians, forced off the already narrow pavements by clusters of haphazardly parked mopeds. He finally screeched to a halt under the portico of the Hotel de Russie.

"You like it?" Richard said, as she stood in the lobby, trying not to let her mouth fall open at the luxury surrounding her.

"I feel like such a peasant." She was acutely conscious of her casual attire and her sweaty body underneath. "It's stunning."

"It's old," he said. "Once the haunt of Russian royalty. They say Picasso and Stravinsky used to hang out here. Be prepared to be treated royally, too. It's one of my favourite hotels."

While the streets outside were cramped and grimy, their hotel room overlooked an oasis of fountains, trees, and winding paths. Sarah imagined whiling away a few hours in the hotel's central courtyard, planning outings or relaxing after the whirl of sightseeing. She was already in love with Rome.

They fell into an easy routine—sleeping late, breakfast in the hotel together before Richard headed off to deal with the day's business and she set out on whatever adventure she'd planned. When he had a spare afternoon, they ventured out together, hand in hand, pottering around intriguing places beyond the tourist trail. In the evening, a drink in the verandah bar, sometimes an interlude in the bedroom and then dinner out, completed the day.

Richard had been modest about his historical knowledge. Being well-educated and well-read, he could hold his own in their conversations. However, she knew there were still surprises she could spring on him. Little gems that other visitors to Rome often missed. So it was with excitement that one afternoon she planned an outing for them beyond the city walls, to a place she'd long to visit and one that she knew he'd enjoy too.

Sarah waited outside the hotel, smiling to herself in delicious anticipation of Richard's reaction. Sitting in the driver's seat of the scarlet convertible, there was a gentle vibration as its V6 motor thrummed. The engine's delicate purr hinted it might easily become a growl on the open road. It was probably excessive to have selected this upmarket Alfa Romeo Spider from the array of rental vehicles, but up till now, Richard had insisted on paying for absolutely everything. It felt good to dip into her savings for something so quintessentially Italian for their outing.

Today they would leave Rome's narrow cobbled streets behind and head for the ancient city beyond the city: Ostia Antica. Sarah couldn't wait to walk its streets and explore the buildings, up till now only experienced through books, photographs and film. This was where ordinary Romans had lived their lives, in the streets of a bustling port at the mouth of the Tiber.

Richard arrived right on time as arranged, looking handsome in a blue polo shirt that emphasised the intense colour of his eyes. Those eyes widened in shock as he realised she was the woman waving at him from behind the wheel of a sleek sports car. She'd told him she'd grab a rental car and meet him under the hotel portico. But he hadn't envisaged this. It was fun to surprise him. And for once to be treated to the sight of him taking delight in some unexpected experience. Most of the time it was he who'd delighted in watching her discover all that lay beyond her previously small world. A broad smile of approval spread across his face as he strode across the driveway.

"So, it seems you have great taste in cars," he said. "I think I'm going to regret saying you could be our driver today. I'd love to get behind the wheel of this beast." He ran an appreciative hand over the tan leather seat before leaning across to kiss her.

"Well, if you're very good, I might let you take a turn with her on the way back."

"No, it's OK," he said. "I think she'd prefer you. You look good in the driver's seat—two beautiful girls who belong together."

Sarah took a deep breath before inching out into the insanity of the streets, navigating the car between crazed scooter riders and frantic taxis. She was relieved when they finally left the narrow streets behind and were cruising along a motorway. On either side, there were green fields, hedges and livestock. She inhaled the fragrance of the country. It was such a refreshing change from the myriad smells of the teeming city that assaulted your nose at every turn.

By contrast, at their destination, the sun-baked cobbles of Ostia Antica gave off a pleasant, earthy aroma. The early afternoon autumn sun lit up the ruins of the city, immersing them in a burnished copper glow of ancient brick. She led him on a winding path through the maze of streets, revelling in the role of tour guide.

"How do you know all this stuff?" he said, as they stopped to admire one of the many colourful mosaics. "You've never been here before, yet you're rattling off all this information like you do it every day..."

"Ah, but that's where you're wrong," she said. "I've been here dozens of times——in my mind. Walked these streets as I read about them. Studied the photographs and maps. Soaked up the knowledge as I watched documentaries."

"Yeah, but other people read stuff and watch stuff, but don't remember a scrap of it. The level of detail in what you know. It's seriously impressive."

She could hear genuine admiration in his voice, and it felt good. To have Richard, who himself was such a clever man, pay tribute to this side of her, reinforced her belief in what he claimed—that to him she was more than just a pretty face, a bit of fun. There was respect in his words. She needed that from a man.

She shrugged. "I don't know. It's just something I've always been able to do. Photographic memory, perhaps?" She didn't understand it herself. All she knew was that once she entered this world of the past, it was as real to her as if she was there, the details imprinted indelibly in her brain.

"OK, so here's a question for you," she said, attempting to deflect the conversation away from herself. Much as she enjoyed the compliments, she preferred not to dwell on them. "These buildings here—what do you think?"

She pointed at the row of multi-storey buildings that flanked them. Their empty window frames, like the vacant eyes of a skull, felt a little melancholy. Once these were homes, real people living their lives inside them, working, playing, laughing, crying, bickering or whispering endearments.

"I'd say they look a lot like a row of terrace houses," he said, "Coronation Street style."

"And you'd be correct," she said. "Apartment blocks. A bit more modest than yours, homes for workers and their families. No kitchens though—too much risk of fire. And so we have this." She pointed to a doorway opposite, and he followed her lead, disappearing inside the low-roofed brick structure. She positioned herself behind the huge concrete slab that dominated the space. "Would you like fries with that?" she said.

He laughed. "McDonalds? Really?"

"Well, yes. People ate out, even the working classes. Nothing new about takeaways."

"I'll never feel guilty about ordering in again," he said, reaching across to smooth a rogue strand of her hair. The open-top car had left it in wild disarray. "You know Sarah," he said, his eyes aglow with pride, "you're freaking amazing. Smart is sexy, and you are very smart. And very sexy." He took her hand, pulling her to him from behind the counter to wrap her close.

She could have stayed there forever, the two of them entwined, still as the rows of statues at the entrance to the ruins. But the moment was interrupted by the arrival of a bustling group of tourists. Their guide herded them into the room, his nasal voice echoing off the walls. "Right people, here we are, at the world's first ever McDonalds."

Zipping along the road back into the city, the warm wind tugging at her hair, Richard's hand resting lightly on her knee, Sarah decided that this was the happiest she'd ever been. She wanted to etch these moments in her mind, knowing that soon they would be just memory.

She'd tried not to think beyond Rome, knowing that in a few days this blissful bubble would burst, and they'd be on the plane returning to New Zealand. She was dreading it. It wasn't just the prospect of having less time with Richard. It wasn't the pain of parting from this city she'd longed to see for as long as she could remember. It was knowing that back in Wellington she would find out what price she'd paid for choosing to be here. She pushed the nagging thought away, instead concentrating on the road ahead as she steered the car onto the motorway exit and plunged into rush-hour traffic.

## CHAPTER 10

Love Story

# Sarah

Rome, Italy – September, 2007

"WHAT KIND OF COUNTRY has cake for breakfast?" she said, biting into a huge golden slice of Madeira cake, enjoying its tangy lemon flavour on her tongue.

"The best kind," he said, looking up from the newspaper.

"So, what's on the agenda today?" she asked. He'd completed his business over a dinner the previous night, and now four more days stretched ahead of them, blissful days, where they could go wherever the mood took them and nothing else would steal him away from her. She'd handed over the decision about those days to him.

"First job is for you to pack a bag. I know you've loved Rome, but you need to take your nose out of the ruins. I'm taking you to *my* favourite city."

There was a touch of disappointment, having found other places around Rome that she'd noted to go back to with Richard in tow. It had been magical for her to see the history she so loved, and sharing some of it with him was even more special.

And she'd be sad to leave the Hotel de Russie. She could understand why some people lived in hotels. She'd settled in there and would miss the rhythm of life within its walls. Now she'd fobbed off the sense of being a scruffy imposter that had overwhelmed her that first day standing in the lobby, Sarah felt a pleasant sense of belonging in this exquisite place. But Italy *was* more than Rome. It had an abundance of wonderful cities. She tried to read his face as she rattled off a list of possibilities.

"Come on Richard," she said. "I told you I'm useless at guessing games."

"No, I'm not telling you," he said. "It's a surprise." And he refused to give her even the slightest clue, not even when they were standing at the doors of the vast old train station.

"Yes, I know—it's a bit cliché," he said, as they arrived at the platform, where a blinking electronic sign told her the waiting high-speed train would whisk them to Venice in style and comfort, taking a mere three-and-a-half hours. "But I'm traditional. You're not going to the latest trendy destination with me, I'm afraid."

"And a closet romantic. Venice has to be the most romantic place in this country, unless you go chasing Romeo and Juliet in Verona," she said, as the helpful attendant stashed their bags.

"Well, the first time round, guys like me didn't want to be seen as romantic. Any notions like that I squashed straight away. But now I don't give a shit. And the world's moved on a bit since then. It's OK for us men to show our softer side."

"I'm glad that I get this version of you," she said with a kiss. They nestled into the wide comfortable seats and watched the Italian countryside rush past them at two hundred and fifty kilometres an hour.

She was unaware exactly how much of a romantic Richard was and how absolutely cliché he could be until their final evening in Venice. They'd found a small restaurant tucked in under the Rialto Bridge. The canal traffic on the water beside them was relentless. But Sarah found it soothing to watch the buzz of water taxis surge past, interspersed with the soft swish of gondolas sweeping by.

"Best time to be here," he said for at least the third time that day. He was right. Both the oppressive heat and seething tourists of the summer months had departed. Autumn had arrived, with clear days and a slight chill in the air. The lagoon's swampy smell was an undercurrent rather than the overpowering stench he'd warned her about.

"I wish we didn't have to go home." She sighed, feeling like a petulant child. She didn't want to spoil their last evening, but she dreaded the thought of returning. "I don't think I want my old life back. I like this one."

"What if I said you didn't need to have your old life back?" His face had a satisfied expression, as if she'd played right into one of his plans.

"I'd say, how do I avoid it?" She wasn't needed on the farm, but she didn't really have anywhere else to go for the next few months. Not now she'd turned down the uni position. And her long-term future in Wellington hung on a very slim chance that she could still win over a group of stuffy professors who weren't exactly enthralled with what she had to offer. "I know I want a change. But I haven't given any thought to what that might be, and how to make it happen."

"I can solve both of those problems for you," he said with a smile that had a glimmer of smugness about it. "You marry me."

She'd noticed on the plane as he'd fussed over fastening her seatbelt that his platinum wedding band had disappeared. She hadn't commented, but she had wondered. Now it seemed he was hellbent on replacing it with one from her.

At first she nearly laughed, thinking it was another one of his jokes. After all, she was fairly sure he'd lured her into this same trap the night at the lodge. For a moment, then, she had actually thought he was going to propose, and she suspected he'd known it.

But this was no joke. He reached into his jacket pocket, producing a small black box. He opened it carefully, placing it in front of her. Around them, other diners' glances became stares of expectation. They didn't need to understand the language, to know what was happening here. Even in the candlelight's gloom, the diamond solitaire tossed dazzling shards of light at her from its velvet nest.

"Marry you?"

This time, he had surprised her. She'd known Richard for two months. In that time, she'd seen his public persona—the cool exterior, the astute businessman, the calculating corporate raider—and learned that in private he was a very different man.

But this seemed one step too far. Richard didn't do sudden, spontaneous, impulsive. He rarely went to dinner without making a reservation. Both his work life and his personal life were constrained by a diary, overseen by Gwen West, his flawlessly organised PA. Sarah wouldn't have been surprised to open his laptop and click on it to find 'Ask Sarah to marry me' typed neatly alongside 6:00 p.m. on Friday 21st September.

"Sarah, you know I don't do anything unless I've thought it through, but I'm good at doing that quickly, making decisions, especially when there's something I want badly, when there's an opportunity that I can't afford to miss."

How alike they were in that respect. That was the sort of decisiveness that had landed her here. She'd seen the opportunity to be with Richard and she'd grabbed it. He perceived an opportunity to bind her to him forever, and he was taking it.

"One thing that comes with age," he said with a smile "is you have a clear idea of what you want and don't want. I want you. I've wanted you since the first time I locked eyes on you, in your red dress."

"In Claire's red dress."

"Claire could never wear it like you. Sarah, I love you. Even when you're in your farm overalls, smelling of cows." He'd not let her forget the state of her that afternoon on the farm. Told her it was wonderful that she was as comfortable in the cowshed as the ballroom. "It's not only the packaging, it's what's inside that's beautiful," he'd assured her.

"Richard, I don't know what to say. It's all so fast."

She felt the weight of her inexperience. Lust, well, that was something she recognised. And god, he'd ignited that in her. But love. How did you know? She only knew she hadn't found it before. The feelings she had for Richard now, the ones that allowed her to laugh with him and cry with him, to be her craziest, most uninhibited version of herself—that could be love. Or it could simply be the novelty of him, after the parade of nice but dull farm boys.

Love needed to be more than the thrill of snatched moments in between his work, or the buzz of a holiday. It would have to be constant enough to withstand the routines of day-to-day life, and resilient enough for the hard times that would surely come. She wasn't so naïve to think that marriage would have the thrill of an endless roller coaster ride, nor lack its terrifying downward plunges.

And even if she actually loved him, there were things they hadn't had time to discuss, things that would need to be addressed. Children for a start. He had his girls. He might not be keen to dive back into changing nappies and broken sleep. She was certain she'd not want to emulate Vivi with her brood. But she wouldn't rule out the possibility of one or two.

Then there was the question of what else she'd do with her life, in between mothering children. With Richard, there'd be no need for her to earn money, but the thought of joining the ladies who lunch and not much else was repellent.

The lure of the doctoral programme was strong, although now it was definitely a long shot. It had been a wrench three years ago to tell Professor Jermaine that his top student was withdrawing before she'd even started. Walking into his office back in July, there had been genuine delight on his face. She regretted causing the disappointment in his voice when she'd called to turn down the job. Yes, she'd stuffed it up royally by coming on this trip, and the chances of resurrecting her dream were slim.

As Richard's eyes searched hers, she knew he recognised the whirl of thoughts in her head. The slight frown of uncertainty on his face was to be expected. He wasn't used to people saying no to him, but she saw him mentally preparing for that possibility. And then he acted to avoid it.

"Too fast," he said, closing the case with a snap and palming the little box with a smile. "Too soon." His hand rested on hers, a gesture of reassurance that he was comfortable leaving it for now. "I understand, and it's fine."

She nodded. Around them, the other restaurant guests turned back to their own conversations, clearly almost as disappointed as Richard, that the evening hadn't ended with a proposal accepted.

"It's not a no. These two months have been amazing. To be honest, I can't imagine my life without you in it anymore. But I need some time."

"Take all the time you want," he said. "I'm not going anywhere. I'll still be here when you say yes." Her response hadn't dented his confidence. Maybe he already knew her better than she did herself. "But you don't have to go back to the farm. Move into the apartment. Call it a trial period with a money-back guarantee."

"That I can say yes to."

"And that makes me indescribably happy," he said, raising her hand to his lips. A woman at the next table turned to look at them again, as if wondering whether the beginning of a great love story was playing out in front of her eyes after all. Sarah didn't want to spoil her night, so calmly returned the smile despite the tumultuous feelings that gripped her inside.

CHAPTER 11

Deal or No Deal

# Richard

Venice, Italy – September, 2007

ACCESS TO THE BUSINESS lounge was essential at times like this. Richard refreshed his laptop screen once more, but still nothing had changed. Even down the phone, he could hear Gwen's fingers tapping her own keyboard furiously, and prayed this wouldn't take long. He'd had no opportunity to confirm all of this with Sarah and hoped she wouldn't mind. She'd said she didn't want their holiday to end, so he was fairly sure she'd enjoy a few days in Hong Kong. She seemed happy enough reading on the iPad he'd bought her, sipping coffee and nibbling a piece of the same breakfast cake she'd fallen in love with in Rome.

"Gwen, how's it looking?"

His PA was a gem. Here it was, the middle of the night in New Zealand and she was onto it. Flight changes, hotel bookings. He'd never regretted nabbing her when one of the other partners retired. They didn't make PAs like the ever-willing and unflappable Gwen these days.

"Nearly there," she breathed, "and... we're done. OK, you should be seeing it at your end now. And I'll make sure Layton has your flight times. I've told him you want to meet straight away."

"Thanks so much, Gwen," he said, refreshing his screen. "And my apologies to Lance. Tell him I'll shout him a beer next time we meet."

Gwen's chuckle bubbled down the phone. "He didn't even stir the lazy bugger. Still snoring so loud I can hear him through the wall. But don't let him know I said that."

"Well, thanks again. Take care and I'll see you in a few days."

"You too Richard."

He made a note to himself to at least take her out for coffee when he was back in the office, as he sauntered over to grab one for himself and then break the news to Sarah.

"Why would I mind? No, I'd love that," she said. "Another country to add to my passport."

"Thanks so much for understanding. I'm pissed off that our guy we sent up there hasn't been able to close the deal. Not his fault. The directors of this company are notoriously difficult. Seems like they want a senior partner in person to nudge them over the line. Not that I mind the trip itself. Love Honkers, it's a great city. Been there a few times."

"You can give me some sightseeing tips." She reached over and stroked his hand. "Poor you, stuck in some office all day while I play tourist again."

---

He reluctantly left her dozing in their vast bed at the Peninsula Hotel. He'd delighted in seeing her wide eyes as they'd stepped from the taxi into the lobby. Watching her experience new things, beautiful things, brought a flutter of joy that had been absent from his life for a long time. He wanted to spoil her. It was the least he could do to repay her for the change she'd wrought in him these last months.

She'd appeared in his life like an exotic bird, loud and colourful, impossible to ignore, impossible not to love. He now recognised he'd been lonely. Tried to fool himself into believing in the image he presented to the world of a man confident, relaxed, independent and possessing little emotion. The women he'd encountered before Sarah had accepted *that* Richard, not demanding anything more of him. They were fooling themselves too, believing that wrapped in the trappings of the material things he could provide, they could exist without a need for his love.

But Sarah had ignored that outer shell, not the least impressed with the job, the car, the apartment. And she'd challenged him to reveal things beyond that, things about himself, some that he'd told no one, not even Victoria, much as he'd trusted her. Not even Paul, who was more father than business partner. This was why he loved Sarah. Apart from his mother, she was the only person he'd ever truly let in.

Sarah stayed with him throughout the day. During the morning meetings, he was distracted. Not like him at all. But he found that his years of experience left him strangely able to manipulate the negotiations in the right direction despite the lack of his usual laser focus, while allowing him to hold thoughts of her in his mind.

She even invaded his thoughts at lunch. He left his junior offsider, Layton, doing most of the work, softening up the other side with good food and drinks even though they all knew it was a ploy, designed to induce early afternoon somnolence, at which time they'd go in for the kill. He excused himself from the table early, citing the need to make a few calls. In fact, he only made one.

"You still in bed?"

"It was tempting," she laughed. "But no, right now I'm on the tram to the Peak." He was grateful for her independence, happily doing her own thing even when dropped in the midst of this unfamiliar, teeming city.

"Lucky you. I'm still trapped trying to massage the egos of these buffoons. At least it seems to be working."

"So you'll be back for dinner?"

"No guarantee, but I think we're on track."

He hoped so. Would do his best to make it so, not only for the sake of the deal, but for the chance to have at least some of this day with her. He didn't go straight back to the restaurant. Instead, he sat gazing out across the towers of Hong Kong Island. The wispy clouds that twisted and turned, shrouding the tops of the tallest buildings, were like the thoughts that tumbled through his mind.

She was going to leave the farm. That was a given. And she'd agreed to come to Wellington. He imagined her there, settling back into life not only with him but also surrounded by her old university mates. And through them a crowd of men her own age: young up-and-coming businessmen, the idealistic political hacks, the passionate journos, the intense academics she was so at home with.

Unfamiliar emotions battled inside his mind. Jealousy surged within him as nebulous images of these imagined other men swirled around. Followed by guilt. That chaining her to him, binding her young life to his own, was an unfair expectation. And the most uncharacteristic feeling of all—doubt. He wasn't confident that even should she say yes now, she might not tire of him later. The difference in age, the crazy anachronisms that for now caused them to laugh, had the potential to morph into something that could instead destroy them.

"Richard, they're going back in now."

With his phone still in his hand, he hoped Layton hadn't noticed his mind was definitely not on business. The two of them sat at the massive white boardroom table, facing down their opposition. He was determined to draw this to a close, the earlier the better.

"You know, gentlemen," he said, facing his adversaries, "it seems we're getting pretty close. I think all of us are on the same page here." The two men opposite maintained their poker faces, but he detected a glint of something in Grantham St Clair's beady eyes. It was time to address it directly. "Grantham, I can see there's something holding you back. Come on, spit it out, man. What's the deal breaker here?"

Grantham took a breath. "Well, since you ask..."

———

Later, with papers signed and celebratory drinks completed, he relaxed back into the taxi. He waved farewell to the grateful Layton as the driver sped him towards the Peninsula Hotel—and Sarah. Mulling over the afternoon's success, he wondered if he should apply some of the same tactics he wielded so skilfully when hammering out business deals to this deal he was struggling to make with her. Probably the most important deal of his life. He could tiptoe around whatever was holding her back. Or ask her outright.

Dinner at the hotel wasn't the right place to do it. His very public proposal in Venice had been a disaster. He'd seen the disappointed, even sympathetic stares of people at the other tables. It had been downright uncomfortable feeling the scrutiny of strangers who didn't know the first thing about the two of them. He wasn't used to being pitied and damned if he'd fall into that trap again.

Although he'd done his best to hide it from her, he'd felt foolish at his lack of judgement. It had hardly occurred to him that she might say no. But this was what she did to him—made him think differently, act differently—and most of the time, that was a good thing. No, if he was going to risk a second rejection, he'd do it in private this time. He'd wait till it was only the two of them. For now, simply relax over the wine and food. But mesmerised by the simple presence of her, the question lurked below the surface, as her every word and gesture told him how important the answer was.

"Oh Richard, the escalators." Her face lit up with excitement. "Now, I know what you're thinking," she said, seeing his smile, "after the airport in Singapore, you think I'm obsessed. But honestly, they go on and on. It's bizarre. It was like being in a sci-fi movie."

Hearing her talk about her day, watching her face so alive with the joy of living, enthralled even by such small discoveries as the bank of escalators in the Central-Mid-Levels, made him feel old and jaded by comparison. He'd lived a privileged life in recent years, and some days, it seemed like he'd seen everything and done everything. But living it anew through her eyes brought a freshness to each new day, and an optimism for the future that he'd lost well back in his youth.

"So, how was your day?" she asked. "Pleased to have the deal signed?"

"For sure. Thought it might take longer. But no, all done. So we have a couple of days. For us."

"I'm pleased. I couldn't help but think of you stuck in an office while I'm out enjoying the city."

He didn't want to tell her he'd been thinking of her all day, too. Then she'd want to know why. And that must wait for the privacy of their room.

---

She sauntered from the bathroom, clad only in a t-shirt and knickers, showing off all her delicious curves and long muscular legs. Not a wispy, stick-like model figure, best suited for languidly adorning the side of a pool. No, Sarah possessed the build of a woman who could take on anything, along with the confidence to do so. He appreciated looking at that body, but preferred it pressed hard against him, slick with sweat, exuding her familiar intoxicating scent, and producing tiny growls of pleasure.

But it wasn't simply that which fed his overwhelming need for her to be in his life. It was the woman behind it, the complexity of her revealed in the ever-changing expressions in those eyes, brown like a fine single malt whisky.

Her constant questioning and wondering, a product of that keen intelligence, excited him. Like yesterday sitting on the plane when she'd casually said: "Richard, I have to admit I know absolutely nothing about the stock market. Can you explain to me how it all works?" So he had. And she was so damn quick to pick it up, he'd have her working on the trading floor in a week if that was what she wanted to do.

And there was that appraising stare when she challenged him—god, he loved a woman who could argue with him so eloquently. He'd seen that tonight when he'd lingered by a shop window, admiring a set of antique cufflinks.

"Oh, Richard, you can't possibly buy those. Ivory is just wrong." He'd tried to protest since they were from an age where that was completely acceptable, but she'd come back at him with a barrage of reasons why that argument wouldn't fly. In the end, he'd been forced to agree she was right and meekly accept her rebuke at thinking otherwise, even for a moment.

The sparkling excitement in her eyes at some novel experience was like a drug he couldn't get enough of. This whole trip had been full of those moments, and he never tired of seeing the world anew through her. Although her youthful enthusiasm reminded him she was closer in age to his kids than to himself, it also energised him, making him forget the years that separated them.

And of course there was the sultry, come hither look that he read in them now, as she sank onto the bed beside him, one hand casually draped across his thigh, the other cupping his face as she kissed him.

"So now that the business is out of the way, let's get down to business." She purred in his ear, dotting little kisses down his neck.

The business he'd thought was top of the agenda could wait. He let her take control. It was another thing he loved about her. She didn't expect him to always take charge. The bedroom was not the boardroom, and he'd discovered the thrill of allowing her to be the boss sometimes.

Despite the air-conditioning, he could feel a trickle of sweat making its way down his back. They lay side by side, not touching, letting the cool draft of air waft across them, dispelling the heat of their exertions. He decided he couldn't avoid it any longer.

"I was thinking about us today. About you."

"You had time for that?"

"Yeah, sitting in a boardroom while they argued over details next door. Wishing they'd hurry the decision so I could go home, take you home. Us. In Wellington. Together."

"Me too. No going back to the farm. Not after this. Falling asleep beside you every night, waking up to you each morning. Everything's changed."

"I don't want to pressure you, but I couldn't help but think about…" He fumbled for words, not wanting to spook her. "…how I'd rather it was us in Wellington together. And married." She was silent except for a small exhalation of breath that could have been a sigh. "And today, while I'm trying to force bloody St Clair to lay his cards on the table, tell me what we have to do to make this deal fly, all I could think of was us. Wondering what's the deal breaker here? What's standing in the way of you saying yes? Is it that you need time? Or is it something else?"

"You want to seal the deal."

She lay on her back staring at the ceiling, and he propped himself up on one elbow, scrutinising her face, her eyes. He could see her brain working, assessing the position he'd put her in. He was still unsure if this was the right thing, forcing her to tell him the things that had been gnawing away at her. Once she did, they'd both have to live with the consequences.

"OK," she said slowly, gathering her words. "I've been thinking about it, too. And yes, it's all happened so fast. My friends and family might tell you I have an impulsive streak—although I like to think it's just I'm decisive. So it wouldn't surprise any of them to find that ring on my finger. They're used to me jumping in quickly when I know something is right."

"So, if it's not the timing, then... are there things you need to know?"

"Only two."

"That sounds promising. I've found in negotiations, there are rarely insurmountable obstacles. As long as you can work out what they are. Depending on what the two are, of course." He thought he'd start with the elephant in the room. "Some things we can't change—like my age."

She rolled to face him now. "Richard, you should know by now the age difference between us means nothing to me. You're just Richard, I'm just Sarah. In many ways, it actually makes it interesting. We pool our different lives, our different experiences and come up with something exciting and new."

She took a little breath, and he knew she was preparing to take that leap, opening the conversation up to answers that both of them might not want to hear. That had the potential to end this coming-together of their lives, parting before it had even begun.

"I'd like to aim for the PhD offer. I need to work. But I know from the first night we met that you're comfortable with the idea of a kept woman. I remember you saying that pretty women don't need to be career-minded."

"I really said that? Oh god, I did, didn't I?"

He'd been desperate to impress her, delivering her a compliment. Now it was backfiring on him.

"Unfortunately, you did." Her face was earnest. "Richard, you can see I'm no good at doing nothing. Can't relax with a book for more than an hour—unless it's one of my history books. I can't be one of those idle rich wives, or pretend to be busy in nice little charity causes where you don't need to get your hands dirty." He knew she was right. She'd wilt amid the other corporate wives. "I need to do something with my life, with my brain. I've been in limbo for too long."

"You do whatever you want. Whatever makes you happy. I couldn't bear to see you anything less. Even if you still want to get up at some ungodly hour and wallow in cow shit, that's fine by me. As long as you let me join you in the shower after." She grinned at him, her eyes wickedly playful. He tried to match the mood. "In fact, how about we try that now?' he said. "The shower, I mean. I'm all sticky."

"It's tempting, but we still need to talk about the second thing." This was the big one. He could see it in her eyes. The one she was worried about. "It doesn't bother me that you've been married before, or that you have the girls. Although I do want to meet them, get to know them. And of course I hope they won't resent me, see me as trying to take their mother's place."

"I don't think that will happen. I've already talked to them about you. They're curious, of course. But Victoria and I were very open with them when we parted. And they were old enough to understand the reasons. I think they'll be fine. So you can tick off that worry."

"Well, that wasn't quite what I was getting at. You have children. I don't. And I don't want to close the door on having a child. In fact, now I've thought about it, it's strangely appealing. Especially a child with you. So I need to know how you feel about that."

He couldn't believe he'd been so stupid. Of course, she was going to want what most women her age wanted. Perhaps her preoccupation with travel and study had lulled him into thinking it wasn't important. He'd assumed she was all about her career. With business, he naturally looked at all the angles. And yet here, where it mattered most, he'd been so blind. This was the deal breaker. Although he'd given it no thought, he already knew the answer. But his words were measured and careful. It was a struggle to look her in the eye, knowing this had the power to finish them before they'd begun.

"I have to be honest with you, Sarah." How he wished he could tell the lie, agree now and then renege on the deal later. But he loved her too much to put her through that, and he knew it could still end the same way. He'd lose her. "I'm sorry, but I can't promise you that. I've been there—sleepless nights, changing nappies. Yes, hard to believe I know, but I was a hands-on father whenever I was home." He tried to make light of it, but her eyes scrutinised his, and her face was serious, already a little sad. "But I don't think I want to go there again. And if I was to become a father now—can you imagine me rocking up to school, and weekend sports? People thinking how nice that grandad comes along to watch the game. Sarah, that time has passed for me."

She didn't speak at first. When the words came, they did nothing to take the edge off the pain that jabbed in his gut.

"OK, well, I'm going to need some more time. To think."

"You take all the time you need."

He needed it, too. This had blindsided him, and he chided himself for his foolishness. He kissed her gently, a grey melancholy drifting in the air between them. It lingered as he turned off the bedside lamp and lay himself along the soft length of her, taking in the fresh smell of her hair. He knew from the rise and fall of her breathing that she was still awake. He drank in the moment, wanting to fix it in his mind, in case this, what he had with her, would soon evaporate before his eyes.

Chapter 12

Change of Heart

# Richard

Wellington, New Zealand – October, 2007

Paul poured the whisky without asking. The oily molecules wafted across from the antique sideboard, its form so opposite to the stark modernity of the office, as was Paul himself.

This was the traditional end to their week whenever they were both in Wellington, a time not only to debrief as business partners, but to reconnect as friends. Richard was going to miss these meetings and this conniving old bastard when he retired. He'd up and follow him if it wasn't for his struggle to find an out for himself. So far, the only ideas that presented themselves seemed to have a sting in the tail. He had no idea how he could walk away without appearing ungrateful for Paul's contribution to their success. Paul trusted him to nurture this creation of theirs into the future. He couldn't simply abandon all they'd worked for.

"So, tell me," said Paul, his calculating blue eyes now lit up by the grin on his face. "I hear you've moved that attractive young lady you took to Europe into your apartment." His shaggy grey eyebrows waggled in anticipation like two drunk caterpillars.

"Yes. Sarah. You may remember her from Jonathan's party a while back."

"Oh, yes, red dress, and god, the cleavage to fill it out. Everyone in the room that night would remember her." He gave a bawdy chuckle. Some people took offence at Paul's lack of filter, but Richard was used to it. "About bloody time, I say. You've been rattling around on your own too long."

"Yeah, well, not sure I won't be on my own again fairly soon."

"What? Don't tell me you've stuffed it up already? What the hell have you done?"

"It's not what I've done. It's what I don't want to do."

Paul looked at him quizzically. "Well, come on then. Better tell Uncle Paul."

He was going to miss this, too. Paul had been more than a business mentor. In him, Richard had found the father figure he hadn't known he needed. It was Paul who'd helped him navigate some of the trickiest times of his life—like the divorce. Both the amicable split and his success at protecting the girls from the fallout directly resulted from Paul's wise advice. If anyone could help him through this brick wall he'd erected between himself and his future happiness with Sarah, it was Paul.

Although Sarah had settled into the apartment happily, and appeared content enough. She'd spent the three weeks since their return working away on her draft PhD proposal. She met him each evening with a smile and a kiss. They cooked dinner together, chatting about their day like an old married couple. She lay draped across him on the couch, watching the ships come in, buzzing with excitement at the progress she'd made on her work. They made love with the same ferocious passion, as if nothing had changed.

It had. But neither of them dared raise the question of children that lay between them, unspoken and seemingly insurmountable. It was like a box of fireworks sat in the corner of the apartment. Both of them tiptoed around it, careful not to speak the words, providing the spark that would blow apart their happy domesticity.

"Oh, Richard." After listening to the details of Richard's dilemma, Paul sculled the last of his whisky and poured them another. "I can't believe you let it go so far without considering what she might want out of life. What were you thinking?"

"I wasn't thinking. That's the problem."

Paul regarded him thoughtfully for a moment, resting his white, neatly bearded chin on the gnarled hands peppered with age spots.

"No. You know what?" He paused for effect, as he always did when about to make some pronouncement. "You've been overthinking it. This fatherhood thing. God man, it's not like you haven't done it before. And you did a bloody good job of it. Those girls are a credit to you. Not to mention you did it with Victoria, when we know you two spent all those years going through the motions of being married. If you really love this girl, well, won't it be that much better the second time around?"

"But starting again at my age? Poor damn kid. Think how embarrassed he'll be when all the others think it's his grandfather cheering on the sidelines at rugby."

"No, you're wrong." Paul was quick to contradict him. "The kid won't be embarrassed. Only pleased that his father cares enough to come and watch. The only one who might be embarrassed is you. And, honestly, why should you be? You know the demographics. Couples are marrying later, having kids later. You'll blend right in. Besides, when have you ever cared what other people think?" He had him there. Shot down his objection in one swoop. But he hadn't finished. "Come on, there has to be more to it than that. For you to leap in and ask her to marry you and then, in the next breath, make it impossible for her to say yes." That was the thing about Paul. It wasn't only in business that he could cut through all the bullshit and demand the facts. Nothing for it now but to put into words the doubt that had been eating at him.

"You said I was a good father to Hannah and Chelsea. And in some ways, I was. But I could have been a lot better. If I'd been there. Instead of working all day and half the night. Instead of spending months living out of a suitcase in every city but the one they were in. Victoria pretended to cope, but she didn't. She wasn't cut out to play both mother and father to them."

There was an awkwardness in admitting this to Paul, the same man who'd been his ally in all of that crazy euphoric time when the company soared and they rode the jet-stream of its runaway success. Also, the man who didn't have his own children left behind. Didn't have the guilt of missed school trips and absences from birthday parties. Didn't have the little voices over the phone asking when he was coming home.

"So, you feel guilty. Well, you can't go back and change what's been. But from what you tell me, this Sarah's nothing like Victoria. You said she's strong, independent."

Richard chuckled inwardly. He couldn't wait for the two to meet. Paul and he were so alike in their admiration for strong women. Maybe it was a welcome contrast after commanding others all day—to go home to someone who issued the commands. God knows Paul's own formidable wife did. In fact, she was the only person in the world that he was even a little afraid of. A now retired High Court judge, Eleanor Whitfield-Crombie, took no prisoners and tolerated no crap from anyone, especially her husband.

"Like Eleanor."

"Yes, like Eleanor. And like Eleanor, she'll tell you if she doesn't like the way things are going. And you'll listen."

"Worked for you."

"Too right it did. But of course the timing is better too," said Paul. "Back then, this company needed us 24/7. It doesn't anymore."

"What are you saying?" The look in Paul's eyes unsettled him. He thought he'd hidden his disillusionment. Difficult when you worked closely with someone that perceptive. Nothing escaped him.

"I think you know. Come on, we're like an old married couple you and I. I can read the signs. You want to get out. And you should."

"But I thought you were only retiring because you knew I'd stay on."

"I'm retiring because it's time. Should have done it a few years ago, while I still had a bit more life about me. I'd never sentence you to do the same." Richard saw the affection—no, the love this old man had for him. And he knew Paul meant it. "Richard, don't wait till you're my age. Start your new family and start your exit plan. This is your chance to do it over again and do it how *you* want."

He arrived home to find her sprawled on the leather couch, asleep. An open book lay where it had tumbled to the floor. He picked it up with a smile. *Caesar's Conquest of Britain*—in the original Latin too, of course.

Coming home to her always felt so right. She belonged here. And that word 'home'. He'd never thought of this apartment as home, merely a place to lay his head. Now it had all changed. Because of her.

Lowering himself with care, not wanting to disturb her, he sat gently beside her, drinking in the sight. He stroked a stray tendril of that wild, dark hair away from her face. He couldn't help but lay a finger on that beautiful mouth, even now upturned in sleep, and stroke the small dimpled curve. She stirred a little at his touch. When her eyes fluttered open, in that moment between sleep and waking, he saw her pleasure at seeing him, read the love in her eyes, as her mouth moulded into a languid smile.

Then, as she slid into full wakefulness, fully registering his presence, he thought he saw a slight shadowy veil come over her eyes, the shadow that hung between them. The shadow that he was about to tear away.

"You're a little late tonight."

"Yeah, I should have said—Friday night session with Paul. It's a bit of a ritual when we're both in town. We always have a drink, chew the fat."

She smiled up at him. "Sounds like *Boston Legal*." He'd never watched it. Never watched TV at all. But he understood the reference. You'd have to have been living in a cave these last years, not to know of the hit show. Sarah was spot on. Paul definitely had a touch of Denny Crane about him. "Though you don't have any whiff of cigars about you," she said. "Just as well."

She wrinkled her nose in distaste at the thought. Such a cute gesture, her small freckles dancing with the movement.

"Sarah, I've been thinking this week. A lot." Now he caught a flicker of fear, a wariness in her face. She sensed he was about to approach the subject they'd shoved deep down since that awful night in Hong Kong, anxious it would wreck the truce they'd forged between them these past weeks. "And Paul helped me out tonight. Put it into perspective."

"You talked to Paul about it?"

Her eyes widened, and her voice had a steely edge. Not knowing Paul, it was understandable she might question involving him in this most intimate of problems.

"He wormed it out of me. Sarah, he knows me too well to not see when there's something big worrying me. But I'm glad he did. He's one of the few people brave enough to tell me when I'm being a dick about something. And I have been."

Her face relaxed a little and now her eyes held a spark of emotion that he read as hope. He took her hand in his, but he didn't have to speak for her to know his answer. The surge of elation at the thought of creating a child with this beautiful woman forced a broad dopey grin onto his face and drew his hand to lay gently on her stomach as if envisioning their child growing there one day. Any remaining doubts had evaporated with the sight of that hopefulness in her eyes.

"It was stupid of me to shut the door on us having children. I have my girls, so if you'd decided motherhood wasn't for you, I could live with that. But having kids is a pretty special experience. I won't deny you that experience. So if you decide that's what you want, I can't imagine anything better than to share it with you."

She'd been holding her breath, and it came out with a rush. He could see relief in her eyes.

"Even if it meant waiting a couple of years? Till I've finished my studies?"

His stomach plummeted at that. Two, maybe three years more? Him that much older? But then he accepted it wouldn't be such a bad thing. It was possible he'd have shaken off the shackles of Crombie Norton by then. Working part time; or not working at all. The more he thought about it, the proposition might actually be perfect.

"Whenever you're ready, my love. Whatever makes you happy."

He'd never handed over such important decisions to someone else before. It was surprisingly freeing.

She placed her hand over his, trapping it against that smooth stomach. The solid feel of her body and her breathy kiss triggered an urge to make love to her right then and there. Take her on the couch. But coming up for air, he remembered what he'd retrieved from his office safe before he'd left.

"Wait, just a second." He prised himself away from her arms, moving to locate his briefcase dumped by the door. Deep in one interior pocket, his fingers grasped the small box. He held it out to her.

She recognised it immediately.

"You want to seal the deal?"

He nodded. "I'd love you to wear it. So everyone will know. I want them to know."

"It will be hard to miss. It's enormous."

She slipped the diamond solitaire on her finger, tipping it this way and that, admiring the lights like tiny stars bouncing off its facets.

"So it's yes?"

"Yes, Richard, I will marry you."

He lay her back gently on the couch, his hands slipping inside her t-shirt, following the beautiful curves of her breasts, while thinking that he couldn't remember the last time he'd been this happy.

## CHAPTER 13

## Stalling

*Sarah*

Wellington, New Zealand – October, 2007

SARAH FOUND A WINDOW seat in the little cafe, where she watched the streams of suit-clad men and women flow along the Wellington streets, hurrying to important meetings with important people. Interspersed between their uniforms of black and navy, scruffy students toting sagging backpacks headed towards the university campus. A homeless guy with a mournful-looking dog jangled a cup at the passersby, two identical sets of pleading eyes locking onto anyone who paused long enough to make contact. She'd grown up in the country, but it was the city that sent tingles of possibility through her body. This was her home again. She belonged here.

"Do I need to leave these on?" Mel quipped, pointing at her sunglasses, as she eased herself into the chair opposite. "From the photographs, I'd say it's quite some rock you have on your finger."

"Ha, ha, very funny." Sarah stretched her hand out, and Mel took it, rotating it with an appraising eye.

"Beautiful. Expensive. Big. But tasteful. He chose well."

"He sure did. I'd have never gone into a jeweller to look at something that size. But I suppose that's because I'd always have been worrying about the cost. No, I love it."

And she did. Apart from the sheer size of the diamond, it was elegantly simple, with no hint of ostentatiousness. Richard had chosen well. Like everything he did, it shouted 'expensive' at those who knew what to look for, but wasn't gauche.

She'd asked him about it once, lying snuggled against the length of his warm body, as they talked, both wanting to move on from their initial superficial knowledge of each other, to understanding the undercurrents of each other's lives, the events that had built the other into who they were now.

His was an intriguing metamorphosis from the child of a single mother living in a shabby state house in a neglected suburb of Christchurch to one of the wealthiest men in the country. He'd told her how, from his first encounters with this other species of human, the super-rich, he'd carefully studied them.

"Old-money people, they have nothing to prove. They're so secure in the generations of wealth and breeding that sit behind them, they don't think like the rest of us. They don't act like regular people."

He'd imitated their ways, their speech, their style. And along the way watched others from backgrounds like his own, clawing their way up the ladder and flaunting their newfound wealth and status with tacky displays of excess. But failing to see how this marked them out as a Johnny-come-lately who'd never find genuine acceptance in the top tier of society, the elite mocking them behind closed doors and sometimes to their faces. He'd vowed that wouldn't be his fate.

Richard was a careful man, who had made himself indistinguishable from those like Paul Crombie, or his former father-in-law who'd been born into wealth and power. They wore it with ease and an innate sense of style, like a well-fitting Armani suit. As he did too.

"So, having rushed into an engagement," Mel said, "do I need to brush up on wedding planning skills? Splash out on some copies of *Bride and Groom* magazine?" Her friend was probing in her quiet way, trying to get a feel for Sarah's thinking without asking outright.

"No, not yet. No hurry. Sometime next year I imagine." She tried to sound casual.

"His schedule or yours?"

"Mine. He'd be happy if we went and did it tomorrow."

"Buying yourself some time?" Now Mel was trying to delve into places Sarah would prefer not to go.

"You think I'm leaving room to change my mind?" she said.

"Well, the engagement was definitely your style. I know once you've made up your mind about something you don't muck around. So I guess I thought you'd have the rest of the plan all mapped out too."

"No. You're reading way too much into it. I want to marry Richard. I *will* marry Richard. But there's no need to rush." She knew her words came across as defensive, a reaction to her friend calling her out on something that bothered her, too.

Most girls, given the freedom to choose the date, and an open cheque book to have the wedding of their dreams, would be all over this. It worried her that subconsciously she *was* buying herself time, and it worried her even more that Mel had seen it. Because if she had, maybe Richard had as well. It might be best to take a few tiny steps towards it. Once the wedding was a reality, perhaps it would steady her nerves. With that in mind, and seizing an opportunity to lighten the conversation, Sarah tried to allay Mel's fears.

"I promise, you are definitely my number one bridesmaid and chief wedding planner. You will be the first to know when we set the date. And in charge of telling me the truth about the dress. I don't want to end up in some nightmare gown based on the flattery of a bridal shop assistant. So how about we finish our coffee and then have a look in that bridal shop on Willis Street?"

This suggestion appeased Mel. Her face lit up at the thought of wasting hours in Wedding Belles gushing over confections of satin and lace. Sarah put on her excited face too, but as she downed the last of her coffee, there was an uneasiness that the emotion didn't come naturally at the thought of the wedding.

They joined the flow of pedestrians en route to the bridal boutique. She tried to push back the sick fear that this lack of enthusiasm might indeed be a symptom of her underlying doubts. Late at night, while Richard slept soundly, she lay awake, her restless mind wrestling with questions: Was Richard really committed to having children, or had he acquiesced to gain her agreement? Would her father eventually give his wholehearted support or forever remain lukewarm at her choice of husband? At some time in the future, would the naysayers be proven right and their difference in ages become a source of conflict? These were the doubts she hadn't dared voice, but Mel sensed were there. Doubts that, given sufficient time, might lead her to change her mind—and cause immeasurable hurt to the man who loved her.

CHAPTER 14

Road Block

*Sarah*

Wellington, New Zealand – October, 2007

THE FIRST HINT OF the approaching summer was in the air. This harbour, so near to the turbulent open sea of Cook Strait, would never be millpond-flat. Today was as close as it came, only faint ripples tossing a bobbing kayaker in the shallows near the motorway.

Sarah zipped along in Mel's little car, windows down to cool the interior in the absence of air-conditioning. The Wellington wind that would normally blast through any opening was uncharacteristically subdued. She was overly warm in her jeans and jumper, but they were the practical choice. Her feet were hot and tingly, encased in work socks and sturdy boots. And the gnawing anxiety that gripped her stomach added another layer to her discomfort.

Richard's idea to introduce her to the girls like this was a smart one. She'd imagined it would happen sitting in some cafe, already divided by a table, set up as opposing forces, eyeballing each other warily while trying to come to terms that their lives and hers would be forever linked through him. But he'd suggested that she do something with them instead, something they enjoyed. That something was horse riding.

On Friday afternoon she'd decamped to Mel's, discreetly removing all traces of her from his apartment. He'd told her not to be silly, that staying at Mel's was enough to give the girls some space. But she preferred not to make her presence in Richard's life too obvious, not wanting her entry into their lives to be confronting. Slow and gentle.

That evening, he drove up to Marton, collecting Chelsea from boarding school. Meanwhile, Hannah flew in from Dunedin. They'd had dinner out together, no doubt a chance for Richard to prime them for today.

It had been the strangest thing, waking up this morning in her old bed in Mel's flat. In the half-wakefulness, she'd reached for him and startled at finding him missing. Then, fully conscious, she'd remembered where she was and why. And that was when the nervousness took up residence in her stomach. The rational part of her brain told it to settle down. She was a capable, confident person. Most people seemed to find her likeable, as far as she was aware. And she was extrovert enough to make her way in most social situations. But this was different. The success of this meeting with the girls was crucial. They were going to be part of each other's lives for a long time.

Richard's Jag looked decidedly out of place, lined up alongside a battered Hilux ute and a sturdy Pajero four-wheel drive. But the stables themselves were new and smart. Already the grooms had tied four sleek horses in an adjoining yard and were now fitting saddles. He was at the door of the car before she'd had time to kill the engine, as if wanting to manage every moment of this meeting from the beginning.

He scooped her into his arms, his kiss filling the yawning gap that even this small separation had created. It was crazy, but they'd spent so much time together in the last two months that even in the space of one day, she missed him. His embrace lingered, as if he too wanted to renew the feel of her, and she breathed in the familiar smell of him, trying to ground herself.

As she looked across his shoulder at the two young women standing by the yards, she smiled at them, hoping to convey the right amount of warmth with no hint of smugness that she'd snared their father. He released her and grabbed her hand, leading her across the driveway.

If you hadn't known otherwise, you would have thought the girls were twins. She could see Richard in the thick dark hair, Hannah's captured in a jaunty ponytail, Chelsea's in a chunky plait that draped snake-like over her shoulder. And the upturned mouths, as if they might smile at any moment, were his too. She hoped they would return her smile. At the moment, they both looked disturbingly serious. Perhaps they shared her nervousness. The two sets of eyes were not like Richard at all. Warm brown, framed with long lashes, they were obviously Victoria's eyes. But the appraising expression in them—well, she'd seen that look nearly every day in the past months.

She'd spent enough time in Richard's world to know that clasped hands, a hug, and air kisses were the expected form of greeting. Hannah stepped towards her, and Sarah sensed an immediate warmth as she extended her hand.

"You must be Hannah. So good you could get away from uni. It's great to meet you."

"And you." The murmured words were as friendly as Hannah's hug.

She turned to Chelsea, who hung back, forcing Sarah to make the move to greet her.

"And Chelsea. Good to be away from school for the weekend?"

"I suppose."

The words were polite, but there was a sullen undertone that put her on alert. This one wasn't so pleased with the state of things. The awkward, angular body that met hers confirmed it.

Richard's wave was cheerful, but she could see a hint of concern in his eyes as they rode off. He, too, sensed their future rode on the success of this outing. Sarah was relieved that at least out here on the two-hour trek, prickly Chelsea wouldn't be forced into conversation with her unless she was ready. Which she obviously wasn't yet. The moment they set off, the girl surged ahead, ensuring her mount's position alongside their guide, and struck up conversation with the woman. It was Hannah who fell in alongside Sarah, and at first they rode along in a comfortable silence. But this was supposed to be a chance to get to know each other, so Sarah decided to test her out.

"How's uni going then? I remember my first year being a delicate balance between work hard and party hard, even at Vic."

That elicited a grin from Hannah. The Otago University students, known as scarfies, were notorious for heavy drinking and outrageous street parties. Their escapades frequently aired in the news, stirring outrage in older generations who conveniently forgot the excesses of their youth.

"Yeah, don't tell Daddy, but I'm having a blast. God, if he only knew what they show on the TV is only the half of it. But the work's fine. Exams soon, and I'm fairly confident I'll get into second year." From what Richard had said, she was being modest. He was proud of his straight-A-student eldest daughter.

By the time they came to a halt by a clear rushing stream, where they dismounted and let the horses drink, Sarah had relaxed and was genuinely enjoying Hannah's company. The small gap in age between them meant they had a lot in common. Hannah also had a maturity beyond her years that left her seemingly unperturbed by Richard and Sarah's relationship. She also had her father's astute nature, and so when it was time to head off on the trail again, Hannah neatly took the place at the front by the guide, forcing Chelsea to ride with Sarah. Buoyed by her success with Hannah, Sarah attempted to strike up a conversation.

"I imagine this trek is fairly tame for you. Richard tells me you're an accomplished rider."

"You could say that." She wasn't planning to make it easy.

"Well, I'm grateful you let me off with a gentle ride. I rode a bit in my teens. My father finally let me have a horse after years of pleading. Dairy farmers aren't too keen on giving up good grazing. Pony club mainly. But nothing like your standard. And it's been a while. Richard said you're in a lot of competitions?"

"Yes. I would have been this weekend too, except..."

The girl resented even being here, let alone having Sarah imposed on her life.

"Well, it's nice you came down here for your dad. I'm sure he appreciates it."

"It's for you that I had to come down here."

The girl flashed her an angry look. Sarah, determined to look past the brattish words, tried to put herself in the girl's place, and responded softly.

"Then Chelsea, thank you. I honestly appreciate it. You are very important to him, and he is very important to me."

She wasn't sure, but she thought she'd glimpsed a slight easing of the hostile gaze. But it was going to take more than one encounter between them to have anything like a harmonious relationship.

Richard was leaning on the fence, busy on the phone as they rode back in. Handing her mount to a groom to deal with, Chelsea headed straight for the car, closing the door with a resounding bang that wasn't quite a slam, but conveyed her mood to all.

Hannah and Sarah unsaddled their horses, leading them over to a green paddock where they set them free to graze, all the while ignoring the younger girl's performance. As they walked back towards the car, Hannah stopped and turned to her.

"I enjoyed that more than I expected. I haven't ridden for ages. And it was good to meet you. I knew when Daddy found someone else that he'd choose well."

Hannah's words quite overwhelmed Sarah. It was natural to hug the girl to her, elated by the knowledge that she'd won over at least one of Richard's children.

"Well, good luck for your exams, although from what he's told me, you don't need too much of that. And be sure to come and spend some time here, after you're done. And I promise, not a word about the partying," she whispered conspiratorially.

Hannah laughed, but then glancing at Chelsea's sulky face, peering at them from the car, became serious.

"Don't worry about her," she said. "She'll get over it. Don't take it personally. She's at that age where she's outraged at everything. I remember being like that myself. She'll grow out of it."

Sarah smiled at this young woman dispensing advice. Perhaps as the eldest child, she'd acquired extra wisdom along the way.

"Thank you, Hannah," she said, hugging her close again.

It was at that moment Richard appeared, tucking his phone in his pocket and beaming with pleasure. "Looks like it went well," he said.

Hannah and Sarah's eyes met, both thinking it wisest to not dispel that thought.

"It did Daddy," said Hannah. "It was fun." And she headed for the car.

"Thank god," he said, with obvious relief that his plan had worked. "That's one hurdle out of the way." She knew she wouldn't have the heart to tell him that blending her into his family was going to take a little more than this one outing. "Right, I'll pick you up from Mel's later," he said. "Chelsea wants to get back. Some dressage event tomorrow that she's determined to ride in. So I'll head up there now. And Hannah's going to spend the night with a friend. Probably so she can go out clubbing all night without me knowing what time she gets in." He bent to kiss her. "And thank you for this. You know how much it means to me that you and the girls can get along."

As she headed back along the motorway, the morning's sick feeling returned. There was a long way to go before Chelsea would accept the finality of a wedding. Another reason it was good that they hadn't set a date—there was plenty of time, hopefully enough for the girl to get used to the idea.

CHAPTER 15

Detour

# Sarah

Wellington, New Zealand – November, 2007

IT HAD BEEN EATING away at her ever since they'd arrived back in New Zealand. And it had grown steadily worse since the ring appeared on her left hand. She'd read it in the eyes of some of the well-wishers who, while offering effusive congratulations with carefully crafted smiles, couldn't completely hide their suspicions.

And she didn't totally blame them. Older man, loaded with money, leaping into a second marriage to a younger woman after only knowing her a few months. Young woman, with no job, and no assets who'd snared an attractive man who would take care of all her needs.

No one came out and said it. They were far too two-faced for that. But behind her back, the whispers were growing louder, and she wanted to put a stop to it before it was out of hand.

She loved Richard for exactly who he was, and considered herself too down-to-earth to be swayed by expensive baubles. And he'd told her many times how refreshing he found her total disinterest in the manipulations of the moneyed social elite.

But unfortunately, they couldn't avoid these people. If she could simply never see them, it wouldn't be such a problem. That wasn't an option. Like it or not, Richard needed to attend the whirl of social events where he did much of his networking for the company. Refusing to accompany him would only give them another reason to criticise her.

At the moment, according to Claire, they were the hot topic of dis- cussion amongst the Wellington set. Sarah dreaded her regular updates prefaced with "I just thought you'd want to know...." It would be better that she didn't know.

"That Sarah knows how to get what she wants. Poor Richard, I don't think he stood a chance!" From the mouth of Marilyn Preston.

"Oh, I know Richard's in pretty good shape for his age, but surely a young thing like her wasn't thinking of *that* when she set her sights on him?" As Cheryl Farmer said to Robyn Middleton.

"God, she's practically a child. Next, he'll be paying university fees for her as well as his girls. What was he thinking?" Karen Gillespie's question to Claire Blackwood.

Never mind that every one of these women lived a life of ease on the strength of *their* husband's money. Dwelling on their vicious words was still tarnishing what should be, and mostly was, the happiest time of her life.

Then there was the question of her doctoral position. The university hadn't said no. Yet. But she knew there were people in the history depart- ment who would seize on the slightest reason to reject her proposal once and for all. And probably the first of those was its head, Professor Raymond Preston, who, in a cruel twist of fate, just happened to be father-in-law to bitchy Marilyn. Labelled as a rich man's pretty trophy wife would make it even more difficult for her to be taken seriously as a historian. She couldn't afford idle gossip to ruin her last slim chance of winning that spot.

She was flipping through the pages of a trashy woman's magazine in her dentist's waiting room one afternoon, when the solution jumped out at her from a headline: 'Signing it all away: Kim doesn't want Ryan's millions'. The article alluded to an apparently poorly kept secret: little-known Australian model Kim Heatherington had signed a prenuptial agreement designed to secure the fortune of her country music legend husband-to-be Ryan Seafield should their impending marriage go belly-up.

"That's it," she thought.

If they could ask Richard's lawyers to draw up a prenup, then make it widely known she'd signed. Not difficult, since she knew exactly which conversations to drop that information into. She could ensure all of Wellington knew within days and stamp out the gossip.

She considered herself reasonably thick-skinned, but the murmured words swirling around her—'a gold-digger', 'mercenary', 'sugar-daddy' to name a few—were unexpectedly hurtful. Resolving to tackle him over the dinner they'd planned at Silver that night, she threw down the magazine as a masked nurse invited her to the dentist's chair.

"No bloody way," he said, eyes wide with incredulity. It was the first time she'd seen them flash icy blue at anything she'd said. "Absolutely not."

She hadn't predicted that reaction. He slammed down his fork, abandoning the plate of pasta that Giulia had set in front of him. It was ironic that the first wobble in their relationship, the first time she'd seen his displeasure directed at her, should occur in the same place it had begun. Her own surge of anger flared, and she spat back at him.

"How can you just flatly refuse? As far as I can see, you have nothing to lose by this. It's not you who's the topic of nasty slanderous gossip. It's not you who they label shallow and grasping."

"Don't you see how it would make *me* look?" he said.

She hadn't considered that. And a twinge of guilt tempered her anger. He was right.

Absorbed in the bitchy comments circulating about her, she'd not thought of what impact it would have on him. Somehow, maybe because he was a man, she thought he'd sail above it. Or perhaps it revealed that she didn't yet truly know him, didn't understand that there was more vulnerability than she'd predicted under that tough exterior.

"If I draw up that prenup," he said, "it makes it look as if I have no commitment to this marriage. Like I'm more worried about my money than about you. Like I'm a pathetic, insecure old arsehole who suspects he might be taken for a ride by a pretty young woman. I can't believe you'd even suggest it."

He was so angry, and she realised they were having their first fight. She took a deep breath and steeled herself.

Two opinionated people, both unused to accommodating the feelings of another—inevitably, this day would come. At least they didn't argue about small things. But tonight would not be easy, and she hoped that their relationship would emerge unscathed.

She took her time, spelling out the facts—what was being said about them, well, mainly about her. Then, deferring to his experience and wisdom, she turned it over to him. If he didn't like her suggestion, perhaps he'd have one of his own.

"I just want it to stop, Richard. It's growing worse by the day, and I'm not sure what to do." Talking about it openly like this had stirred up her emotions, and tears prickled behind her eyes. She wiped them away, annoyed that she'd let it get to her so much. "The prenup was only one idea. But you possibly have a better one? There has to be something we can do."

He softened a little at that, seeing her welling eyes. He already knew not much made her cry. Or perhaps it was because she'd offered him the role of fixer—one he was comfortable in.

She wasn't sure that navigating the treacherous waters of international business was a suitable apprenticeship for solving problems of the heart, or for tackling a bunch of nasty, conniving, idle wives with nothing better to do than find a victim for their disdain. But she was willing to let him take the lead.

"Well, I could pay some heavies to go round and rough them up," he joked. The thought that suave Richard would even know those sorts of people was so ridiculous that it elicited a smile. "Or threaten them with my lawyers. They're pretty scary."

That brought forth a giggle as she imagined Josephine Morgan, head of the legal team at Crombie Norton, going into battle on her behalf. She'd met her once, only last week at a company barbecue hosted by Claire and Jonathan. 'Dress casual' didn't quite mean the same in these circles—not a pair of shorts or jandals in sight. But it appeared Josephine hadn't got the memo, looking totally out of place in a business-like pantsuit.

She was a truly formidable woman in her fifties, no hint of silver in the dark hair pulled back in a severe bun. Intelligent eyes peered critically from behind stylish dark-rimmed glasses, and her serious mouth sported an unexpected smear of fiery red lipstick.

Sarah could imagine Josephine on the doorstep of a Khandallah mansion, squaring off with smarmy Karen Gillespie, the alleged ringleader of the group spreading ugly gossip. God, she'd loved to be there to watch Josephine squash that poisonous bitch.

"Yeah, the thought of Josephine would definitely deter me from speaking out of turn. She terrifies me."

"Me too," he admitted with a rueful smile.

He reached for her hand across the table, stroking it with calming fingers, and stopping to dwell on the enormous diamond that now marked her as his future wife. She breathed a sigh of relief that the fight was over.

But he still didn't like her solution, nor had he offered one of his own.

Josephine Morgan's corner office was an emblem of the quiet power she wielded within Crombie Norton. She was like a spider in the centre of the complex web of companies and trusts spawned from Richard and Paul's partnership, and not the least intimidated by her employers. Rarely deferential in her manner, she told it like it was. That's why Richard had hired her. He needed someone who wasn't afraid to disagree.

Behind the large white modernist desk, a massive window framed a view of the harbour, today etched with choppy whitecaps, the turbulence mirroring the feeling in Sarah's stomach. The desk itself was bare, the office sparsely decorated, but with no expense spared. The moody, abstract landscape on one wall captivated Sarah. She hoped she could get close enough to see if it truly was a Colin McCahon. Paul was passionate about art, and the corporate collection was impressive. That this was a genuine McCahon was entirely possible.

Josephine's handshake was surprisingly warm, as was the look in the brown eyes that fixed on Sarah from behind designer spectacles.

"Good to see you, Sarah," she murmured, her voice soft and melodic, quite at odds with her serious demeanour. They sank into comfortable leather tub chairs drawn up around a low table. An assistant discreetly delivered coffee and disappeared. "Richard will be through in a moment," she said. "So while I have you here, I thought I'd share something with you, something I wouldn't share with him. Oh, he probably knows the gist of it. But it's not the sort of thing you chat about with your boss."

Sarah couldn't help her raised eyebrows, but cast her eyes downward as she sipped her coffee, hoping to disguise the nervous lurch as she wondered at the content of Josephine's off-the-record conversation.

"Sarah, I've been in your shoes. So I know it's an unpleasant situation." Sarah placed her cup down, eyes now fixed on Josephine's, and read empathy there. "I was like you, an outstanding student. Graduated top of my law school class. So, even though I was a woman, it was a ticket to an excellent position—at Morgan & Pierce." Sarah knew of them. Everyone did. They were the go-to firm for businesses wanting the best and, of course, the most expensive legal advice.

"They rarely took on graduates, so I didn't expect to get the job, but I did. I also didn't expect I'd fall head over heels in love with Robert. He was a senior partner—and twenty-five years older than me." Sarah had met Josephine's husband at that same barbecue. Silver-haired, but still handsome. She recalled thinking he had to be at least seventy, but also rather dashing.

"Well, for a while there, we were the scandal of the city's professional and business community. Worse still, he was married. Not happily—but people don't care about that when they judge you." Sarah considered the vitriol she'd experienced was nothing compared to what Josephine must have endured for the crime of falling in love. "So, you see," Josephine went on, "I'm uniquely qualified to advise on your current situation. And I can tell you, it will pass. We need to steer you a course through these shark-infested waters."

Sarah smiled at Josephine's apt description of the women whose hatred plagued her, all big-toothed smiles that only barely disguised the malice behind them, circling around her, waiting for an opportunity to rip her to shreds with their vile words.

"Thank you Josephine," she said. "Richard trusts you. And I do too."

Almost on cue, he appeared in the doorway, leaned in to kiss her lightly and positioned his large suited frame into the vacant chair. Josephine took up residence behind that enormous desk. Sarah wondered if it was a force of habit to seize the high ground, or because Josephine knew she'd need every advantage to convince her boss to take the unpalatable path she was about to suggest.

She opened a folder, flicking through the pages as if checking her notes, although Sarah sensed Josephine didn't need them to dispense her wisdom about their problem. Then peering through those huge glasses behind steepled hands, she spoke, her words direct.

"So, Richard, you asked me to look into options as to how we might damp down this rather unpleasant gossip, in particular Sarah's suggestion of a prenuptial agreement. Now, I understand you had some reservations about that course of action. So I took the liberty of having a quiet chat with Camilla."

"Good move," Richard said, nodding in approval. Sarah liked Camilla Lowell. She was another of the highly competent women who occupied the upper echelons of Crombie Norton. While the company projected a conservative image, they were progressive in their hiring practices, and grabbed talent when they saw it, irrespective of gender. When she'd encountered Camilla at a company dinner, Sarah thought it rather ironic that the head of corporate PR should bear a striking resemblance to TV's fictional PR guru, Patsy from 'Absolutely Fabulous', with her French-knotted blonde hair, stylish designer clothes, a cigarette in one hand and champagne in the other. But that's where the resemblance ended. Camilla lacked Patsy's supercilious and sarcastic tone. She was sweet and funny, qualities that had lulled many a journalist or politician into underestimating her to their detriment.

"OK, you're probably not going to like this, Richard—but Camilla and I agree that the simplest way to squash this nonsense is to do exactly as Sarah suggests." Richard opened his mouth to reply, and then thought better of it, and Josephine continued. "I understand your point of view. However, it seems we are caught between them trashing Sarah's reputation and denting your own a little. But, if you think about it, they will expect you to tie things up legally. And if you make it known that you have indeed done so? Well, it will be no surprise. And for that reason, it will become yesterday's news quickly. Whereas if you don't—then I'm sorry to say that poor Sarah will find it difficult to avoid that mistrust of her motives for some time. I know what they're like."

The paperwork appeared quickly, with Sarah signing away a tiny part of her entitlement to Richard's vast fortune. In the unlikely event of him dying or the equally unlikely situation that they should divorce, a large amount of money would still come to her. But their critics didn't know that.

Josephine and Camilla's carefully placed snippets of insider information would reveal that she wasn't marrying him for the money. Staring down at her name written there, in the indigo ink of a Montblanc pen, it seemed too easy. The simple act of placing two signatures on a piece of paper. She just needed to summon her trust in older, wiser heads and hope that it would have the desired effect. And face the fact that there was no good reason to stall on a wedding date for any longer.

## CHAPTER 16

Merger

# Sarah

Wakefield, New Zealand – April, 2008

SARAH ASSESSED THE SCENE in front of her, eyes flickering from one group of people to the next. She'd been nervous about this day for weeks, not only the usual pre-wedding jitters, but a deep concern that their two worlds colliding for the first time might reflect unfavourably on their future together. She needn't have worried. When you drilled down to the heart of it, as Richard kept reminding her, they weren't so different. And even the people each had cared enough to invite were now in person not as different as they'd seemed from their names on the guest list.

Richard still slouched in his chair at the top table, sharing a joke with his best man and regular squash partner Stu. Partnered at random in a tournament years ago, the two men had developed a strong friendship. After their weekly game, they'd skive off to a suburban bar, Richard arriving home often a little merry after one too many beers, with an air of lightness about him. For Richard, it was an escape from the expectations of his work and position to spend time with Stu, who ran a small but successful construction company. In some ways, they were unlikely friends, walking in different worlds. But it worked, each of them relaxed in the other's company.

Meanwhile, Paul Crombie was in earnest conversation about local body politics with Neil Hoskin, who owned a neighbouring farm as well as holding the esteemed position of mayor of Wakefield District. Paul's wife, Eleanor, a stylish sixty-year-old dressed in a silk pantsuit and pearls, had found unexpected common ground with Mrs Hoskin, both sharing a love of cultivating rare orchids.

Claire and Jonathan Blackwood had gravitated to the most hip looking younger couple in the room. Sarah's school friend Teena had thrown off the shackles of her provincial upbringing to become a leading interior designer, and marry Mikey Maverick (not his real name) an Auckland radio jock. The four were happily working their way through a rainbow of cocktails, while each couple made an animated case for their home city to be the nation's capital of cool culture.

The huge marquee was light and airy, but guests spilled onto the man-icured lawns, enjoying the autumn sun. Richard's scepticism at her sug-gestion of wedding venue had long evaporated. He'd envisaged an exclusive country estate or an elegant vineyard retreat. But he'd trusted her, and their romantic country wedding still projected an air of simple sophistication.

Two roads over from the Mitchell farm, another dairying family had sacrificed acres of their precious grass, transforming it from a source of lush feed for their cows to a subtropical paradise. Riverlea Gardens attracted bridal parties from all over the country, offering couples their dream wedding. From the historic country church moved on to the property, to the cute retro caravan repurposed for a bar, it was flawless.

A broad arm slipped around her waist, and Richard leaned over her shoulder to press a kiss on his new wife's cheek.

"How you doing, Mrs Norton?" he whispered in her ear.

"Never better," she said, turning to demand a proper kiss from her handsome husband. She loved turning that word over in her mind—husband. It was so solid, like an anchor that would help her ride out any storm that came their way. And strangely, she loved the thought of being Mrs Norton. Her younger self would have stolidly hung onto her birth name, and refused the title 'Mrs'. But that had changed. Her love for Richard overrode any notion of rejecting his name.

Like a teenager with a crush, she'd tried it on for size, rehearsing it to herself, imagining extending her hand saying "Hello, I'm Sarah Norton", or on the phone, "Yes, I'd like to make a reservation for Sarah Norton". Even more embarrassing were the pieces of paper, filled with flourishes as she experimented with options for her new signature.

"Looks like the girls are enjoying themselves." He nodded to where his daughters, outfitted in the latest fashion, were flirting with two young men. It was as if a pair of exotic birds had landed in a field of sparrows.

Sarah was relieved that she'd finally forged a friendly relationship with both of Richard's daughters. Chelsea had been hard work, but eventually capitulated. She'd dropped her sulky opposition due to Sarah's unexpected ally: Richard's ex-wife Victoria.

Backing up Sarah's claim that she had no desire to be a stepmother to them, Victoria had moved Chelsea from terse conversations with her father where she'd stated unequivocally that she would *not* attend the wedding to choosing outfits with Hannah. It had been a huge surprise to see two smiling faces when Sarah collected them from the airport. And they'd been totally immersed in the inner circle of women, part of the excited female chatter as they'd all dressed for the wedding earlier that day. Sarah breathed a silent thank you to Victoria as she watched the boys hanging on Chelsea's every word.

"They could do worse than to hook up with the Thompson boys," she said. "They're nice kids, not to mention their parents own three huge farms, so there's plenty to go around. Chelsea wouldn't be the first horse-mad girl to snare herself a young farmer so she can have her horses while he makes the money to keep them."

Richard laughed. "I'd like to think I've raised them to be a little less mercenary when picking their future husbands. But it certainly wouldn't hurt for them to fall in love with a rich man rather than a poor one."

"Like me," she said with a giggle. Richard knew that getting her hands on his money was the last thing on her mind when she'd accepted his proposal. If anything, the social circles his wealth forced them to navigate was a drawback to being his wife. She'd already learned the art of feigning polite interest in the conversation at dinner parties, when all she wanted was to escape. At least Richard saw these events as a necessary evil, and more often than not begged off early, protesting he was tired and had an early start. They'd be home in his bed by ten, with all pretence of tiredness abandoned as he whipped off whatever confectionery she was wearing and made love to her, obliterating all memory of the previous tedious hours.

"The music's going to start soon," she said, noting the smartly attired band members taking their places at the end of the parquet dance floor. "You know what that means."

He pulled her in close. "Yes, it means I get to dance with you like on the first night we met. That one dance and it was all over. It was always going to end up here."

"Yes, I didn't know it back then, but it was." She marvelled at how fast life could change in such a short time. In one short year she'd gone from stuck in a rut, with no obvious way out, to living the dream. It had been touch and go with her studies, but she'd have always predicted that in the end she would win through. But she would never have predicted that she'd meet someone like Richard and fall hopelessly in love.

It intrigued her that such a nebulous concept as love at first sight could apply to these two practical people: she the historian with a penchant for correct names and dates, and he the money man, obsessed with facts and figures. But it was undeniable. It happened. Perhaps she'd not associated the word love with that magnetic attraction between them from the moment Richard had zeroed in on her in a crowded room.

He led her onto the floor as the first strains of music floated across the early evening air, and the bandmaster called for the bride and groom. She looped the filmy train of her gown over one wrist, and they whirled together, not the least bit self-conscious as they locked eyes and went to that place where only the two of them existed.

As the music died down, punctuated by polite applause, other couples made their way forward. Noel Mitchell arrived with a broad smile, ready to claim a dance with his daughter. Richard passed her over to her father and grabbed Mel before she could protest.

With her spiky blonde hair tamed into a smooth swirl, and the deep rose bridesmaid's dress, Mel looked beautiful. And surprisingly relaxed, dancing with Richard. He'd found it hilarious when Sarah confided Mel was frightened of him, and he had bent over backwards to build a relationship with her. Sarah loved him for it, that he should work so hard to win over her best friend. And yes, even Mel, who'd been their biggest doubter, had finally admitted that Richard was her Mr Right.

"You do know how happy it makes me to see you so happy?" her father asked as they drifted around the floor, his arm on her waist guiding her lightly in perfect time.

"I do, Dad. And I can see you're enjoying yourself. Hope you haven't downed too many beers? There are cows to be milked in the morning."

He laughed at that, hearing her echo back the words he'd uttered so many times, their lives chained to the demands of the farm, rarely staying out late, always rising early. Of course, now he didn't have cows to milk. The sharemilker would see to that. But it was hard to let go of the habits of a lifetime.

"Your mum would be so proud of you."

"I think she's here, Dad, watching over us."

"She'd like Richard. He is a good man. You know I was unsure at first—about him being older, and a big city type. Not at all like us little small-town people. But he loves you and that's all that matters."

Yes. She'd had her doubts too, and they still lingered on the periphery, tenacious in the small hold they still had on her. Seventeen years of life he'd lived before she was even born. A marriage, children, divorce, while she was navigating childhood, school, university. She flipped those doubts aside once more, annoyed that they should dare to intrude on the day, and enjoyed the solid feel of her father's arms and his approval of her choice.

---

They indulged the local guests with the quaint old traditions, driving off with a 'Just Married' sign in the back window and a clatter of cans trailing behind Richard's Jaguar. She'd deterred them from decorating it with shaving foam, fearing stripped paint. That would have been one too many rustic traditions for Richard.

They headed for the lodge, the perfect place to begin their honeymoon, and one where they'd already created memories in their short time together. She wondered if he'd truly been toying with a proposal that night. Maybe he had known he loved her, even then.

"We can't arrive with that lot clanging along behind us," he said. "We'll wake up every guest in the place. I'm going to pull over."

At the next small bush-shrouded layby, Richard parked up off the road and set about untying the decorations. She leaned against the car, barefoot on the grass verge, her spangly high-heeled wedding shoes abandoned on the floor inside. Ahead of them the mountain loomed up, bare of snow, but the full moon illuminating its navy slopes against the deeper indigo sky.

Slamming the boot on the rubble, he came around the car to meet her. His tie and jacket were long-discarded, white shirt sleeves rolled up revealing muscular tanned arms. He was so damn gorgeous, and he was hers.

"By god, you're beautiful."

His voice was husky, and she was acutely aware of the solid bulk of his erection as he pressed in close, his body pinning her against the car. His mouth covered hers, one hand behind her head, insisting she meet his hunger. Pausing for breath, he drew back a little, only to plunge his hand down into the strapless satin gown, seeking her breast. She shuddered as his fingers grasped her nipple, triggering a rush like an electric current. It lit up every nerve deep down into her very centre.

"I think we start the honeymoon now," she said, struggling to speak, almost struggling to breathe, as he continued to roll her erect nipple under his thumb, while his warm, damp mouth poured hungry kisses over her bare shoulders. "In there," she gasped. "What do you think?"

She nodded at the broad back seat of the car. There was little chance of anyone discovering them in this secluded spot, yet it felt thrilling and dangerous to even suggest they make out here, parked up like two high school kids.

"I'm thinking," he said, his words almost a growl, "if we don't, I might have to take you right here on the grass." He wrestled the door open and pushed her backwards onto the seat with a shove. No longer the elegant bride, she sat, legs sprawled, his frantic hands ruching up the layers of tulle, to loop a finger in her filigree lace panties, removing them with one swift tug.

She grappled with his belt: her need as urgent as his own, between her legs, molten with desire. She placed her hand on him, huge and hard, guiding him into her, drawing him close, her whimper of need drowned out by his quivering groan.

They lay there afterwards, in a tangle of legs and lace, the afterglow of their lovemaking insulation from the chilly autumn air. Neither spoke. There seemed no need, with both of them content to just be. To just be together. Falling in love with Richard, marrying Richard, may have been impulsive, but as he made love to her, their bodies perfectly in tune, as they lay here in perfect happiness, Sarah knew it was right.

CHAPTER 17

Secret Weapon

# Sarah

London, England – August, 2008

SARAH LANGUISHED IN THE queue, the damp air persistent in permeating the layers of wool and waterproofing she'd sensibly chosen for her outing. The line waiting to go into the British Museum was moving at glacial speed. She regretted not joining it earlier. By this time of the morning, uniformed school groups, with teacher minders hurrying them along, jostled with tourists, conspicuous by the guidebooks in their hands. The museum's free entry appealed to her egalitarian notions of education for all and shared ownership of history. But today she would have gladly paid an exorbitant entrance fee to leapfrog the crowd.

Although the British weather was living up to its dour reputation, she felt at home here. It probably helped that Mel was in London, too. Jonathan had taken up a one-year project to expand the bank's interests in Europe, bringing to life Richard and Paul's carefully laid out plans. He'd brought a small team from New Zealand, along with Claire and the kids. Crombie Norton had sweetened the deal by allowing Claire the luxury of a nanny. For Mel, the chance to spread her wings beyond Wellington, and actually be paid for supporting her sister, was the perfect arrangement. But today Sarah was on her own. Mel didn't share her fascination for history and anyway, she preferred to potter by herself in a museum, going wherever her querying mind led her.

After the eternity of her wait, she sidestepped the huddles of people attempting to decipher the museum map. She knew her destination, and had memorised the route in advance. Head up the marbled south stairs, third floor, rooms 33-39. She'd been impatient to see the gallery of Roman Britain, frustrated by the multitude of mindless tasks as they settled here this first week in London. At last, there was a free morning, and she was grabbing it.

Two hours sped by and she'd barely visited half the rooms, but was feeling buoyant at the treasures she'd seen. Home in Wellington, she'd spent the months since their Tahitian honeymoon with head down in reading and research for her PhD, endlessly typing notes in the huge, convoluted file system that had sprouted on her computer. This month in the UK was a welcome respite. It was difficult to force herself to leave the museum today, but they'd be here a few more weeks. Plenty of time to come back and immerse herself in this place, while Richard attended tiresome business meetings.

And now she kicked herself for not leaving sooner. She'd seriously underestimated the time it would take to navigate the crowded pavements. It was particularly difficult on such a wet day, dodging wayward umbrellas and the bow waves of buses as they roared through puddles, splattering her lovely wool pants with mucky water. What she'd give for a solid pair of gumboots and a set of farm overalls. And a solid excuse to offer Richard for not being exactly where she needed to be this minute.

Richard's displeasure was stamped on his face. She saw his eyes taking in her hair turned unruly by the damp, her sodden coat, and rain-soaked boots. His companions seated behind him at the white-clothed table were oblivious to his exasperated expression.

"Sarah, at last," he said in a pleasant, neutral tone as he stepped forward to help her out of her wet things. But the whisper in her ear left no doubt that he was seriously pissed off.

"About bloody time." His voice was low and angry. "You knew this lunch was important. The least you could have done was turn up on time." She'd never heard him use this tone of voice with her before. This deal had him on edge in a way she'd never seen before, nor expected.

Richard's need to be in London for the bank neatly coincided with a personal venture he was desperate to advance. Her passion was history, his was whisky.

He'd caught a whisper that MacFarlane's, a high quality Scottish distillery, was teetering on the edge of collapse. He was a huge fan of their product, having several ridiculously expensive bottles of MacFarlane's whisky in his stash. His plan was to offer them a massive investment of his own money, and provide them business expertise to ensure it was well used. Not only would it guarantee the supply of his favourite tipple going forward, it was the perfect first foray into building something for himself, for them, outside the Crombie Norton web. She'd lain awake many nights listening to his excitement. He had high hopes for this project. Now he was pouring all his energy into realising them.

She damped down the spontaneous flash of anger that rose to meet his. It was replaced with a rush of guilt. His criticism wasn't unfair—she was very late. He'd supported her so wholeheartedly in going for her dream. It was only right she should do the same for him.

He handed off her coat to a staff member who had materialised beside them. She was acutely aware that she smelled like a wet farm dog and wished she'd at least puffed a quick spray of perfume in the foyer, or even found a bathroom to tidy up. Switching back into his usual gracious manner, Richard introduced her to the three people at the table.

"My wife Sarah," he said. "Sarah, meet Hamish MacFarlane, owner and founder of MacFarlane's distillery." The serious dark-haired man in his Aran jumper and corduroy pants looked out of place in this smart dining room. If Richard had hoped to make his guests comfortable, an upmarket London hotel wasn't the right choice of venue. Hamish stood, extending a paw-like hand to shake hers with a firm grip.

"Hello, Sarah," he said, even those two mumbled words betraying his thick Scottish accent.

"And his wife, Heather." The blonde woman's smile was warm and open, and she seemed more relaxed than her husband in the surroundings of the expensive restaurant.

"Lovely to meet you, Sarah. Richard's been explaining you're a history buff."

She'd been told that this was who she needed to impress. Heather was the major obstacle in the way of Richard's acquisition of the whisky distillery. Although their business was struggling, Heather was wary of Richard's overtures, and he thought striking up a camaraderie between the two wives might smooth the negotiations.

"Yes, I'm sorry," she said. "That's why I was late. I've been to the British Museum. It's so amazing. I lose myself in there and time flits by."

Richard cut off her attempt to explain herself, turning to the third member of the group.

"And Joseph Brodie, distillery manager."

"Sarah, good to meet you," said the attractive man in a velvety voice. He had the most striking shock of unruly hair, a colour so deep that it was hard to say if it was more red or brown. Once she'd not have looked twice at a man over forty, but she'd found that since meeting Richard, this barrier no longer existed. *My, aren't you the handsome one?* Her traitorous brain admired the startling green eyes and firm chin. He had that same touch of a smile around his mouth that had so intrigued her about Richard. Not that it was visible on Richard's face today, her lateness destroying any good humour.

"And you," she said, clasping the man's outstretched hand and feeling a little shock of attraction. She was stern, admonishing her mind for supplying these inappropriate impulses. *Stop right there. One, you're married and two, Richard would never forgive you for jeopardising this deal in any way.*

She took her seat opposite Heather and focused on how she might tackle her work as Richard's secret weapon.

She should have learned from her late arrival to that first lunch with the MacFarlanes two days earlier. What she should have done was stay at the apartment for the day, supervising the preparations for that night's dinner with them. But the alternative offer was too good to turn down.

The moment she'd known they would be in the UK for a month, Sarah had reached out to a former colleague from the history department at Victoria, now on an Oxford scholarship. She had to admit to a tweak of jealousy. The allure of Oxford was strong. What it would have been to do her PhD there. Her friend Aaron was living the life she could have had if things had been different. If her mother hadn't died, triggering her father's slump into a dangerous depression. If she'd not allowed herself to be submerged in the routine of the farm. If she'd not succumbed to Richard's charms, linking her future to his. But she consoled herself that given the chance to do it over again, she would make the same choices.

While Richard was out on his early morning run, she'd put on practical clothing and footwear, organised a daypack, walked the few hundred metres to Kensington train station and was now on a regional train heading south west. She'd left a note for him, its careful wording not betraying any hint that this outing was a day trip out of the city. It wasn't a lie, merely a sin of omission.

But there was a nagging worry that it had come to this. Five months of marriage and she was keeping secrets from her husband. But it was a neat solution. Far better than going head to head with him and the unpleasant scene it would have created when she'd refused to back down. Because she *would have* refused. Instead, she'd applied the old the saying 'It's easier to seek forgiveness than permission' to the situation. She hoped it would prove true.

Aaron was working on a recently discovered Romano-British settlement. It was irregular to invite visitors onto a site so early in an excavation. But he'd pleaded her case, given she had a Masters with First Class Honours in this field of interest and the strong links to her doctoral work. He'd intimated to his supervisors that Sarah was possibly interested in applying for a doctoral scholarship like his own, and transferring to Oxford. And so they'd agreed she might join them for a day, an opportunity to check her out. Sarah's practical archaeological experience was virtually non-existent, but she figured she knew enough to bluff her way through. She was excited by this chance to see artefacts in the field, rather than inside museum cases.

On the return journey, this sense of exhilaration still buoyed her. She'd scraped the worst of the dirt off her boots, but they still bore a coating of the Hampshire mud. Her hair, now released from its ponytail, was a tangled mess. There would be no choice but to give it a thorough shampoo if she was going to tame it into a more respectable state for that evening's dinner party. Richard had organised caterers, and the MacFarlanes were due at seven. She was cutting things fine, not helped by the fact she'd missed her planned mid-afternoon train, losing an hour while waiting for the next.

It was six forty-five when she slipped off her boots on the doorstep of the rented Georgian townhouse and braved Richard's wrath awaiting her inside. The moment she stepped into the apartment, his hand closed around her arm, his grasp rough, as he jerked her into the small study, out of sight and earshot of the catering staff who were busy preparing for their guests. She'd never before had him show aggression to her, nor had she ever seen such a look of anger on his face. The words that spewed from his mouth were equally incongruous with the man she knew.

"What the fuck do you think you're playing at, Sarah? Are you deliberately trying to embarrass me in front of these clients? Sabotage this deal? You know how important this project is to me." He stopped for a moment as if to come up for air and then plunged back into the barrage. "First, on Tuesday, you turn up late for lunch, looking like something the cat dragged in. And then, today—well, it's fucking unbelievable. You know they'll be here any minute." She opened her mouth to reply, but he cut her off. "I'm not even going to ask why. I don't want to know."

Her first instinct was to fire back at him. She wouldn't put up with any man speaking to her like that. When cornered, she was always going to come out fighting.

"Since when have you told me what to do? I am your *wife*, not your child. You might get off with telling Hannah and Chelsea where to be and what to do, but you don't do that to me."

But he wasn't having that. It was the first time they had fought, properly fought, and she could tell he would not let her set the terms of engagement.

"No, you're right. I don't tell you where to go and what to do. In fact, what do I ever ask of you, Sarah? Not a fucking thing, that's what. From the moment we met, I've done nothing but cater to your every whim, do everything I can to make you happy. Because you are my wife and because I love you. But it's a two-way thing, you know. The first time I ask you to do something for me, you just carry on your own merry way, as if my happiness doesn't matter to you one bit. If you want me to treat you like a wife, you need to act like one. Since you've been acting like a spoiled child, then maybe I need to treat you like one. Now go, clean yourself up and get back out here with a smile on your face."

Her anger flared more brightly. The words tumbled out, her bitter tone grabbing them and twisting them into ugliness.

"Oh right, you say you love me, but you know, Richard, I have to wonder if that's true. You're pissed off with me because I'm not here on time to be your pretty little hostess, flashing my cleavage and fluttering my eyelashes to sweeten some deal for you."

The doorbell rang, piercing his stunned silence at her words, distracting her from the hurt she'd seen in his eyes and her surge of regret at recognising it.

"Bugger, they're early," he said. They stepped back into the entranceway, his parting shot ringing in her ears as she headed for the bedroom. "I will cover for you, but believe me, you need to be back in that lounge, and soon."

She stood under the shower, the water mingling with her tears. She was still reeling from the shock of the argument. It rocked her that he should speak to her like that. Richard never swore. Most of his cronies had such a high opinion of themselves that they never moderated their language or behaviour, no matter whose company they were in.

But the insecurities of Richard's childhood still drove him to be more gentlemanly than the gentlemen who'd been born to it. He'd worked to overcome the stigma of his childhood. He'd moulded himself into a person who might be judged but never found wanting by the elite society he'd clawed his way into. He was the boy on a scholarship to a posh boarding school who studied the correct etiquette of the wealthy families when his friends invited him home for a weekend. He was the man who considered outbursts and foul language a lack of control, and he despised people who couldn't control themselves.

Shame at having provoked him into lashing out in a way so out of character fought against indignation that he was questioning her right to determine her own life. She hadn't given up that right when she made her marriage vows.

But there was an unsettling thread of truth in his accusations. Had she subconsciously decided that she'd kept her part of the bargain simply by supplying him with a wife almost twenty years his junior, to be envied by his compatriots and admired by his clients? By gifting him a passionate lover, offering her young body for him to enjoy? Had she assumed this was enough, that she needn't consider the things that he wanted out of life? Like this whisky distillery. He certainly didn't need it in his portfolio. It wasn't the sort of troubled business that was ripe for buying up cheap and selling all the assets for a tidy profit. Richard wanted it because it had sparked an interest in him, not only as an investment. Her stomach clenched, nausea now overwhelming her, as she flung herself from the shower and hunched over the toilet, vomiting.

That was how he found her. Naked, wet, her hair trailing in dank lengths over her face, the sour smell of vomit, a lingering miasma in the room. He enveloped her in one of the large towels, lifting her from the floor, cradling her against him, his arms strong and comforting. He carried her through to the enormous bed, laying her down softly, brushing back the hair.

She pulled the covers over her head. He sat beside her, and with tender hands, pulled back the sheet.

"Go, Richard. I don't want you to see me like this."

"No, I won't," he said, his voice gentle. "When I married you, it was all of you. For better or for worse. And yes, I've seen you better, but it doesn't mean I don't love you at your worst. You are always beautiful to me." He stroked her face, his hands tender. "But it's me who's been at his worst today. Not you." Ignoring the fact he was fully dressed, he climbed under the sheets beside her, wrapping himself around her, his arms protective. "I let my obsession with this deal get out of hand. Made it more important than the most important thing in the world—you. I am so very sorry that I forgot that. That I hurt you."

She let the words sink in, but remained silent. His other self, the hard-nosed businessman, apologised to no one. Sensing his concerned gaze upon her, she flickered her eyes open to meet it.

"I love you, Richard Norton," she said, her voice coming out small. "Even if you can be an obnoxious bastard."

"This obnoxious bastard loves you, Sarah Norton—even if you can be an argumentative tart."

An unexpected giggle rose in her throat at that. He'd called her that before, always with a touch of admiration in the label. He'd never wanted a doormat for a wife. Liked that she told him what she thought, pulled him back when he was out of line. Understood that her doubts were unfounded—she was more than an accessory to him.

He smiled and kissed her forehead lightly. "Skip the dinner. The MacFarlanes aren't even here yet—the doorbell was a delivery for the kitchen. You stay here and I'll tell them you're not well. Ask the staff to bring you up a tray."

"Thank you, Richard. I'm not sure I'm the best company tonight."

After he left, she drifted into sleep, her body succumbing to exhaustion from the long walk across the Hampshire countryside, and the complete draining of her emotional well on returning home.

When she stirred, she saw that she'd only been asleep for an hour, but to her surprise, found an aura of calm surrounding her. A gentle tap on the door announced a nervous young woman bearing a tray of food. Sarah propped herself up in bed and picked at it for a while. She could hear faint conversation, the clatter of glassware and cutlery, the odd burst of laughter.

She'd enjoyed Tuesday's lunch with the MacFarlanes. Hamish was clearly a man of the land who reminded her of her father. In response to her questions about the distillery, he'd put aside his awkwardness in the lavish surroundings. The fire that sparked in his eyes when he spoke of his whisky was contagious. She'd immediately liked Heather, warming to the older woman's open, no-nonsense style. And then there was the charismatic Joseph Brodie. He was a man of few words, which made his green eyes even more beguiling as she'd wondered what really lay behind them. Pushing aside those curious thoughts, she set down the tray and made the decision to join them. If she worked quickly to make herself presentable, she might even be in time for dessert.

"Sarah, are you sure you should be up?" Richard met her with a look of surprise as she stepped into the warmth of the dining room.

"Yeah, I'm fine," she said. "Decided I shouldn't miss the fun." She sat in the vacant chair and plunged a spoon into the creamy tiramisu placed in front of her. Between mouthfuls, she leapt into the conversation about a distillery and what it would take for it to become theirs.

After they'd gone, Sarah remained downstairs, out of habit checking all was in its place. She scanned the kitchen one last time. Noting with approval the catering staff's attention to detail, every single part of the room left neat and spotless, she climbed the stairs to their bedroom.

She paused at the door, in silent appreciation of her husband. He'd discarded his shirt. In the dim room, he sat illuminated by the bedside lamp. She thrilled at the thought of that body blanketing hers, the lean hardness of him honed by a rigorous adherence to routine. At home or away, on business or on holiday, he ran. His meditation, he said. And the lightly muscled arms, toned to perfect curves by the rhythmic lifting of weights in a twice-weekly routine at the gym. Although she'd never felt the need to be protected, there was always a blissful sense of safety in those strong arms. Until tonight. The memory of him using that strength against unsettled her.

As he performed the mechanics of undressing, his mind was elsewhere, thoughts rippling across his face, the hint of a smile. Relaxed like this, his expression was boyish, and an aura of excitement surrounded him. The distillery was all but his. A successful evening. Seeing her in the doorway, he stretched out his hand.

"Come here," he said, his words slurring a little from the effects of the whisky. She obliged and, twirling her like a dancer, he pulled her downwards in one seamless movement, onto the bed beside him. She spun herself onto his lap, sitting astride him, her dress bunched up by her thighs, and she was aware of her own scent drifting from the point at which they connected. "You were amazing," he said. "This wouldn't be happening except for you."

They sat, foreheads touching, eyes closed, as she drank in his happiness, savouring her own exhilaration at the part she'd played in it. He slid a finger under her chin, tilting her head into a kiss, the smoky, sweet taste of the whisky still on his lips.

"I mean it," he said, threading his fingers in her hair, twisting it playfully in that way he did. "I'm not used to putting together deals like this. It's all so personal—negotiating with people who've put their heart and soul into something that you want to prise away. Even though deep down she knew it was the right thing to do, it took you nudging Heather. And now it's mine. Ours. Something we can have fun with together."

She leaned back a little, trusting his arms not to let her fall. "So, how do you intend to thank me?" she said, and saw the spark ignite in his eyes.

"Oh, I have a fairly good idea of how I might do that." He tried to sound casual. "First, by ridding you of this."

One deft tug on the sash at the front of her dress and it fell open. She wiggled free of it, letting it pool around her waist, amused by his gaze as it revealed her bare breasts. It was a game they played. It turned him on, the thought that she might not be wearing anything under a dress. So she kept him guessing, him never knowing what he would find when he unwrapped her, like a surprise gift.

"And then, this." He let his head fall forward, his tongue lightly tracing a teasing trail between her breasts. His hand cupped each in turn, raising it to his lips where he suckled the nipple, gentle at first and then dangerously brushing it a little with his teeth. She whimpered at the thrill. She leaned back, secure only by the grip of her legs around his waist, revelling in the waves of pleasure and a faint exquisite tweak of pain as he sought her out more hungrily.

"Have I thanked you enough?" he said, coming up for air.

"Not nearly enough." Her voice was ragged.

He stood, and she released her legs as he placed her gently on the bed. "Maybe this then."

He sank to his knees before her, his head bowed. She twined her fingers in the dark silkiness of his hair as she pressed his mouth to that warm nerve-charged spot at the very centre of her. She let herself succumb to the pleasure of the moment, let it drown out the nagging worry that tonight they'd strayed into dangerous territory, revealed hidden cracks in what this was between them, this marriage, this relationship.

## CHAPTER 18

MacFarlane's

# Sarah

Stirlingshire, Scotland – August, 2008

"CLOSE YOUR EYES," HE said as he eased the car off the country road into a gateway. The hanging sign was emblazoned with a single word: 'MacFarlane's'. Sarah did as he asked, enjoying the playfulness of a surprise. It had all been so serious lately, with Richard's intense focus on his goal of buying this distillery.

Loose chips from the gravel below rattled beneath her feet, the car swaying gently as they travelled along an undulating driveway. She sensed the gradual climb and, even through her closed lids, could feel ripples of sunlight bouncing off trees as they wound slowly towards the distillery complex. The car slowed to a gradual halt.

"Now," he said. "Open them."

"Oh, my god. That's amazing."

The tower house loomed ahead of them, earth-coloured stonework silhouetted against a brilliant blue late summer sky. Framed by massive oak trees, the sun reflected off their waving leaves added a surreal gilded edge to the scene. She'd seen photographs, but they were nothing compared to the reality ahead of them. They drove through an arched stone entranceway, where Richard parked. As if catapulted back into some period drama, staff appeared through massive wooden doors, standing to attention, waiting for their guests to alight.

"Yeah, there's no doubt they did a magnificent job of the restoration," he said. "And the distillery is second to none. But unfortunately, you don't save a crumbling sixteenth century ruin, or create a world-class whisky distillery without spending serious amounts of money."

"The accommodation fit out wouldn't come cheap either," she said. "In the brochure, it looks like the interior of Holyrood Palace, no expense spared." She couldn't wait to see their room on the top floor.

"Yes, that was the final straw. Came in way over budget. And sadly for Hamish, he was up to his eyeballs in debt and in bed with investors he couldn't count on. Tried to do the dirty on him by pulling out their money, knowing he had nowhere else to go."

"But he did. He found you."

"More like I found him, thanks to that tip off from Jeffrey. Hamish was bloody naïve to go into that sort of deal in the first place. Fortunately, my lawyers are one step smarter than the investors. My guys have earned their exorbitant salaries this time."

"It's sad to lose everything you've worked for."

"Well, they're not going to. Those bastards who tried to screw him are going to get a rude shock when they see the paperwork that's about to arrive on their desk. I have them cornered, and they have no choice but to walk away."

Pride surged in her. That he would do this. Put his money and his reputation on the line. Of course, he was buying his dream, but he was also buying back Hamish and Heather's dream, too.

———

From their rooms, which occupied the entire top level of the stone tower house, they had a view out across the property. To the west was a cluster of buildings that housed the distillery itself. Although far newer, they echoed the history of their neighbours. They were built of a similar stone, but with an expanse of glass and the flash of steel beams providing clues to their far more recent construction. She glimpsed Richard, already engrossed in a tour of the whisky making facilities, trailing behind Hamish and his manager Joseph Brodie. It made her happy to see him so happy, freed from the pressure of making money for the bank, immersed in a project he was passionate about.

She pushed open the huge sash window, impressed with the hidden modern mechanism that allowed it to glide upwards with the slightest touch. The smell of the country wafted in on the breeze, the green fragrance of grass and the barest whiff of cows, even though the herd were only black and white dots in a distant field.

Closer in, no longer occupied by animals, were the original barns and outbuildings, which, like the manor house, had once been ruins. But the visionary MacFarlanes had recreated them as boutique cottages. Soon Jonathan would meet Claire, Mel and the two children at Edinburgh's Waverley Station and drive them up here to stay in the largest cottage.

"Can't understand the attraction of the train myself," Jonathan had grumbled, annoyed that he wouldn't be here to start the celebrations early. Mel was more miffed that she wasn't staying in the manor, its age and history appealing to her romantic side. But nannies had little say in their accommodation, even when they were family.

Below the ancient tower house, beyond the distillery, was Hamish and Heather's own home, mostly obscured by fences and shrubbery, preventing its modern lines from jarring against this sixteenth century fairytale they'd brought back to life.

She left the window open, allowing the country air to permeate the room. Next, she pulled off her shoes and lay back on the expanse of the bed, considering how to fill the two hours available to her before pre-dinner drinks. Closing her eyes, she drank in the smell, thoughts of the farm washing over her as she unexpectedly gave way to sleep. She awoke to find Richard standing over her, a bemused smile on his face.

"Hey there sleeping beauty. How you doing?" He leaned over, placing a delicate kiss on her forehead, his large warm hand cupping her face.

"Hmmm, I'm good," she said, the pleasant languid feeling of sleep still heavy in her bones. "What's the time?"

"Five-thirty," he said, making his way around the bed, where he stood stripping off his clothes before lying alongside her. "No need to get all dressed up tonight. Heather said to come and join them for dinner at their house tonight, so it's casual." One hand slid up under her shirt, and was exploring the curve of her breast.

"Oh, good," she said, closing her eyes as he delicately traced her neck with his lips, his breath sending a small shiver through her body.

"Yeah, I thought you'd be pleased." He knew that despite her having mastered the hair and makeup skills needed to transform herself from farm girl to sophisticated corporate wife, she was over the novelty of formal clothes and killer heels. Fortunately, this weekend it would only be required for tomorrow's big dinner to celebrate Richard's partnering with the Mac-Farlanes.

His hand trailed down her stomach, to neatly unbutton her jeans, and all thoughts of dinner preparations evaporated.

"Which means we have loads of time..."

"Exactly what I was thinking." Now fully awake, she pulled herself away from him, and stood, rapidly freeing herself from jeans and shirt. His unwavering gaze fixed upon her, as she discarded underwear, triggered an electric tingle of anticipation.

---

Richard had modelled the programme for their stay on a traditional shooting weekend, and although they lacked the titles of English gentry, he had spared no expense making sure his guests had access to the typical activities of the landed classes. While the only guns firing would be aimed at clay birds, there was plenty of choice in how they could fill the day before a celebratory dinner that evening.

"My god it's early," she moaned, as he rose before dawn, waking her despite his attempt to be considerate, as he tiptoed around in the gloom.

"Sorry," he said in a whisper as he crashed and banged, "but those trout are calling and Hamish will be waiting."

The property came with its own lively stream, which lured Richard with the opportunity of world-class fly-fishing and tales to tell his mates. Sarah dozed, unable to reclaim proper sleep as, like a small child, her brain buzzed with excitement at the prospect of the day.

By ten a.m., she'd eaten a hearty Scottish breakfast served in the elegant dining room, and was ready to ride out with Heather. Their host was an accomplished horsewoman. Only by using her mounts for guests to ride had she saved them from being sold alongside other assets to prop up their ailing business.

Sarah leaned low over the gelding's neck, inhaling the intoxicating smell of its pristine mane. She'd ridden since she was about ten, even having her own pony in her teenage years. But she was decidedly out of practice, the tame trek with Richard's daughters barely counting.

The first sight of the sixteen-hand grey was intimidating, but reassured by its kind eye and steady gait, she settled into the saddle. She was further heartened to discover how quickly her latent instincts could surface when Richard and Hamish, clomping along in their waders, emerged without warning from the bushes behind them. Her quick reactions saved her from a tumble as her startled horse danced wildly, spinning around to fix a wary eye on the two men.

"Nice save honey," he called up at her. "Have fun."

"Bloody stupid men," Heather muttered at their husbands' retreating backs before leading them off on a pretty bridle trail through the woods.

Coming out of the trees, Heather urged her horse into a gallop and Sarah, sensing her own horse's desire to follow, let him have his head. They came to a halt on the crest of a hill; the horses blowing with happy snorts, thrilled with their own speed. From this vantage point, they looked out over the expanse of the property. Sarah realised it was the first time she and Heather had been alone, away from their spouses' talk of business and whisky.

"It's beautiful, Heather," she said.

"That it is." Her voice was soft, her expression wistful. "I've lived my whole life here. My family, for two hundred years. I hoped that in another hundred, my great-grandchildren would look out on this same view and call it their own. It's not wrong to hope for that, is it?"

"No," said Sarah. "I get it. I hope my children will spend time on our family farm, too." In fact, given her sisters' total disinterest, there was a fair chance that one day it might fall to her to keep it in the family.

"You plan to have children?" Heather asked.

"Not yet."

"You're young. Plenty of time." She smiled a wry smile. "I need to keep telling myself that about my son. He's about your age, but not ready to settle to anything, let alone a wife and children. I have to be patient. All in good time, as they say. In fact, he doesn't see the attraction of all this.

Not sure he appreciates how hard we've tried to build something worth inheriting. But he will one day, I'm sure of it."

"He'll come back to it?"

"I hope so. He's here at the moment, you know. But you won't see him. He and his father are at loggerheads all the time. He's lying low in one of the cottages. Off to the army soon. That's one of the things his father's unhappy about."

"And you?"

"Well, of course I have a mother's usual concern for her child, who is about to go off to a job where people may try to kill him. So part of me is terrified for him. But part of me knows that it's a good decision for him. The army life will suit him well. And he's smart, and careful. Knows how to handle himself. I'm not really religious, but on this one, I just have to trust that God will bring him back to me. To this." She gazed out at the hills, sheep dotted between stands of trees, the buildings, doll-house sized in the distance, and sighed, a deep melancholy sound. "Yes, I'd do a deal with the devil to save this place for him."

"So Richard's the devil?" Sarah grinned at her.

"No, no, far from it," said Heather with a smile. "More like our saviour to be honest. That's how I describe him. We used to think that about those bastards who came to us with their big money and false promises. The deal we did with them—well, let's say we've certainly been to hell and back this last year as they tried to screw us over." The lines of tension etched on her face deepened as her mouth turned down in a bitter scowl. "No, your husband is like them, in that he has the money. But he also has a passion for what we do here. You've seen it."

"I have. This is a dream come true for him."

"And hopefully he'll make our dream come true as well. Generations of my family worked this land, each one a little less successful, the property less productive, but I'm the one who stood on the brink of losing it. Hamish and I were foolish with our grand plans. Thought we'd be the ones to stop the decline."

"And now you will."

"We'll see. At least we have a chance."

"Failure isn't in Richard's vocabulary. He wouldn't have come in alongside you if he thought it would fail."

"No, you're right. That's why we're celebrating tonight, aren't we? Speaking of which, there's a lot to do, so I suppose we should head back. How about we give these two a chance to do what they love best, eh?"

She wheeled her chestnut mare around, and with a slight flick of the reins, urged her forward. The mare, knowing exactly what lay between her and home, sprang into action. Sarah's gelding pricked his ears, and with a small whinny, as if to seek her permission, took off in the same direction. This time they went cross-country, no path marked, but the horses knew the way.

At the first hedge, Sarah took a deep breath and attempted to summon all she knew from her limited experiences with the hunt club. The horse sailed over effortlessly, landing with a stable thump. She was relieved to still be in the saddle, but had no time to relax as he veered off towards the next obstacle, a bramble-covered fence.

The gelding took the second fence with the same casual grace, but this time as he landed, Sarah tried to adjust her position in the saddle and failed. In a flurry of limbs, she toppled awkwardly to the ground, the world spinning in front of her. She landed with a thud. Her head jerked backwards, hitting the ground, vibrations ricocheting through her helmet. For a moment, the world went black. When she regained awareness, the gelding's velvet muzzle and spiky whiskers were tickling her face. Seeing her eyes open, he moved off to pluck a few blades of grass, as if it was an everyday occurrence to see a human sprawled in the middle of a paddock.

She could feel the ground vibrate as Heather's horse approached, sliding to a halt alongside her own. Heather leaned over her, her face pale with worry. Seeing Sarah conscious, relief replaced her frown of concern.

"I'm sorry. That was a bloody stupid thing to do. You seemed a capable rider, so I assumed you'd be OK with it."

Sarah propped herself up on one elbow, in her mind checking each part of her body to establish where it hurt.

"No, it's fine. It's not your fault, or his," she said, looking over to where the grey was chomping his unexpected snack of lush grass. "I was enjoying myself. But then misjudged a little there and became airborne. I'm fine, honestly."

Heather's motherly instincts took over, insisting Sarah wiggle each body part in turn, submit to having her vision checked by following Heather's wavering finger, and tolerate her fussing. The final verdict was that there'd most likely be a few bruises coming out later, but otherwise, there was no major damage. She then took both horses in hand and surveyed the distance between them and the stables.

"Well, we could walk, but it's still quite a way," she said. "Or we could follow the traditional wisdom and get you straight back on the horse?"

"I vote for the horse." There was no way Sarah was prepared to walk that distance, not with a banged head and a throbbing leg. "On one condition—we take the track. I think I've used up all my luck for the day."

They arrived back at the stables to find Mel sitting on a bench with a bored expression, attempting to ignore her sister, who sat alongside. Claire was gushing words of encouragement to seven-year-old Abigail and five-year-old George, who were having a riding lesson. The two children circled the arena on sturdy Shetland ponies, each led by a groom giving gentle instructions to the little riders.

"Thank god you're back," said Melanie, as she sidled up to Sarah, while keeping a wary eye on the horse she was unsaddling. "Do you think when you're finished there, we could find something to do that doesn't involve horses?"

"Richard says there's a great pub down in the village. We were going to have lunch. Sound OK?"

"Perfect. Since I'm officially off child-minding duties for the weekend, I need to have some fun."

As if speaking his name had summoned him, Richard appeared, his smile turning to a frown as he noticed her dishevelled appearance.

"What's all this?" he said, pulling a stray twig snared in her hair. "You're filthy. Even here." One finger traced a smear of mud on her cheek.

"Let's say I may have been a little overconfident. Hit the dirt. Nothing broken. Only a bit of bruising, mostly to my ego."

"Don't make light of it, love." Heather strolled over from where her mare was already gorging herself on an overstuffed hay net and reached to take Sarah's mount so he, too, could enjoy a reward. "She banged her head quite hard. The helmet did its job, but we need to keep an eye on her. Could still have a concussion," she warned.

Richard's concerned expression deepened, his eyes fixed on hers, as she tried to appear composed despite a lingering feeling of disorientation.

"I'm fine," she said. "We'll go for lunch, I'll have a relaxing afternoon and I'll be good as new by dinnertime."

Her head was tender in one spot, and she suspected he'd notice bruises when she stripped off her jeans, but she was determined not to let one moment of carelessness on her part spoil the weekend.

# Sarah

Stirlingshire, Scotland – August, 2008

Sarah relaxed in a vast leather chair, drink in hand. She noticed with pleasure how Richard's jubilant mood infected the entire party. This was his triumph, but he was determined that everyone present would enjoy it.

Even Claire and Jonathan, a little unbalanced by the ordinariness of their hosts juxtaposed against the extravagant room and lavish canapés, had immersed themselves in the conversation. Claire's tinkling laugh bounced across the room, contrasting with Jonathan's animated baritone. They saw Richard as a reliable yardstick for measuring social acceptability. Observing his obvious growing friendship with Hamish and Jo, and his easy familiarity with Heather, they took it as permission to drop their usual haughty scrutiny and simply appreciate the evening.

With Mel's encouragement, Sarah had last week bought a stylish dress in a young designer's store just off Oxford Street. Despite its confines, and the layer of makeup she'd applied (with what she noted was growing speed and skill) she relaxed too. This was a pleasant alternative to bank functions. The ambience of the room was far removed from the stiffness of some trendy restaurant or a carefully curated dinner party overseen by one of the formidable corporate wives. The ruby velvet drapes, gold patterned wallpaper, and fire crackling in the most enormous fireplace she had ever seen gave it a homely feel despite the expensive decor.

And she felt at home with these people. She too sensed the beginnings of a friendship—with Heather. Old enough to be her mother, Heather had a warmth and wisdom that attracted Sarah, perhaps because of the absence of her own mother. But there was more to it than that. United by their menfolk's passion for whisky, and their shared love of country life and down-to-earth sensibilities, Sarah welcomed the future link between them forged by Richard's venture.

However, Heather, despite her humble manner, easily fell into the role of gracious hostess as she deftly herded the guests into their designated places at the table. Hamish took his spot at the head, Richard sliding into a chair beside him.

"Sarah, sit here by me," said Heather. "I'll be glad of your conversation. These men aren't likely to even draw breath in between talk of whisky."

As she took her seat, Sarah started at her own unexplained nervousness when the enigmatic Joseph Brodie took his place opposite her. Although he was pleasant, since her unexpected visceral response to the man at their first meeting in the London restaurant, she'd felt more comfortable by avoiding him. Now she'd have to look into those perturbing green eyes for the whole evening.

"Melanie, you sit here by Sarah." That was kind of Heather to leapfrog Mel up the ranks. Claire, with her acute understanding of the social ladder, even here in unfamiliar territory, threw Mel a sour glance as if her sister had engineered the promotion herself. For a moment, the unflappable Heather paused, eyeing the seat opposite Mel with an expression of indecision.

"He's not coming, Heather. Told me himself, only an hour gone." Joseph's voice had an air of resignation, as if saying 'I told you so' without putting it into words. "The laddie doesn't ken what he's missing. Done himself out of a night opposite a bonny young lassie," he said with a smile at Mel. "Sorry Heather, if you were hoping for a bit of matchmaking, he's thwarted your plans."

Sarah understood now. The MacFarlane's mysterious son. Mel's placement at the table hadn't simply been to give *her* some company. After all, Heather was keen for her son to produce the next generation of the family, and he couldn't accomplish that alone.

Hamish glowered from the end of the table. "He should have let us know, but it's typical of the bloody boy. No manners, despite all our efforts in raising him to be better than that."

Heather shot Hamish a glance of rebuke, as if warning him not to air family tensions in public. Regathering her composure, she waved Jonathan into the empty seat and then resumed her job of encouraging the remaining guests to their places. Wait staff noiselessly appeared with wine, soon followed by three courses of food that, while distinctly Scottish, had a sophisticated edge.

"You're quiet," said Mel. She'd taken a breath from her flirtatious conversation with Jo. Deprived of the chance to win over the evasive younger MacFarlane, Mel had focused instead on the only single man in the room, although he was of her father's generation, not her own. Sarah knew it wasn't serious. Emboldened by a few drinks, and Jo's attentiveness to making all of them comfortable, Mel was enjoying it for what it was. It seemed Jo was too. Now Richard commandeered his attention to elaborate on some point on distillation.

"Well, since I'm the married one, I thought it was better to leave you to chat him up," Sarah replied quietly, a grin on her face.

"He's quite good-looking, isn't he? In a rugged sort of way." She turned towards Sarah, voice still low, keeping her words discreet.

Sarah replied in the same hushed tones. "Of course you know he's old enough to be your father?"

"And this from the woman who has found the love of her life with an older man."

"Not quite *that* old," she retorted. "But don't let that stop you from having a go."

"A go at what?" asked Jo, turning back from providing the nugget of information Richard required.

"Oh, Sarah was saying that I shouldn't let her falling off the horse today put me off learning to ride," said Mel. "Claire wants the kids to have lessons when they get back to London and I thought I might join them."

Sarah smiled to herself, thinking what an adept liar her sweet, innocent friend had become. Talk of her inelegant tumble from the horse drew her attention back to the niggling headache that still plagued her. Her temple pulsated with a dull ache. Even the most gentle pressure of her finger elicited a sharp jolt of pain. Earlier, she'd thought that apart from the shock of being briefly knocked unconscious and an ugly bruise on her thigh, she'd come out of it unscathed. Now she wondered if this was the result. There was a rhythmic quality to the sensation, as if John Bonham was playing his drums in her head. The warm room was cloying rather than cosy. Heat flashed in her cheeks. She needed to get out of there.

She pushed back the sturdy wooden chair and rose from her seat, her hands shaky.

"Are you OK, Sarah?" Hearing Heather's voice of concern, Richard's attention flickered from his conversation with Jo. No doubt he was scrutinising her for signs of concussion. His attentiveness always made her feel special for an instant, but then her fierce independence would rear up and she'd fob him off. So, not wanting a fuss, she injected a casual note to her reply.

"Yeah, I'm fine. Just need a little air." She shot him a reassuring smile, and he acknowledged her with a slight nod, relaxed his frown, and resumed his earnest discussion with Jo, the pair of them now engrossed in the finer details of peated whisky. She grabbed a tumbler of water from the table and gulped a slug as she headed for a set of double doors that led into the garden.

Outside, the night was clear and crisp. Scotland was experiencing an unseasonal bout of fine weather, with no sign of the rain and gloom they'd expected. The faint chill was like a welcome kiss, brushing over her burning face. Above her, the Milky Way sprawled across the dark bowl of the sky, misty patches of star clouds adorned with bright blinking pinpricks. Dark sky country, far away from the pollution of city lights. She spun like a dancer, head arched back, taking in the full expanse of the sky, marvelling at the magnitude of that sprawling galaxy, so vast that one could both observe it and be a part of it.

Drawn by the soothing coolness of the night air, she followed a path that wove around behind the tower. Here, flanked by the remains of a high stone wall, it hemmed her in close against the soaring outer facade of the structure. Built to deter intruders back in a time when rival clans might seize any opportunity to take the inhabitants by stealth from behind, it funnelled the meandering pathway close to the building itself.

She paused, craning her neck to take in the full height of the ancient mansion, outlined against the ribbon of stars. An unexpected sensation of vertigo washed over her. Her hand released its grip on the tumbler, and it smashed to the cobblestones beneath her feet. She stepped towards the wall of the house, placing her palms flat against the rough stones, hoping its stable presence would ground her. She steadied herself, eyes closed, blocking out whatever vision had given rise to the nauseous feeling.

However, the absence of sight only heightened her awareness of the existence of a sound. It had the low whine of a distant jet engine, reminding her of her childhood. She recalled days when the air force fighter planes based south of the farm would fly the length of the North Island on training runs, and she and her sisters would run outside in delight, whooping and waving at some faceless pilot as he roared over them. Of course, the British military would have a presence in Scotland. It seemed entirely possible that the RAF would do night training. A totally plausible explanation that she quickly rejected, realising that the sound wasn't coming from above her, but somehow emanated from the actual walls of the house.

Not only could she hear it, but she could feel it. A vibration that passed through her hand shot along the length of her arms and coursed through her body like an electric current. She tried to wrench her hands away. If she could disconnect from it, break the circuit, the sound might stop. But it was impossible, as if a giant magnet held her there by a force so compelling she could not escape.

Unable to step away, she found, however, that she could slide her hands vertically, and she let the weight of her body pull her down, dragging her hands over the stonework, feeling the skin of her palms sandpapered by the rough surface. Slumped on the ground, the sound followed a new path, absorbed by the earth itself, her body a conduit. And having found an escape route, it subsided. Her hands fell to her sides, abruptly freed from the wall and she sprawled backwards, exhausted by the intensity of what had only been minutes, possibly even moments. Keeping her eyes still shuttered tight, she marvelled at the beautiful silence, while fear of what it might reveal simmered in her mind.

Part Two – There

CHAPTER 20

Arrived

# Sarah

Stirlingshire, Scotland – August 2008

Too drained to sit up at the approaching footsteps, her thoughts too scrambled to consider any response to the arrival of another, Sarah lay motionless. Through the first flutter of her eyelids, she saw a set of laces attached to heavy leather boots and above them a pair of hairy male legs. The newcomer crouched beside her. His fingers drummed on her collarbone, beating a sharp staccato, while his voice urged her to wake up. The unpleasant, almost painful rhythm brought her eyes fully open.

"Oh, thank god," he said. "I thought you might be dead."

"I thought I might be too," she said, as she encountered a set of green eyes, their intense focus on hers. "Are you sure I'm not?"

His eyes sparkled with amusement. "Nah, this doesn't look like heaven or hell, so I think it's fair to say you're still in the land of the living." She couldn't help but return his smile and attempted to prop herself up on one elbow. "Be careful," he warned, stooping to scoop up shards of glass from a broken tumbler that lay scattered around her.

"Hope it wasn't one of their best ones," she said.

"No, Mam's a bit of a hoarder. I'm sure she has dozens more."

"Your mother? Heather?"

"Yeah. Calum MacFarlane," he said, extending a large hand to shake hers in greeting, and then lever her to her feet.

"Nice to meet you, Calum. I'm Sarah Mitchell. I believe the empty chair opposite me at the dining table was meant for you?"

His eyes were unusual, the moody green of the forest, edged in thick lashes that would be the envy of most girls. They betrayed a flicker of discomfort at her comment and then, with a blink, returned to their friendly, inviting expression.

"If I'd known Mam had set a place for me next to a pretty girl like you, I would have turned up."

It struck her that, for a moment, there was something familiar about him, despite her never having seen him before. Perhaps there was a look of his mother. He certainly didn't resemble the gruff man who was his father in either looks or manner. Mel had decided that Mr MacFarlane was even more intimidating than the rest of the assembled group at dinner. Sarah had to agree he wasn't a welcoming man, unlike Heather MacFarlane who'd been a charming hostess, making the girls feel part of the event, even though in reality they were on the fringe of the major players.

"So, you're one of the saviours, are you? The ones who are going to halt this family's descent into ruin." His Scottish accent was alluring, the voice low but melodious.

"Not quite," she said. "A friend invited me to tag along. She's here as the nanny for her sister, whose husband is a friend of Richard. He's the guy doing the deal. So I supposed you could say I'm a saviour three times removed."

"Well, that's a rather convoluted way to introduce yourself, Sarah Mitchell. The fact that you're out here rather than with that lot in there suggests we have something in common. How about instead of going back to join those boring old farts, come and have a drink with me? That's if you're feeling up to it."

He turned and wandered off, not waiting for her answer. Assumed she'd follow along. But she saw no reason not to. And she'd be able to report back to Mel about the mysterious younger Mr MacFarlane, conspicuous by his absence at the dinner table.

The cottage was a replica of the one she and Mel were staying in, an old farm building, converted into a space that sported every modern convenience while retaining the charm of the weathered stones. The tangy pine smell of an open fire filled the room. In the hearth, flames crackled vigorously. As he passed, Calum hefted a large lump of wood to feed its hunger for fuel, unleashing bright trails of sparks that spiralled up the chimney.

"Have a seat, and let me check you're not bleeding. There was broken glass all over the ground beside you." He directed her to an armchair and proceeded to examine her hands and arms. "That was lucky, no cuts," he announced. "Only these grazes."

He gently traced the outlines of the abrasions on her palms, the result of her sliding down the wall when she fell. She suspected she'd have bruises as well, but didn't suggest he check those. There was pain in parts of her body that she wasn't prepared to reveal to a stranger, even if he was a handsome one.

He ambled into the kitchen, returning with a small first aid kit. Unwrapping a foil packet, he cleaned away the fine grit embedded in her raw hands with cautious dabs of a sterile swab. She winced a little despite the delicacy of his touch.

"How did it happen? Did you trip over something?" he said. "I'll check it out in the morning. Need to make sure there are no hazards for guests—even ones wandering around strange parts of the property in the dark."

"It was that horrendous noise. It caught me off guard. I think I stumbled over while I was searching for where it was coming from. What on earth was it?"

Not understanding its source, she hoped he could enlighten her. He had to have heard it too, but not thought to mention it. It would have even been audible in the house. Surprisingly, no one had come running out to check. Maybe the MacFarlanes had told them not to bother. That it was some regular occurrence. Nothing to be alarmed about.

"Noise?" He shot her a quizzical look, his dark brows knotted in a frown.

Seeing his confused expression, she wondered if she had imagined it. If so, that was even more worrying. Desperate to put the embarrassment of having flung herself onto the ground simply to avoid a sound, one that he didn't even acknowledge, she diverted the conversation elsewhere.

"So tell me Calum MacFarlane, why did you shun the chance of having dinner with me tonight?"

"Because the invitation came from my mother and not you. You need to do it in person next time." He rose, neatly packed the first aid supplies, and moved to put them away. He returned from the kitchen clutching a bottle of wine and two glasses. "Red OK?"

She nodded, accepting a glass that was brimming with a garnet coloured liquid that gave off a spicy aroma. The first mouthful was smooth, with only the slightest touch of tannin on her tongue.

"So, is there a reason you didn't want to go to dinner tonight?" she said.

"You're a nosey wee thing, aren't you? First, I find you snooping around the back of the building in the dark and now you're interrogating me like DCI Tennison."

She knew he was teasing from the enticing sparkle in his eyes. And if he was trying to hook her in with more than his good looks, well, referencing *Prime Suspect* one of the few TV series she'd watched regularly, was certainly a fortunate ploy on his part.

"Very flattering. I'd love to be even half the detective she is. But go on then. Tell me."

"Well, you might say my relationship with my parents is somewhat strained at present. It always has been with Da. He makes no effort to hide the fact that I'm a massive disappointment to him in every way. Not interested in the farm. Not interested in making whisky—although I don't mind drinking it. Having no other siblings, he's always pinned his hopes on me. And I haven't lived up to them. And now Mam's upset too. They've been on at me for years to commit to something. According to Da, I've been an 'aimless drifter', and I need to 'take some responsibility'. So when I finally do—well, neither of them are exactly thrilled with my choice."

"Which is?"

"I've joined the army. In two weeks I'm off to RMA Sandhurst. That's the officer training school." She could hear the quiet pride in his voice.

"The army? What made you choose that?"

She'd never met anyone in the military, couldn't understand the attraction. All that discipline, not to mention the possibility of being killed.

"I like the outdoors, like to travel, even pretty handy with a gun—only shooting game, mind you—but yeah, it suits me. Been working on construction sites down in London these last two years. Didn't particularly enjoy the work, but it did teach me I'm also good with people. Can organise and lead a team. Skills they want in an officer."

"So, you're just home catching up with your parents?"

"Yeah, that and trying to reassure them that it's a good move. You think they'd be pleased—especially being accepted into officer training. But Mam's so protective. She's not totally against it, but she'd prefer her only child have chosen something a little more tame. I'd like to think I went off with her blessing. And then there's Da who's pissed off because he always is. Can't bloody win with him."

"I'm sure you'll make them proud one day. They may need time to get used to the idea. I don't think I'd be too pleased about my son joining the army."

"Your son? You have a son."

"No, no, only speaking hypothetically," she laughed. "No children, no husband."

"Well, that's fortunate. At least I know some big bloke isn't going to burst in and thump me for entertaining his wife in secret. OK, so you know the only things of note about me. What about you?"

"Sarah Mitchell, twenty-seven, a farmer's daughter from New Zealand. Been here three weeks. I'm starting on a PhD at Oxford next semester—history of Roman Britain. Dream come true."

"History, eh?"

"I know, boring." She was used to people, particularly those of her own age, having that reaction to the thing she loved. She'd found getting in first a useful tactic for deflecting their unwanted opinions on the subject.

"No, no, not boring at all," he said, sounding genuine. "We Scots as a rule are pretty proud of our history. Can't help it, I suppose, when you live amongst it." He waved a hand at the stone walls that surrounded them. "This might seem an odd thing to ask, but..." Leaning forward in the chair, he paused, his expression hesitant, but with a question on his lips. "Would you like to come on a little history field trip with me?" he said. "I'm heading off north tomorrow for a few days, a bit of a road trip up to the Highlands and then out to the Islands. Taking some time for myself before I sacrifice my life to the whims of the army. And it will be a nice change from the city. So I could show you some Scottish history. Far more interesting than reading about it in history books."

It was an unexpected offer, given they'd literally just met. And to take him up on it might lead him to make assumptions about her that weren't at all true. But on the other hand, she hadn't made definite plans for this week. She weighed the options.

Option one was five hours on the train back to London tomorrow with Claire's children complaining of boredom, Claire complaining they didn't appreciate the experiences she was giving them, and Mel complaining how she wished she hadn't taken on the job of nanny and tutor to her spoiled niece and nephew.

Option two was looking way more appealing—a trip with a rather attractive young man into the wilds of Scotland to check out some mysterious historic sights.

Definitely option two.

But before she could tell Calum she would sign up to be his travel companion, there was an almighty hammering on the door. He rose to open it but was thwarted as it flung open, nearly bowling him over, and his father stormed into the room. He stood, surveying the two of them with a stony glare. Like clouds in a stormy sky, expressions raced across Hamish MacFarlane's grizzled face—concern, relief, anger. He whirled around, accosting Calum.

"They've all been looking for the lassie. Did you not think it would be a good idea to tell someone that she was here?"

"Da, how would I have known that?" Calum grew in the moment, towering over his father, hackles raised.

"Bloody common sense should have told you, but as we well know, you're sorely lacking in that."

"Mr MacFarlane." Sarah rose to her feet, placing herself between the two warring men while attempting to put a conciliatory note in her voice. "I can't let Calum take the blame for this. It's my fault for wandering off outside like that. *I* should have had the common sense to tell someone. Calum simply came to my rescue when I took a tumble in the dark."

Her ploy worked. Hamish turned to meet her calm gaze, obviously flustered at her unexpected intervention.

"Well, I guess I can tell your friends to call off the search party," he said, somewhat appeased, before turning back to Calum. "Could have saved us all a lot of fuss though, if you'd used your bloody brain."

He flashed his son a last glowering look and stomped to the door. Sarah placed her wineglass down and smoothed out her rumpled, dirt-stained dress, preparing to follow him. Catching the movement, a more subdued Hamish glanced back at her.

"Don't hurry yourself, love. Finish your wine. As long as we know you're safe." And with a few inaudible mutterings, he left them alone.

Calum sighed deeply, flopping back into his chair.

"Calum, I'm so sorry." She regretted her stupidity had caused the unpleasant scene. "Guess you didn't need your father any *more* angry with you."

"No, don't trouble yourself. If it wasn't this, he'd have soon found some other fault to berate me about. He's right—enjoy your wine while we plan what you'll need for the trip."

Arrogant bugger, already assuming she would take him up on his offer. But she wouldn't change her mind simply to contradict him. Spending a few days with the intriguing younger MacFarlane opened up all sorts of possibilities.

CHAPTER 21

The Munros

*Sarah*

Stirlingshire, Scotland – August 2008

"Are you sure? Off on a jaunt with a guy you've just met? What if he's actually a serial killer?" Mel's pixie face clouded in doubt at hearing Sarah's plan for the week.

"Not likely," she said. "I'm sure he had to pass all kinds of personality tests before the army decided he's officer material. Besides, Heather's lovely. I doubt she'd have raised a psycho. You're way too suspicious."

"You're too trusting. Well, last chance to change your mind. But you'll have to be quick."

Claire was busily buckling her offspring into the spacious Volvo four wheel drive, while Jonathan tossed bags into the rooftop pod. Soon they'd be summoning Mel for the drive to Edinburgh to meet the train.

"No, enjoy your train trip and I'll see you in London in a week."

"Unless we see you on the telly in a missing person's investigation."

"You've been watching way too much telly. That's the problem. Anyway, I can look after myself." Mel wrapped her in a farewell hug tight enough to be her last, and with a "Be careful," joined the family.

Sarah did one final sweep of the cottage, and, assured all her belongings were safe inside her overstuffed bag, went in search of Calum. Spotting a tall, ruddy-haired figure bent over the bonnet of an ageing Land Rover, she headed that way, dumping the bag with a thud beside the passenger door. The man turned, and she saw she was mistaken. There was the same thick brush of deep chestnut hair and surprising green eyes, but the face was lean and narrow, and certainly older, small wrinkles around the eyes and mouth giving the impression that he was about to break into a smile. It was the distillery manager. He'd been at the dinner last night, but she couldn't retrieve his name.

"You'd be looking for Calum, would you? You must be the young lassie who's agreed to go off on an adventure with him. You're a brave lass." He gave a snort of laughter. "Joseph Brodie," he said, extending a hand. "I manage the distillery for the MacFarlanes." He paused and scrutinised her for a moment. "And you're also the one who went wandering off in the dark last night. Best you don't do that out where Calum's off to take you." Sarah inwardly cringed with embarrassment, discovering that her night time excursion was coming back to haunt her today.

"Yes, I'm Sarah," she said, accepting the firm handshake. "And yes, I'm the wanderer. I've promised Calum I'll behave myself."

She couldn't help but stare at Jo Brodie, struck by the uncanny likeness between him and Calum, now that she'd met both men. Same deep copper hair, same black-fringed eyes of that surprising green hue. He had to be more than the manager, somehow related to the family.

"Can you tell him that this is the map he was wanting? I have some things to attend to."

And with that, he made a beeline for the distillery, leaving Sarah to ponder over the topographical map of the northern half of Scotland with its trail of islands, a ragged coastline, and the contour lines, densely clustered in places, marking the rugged terrain of the Highlands.

When Calum himself emerged from inside the nearby shed, she decided perhaps the similarities between him and Joseph Brodie weren't as pronounced as she'd first thought. After all, she'd been expecting Calum, and her mind may have filled in his features on the other man.

"Worked out where we're going?" he asked.

"Not exactly, but looking at the map, I don't have the kit for this journey."

He looked at her critically, the sweep of his eyes assessing her choice of clothes: jeans, sneakers, sweatshirt and a windbreaker thrown on to ward off the breeze that had sprung up this morning and was now toying with the gold-tinged leaves overhead.

"You'll do for now," he said. "Not going too far off the beaten track today. But you possibly need something different for the Munros."

"Munros?" What on earth was he talking about? She'd thought they were going to explore the countryside, not meeting up with any Munros. "Who are the Munros?"

He laughed at the bewilderment on her face, taking obvious pleasure in being obscure.

"Not *who* are the Munros. It's *what* are the Munros you should be asking."

She obliged him with the question. "OK," she said, with a touch of exasperation, "*what* are the Munros?"

"That's a Munro," he said, stabbing his finger at a spot on the map. She could see the concentric rings clustered tight around a red triangle. She knew what that meant.

"It's a bloody mountain," she said. She hadn't expected mountain climbing to be on the itinerary.

"I suppose it is. But here it's a Munro. Anything over three thousand feet. This one's a smidgen over."

She peered more closely, reading the Gaelic hesitantly. "Beinn Alligin."

"Not a bad attempt." He smiled. "Maybe I can give you a few lessons in the Gàidhlig on the way. You could be a natural. Yes, so Beinn Alligin is where we're headed. This isn't the tallest of the Munros. That's ..."

"Ben Nevis?"

"Yes, well done. But Beinn Alligin is my favourite. A good workout, but not too challenging, even for a novice. And a pretty drive up there, too."

"I thought you were taking me to see some historic sites, not climb mountains."

"Oh, I am. After we've done a quick sprint to the summit and back, we'll hop on a ferry to the islands. And across the water, I'll show you some truly special history. Now, I think we need to pop in and see Mam. You look about her size. I'm sure she has a jacket and possibly even some boots."

Sarah trailed behind him to his parents' house, wondering what she'd gotten herself into. She'd spent many happy weekends on the mountain trails at home, tagging along with her sister and her friends. But that was years ago. She hoped there was some residual fitness in her muscles. After all, hefting hay and calves on the farm was a reasonable workout, and she'd been doing that up till a month ago. Not the same as scaling the heights of a mountain, even a small one, but it would have to do.

Without sunlight to pick out the surface ripples, Loch Ness was a dense foreboding navy blue, a reminder of its immense depths, perfect for cloaking mysterious life forms within its chill waters. They were skimming along the eastern side of the lake, taking the road less travelled, and also one that gave her an uninterrupted view from the passenger's seat.

"No sign of Nessie yet?" he teased. "As I'm the driver, the role of monster-spotting falls to you."

"Keeping my eyes peeled, but no, she's not bothered to pop her head up yet. So—you're a believer?"

"Absolutely," he said. "It must be my Scottish blood that allows a rational scientific view of the world to coexist with a belief in Nessie, faeries, ghosts, and people taken for two hundred years by the wee folk." He seemed deadly serious. "What about you? Does your historian's perspective allow room for the unexplainable, the unexpected?"

She was thoughtful for a moment, not having examined her beliefs about the supernatural in any detail before.

"I suppose it does. I do think some of the strange stories are simply where actual events have been embellished with the telling over the years. But on the other hand, I'm pretty sure we humans have barely scratched the surface of all there is to know. So anything is possible."

They drove along in silence, apart from the rough noise of the vehicle, its voice as rugged as its exterior and the distant mountains that beckoned them. The road hugging the lake was all but straight and she relaxed to the point she even dozed a little. She noticed the signs for Inverness, but rather than heading the way of the town, they skirted around its edge, veering off to the northwest.

"We'll stop in there on the way back," he said. "Must check out the battlefield nearby, warring Jacobites and redcoats. We're a bloodthirsty bunch."

The Land Rover wasn't the most comfortable of vehicles and as they left the straight road behind, it became less so. Calum threw her an apologetic glance, noticing her lurching from side to side at every turn. She'd tried to look unperturbed, but was unable to prevent the tension from seeping onto her face.

"The old girl has a bit of body roll, unfortunately. But I figure if it's good enough for the Queen, then I suppose it's good enough for us."

"The Queen?"

"Oh, yes, Her Majesty loves to hack around the back roads of Scotland in her Land Rover. Keep an eye out, you never know," he said with a laugh.

Soon he was nursing the heavy vehicle further, as it wallowed around winding corners. Despite Calum's levity, she found the sensation disturbing. She gripped the edge of the seat, her usual nervousness inside a vehicle on the open road taking hold, her knuckles white.

"Time for a stop," he said, noticing her tense face. He pulled over in a layby where a coffee vendor's sign warned 'Last coffee for 200 miles'. "Not really," he said with a smile. "We Scots like to exaggerate. Always a bit dramatic."

The coffee was surprisingly good, considering they were now far from civilisation, with steep peaks surrounding them on all sides.

"I'd have not taken you for a nervous passenger" His voice was gently teasing. "Otherwise I'd have dropped you in Inverness."

She stared at him over the edge of her coffee. May as well get it over with.

"Sometimes I am," she confessed. "My mother was killed in a car accident. Now and then, the fear creeps up on me. Like back there."

His green eyes were sympathetic. "I'm so very sorry," he said, placing his hand over hers, the touch comforting. "If I'd known, I'd have thought twice about bringing you this way. The road from here on is—well, challenging, to say the least. If you want, we can backtrack a little, take the easier road, not a problem at all."

"No," she said. "I'm not one to quit. I won't let stupid fears stand in the way of me seeing the world."

"They're not stupid," he said. "I understand. But good on you, this drive is well worth it. So, if you're ready, let's go."

Soon they were climbing steadily up Bealach na Ba, the aptly named 'Pass of the Cattle'. It was certainly more cattle track than road: narrow, mostly one way with the odd passing spot; and winding as if following the footsteps of a meandering hairy Highland cow making its way slowly along, stopping to graze here and there, but in no particular hurry. As they climbed, ever upwards, it seemed as if they travelled on a road to the sky, but each time they crept closer, the mountains on either side pushed it further out of reach.

It was spectacular; the mountains soaring above and valleys plunging deep below. And now as they wound down the other side, tantalising glimpses of royal blue ocean.

"Applecross," he said, pointing to a distant cluster of houses. "Our stop for the night. I've booked us a caravan at the campground. It's a nice spot. I've stayed there before."

Sarah gazed at the village tucked into the shoreline below. The village where they'd be spending the night. Together. She'd been having so much fun, Calum laughing and joking with her to take her mind off the winding road, that she'd given no thought to the details of their accommodation. Now, hearing the word caravan, worry crept in. She'd spent nights in caravans before: tiny single-roomed cabins on wheels, usually with only one bed. Much as she felt at ease with Calum, and physically he was rather delicious, sharing a bed with him had not been on the itinerary.

Having descended the last few bends onto a straight road, they almost immediately came upon signs directing them to the campground. Calum edged the Land Rover into a parking spot outside a small office.

"I have this sorted," he said, leaping from the vehicle, leaving it idling as he headed inside. The cheerful red door sported a sign that read 'Fàilte Gu A' Chomraich'. The Scottish Gaelic had popped up everywhere since they'd entered the Highlands, and Sarah already recognised the word for welcome.

She sat mulling over possible tactful solutions to her problem. He could be the gentleman and sleep on the floor. From what she knew of the inside space of caravans, even that was going to be intimate. Or they could build a pillow wall along the bed marking out territory, a line not to be crossed. And oh, how awfully embarrassing it would be if she snored! Her sisters and Mel both swore she did, although usually when she'd drunk too much alcohol. Or what if he did? Like her father's freight train noises that rumbled through the farmhouse. At least if he did, it would quell any lustful thoughts stirred up by such close proximity to an extremely sexy man.

Calum returned a few moments later, jangling a small set of keys, a wide smile on his face. Uncharitably, she wondered if the smile was to celebrate a mission accomplished: trapping her in a tiny room for the night with no way of avoiding his attention.

They wound slowly along the network of lanes that criss-crossed the campground, Calum reading the numbered signs, turning left at this one and right at another. At each turn, she expected to see the dreaded caravan, but none appeared. Bewildered when he finally cut the engine outside of a rather large cabin, she grasped that this was their home for the night.

'Caravan' obviously meant something totally different in this part of the world. This caravan accommodation was in fact a spacious, self-contained two-bedroom cabin even having its own kitchen, although Calum had already booked dinner at the nearby Applecross Inn. She was happy to claim one bedroom for herself. As much as she found Calum decidedly attractive and good company, her relaxed attitude to relationships didn't usually go as far as leaping into bed with someone she'd known less than a day.

"Fancy a stroll on the beach?" he suggested, after they'd indulged in a delicious seafood dinner, sampling the bounty of the sea that lapped on the doorstep of the little village. "After all, I know you're not averse to a walk in the dark."

"I'll try not to require rescuing this time."

Although she said the words with a laugh, the reminder of the previous night's bizarre experience now resurfaced. She'd buried the sickening memory of that sound for most of the day. Her rational mind told her that there had to be some perfectly sensible explanation, but something deep inside of her argued otherwise. She thought back to their earlier conversation. Somehow in Scotland, there was room for the unexplainable.

They crossed the narrow street onto a pebbled shoreline. The smooth rocks were slippery underfoot, and he took her hand to steady her as she wobbled a little. There was a comfortable feeling with her hand in his, and she made no move to wrest it from his grasp when they found themselves on firmer footing. He guided her to a set of steps, and they sat there watching as the moon lit the rippling water that met the shoreline. There was a slight hiss as the waves jostled the stony seabed, barely audible above the chatter and laughter of punters in the bar opposite.

Sitting shoulder to shoulder, she was intensely aware of his male smell, lightly overlaid with the freshness of soap that had earlier wafted from their tiny shared bathroom. Without thinking, drawn to that smell, she lay her head on his shoulder. His strong arm slipped around her, holding her close against the chill of the breeze off the sea. It felt like the most natural feeling in the world, the two of them there drinking in the view, not needing conversation.

She liked this man. He was straightforward, uncomplicated, and under that rugged exterior, projected a gentle kindness that she found strangely attractive. She'd always been drawn to strong-minded men. Being strong-minded herself, she enjoyed the cut and thrust of pitting her will against an equal, enjoying the small victories when they gave way to her needs and desires. And she loved the intellectual challenge of arguing a point using her razor sharp mind and keen memory to win an argument.

Not that she considered Calum a lightweight in that regard. He'd chatted away knowledgeably about the Highlands and its history. He knew the details of each bird or tree, keeping up a running commentary covering everything from scientific names to estimated numbers of the more-endangered species in this fascinating ecosystem.

And he wasn't pushy. He obviously recognised that glimmer of attraction too, but presumed nothing. Many men would expect a woman so rash that she'd agree to go on a week-long trip with him after knowing him for a matter of hours was equally impulsive about taking things further. Not that she wasn't tempted...

Later, as he left her at the door of her bedroom, his chaste kiss goodnight sent a small thrill through her body. It would have been so easy to wrap her arms around him, thread her fingers in that thick, dark red hair, and seek out that sensuous mouth with her own. As she closed the door, it was all she could do not to fling it open again and invite him in. She wondered how she was going to hold that feeling at bay for a week, or if she even wanted to. There was a small twinge of regret that the caravan was not what she'd imagined.

## Beinn Alligin

## Sarah

Applecross, Scotland – August 2008

SARAH GAZED UP INTO the clear early morning sky, breathing in the pure Highland air that carried a trace of the nearby sea in its breath. It felt good to be up early. Calum was clearly impressed with her ability to haul herself out of bed at that hour.

"Thought I'd have to hammer on the door," he'd said, rising at five to find her already at the tiny dining table, coffee made and munching on an apple.

"I'd usually be in the milking shed by now if I was at home. No room for slackers on a dairy farm."

"Well, it's a good thing you're ready. I want to be on the track by seven, and it's about an hour from here."

Throwing their belongings in the back of the vehicle, they set off on the winding route. Sarah stared down at the thick woolly socks and tramping boots that encased her feet. Heather's well-worn boots were a comfortable fit. She wasn't a total novice at hill walking, having spent many weekends scrambling around the tracks on the mountain above her home. But it had been a while. Although dressed only in a t-shirt and shorts, her generous daypack, another loan from Heather, was stuffed full of clothing. It was an insurance against whatever weather the Munro might throw at them despite a reasonable forecast.

Calum's own pack was three times the size, and carried not only clothing, but first aid supplies, a sleeping bag and a compact tent. Not that they were intending to camp out. The walk would take them seven to eight hours and, allowing for stops, they should be back in the car park by late afternoon. She hoped she wouldn't hold him back. She was reasonably fit, but since arriving in the UK, her activity had largely comprised exploring London with Mel. Traipsing round the tourist sights and investigating parks and markets wasn't exactly suitable training for climbing a mountain.

"Give me a minute?" he said, leaving their unloaded packs leaning on the front bars of the Land Rover. She, too, rested against the heavy grill, enjoying her legs outstretched after the confines of the vehicle while soaking in a little warmth, the metal already having absorbed the first rays of the day. Her eyes followed the line of the path, barely visible as it rambled between clumps of heather and rocky outcrops. It looked reasonably benign, lit by the early morning sun.

Calum disappeared around the back of the vehicle, and after some rustling and door slamming, emerged with a shy grin.

"Well," she said, lost for words at the sight. He'd abandoned his shorts and his shapely knees now peeked out below the hem of a kilt. It had a palette of muted greens and browns, shot through with a small bright band of sky blue. It was as if some weaver had sought to capture the authentic colour of the Highlands in the fabric.

"Not just a historical relic," he said, responding to the surprise on her face, "but, in fact, a very practical garment for hill-walking. A tried-and-true piece of outdoor clothing. After all, my ancestors had hundreds of years to find that out."

"You should have said." She grinned back at him. "I might have found a skirt for myself if I'd known."

"*Never* call it a skirt," he warned, with a mock glare at her. "Wash your mouth out."

She laughed, raising her hands in surrender. "Point taken. Now let's get moving. It may take longer than you think with me in tow."

From the carpark, the track snaked alongside a river, and Sarah stopped on the bridge to take in the view. The lively current burbled beneath her feet and she could hear the mellow tumble of waterfalls in the distance. They veered off onto a smaller pathway, and soon they were climbing.

Calum had the gait of a mountain goat, taking the narrow zigzagging route with ease. Ever the gentleman, he insisted on numerous stops to take in the view and top up with water. Without them, she knew she'd be lagging far behind, and appreciated his quiet consideration. She was grateful when at last they reached more gentle ground and Calum declared an early lunch break. She slumped onto the rocky earth beside him, leaning back against a stone cairn, thankful for its support despite the uncomfortable, rough surface prodding her back.

"Congratulations," he said with a smile. "You've bagged your first Munro."

"This is it?" she said. "I thought we had miles to go."

"Yes, and no," he said. "It's a bit of a sneaky way to bag two Munros for the price of one. This is Tom na Gruagaich. It's only been classed as a Munro for about ten years. The higher peak's a way off yet." No doubt seeing the look of weary disappointment in her eyes, he tossed her a crumb of hope. "And the other good news is that the worst is behind us. While we are going a lot higher, the climb's not so steep."

"Thank god for that, every muscle in my calves and butt is begging for mercy."

She knew tomorrow she was going to regret this unless she could find someone to give her a good massage. She wondered if Calum had any skills in that area, then checked her brain from heading off in the direction those thoughts led. All morning looking at the rear view of his taut muscular body in a tight t-shirt had given her something to focus on besides the pain, but hadn't diminished her growing attraction to the man, even if he was leading her on this torturous trail. Not to mention the hypnotic sway of his kilt. There was a definite allure in a kilted Scot.

The view in front of her now was also spectacular, the height of their vantage point and a clear late summer sky revealing the landscape all the way to the Hebridean islands. As they ate, he named the landmarks in the distance, his tongue rolling gently over the Gaelic names of peaks and lochs displayed before them.

"So, over there is An t-Eilean Sgitheanachthe, the Isle of Skye, to you. We're looking at the northern end, the Trotternish. So the peninsula further away, that's Rubha Hunish, and see the one a bit closer to us? That's Rubha nam Brathairean."

He had a voice like velvet, and she tilted her head to the sky, letting the sunshine play over her face, and that lilting Scottish accent wash over her. But soon he decided that the rest time was over, jarring her from her lazy dream.

"OK, time to move. Unless you want me to carry you?"

"Good luck with that. I think I weigh a bit more than even you can manage," she said with a grin. He hoisted his substantial pack onto his back as if it weighed nothing. She pulled on her own and followed him as they set out for their next conquest.

An unexpected concern overshadowed their triumph at reaching the top of the second peak. Although he'd checked and rechecked the forecast, the fickle Scottish weather had a mind of its own. The temperature was plummeting as a towering bank of cloud rolled in around them, holding the promise of rain in its moist centre. A brisk wind clutched at them with icy fingers, whipping the escaped strands of Sarah's hair across her face.

They sat in the lee of the cairn at the summit, taking what little shelter it provided while they dived into their packs for jerseys and coats. Sarah pulled an old beanie of Heather's low on her head. They huddled close together, and she saw his eyes darting back and forth as he turned over options in his mind.

"So, two choices," he said after mulling over their situation for a while. "We make a run for it, probably back the way we came, as the descent in the other direction is pretty steep. But we are going to get wet and cold, even though we have the right gear. The visibility will be shit so it'll be slow going. "

"Doesn't sound like fun, but I'll give it a go if you think that's best."

"Second option, we find a sheltered spot and I throw up the tent. This weather will most likely blow over in a few hours."

"Won't the light be gone by then? I don't fancy clambering back down in the dark." She knew downhill was always deceptively more difficult, and in darkness, it would be doubly challenging.

"Yeah, we'd need to stay over. Head down at first light. People camp on the summits all the time. It won't be luxurious, but it will be safe and warm."

"What about down below? Will anyone be worried about us?"

"Nope," he said, producing a handheld radio. "I'll send a message saying we've decided to summit camp and check in a couple of times to let them know all is OK. So, stay or go?"

The thought of a warm shelter for the night, even if it did mean sharing Calum's tent, won out over the prospect of a lengthy night time scramble over steep paths.

"Stay," she said, already aware that their sleeping arrangements were going to be unexpectedly intimate. But after last night on the beach, and a day following him wherever he led, she wasn't sure that was actually a problem.

Tucked into the shelter of a rocky hillock, inside the protection of the jaunty yellow tent, Sarah felt like a kid on an adventure. Thrust together in this space with nothing else to occupy them, they talked and laughed, oblivious to the rain peppering the nylon exterior and the odd blast of wind that slapped at their place of refuge.

The light inside the tent was as gloomy as if the heavy rain clouds themselves had infiltrated the space. His hand reached towards her, looming out of the dimness. He peered at her face, lightly brushing aside a corkscrew of hair that had burst free from the edge of the beanie. His finger softly traced the zigzag scar on her forehead, and she shivered at his touch. His eyes were questioning. Everybody wanted to ask about that scar, but she'd become so accustomed to it after all these years that she never noticed its silvery line any more.

"Don't tell me you're really Harry Potter?" He grinned at his little joke.

"Sorry to say I didn't gain it by such dramatic means. You're a fan? I wouldn't have picked you for one."

"No, but somehow I got roped into taking my younger cousins into Cluanie to see all the movies. They weren't too bad, actually."

"I read all the books," she said. "I love fantasy. It's about the only fiction I've ever read. Escapism."

"So," he said, again brushing the scar ever so gently, again sending a thrill of excitement—or was it anticipation—down her spine. "Your lightning bolt—it wasn't a battle with Voldermort. But it tells a story all the same?"

"Yeah, an embarrassing childhood one."

"Come on then. Tell me," he said. "After all, we've got all afternoon."

"OK, well, I blame my sisters for this one. They considered me the spoiled baby so they loved to set me up whenever they could."

"I can't imagine you being gullible."

"Well, I was only six, and they were years older. Anyway, us farming kids always raised a lamb or a calf for our school's annual ag day."

"Me too," he said. "And it was fun. Back then, Mam still thought the farm might tempt me."

"Yeah, it was Dad who encouraged us. He'd pick out a nice wee early baby for us to train up. It didn't matter if the calf was bigger than you, you just did it. I loved it. Every year I was so excited, and I'd spend hours walking the poor thing round and round and grooming it till its coat shone."

"Did any take you for a bit of grass skiing? Mine did."

"Oh for sure, that happened a fair few times. But that's not how I cracked my head open. We started to get a lot of town kids coming to our school as well. Parents wanting an idyllic rural education for their children. And, of course, they didn't have livestock. So the school came up with a bright idea that they'd get day-old chicks for the town kids and let them raise those for ag day. Not too big, easy care, manageable for a townie family.

Well, the day came when those chicks arrived at school and they were so beautiful, soft, fluffy down, the most incredible shade of yellow, cheeping away with the cutest sound. I was totally mesmerised. So I went home and begged my dad for a chick. But he said no, I already had the calf to raise. I thought he was so mean."

"Not quite the spoilt baby," he said.

"No, he was a practical man, and he was right. I had plenty to keep me busy. Anyway, I was having a little cry about it in my room when my sisters came in. Told me that they knew a way I could get a chick. All I had to do was take an egg, wrap it up snugly, put it in a dark place, and turn it every day. And eventually, a chicken would hatch. So that's what I did. Every evening I'd stand on a chair and reach up into the top shelf of the wardrobe, carefully take my egg out of its box, turn it over and place it back. I fully believed that one night when I opened that box, there'd be a fluffy yellow chick waiting for me."

"Definitely gullible!"

"I *was* only six," she repeated. "Well, one night I was teetering on tiptoes on my chair when Mum walked in and asked me what on earth I was doing. I got such a fright I overbalanced, fell off the chair and bashed my head on the corner of a dresser on the way down. A trip to the doctor, seven stitches, a scar for life—and worst of all, no chicken."

"Hearing stories like that, maybe it's a good thing I didn't have siblings," he said.

"No, but I'm sure you've still got some stories from when you were a kid. Come on. Your turn."

"OK," he said, before launching into the tale of how, without asking, he'd taken out the feistiest of his mother's horses and it had tossed him in a ditch. He didn't have a scar, but had broken his nose. "See, just here," he said. Even in the dim light, she could see the slight bump halfway down. It felt natural to reach out at his invitation, to trace the shape of it.

"Mine too," she said. "A stray cricket ball. Just here."

His finger followed the ever-so-slightly crooked line of her nose, lingering for a moment on the tip, before he drew it back with a smile.

"Even a broken nose and a scar couldn't spoil your face."

She dropped her head a little at that, an unexpected blush creeping up her cheeks. Then steered the conversation away from his compliment, glad that the dim light meant he was unaware of its effect on her.

They were so engrossed in swapping stories that neither noticed when the sounds of the weather subsided. It was only as the light of the distant sun peeking through clouds out over the western sea turned the side of the tent a soft gold that Calum thought to unzip the entrance and survey their situation.

"Still got it," he said.

"Got what?"

"My weather forecasting abilities. I said it would clear in a few hours and it has."

"So we won't mention the earlier decision to come up here in the first place?"

"No, that was the fault of the good old Mountain Weather Service. You can usually rely on them, but no forecast will be perfect. That's why we carry all of this."

She shuffled alongside him to peer out through the door. Far off over a dove grey sea, the late afternoon sun gilded the peaks of the Isle of Skye.

"Wow, that's stunning." She turned to him with a smile. "You know, I'm glad the forecasters had it wrong. Otherwise we'd have missed all this."

"And this," he said, his green eyes no longer projecting the playful sparkle of their earlier conversation, but a soft, longing look that matched the quiet tone of his voice. "Us, together this afternoon. I honestly didn't lure you up here, planning to trap you in this tent for hours. But I'm glad it happened."

"So am I," she said. And instinctively she reached for him, her finger following the line of golden stubble on his chin, her touch a little shaky from the nearness of him. "Very glad."

He leaned in to her, cupping her face gently in his large hand, and his lips brushed hers; a tentative question. She responded, her answer leaving no doubt as she invited him with hungry kisses. She didn't care that her hair was a tangled mess, or that she was clad in his mother's woollen jumper and leggings. In this moment, all that mattered was the thrill of his touch.

Their eyes met and without words, she offered her permission for him to explore further. His hands edged inside her clothing, seeking the curve of her breasts, exploring the hardness of her nipples, then gliding downwards, finding the wet warm centre of her arousal. Her own hands alighted on the hardness of his erection and he groaned in pleasure as she fumbled under his waistband to connect skin to skin.

"Stop," he said, his voice rough and ragged. "Let's get rid of these bloody clothes."

She extracted her hand, allowing him to sit up, where he stripped off the layers as she hurried to do the same. The air was cool, but he dragged her back down beside him, laying his warm body over hers, one half of the rumpled sleeping bag cushioning her against the rocky ground, the other swept up over them, trapping them within its soft folds. His eyes were an even more intense green, in the strange half dark of the sun-brushed tent.

"Are you sure you want this?" he said, his voice softer now that the first wild rush of lust had subsided a little. "After all, this time two days ago we hadn't even met."

"My friends tell me I can be impulsive," she said, "but I like to think I'm quick to know when something's right. And this feels right."

Her voice came out as a whisper, choked not only by physical desire, but by her struggle with the emotions that spiralled inside. All her life she'd been fiercely independent, not needing anyone to look out for her. And now here was someone who she wanted to do just that. Someone who made her feel she could be vulnerable. Someone who made her feel safe. She abandoned her attempt to make sense of the sudden unexpected connection she felt with this man and simply relaxed into the moment.

"Give me a second," he said, pausing to rummage in the depths of the pack, finding the condom he needed tucked in a battered leather wallet.

She let her legs fall apart a little, allowing him to nudge between them. The smell of their arousal drifted in the close air, mingled with the sweat of the day's exertions, a primal smell that only served to heighten her need for him. He entered her gently, those green eyes locked on hers, scrutinising her face, scanning for each nuance of feeling that played out there. She'd not been promiscuous, but she was no novice when it came to sex. However, there was an intensity in their coming together that was new. This is what they call it making love, she thought, as she gave herself over to him, and he to her.

---

Calum unzipped the doorway of the tent and they sat, limbs still entangled, the sleeping bag wrapped to cocoon them from the approaching night's chill. Now a blaze of red clouds wreathed the distant island, the water taking on the same fiery hue, as if the heat of their lovemaking had poured out into the universe.

"Hungry?" he said. "I can fix us something from my stash. On the menu tonight we have dehydrated food or, if you prefer, dehydrated food."

She laughed. "I promise not to judge your culinary skills on tonight's meal. Chef's choice."

She reluctantly released him from her arms and he produced more surprising goods from his pack: a tiny gas stove, a cooking pan, and two foil pouches. Once the water was bubbling, sending curling wisps of steam into the night air, he poured in the sad-looking shower of dried meat and vegetables. Within minutes, a strangely appetising aroma wafted from within the pan.

They sat facing each other, legs crossed, now both clad in their woolly jumpers, warming the outside while enjoying the warmth of the food in their stomachs. It was far tastier than she'd expected, and enhanced by the intimacy with which they ate. There was something sensual about him feeding her from the one dish, the one spoon. She parted her lips gently to take it in, thinking of how she'd welcomed his tongue between them earlier. In his eyes, she could see that while they had met their hunger for food, their other appetites were far from satisfied. The heat ignited between her legs just thinking about the whole night that lay ahead, with only the two of them, and only the stars for company. The moon had set, and millions of tiny distant suns sprawled above them, filling the basin of the sky.

Calum insisted they wash down the meal with a dram of whisky from a flask that somehow he'd also made room for in the pack.

"A toast to conquering two Munros today," he said, taking a swig first, then offering it to her.

She took a large gulp. The strident first pass of the liquid over her tongue was followed by a pleasant warmth that travelled all the way down to her centre. Before handing it back, she held it up with a smile.

"And to our other conquests," she said, taking a second hit while shooting him a flirtatious look. He snatched the flask from her, took a quick mouthful, and then fastened the lid with a knowing grin. Thinking how sweetly that smokiness lingered on his lips as they pressed against hers was her last coherent thought before she pulled him back down into the dark of their refuge.

CHAPTER 23

The Island

*Sarah*

Isle of Lewis, Scotland – August 2008

SARAH LEANED OVER THE railing, watching the small town of Ullapool disappear as the ferry chugged towards the open sea. Away in the distance, not yet visible on the horizon, was their destination: an island that, for some bizarre reason, bore two names. The Isle of Lewis and the Isle of Harris were, in fact, one island, divided only by mountains. Officially, they were on their way to Lewis, its main town, Stornoway, their base for the next few days.

She pulled on Heather's beanie, unattractive as it was, not for warmth but in an attempt to tame her hair. She had luxuriated in the hot shower, washing away the grime of the hike in the little campground in Torridon.

Although she could still smell the lightest touch of Calum still upon her. Her newly washed hair had sprung back to life, a mane of irrepressible curls that would become a knot if she let the wind toss it around.

Calum appeared with two coffees, demanding a kiss before he'd hand one over. She had to oblige with a second kiss before he produced her late breakfast from his pocket, a brown paper bag, inside it a crusty muffin. They sipped and ate as the ferry rose and fell more vigorously, ploughing through the water of the open sea.

The view reminded Sarah of being a tourist at home; the sea dotted with islands and mountains rising up in all directions. But thoughts of home didn't induce any feelings of longing to be there. It had taken her years to escape, and she wasn't heading back anytime soon. The lure of her studies, the joy of being a historian at last immersed in a land with history, and the excitement of a new adventure, extinguished any small flicker of homesickness. And now there was Calum.

"Today's for you," he said. "As a reward for indulging my passion by scrambling up a mountain yesterday, today we get to do your thing, my studious little historian." He kissed her lightly on the forehead, sealing the bargain.

True to his promise, they'd no sooner driven off the ferry in Stornoway, and he was straight into tour guide mode. He started at the impressive Gothic-revival castle that stood guard over the harbour. "This is what success in the opium trade bought you back in the 1800s," he said. "Not just a castle, but a whole island."

They wandered in the overgrown park where the wild threatened to steal back the once carefully tended castle grounds. Seeing the building derelict made her feel a little sad. She'd been told many Scottish castles lay in ruins simply because the owners couldn't afford to maintain them. It looked as this one was in danger of going the same way.

They headed north, intending to loop up around the tip of the island and back to Stornoway for the night. The drive around Lewis was like stepping into a time machine and leaping back and forth through history. Sarah was busy snapping away with her tiny camera at each new stop, revelling in the parade of the past encompassed in this one island.

"How on earth do you know all this stuff?" she asked, as they left a quaint village where once derelict crofts had been painstakingly restored. She marvelled at the barrage of facts and dates he'd tossed out effortlessly as they explored.

"Aw, well," he said modestly, "I suppose you could call this my second home." That explained it, local knowledge. "Mam has some family and a few friends out here. She's always come over to visit a couple of times a year. And as a teenager, given the choice of staying home and fighting with Da for a few weeks without her to referee, or coming here—well, the choice was easy. Soon made a few friends. Learned to drive, learned to drink."

"Hopefully not both together?"

"Only now and then. Some of the lads over here are pretty wild, but good blokes all the same. Don't worry, we're going to stay with one of my less disreputable mates. I warned him you're coming so he'll be on his best behaviour."

"I've saved the best for last," he said as late in the day they leaned on the Land Rover, eating a sandwich they'd picked up from a small roadside store in one village, and soaking up the afternoon sun.

She wondered how anything could top the places they'd been so far. What could better this? Here at Dun Carloway was an Iron Age broch, standing sentinel, gazing across the Atlantic, with virtually nothing between it and the shores of Newfoundland. She'd marvelled at its antiquity, running her hands over stones placed there by long ago builders. Or the little stone church of St Moluag they'd visited earlier—standing since 560, when even her homeland's Polynesian ancestors hadn't yet navigated their way across the Pacific. Intrigued, she leapt into the passenger's seat, keen to get to the last stop of the day.

He knew her well already. From her first glimpse of them, the standing stones captivated her, and it was all she could do to prevent herself running towards them like a gleeful child, wanting to press herself against them, as if to absorb all they'd seen, all they'd known over five thousand years.

She had a sudden wish that Mel was here. She'd have to bring her one day. Mel was a passionate fan of a series of books, where people were sucked through time simply by laying their hands against stones such as these. And they begged for her touch. She traced the swirls of the three billion year old layers, rubbed her hand over sparkling black crystalline eyes embedded there and marvelled at the ancient hands who had shaped and placed them with care.

"Take a picture," she called to Calum, as she stood hands braced against the massive central monolith, hoping that she wouldn't actually travel, as she was blissfully happy in the right here and now. But Mel would love the image, and Calum obliged, although his expression suggested he thought her behaviour a tad bizarre. She'd explain later—surely a Scot would understand.

They sat in the centre of the largest circle, guarded on all sides by the silent watchmen, and she lay back on the ground, as if she might feel the power pulsing up from beneath her, tap into the magic that had drawn people to labour in creating this temple. Calum lay down beside her, taking her hand, and, not caring if anyone thought they were totally mad, they stared into the blueness of the late afternoon sky, letting the sound of the nearby sea wash over them with a soft hiss.

---

Calum's mate, Gary, looked rather like a modern day Viking, with a large intimidating presence, a long beard, and arms the size of a weightlifter. Underneath that gruff exterior was a quietly pleasant young man who'd followed his father into the fishing industry and made himself sufficient money to buy a decent house for someone of his age. His muscled arms, the result of hauling on nets and lines, belied a gentle grip as he clasped her hand in welcome.

"Good to see ya mate," he said, clapping Calum on the back. "And what do ya think of my new abode? Come in and I'll show you around."

Calum shot her a sly smile behind Gary's back as he ushered her into one bedroom while showing Calum into another. She hoped the house didn't have creaky floorboards, as she doubted they'd be able to spend the night apart after what they'd started the previous one on the mountain. Even thinking of it now sent a flush of heat to her face and other parts of her body.

Once he'd overcome his initial shyness, Gary proved to be great fun. He reminded her of boys from home, down-to-earth and with an inherent kindness. Dinner at the local pub was a lively affair, and the first decent meal in two days. They drank rounds to celebrate Gary's new status as homeowner, Calum's acceptance into the army, and her place at Oxford. Calum headed to the bar to purchase another, although they hadn't yet decided what to toast next. But after stopping in conversation with a man at one of the leaners, he returned empty-handed. His face was lit with excitement. He had a quiet word with Gary, who nodded in approval.

"What is it?" she pleaded, on the walk back. "Come on, it's not fair."

"No, it's a surprise. Go in and get your jacket, and Mam's hat too. We're going out."

She did as she was told, and Gary waved them off with a knowing smile. They hurtled along the road, leaving the town behind, plunging into the dark countryside, where only the odd light here and there marked the imprint of humans on the landscape.

Calum swung the Land Rover into the empty car park, and she recognised they were back at Calanais. The moon had disappeared, and now only the band of stars across the sky lit the stones. He took her hand, and they walked along the central avenue, the aisle of an ancient temple.

"Good, we're the only ones here," he said, his voice hushed, respectful of the special place. He spread out an old tarpaulin, and pulled her down to sit in front of him, wrapping his arms tightly to protect her from the chill. "And now we wait."

The first hint was a faint silver shimmer, appearing so briefly that she thought she'd imagined it. But soon it returned, accompanied by waves of other colours, yellows and greens and golds, giving way to a startling magenta. Like gauze curtains blowing in a gentle breeze, the aurora floated across, edging out the stars, taking the entire stage of the night sky for its own.

She stood desperate to be nearer. She stretched her hands upward as if to touch the fluttering fabric and whirled in delight. Calum caught her in his arms and they spun together, heads thrown back in blissful happiness, and the heavens above danced in celebration.

## CHAPTER 24

Enough

*Calum*

Isle of Lewis, Scotland – August 2008

GARY'S EYES JERKED UP from the mound of fried food, his fork paused in mid-air. Calum abandoned his own heaped plate for a moment. He glanced over his shoulder to see what was interesting enough to halt his friend's assault on the massive breakfast in front of him. Gary's appetite was legendary. Calum had never seen anyone who could put away so much food. His weekly grocery bill must be horrendous. The advantage was that as well as loving to eat, Gary loved to cook. You always knew the catering would be good when you stayed at his place. But something had stopped him in full flight.

Sarah. Her attempt to leave his bedroom and discreetly slip back to her own had failed. She stood framed in the door between the hallway and kitchen, her mouth open in surprise, a faint blush blooming on her cheeks. She looked beautiful standing there, her hair tousled from sleep. No, not just sleep. It almost made *him* blush to think of how they'd filled the hours between returning from Calanais and finally giving way to tiredness.

But it wasn't just her body's response to his in bed that mesmerised him. Or how damn sexy she looked standing there, clad only in her shirt that barely covered those shapely long legs. Or the thought of what lay underneath the flimsy white linen. It was that big personality. He loved her boldness. And he saw it re-emerge now as she gathered herself up, as if she wasn't really standing there half-clothed facing his friend who she'd only met yesterday.

"Morning," she said. She sniffed the air. The tantalising aroma of bacon that hung heavy in the room had reached her. "That smells good. Hope you've left some of it for me?"

"Sure," said Gary. "Plenty more where that came from. I'll even cook for you. Did you sleep well?" He kept a poker face.

"I did, thanks, Gary," she said, with no remaining shred of her initial embarrassment, and disappeared in the direction of her room.

"So..." Gary said, his face thoughtful. "Moved fast there Cal. Well, faster than usual."

He was absolutely right. On nights out with the lads here on the island, Calum had done his fair share of chatting up women, sometimes walking one home. But it had always stopped there on the doorstep, at least on the first few nights. He wasn't like a lot of the others, hell bent on getting laid, sweet-talking a girl into bed when you barely knew her name, or anything of note about her. The few times he had rushed into something, he'd regretted it in the morning. So when he'd phoned Gary to say he was bringing Sarah with him, his friend naturally assumed they'd be needing separate beds.

"Yeah, mate," said Calum. "Didn't see it coming, to be honest. But when someone like her walks into your life, you'd be a fool to hesitate."

"Can't say I blame you. She's great. Not just a pretty face."

Calum had discovered a lot of things about Sarah in the last few days. One was the ease with which she moved between different people, different situations. He'd listened to her as relaxed in banter with Gary over a pint at the pub as she was having a friendly natter with his mother, or on the phone to her academic supervisor at Oxford. She moved through the world with a confidence that was attractive rather than abrasive. People warmed to her.

He'd also discovered that she was as surprised as he was by this thing that had exploded between them. She'd admitted that, like him, she was more likely to take her time before crossing that line. He wasn't sure where it was all heading. Was it going to be a short, intense fling—a sudden blaze that would burn out in a flash before they both headed off to their new lives? He recognised that this thought disappointed him. But the alternative—that this was the start of something more enduring—well, that frightened him. He hadn't had the best of models on how to sustain a long-term relationship. His parents were an example of what not to do. And so far he'd never met anyone that he'd seriously considered committing to long-term. Until now.

"Shuffle over," she said, as ten minutes later, she edged onto the bench seat beside him. Her damp hair hung in loose tendrils, and the steamy warmth of her-freshly washed body beside him exuded a sweet clean tang.

"Right," said Gary, lighting up the gas hob and sliding the enormous cast-iron pan back onto the dancing flames. "One good Scottish fry up coming your way."

"That sounds perfect," she said. "As long as I'm not holding you up from getting to work."

"Nah, all good," he said. "That's one thing I like about fishing. No nine-to-five routine. We go with the weather and the tides."

Calum sat and watched while the two dived into a detailed conversation about the fisherman's life. There it was again: her so completely at home with someone new, asking questions, listening to their answers, showing genuine interest in getting to know them. And he pondered for a moment, wondering if that was also what he was to her—someone who'd piqued her curiosity, interesting for now while he was still a novelty. But too ordinary to hold her attention for long. Especially since in ten days or so, they'd be going their separate ways. Their paths had intersected for this brief moment in time before winding off in opposite directions. He wasn't sure they'd find their way back to each other. He clenched his eyes shut, trying to ward off the unexpected stab of anguish that he felt in his gut at that thought.

"Calum? Are you OK?" she asked, distracted from Gary's description of the process of mending nets, a job he intended to start on after breakfast.

"Oh, yeah, for sure," he said. "Probably just too much of Gary's cooking, sitting a bit heavy in my stomach."

"I'll take that as a warning," she said, clasping her hand over his, offering a cheerful smile.

He smiled back, soaking up the simple pleasure of having her next to him, their bodies comfortably resting against each other. This was enough for him. These simple comforts. If he could have her alongside him like this, doing such ordinary, everyday things as sharing breakfast, he was certain it would be enough for him. The question was: would he be enough for her?

CHAPTER 25

Past Imperfect, Future Perfect

*Sarah*

Stirlingshire, Scotland – August 2008

THE GAP BETWEEN CALUM and his father was so immense they may as well have been sitting at opposite ends of the ten-foot dining table in the mansion house next door. Hamish MacFarlane glowered at his son from the head of the small family table. Beside him, Heather made a brave attempt to keep the conversation light and deflect the waves of disapproval rolling towards her son. Hamish's dark eyebrows knotted in a permanent frown, and the odd words he uttered between mouthfuls were single-syllable responses to Sarah's polite attempts to engage him. The only other sounds he emitted were disparaging snorts as Calum and Sarah relayed the events of the previous five days.

"This is our last meal together for a while," said Heather. "I do hope they feed you well at Sandhurst."

"Well Mam, they say an army marches on its stomach, so I imagine the cooks do a reasonable job."

"At least we know it will outdo the meals on your last march," said Sarah. "Though I was glad of that dehydrated food. It was better than starving."

"Bloody foolish, what the hell were you thinking taking the girl up there so late in the summer?" Hamish's glare was almost palpable.

"Calum knows what he's doing." Heather leapt in to defend her son. "We had Sarah all nicely kitted out in my gear, didn't we?"

"Yeah, thanks Heather. It was perfect. I was warm and comfortable the entire time."

She tried not to colour at the thought of how it wasn't the clothing, but Calum's warm and comfortable body wrapped around her that had made the little tent so cosy. Heather had made no comment when they'd un-loaded her things into the cottage. Simply smiled and carried Sarah's bags into his bedroom. And now here at dinner, she was pleased at Heather's unspoken acceptance of her into the family, not only for her but for Calum. At least one of his parents approved of this new direction.

Calum ate in silence, not engaging with his father's jibes, ignoring Hamish as if he didn't exist. This father and son relationship was badly broken, most likely to the point of irreparable. She thought of her own father's mild nature and unwavering support and wondered what had caused such a deep divide in this family.

They'd agreed that they'd head down to London for a week before their commitments forced them to go separate ways for now: Calum, down to Sandhurst, to his new career; she to share Mel's company for a week after that before heading to Oxford. Claire and Jonathan had graciously given Mel another few days off and offered that Sarah stay with them. She hoped time with Mel would help ease the parting and fill the hole that she already knew Calum's departure would leave in her life. At least she could soon plunge into her studies.

Back in the cottage, she showered and then pottered around in her robe, making a half-hearted attempt to pack some of her things. Leaving made her a little sad. While they were here, she could pretend their separation was a long way off.

"Leave that," he said, coming to wrap his arms around her from behind and nuzzling at the nape of her neck. "Plenty of time in the morning."

He turned her to face him, enveloping her in a first slow kiss, as if seeking to prolong every second of the time left to them. Then bowing his head, he ran his lips along her bare shoulder, where he'd nudged away the robe. His kisses were becoming more insistent now, and she welcomed the hand that traced a pathway down between her breasts, hovering lightly over her stomach, before gently parting her thighs. Soon his lips followed that same pathway, with delicate kisses and his flickering tongue lighting her up like a firework.

"No, stop," she said, wanting to take him with her. He rose to fit his body to hers, his kisses sweet and salty with the taste of her upon him. She gently rolled him away, climbing astride and lowering herself to take him deep inside, rising and falling with the waves of desire, his breath coming in harsh gasps, hers a ragged echo.

After, she lay still tangled with him, as his breathing slowed into a peaceful slumber. It was comforting to see his face relax into softer lines as he let go of the tumult of his father's scorn. She was still reeling from the toxic atmosphere at the dinner table, still incredulous that a parent should not love this beautiful man. He was easy to love, and she admitted to herself that this word was the one that came to mind when she analysed her own feelings. It was an impulsive leap for sure, but one that felt undeniably right.

They lay awake in the night, her head tucked into the curve of his muscular shoulder, one hand flung across Calum's broad chest. She'd awoken to find him lying there, staring at the ceiling. Sarah could feel the tension had returned, like steel rods rammed through his body.

"Sorry to put you through that tonight," he said after a while. "If it wasn't for Mam, I wouldn't have gone to dinner. She's still trying to play happy families when we all know that we haven't been one for years. You think the old bastard could at least pretend for one night, even if he sat there and said nothing?"

Even in the darkness, she could make out the set of his face, rigid with hatred, and in that moment hatred flared in her too, for the circumstances that had robbed her of the funny, cheerful Calum who she'd fallen for over the last few days.

"It's OK," she said, "I'm fine. It's you I'm worried about." She trailed her fingers through the soft hairs of his chest, trying to soothe his rage.

"You don't need to worry about me. I've had so many years of this that it's just water off a duck's back. What makes me so fucking angry is that he uses that prodding at me to hurt Mam. I don't know why she puts up with him. I suppose they loved each other once, or thought they did. But there's no trace of that now."

"Why do you think they stay together? If it's that bad?"

"Well, I guarantee they're not doing it for the kids," he said with a savage grin. "I'm pretty sure my father regrets my very existence. Nah, it's the business. Mam brought this property with her into the marriage. It wasn't much at the start, but now it's certainly something—the farm, the distillery and the lodge."

Sarah understood perfectly. She'd seen their neighbour's family farm lost to the next generation through divorce. Unravelling the MacFarlanes' complicated ownership to divvy it up between them was likely to see it sold and Calum left to inherit nothing and Heather wouldn't have that.

"Give the bastard some credit, he has worked his arse off here, as has Mam. So I understand they don't want to lose what they've created, but you think they could at least move into separate houses instead of keeping up this charade. Maybe she'll move in here when I'm gone."

"How long has it been like this?" she asked, wondering how anyone could endure such outright disharmony.

"Years. I have memories of my father when I was small—good ones. Him taking me fishing. I was so damn proud of myself bringing home my first trout. And he was too. We'd go out hiking. It was him who instilled my love of the outdoors. I suppose I have to at least thank him for that." She smiled, imagining him a boisterous small child, thinking that parts of that little boy were very much still there. "And I'd trail around behind him in the distillery—wouldn't happen these days, health and safety and all that. I suppose it was when I was about eleven or twelve, things changed. I know lots of my mates clashed with their fathers in their teens, but somehow they moved beyond it. Didn't happen with us. It was as if one day he decided I could do nothing right in his eyes and he simply wrote me off. He's never let me back in, never tossed even the slightest olive branch my way. I've learned to accept that there's never going to be a father-son relationship there." He rolled towards her, placing a warm, deep kiss on her waiting lips. "Anyway, let's not talk about that. Shouldn't let dwelling on my disastrous family situation steal away any more of the time we have left."

"It's OK," she said, stroking his hair, as he nestled into her, his head heavy on her breast as if seeking refuge there. "Families can be complicated."

"Yours isn't, though. Your parents loved each other, loved their kids. That's how it's supposed to be."

Sarah was glad she'd opened up to him about her mum and dad. One night in the pub in Stornoway, clad in his kilt, he'd jokingly asked what her father would think of her bringing home a man in a skirt. She could have given him a flippant, superficial answer, the sort she gave to most people who probed about her family circumstances. But she trusted Calum and knew the growing relationship between them meant she owed him more than that. And so she'd told him about the gentle man of the land who'd raised her, been her rock. And how she'd been the same for him, when the loss of his wife had left him stricken with grief. Few people knew how much her mother's death had cost her. Calum knew and understood.

As if deciding it was time for action, he pulled himself away, and she could see thoughts rippling across his eyes as he propped himself up on one elbow.

"I know it's early days." His voice was hesitant, and he let his gaze fall downwards, an unexpected shyness as his hand traced the line of her neck.

"But... do you think it could be that way? With us? I don't want to pressure you. But beyond this...we might have a future together?"

Her heart raced while her mind, lagging behind, slowly processed what was happening here. She struggled for words, but knew she must find them. Couldn't leave him hanging on her answer. Not when he'd made himself so vulnerable before her, risking her rejection on top of the other bitter disappointment he lived with.

"Calum, I don't think it *could* be that way. I feel like it already is." And now she took a risk of her own, feeling both elation and fear, the competing emotions tugging at her, alongside the awareness that these next words could trigger the best or the worst thing to happen that day. "I think I love you Calum MacFarlane."

He didn't hesitate, and she loved him even more for that. "I think I love you too, Sarah Mitchell."

So there it was. The two of them. A future together. Oh, for sure, its outline was a little hazy for now, but they'd work it out over the months ahead. Out of an imperfect past, a perfect future.

CHAPTER 26

Worlds Collide

*Calum*

London, England – September, 2008

"SMITTEN, I'D SAY," SAID Rev, as he slid the pint of dark ale across the leaner towards Calum.

Both men's eyes followed Sarah's bobbing figure as she wove her way across the bar through the lunchtime crowd, heading for the door. She was off to meet Mel at the train station. In the background, Calum acknowledged a twinge of nervousness, knowing how he was going to be measured at this meeting. He pushed it away and turned to his friend.

"Yep, that's about the state of it," he said.

He couldn't help the stupid grin from edging across his face at the thought of just how far he'd fallen for this woman. At least with Rev he could own it. Malcolm Harrop, known to all on the building site as 'The Reverend' but generally referred to as Rev, was one of those men who invited confessions. He was the kind of guy whose companionable silence encouraged you to share things that you'd not normally confide to anyone else. Tall and lanky, an angular face to match his awkward body, Rev was a man who said little but was a great listener. And when he spoke, his words embodied a quiet wisdom that you couldn't ignore.

"Sudden. You're gone three weeks and then you're back with her."

"Yeah, took me by surprise as much as you. The timing sucks. Just my bloody luck when I've promised myself to the army and then she drops into my life."

"Not thinking of changing your mind?"

"Nah, signed my life away for now. Only way out would be for me to fuck up so royally that they boot me out. And to be honest, I wouldn't throw it away like that. I still want to go. Having the army doesn't mean I can't have her too."

"You sure about that?"

"I am. She's chasing a career too. We just need to work out how to make sure our lives collide often enough to build something long term."

"Well, good luck to the both of you then," said Rev, raising his glass. "You deserve it, mate. And I can see you're not the only one smitten. She's only got eyes for you."

"Hope so. Don't want her taking up with one of those Oxford boys while I'm off doing night marches and blowing shit up."

"Well, if you ever get tired of it, I'm sure the boss would have you back without hesitation. The new foreman is struggling. Those young blokes have no respect for him. They're getting careless along with it. Only a matter of time."

"Watch yourself Rev. Don't get hurt through some other bastard taking stupid risks."

"Will do mate. But you're missed. They always listened to you."

Two years on construction sites hadn't been great, but it hadn't been all bad. It had put enough distance between Calum and his father for a start. The money was good too, almost enough to compensate for life in that grey, teeming city. But the best thing about the job was it had taught him what he was good at and that had led him to this new path. He wouldn't go back.

"So, tell me more about this new lady of yours," said Rev. "Don't think I've ever seen you this happy. Not even with Kristin."

"I wasn't happy with Kristin. And in the end, she definitely wasn't happy with me."

Kristin. It had been a mistake from the beginning. A workmate's sister. They'd met at birthday beers at their local. She'd set her cap at him and chased him hard. He'd been lazy, letting her move their relationship along, steering it carefully towards the end goal. Except her end goal hadn't been his. If only he'd seen it sooner and broken it off. At least she wouldn't have been so angry at him. He'd allowed her to invest herself in a future that was never going to happen.

Subconsciously, he'd hoped she'd decide for herself that he wasn't marriage material. But she hadn't, and he'd realised too late, when the only choice was to be blunt. The breakup had been a circus. He'd deserved her screaming, yelling, throwing things, tossing his stuff out the front door, with the neighbours peering down at him, some shocked, others amused. He regretted putting her through that, but luckily she'd picked herself up, found a new guy who did make her happy.

"So what is it about this one that's got you hooked? I mean, she's an attractive woman, and she's funny and smart. One hour of conversation and I can see why a guy would be interested. But it looks to me like you're in it for the long haul, mate."

"Yeah, afraid so. It's the simple fact that she gets me, Rev. She's even seen the shitstorm that's my family and still believes in me enough, believes I won't repeat it. And makes me believe it too. For the first time in my life, I can see myself with a wife, kids. Not a total fuck up like my old man. With her, I can be the person I want to be. And she wants me to be that too."

"So this is the real deal, then? Love at first sight, huh?"

"Stupid as it sounds, I guess it is."

"And she sees it the same way as you?"

"If there was one thing I learned from the Kristin debacle, it was to check it out from her side. This time I have. And I will continue to do so. I'm not going to stuff this up. "

He ran his hand over his jacket pocket. Tucked in there was a small silver ring. His mother had entrusted it to him, to keep safe until he found the right person to give it to. It wasn't an engagement ring, but nevertheless, once he'd put it on her hand, it would feel like a promise to each other.

He'd been watching the door, and saw Sarah the moment she returned. She carved a path through the maze of people. Trailing behind her was a petite blonde woman with wispy elfin hair framing a pale face. As he smiled and waved at them, Calum caught the appraising flicker in Mel's grey eyes. This was worse than meeting a new girlfriend's parents. A girl might not listen to her parents, but she takes her best friend's opinions seriously.

"Mel. Hi, I'm Calum." He stretched out his hand and clasped her tiny one. "I'm afraid I've got you at a bit of a disadvantage. I've heard all about you, but you know almost nothing about me."

"Only a little bit," she said. "Most of it good." Her tone was light, almost teasing, but there was still a hint of wariness in her eyes. He was going to have to work on this one.

"And this is Rev," said Sarah. "Calum's friend."

"I'm off to get us another pint. How about I get you ladies a drink?" Rev offered. While the two women debated what to have, he leaned in close to take Calum's empty glass. "That's where you've got your work cut out for you," he said with a discreet nod towards Mel.

"Don't I know it," said Calum, as he prepared to do whatever it took to win her over.

CHAPTER 27

Torn Apart

*Sarah*

London, England – September, 2008

SARAH LAY SPRAWLED IN pleasant drowsiness, the mid-afternoon sun filtering through the curtains of their hotel room. The elegant interior, although modern, hinted at the beautiful Georgian building that encased it. The soft hum of traffic moving along Bayswater Road provided an undercurrent to Calum's breathing. His face nuzzled into her neck, one muscular arm cupping her to him even now as he slept.

While nearby Hyde Park had beckoned that morning and they'd spent pleasant hours strolling hand in hand, the London drizzle that descended around lunchtime was a convenient excuse to dive back into their room and each other's arms. They'd had these five days, not to explore the city, but to explore each other and the love that had blossomed between them, so sudden and unexpected.

She mused over their first meeting. The indignity of him finding her there on the ground, curled into a ball, taking refuge from a sound so excruciating to her own ears, but not to anyone else. But him seeing her like that, vulnerable, stripped back to the scared little girl that lurked beneath her confident exterior, may well have kick-started their relationship.

Just like she'd seen him in the depths of misery, shunned by the father who had once loved him. It affected him deeply, despite his protestations otherwise. It had given her insight into the core of Calum, the part of him he didn't show to the world. And that's what love was about—for better, for worse, seeing someone at their best and also when it seemed the only thing good you had in the world was each other.

He stirred a little, and she rolled towards him, taking in the sharply defined nose with its slight bump, the sensuous mouth, the dark hair shot through with ribbons of red, like the last threads of a sunset lingering into the night. She couldn't help herself, grazing his lips with her own, and he nudged into wakefulness, eyes still drowsily closed, but giving a little sleepy smile.

"Be careful, you'll awaken the sleeping beast." She immediately felt the aforementioned beast gently prod against her thigh.

"It's bloody insatiable," she said, acknowledging its presence with a gentle tap. "Well, I suppose we are getting our money's worth out of this bedroom."

"It's only hungry for you." His green eyes were now wide open, the hunger written bright within them, the dark pupils dilated. "How about you feed its need, and then I'll take you out for some food too?"

After seeing him with his mate in Stornoway, it was no surprise to Sarah that gregarious Calum should have a tribe of friends in London who all wanted to meet up with him. Given they only had a few days, she might have resented the time spent with them, but she didn't. It was an opportunity to see the whole person, Calum reflected in the company of those who knew and loved him, and observe dimensions of his personality that he hadn't yet revealed in their time together. It was the chance to take the first tentative steps outside their little bubble of two, emerging from a world with only them in it, to test what it would be like as a couple in the real world. And it was wonderful.

She'd been quite at home in the boozy group at a London pub that first night, slotting easily into the banter. The construction site team were an earthy bunch who attempted to tame their bawdy conversation in her presence and failed. But they were likeable, and she sensed they liked her too, each taking the time to peel away from the group to chat with her. No doubt they were taking the opportunity to weigh up this new woman who'd made a sudden appearance in their mate's life.

"So Sarah, do you have any nice Kiwi friends here that you can hook me up with?" Matt had placed a drink in front of her and edged himself onto a vacant bar stool. "Guess I can't make a move on you now Calum's got in first."

OK, Matt was a tad drunk, but he and the others seemed genuine in accepting her into their crowd.

"I do, actually," she'd replied. "She's single and looking for a good man. How about we go out for drinks one night when Calum has some leave?"

The next night Sarah had been anxious, putting Calum and Mel in the same room for the first time. She desperately wanted her friend to like him, see that he was certainly no psycho, and far more than an impulsive hook up on her part. And she wanted Calum to like Mel too. She was closer to this woman than her own sisters, and any future would always have Mel in it.

By the end of the evening, those anxieties had dampened down a little. Having Calum's friend Rev there, a quiet friendly presence at the table, had helped. It gave Mel the opportunity to see Calum against the backdrop of someone else who cared about him, not just through Sarah's love-blinded gaze. Calum was his charming self, and despite her initial wariness, Mel couldn't help but fall a little under his spell. She'd giggled and flushed with pleasure as he teased her like a new big brother.

They'd gone to the loo as a pair like two silly teenagers, and sounded like that too, Mel's high-pitched voice echoing off the bathroom walls. "Oh-my-god! He is rather gorgeous. Now I know why you decided to go off climbing mountains with him. Even I'd consider putting on some walking boots for a guy like that."

"Well, he does have a rather nice single friend..."

It was a relief to have Mel's approval, although Sarah wasn't quite ready to share everything with her friend. Mel saw him as her interesting new boyfriend. Sarah saw him as her future.

―――――

On the final night, they carved out a space for just the two of them. It would be a long fourteen weeks before Calum's first leave. Her first priority when she arrived at Oxford was to hammer out her academic programme with her supervisor, making sure nothing stood in the way of those precious times when Calum was free.

He'd promised to take her back to Scotland to walk parts of the old Roman Antonine Wall. They'd revisit the Highlands and climb some Munros together. They might even venture across the Channel into Europe. There was so much world to explore and the thought of doing it alongside Calum was exciting.

They sat at a tiny inner-city restaurant; the minutes rushing by too quickly. Tucked in under an old brick warehouse, Sarah watched the ferries on the Thames, and the lights of The City across the water, dancing merrily in contrast to her flat mood. Not wanting alcohol to dull the moment, she opted for water. They needed to make memories tonight that would carry them through the long weeks ahead.

"Just think, at least we have plenty to occupy our minds while we're apart." Ever the optimist, but she had to agree he was right. Although she'd been a confident student, flying through her degrees with relative ease, Oxford's daunting reputation preyed on her mind. She'd need to bring her A-game. "And there's always phone sex," he said with a grin.

"Then it's probably just as well I have my own room at the College. Not sure you'll be so lucky. No privacy in barracks."

"Well, as they say, love will find a way—or lust."

They hadn't talked beyond the next year. It was too soon, although Sarah had a lurch of both delight and fear when she thought what the future might hold. Right now she couldn't imagine a life without Calum in it. This was more than a two-week wonder. Fate had tossed them together. She'd been in the right place at the right time. But she preferred to keep the details of that future a little fuzzy for now.

The words 'army wife' held an ominous tone. He'd be away a lot, in places she couldn't follow. Dangerous places, and she would be forced to somehow conquer the ever-lurking fear that one day he wouldn't come home. She prodded the disturbing thoughts back where they'd come from. Thoughts of an uncertain future would not spoil their present.

"Where's that million-dollar smile?" He'd read the ripples of uncertainty on her face. "Come on, you'll blink and before you know it, I'll be back."

She flashed the requested smile. "Sorry, it's not like me. Guess this is the first time I've cared enough."

He took her hand, stroking her fingers, eyes bright with some simmering excitement. Then, with one smooth movement, his other hand pulled something from his pocket, and he extended it towards her, palm closed.

"This is the first time I've cared enough as well." He unfurled his fingers to reveal a small silver ring. Its band sported a delicate engraved pattern, interlaced thistles with Celtic style flourishes between. "It's Mam's. Handed down in the family, so it's old. Would you wear it? See, I feel this need to mark you as mine."

"You've already marked me as yours," she said, looking into his dark-lashed eyes. "In two weeks, you've made an indelible mark on me. Whatever happens from here—who knows—but my life will never be the same. Yes, I'd be proud to wear it."

He threaded it onto her right hand. She had a flash of the future, maybe the not too distant future, maybe a wedding ring to match on the other. It was weird admitting to herself that if he asked her to marry him right now, she'd say yes. But he was sensible enough to know they needn't rush. There was plenty of time.

Leaving the restaurant, they stood on the Millennium Bridge, where tourists meandered and laughing theatregoers spilled out of The Globe, oblivious to them all. Like a stone in the middle of the current, the people flowed around them, but Sarah was aware of only one thing: she was in love.

---

Their actual parting was anticlimactic. The taxi pulled to a halt in the pretty square ringed with elegant terrace houses. Ignoring the driver's surreptitious glances in the rear-view mirror, they'd sat clasped together in the backseat for the entire fifteen minute journey, like two youngsters making out. Reluctantly, they pried themselves apart. Sarah pushed back the tears that were threatening to spill over, despite her resolution that there'd be no ugly crying. She ran her hands one last time through those thick waves of hair, already mourning their loss to the army's strict rules.

"I'll call you tonight," he promised, giving her one last quick kiss, before clambering back into the vehicle. "Wish me luck." And with a wave and a last flash of that smile she loved, the taxi whisked Calum MacFarlane away.

Sarah turned to make her way towards the door of number fifteen, Jellicoe Square. Like its neighbours, it was old, beautiful, and expensive. It was nice of Claire and Jonathan to have her back for a few days. Mel would be there if she needed a shoulder to cry on. Her friend's perky optimism was a safety net, and she was grateful knowing that it would prevent her from slipping into a morose mood in Calum's absence.

She hesitated at the edge of the footpath, her passage to ring the doorbell interrupted by a disturbing sensation. The lingering warmth of Calum's kisses drained from her body, replaced by a nasty seeping chill, as if an infusion of iced water pumped into her veins. She shivered.

Prickling goosebumps appeared on her forearms, multiplying rapidly to the point of pain. And then the sound came, reverberating off the houses, circling around her, capturing her in its midst. It seemed as if the sky above her was falling to earth, about to crush the elegant portico and her with it. Sarah flung herself to the ground, her screams merging with the sound as she became one with it. Her eyes scrunched tight shut against the pain as the world around her was brutally torn away.

Part Three – Here

Puzzle Pieces

# Sarah

London, England – September 2008

"Sarah. Fuck. Claire—go get Richard."

Frantic hands rolled her over, her head flopping back onto the hard ground with a painful thud. Warm hands cupped her face, traces of a familiar perfume wafting from the wrists. *Mel*. But Mel didn't swear. No. Not Mel.

"Fuck, Sarah wake up." The voice was urgent. The shaking was insistent. It was Mel. God, her mother would be appalled at that potty mouth. There was a clatter of footsteps. More people. And tiny pats of liquid dotted her cheeks. Rain.

"What the fuck's happened?" The man's voice was demanding.

"I don't know Richard. I heard a scream. There was a thud. I opened the door and there she was. Lying on the footpath, huddled up like she expected someone to hit her. Or like someone *did* hit her."

"Shit, do you think she's been mugged, right on our doorstep? Oh, how horrible. Surely things like that don't happen around here? I thought this was a nice neighbourhood." The second woman's outraged voice grated on her ears. "We don't pay all that money to live somewhere where there are thugs waiting to pounce."

The man interrupted. "Shut up, Claire. No one cares about your bloody rent money. Stop fussing, the two of you, and let's get her inside out of this bloody rain." The intermittent drops were becoming a persistent patter.

Sarah sensed muscular arms underneath her, plucking her from the pavement, lifting her into the air as if her body had no weight at all, even though her limbs were leaden. Cradling her to him like a small child, the man carried her up the steps. He smelt good, comforting, familiar. What had the woman called him? Richard. There was a flash of recognition.

"Richard." She said it out loud, tentatively, and the confirmation came back. She knew the firm voice, those strong arms.

"Yes love, it's me. Don't try to talk. You're going to be OK."

When she woke, the daylight was ebbing, the last traces of a sickly sun giving way to evening. She could hear faint voices, activity elsewhere in the house. Above her, the ceiling was so white it glowed in the dimness. She focused on the centre, an ornate leafy wreath surrounding a modern pendant light dangling above her head. The bed was vast, comfortable, but not her bed. Low voices came from outside the door, and assuming it involved her, she strained to hear the conversation.

"Why don't you stay the night, Richard? I think it's too soon to move her."

"I thought she might be better in her own bed. You know, familiar surroundings."

"Do you think she needs to see a doctor? After all, it's pretty strange to collapse like that. Someone young and fit. It could be something serious."

"I've already made an appointment for her tomorrow. No, I want to take her home."

The door opened a slit. A pair of concerned blue eyes peered at her. Richard's tense face relaxed. Seeing her return his gaze, a smile bloomed as he pushed the door wide. She could see Claire hovering at his shoulder.

"Hello love, good to see you're awake." He moved to lower himself onto the bed beside her, his hand caressing the strands of her tangled hair.

"Richard." Her voice was a whisper, and she was grateful for the glass of cool water he passed to her. She gulped at it, feeling the soothing chill ease the rasp in her throat.

He turned to Claire, still lingering in the doorway. "Do you think you and Mel could keep an eye on her, organise her things? I'll bring the car out front."

Turning back to her, he leaned forward to place a delicate kiss on her forehead.

"It's OK love. I'm taking you home."

---

Sarah sipped at her water, longing for a glass of the weighty Bordeaux that Richard was pouring for their guests. Its earthy smell drifted towards her and conjured the taste of ripe plums, the ruby red depths taunting her, whispering how perfectly it would complement the lamb rack on her plate.

"Oooh, that's good." Mel rolled the liquid in her mouth, then shot Sarah an apologetic look, guilty at her enjoyment of something forbidden to her friend.

Sarah smiled and tried to look enthusiastic about the water. She needed to be a good girl, doing as instructed—including no alcohol for a while—if she could curb her natural impulse to dive back into normal life like nothing had happened. She must convince them all that she was looking after herself. Then, soon, she would be free from the doctor's list of silly restrictions and Richard could cease monitoring her like a probation officer.

But there was one thing that might clinch the deal—if she could drag up the elusive memories of the past two weeks of her life. While they continued to lurk in the shadows, dancing with glee tantalisingly just beyond reach, there would be suspicion. Suspicion that she was harbouring some undetectable neurological condition. Suspicion that her tumble from Heather MacFarlane's horse had caused a concussion and messed with her brain. Suspicion that the bump to her head when she'd fallen to the pavement outside Claire's house was more serious than it seemed.

She thrived on the conversation that whirled around her, snatching snippets about their trip to Scotland, each tiny fact adding a piece of the puzzle. In the days since they had found her barely conscious on Claire and Jonathan's doorstep, she'd eavesdropped on conversations and asked surreptitious questions, desperate to gather information. She noted facts on her mental list and then in secret jotted them in a little notebook, reading them over when she was alone. Tonight was a brilliant opportunity to make a big leap forward in her detective work.

"That smoked trout was delicious," gushed Claire, paying tribute to the recently cleared entrée. "And you caught it yourself, Richard."

"Yeah, that stream of Hamish's is a beauty. Not quite up to the Tongariro, but to think it's right there on his doorstep. Trout for the taking whenever he wants."

Sarah could remember Richard stepping out of the bushes clutching the fish, pride written on his face, and her horse dancing a jig at the unexpected arrival. In fact, she had pinpointed that her memories were clear leading up to the moment during dinner that night, when she'd stepped outside for some fresh air, even as far as to remember the arc of the Milky Way above her head. And then nothing.

"Tell me, Sarah, what did you think of York?" Jonathan turned to her. "With your obsession for all things historic, I imagine you would have been in your element."

She'd already worked out that Richard had opted to leave MacFarlane's early and strike out for York so Sarah could explore the historic city at leisure. He'd worked at the hotel while she'd visited the sites on her own, unable to drag him away from assembling the last pieces of the distillery deal.

"It's amazing," she said. "You know, it was a Roman settlement long before all the Viking stuff. So yes, I loved it."

In fact, her day in York was still largely a mystery. But she knew, given her interests, what must-see sights she would have visited, and so she'd jumped online to grab some details to prepare for awkward questions. Somehow, she'd need to engineer a 'return' visit.

"Sarah and her love affair with the Romans," said Mel with a smile. "She's still trying to convince me. How long did we spend in the Roman Gallery at the museum the other day?"

"Hours, I know. But I'm not going to apologise for my obsession. And I don't think there's any sign I'll grow out of it."

Another blank. Another lie. Sarah had no idea as to why she'd dragged Mel to the British Museum three days ago. No memory of lunch at a cafe overlooking the Thames. No recollection of which shop she'd found the two new pairs of shoes in her wardrobe that looked at her accusingly. Did she love them so little that she couldn't even remember why she'd selected them?

The refracted light from a low-hanging chandelier bounced off the glass of water, highlighting the filigree of the sweet little ring on her right hand. She couldn't recall purchasing that either, but presumed it was from a visit to the antique market in Marylebone.

They'd been to Alfie's, according to Mel. But her fickle mind could not retrieve the details of the outing, let alone the items she'd bought. A shame, as the ring was of an interesting design. Knowing her own obsession with history, she would certainly have inquired as to its provenance. But that conversation too was consigned to the odd in between time, where it seemed the real Sarah had been strangely absent, an automaton in her place.

"Pretty," said Claire, seeing Sarah twirling the ring thoughtfully. "Antique?"

"Yes, a little souvenir from the trip."

She was becoming skilled at providing the right answers. Most people were content with vague, generic responses. It was like being trapped on a TV quiz show, with a return to her normal life, the prize for success. Sarah was determined to win this game.

CHAPTER 29

Dilemma

# Sarah

Three years later, Wellington, New Zealand – March 2011

SARAH STOOD AT THE basin, the now-empty foil packet lying on the marble top, a smooth round tablet balanced on her hand. It was the last one. She stood contemplating these past four months, and the lie she'd been living. As far as Richard was aware, they'd reached a comfortable compromise about the question of children.

Almost four years ago, when it had threatened to derail their marriage before it even started, they'd hammered out this arrangement. He'd agreed that it was wise for her to concentrate on her studies, not attempt to balance motherhood with the demands of her doctoral work. She'd agreed that once she was done, out of regard for the years ticking by and his concerns about being a father so late in life, they'd try for a baby straight away. But she'd reneged on the deal. Unbeknownst to him, she'd continued to take these small pink pills each morning.

He'd been gentle with her, only raising the baby topic once directly. It would have been better if he'd been less subtle, less patient. She'd have likely felt more guilt at deceiving him. But he was a practical man and knew that pregnancy didn't happen instantly. And so he hadn't pressured her. She wished he had. She may have abandoned the pill sooner, might not have the new packet sitting in the drawer tempting her to continue.

Too late, she was aware of his footsteps behind her. Lost in thought, she had been oblivious to his presence in the bedroom next door. He rested one hand on her shoulder.

"I can't find that..." He stopped, and his eyes met hers in the mirror. Emotions flicked through them in rapid succession—shock, a flash of anger, and then a look that she would come to see often in the coming days: a gutting disappointment. He said nothing, simply turned and walked away. Even his retreating back gave off waves of dismay.

The chill between them when she joined him at the table hung in the air; an almost tangible presence.

"Richard," she said, laying her hand over his, hearing the pleading note in her voice, hating that it was necessary. He jerked his hand away, his eyes not leaving the newspaper.

She moved to the fridge, spooned dollops of yoghurt into a bowl, rained granola on top of it and returned to sit beside him. His silence was unnerving. She had been so stupid. Finally he folded the paper neatly, laying it beside him, sipped at his coffee and then spoke. Only one word.

"Why?" he said, his eyes on her now with that piercing gaze, the one that Mel had found so intimidating, the one she'd only seen on rare occasions. Except for her it wasn't the gaze that scared her, it was the knowledge of the damage her foolishness in not talking to him had already wrought.

She'd deluded herself into thinking that if he didn't bring up the subject, he didn't care. But he did.

Unexpected tears welled in her eyes, tears of anger at her own stupidity. She tried to hold them back. She didn't want to risk him thinking it a deliberate ploy to escape the trap she'd made for herself.

Why? Why had she done it? She had no answer.

"If you've changed your mind about wanting children, you only had to say."

"And would you have minded?"

"Yes. I won't lie. I would have. I do mind." He was holding up his end of their arrangement. It was she who'd changed course without telling him. "You know that at first I didn't entertain more kids as part of my future. Wanted to leave it in the past. And to be honest, at first I only agreed because I feared losing you otherwise. But you know what? I grew to love the idea. How could I not want to share that with you?" Her tears spilled over now. Anger replaced by guilt. His voice softened a little, seeing her distress. "I've been lucky. I have my girls. If you'd decided that you didn't want to have our baby, don't you think you should have talked to me about it?"

"But I do. I do want a baby."

"Then what the hell are you doing still taking the pill?"

She looked away, couldn't face him, couldn't put into words the knot in her stomach. The fears, like strands of heavy coiled ropes, twisted and turned, holding her back from taking that next step, while forbidding her to speak of them.

"OK, well I'm going to the office," he said, taking her silence as unwillingness to discuss it further.

***

The students filed out of the lecture theatre. To her, their animated buzz of chatter was the equivalent of a scorecard that read ten out of ten. She was good at this. History had the potential to captivate people or bore them to tears. Sarah prided herself on her classes, always ending the lecture on an intriguing thought or a provocative question. When students left the room, they carried with them a little spark of the magic of the past that had enthralled her since she was a small child. But it was no random accident. It took hours of preparation, at least now, while she was still a relatively inexperienced member of the faculty. Seeing her students like this emphasised even more how much she loved it. And brought to the surface what she now recognised was her paralysing fear: that having recently gained this position, the arrival of a baby would force her to give it away.

"Dr Norton?" A timid-looking girl with wispy blonde hair stood at her elbow, a hesitant note in her voice. The girl couldn't know how much hearing someone address her that way sent a thrill of elation through Sarah. Although technically she wasn't entitled to use the title until after the official graduation ceremony in a few weeks, she'd found the nameplate on the door of the pokey office she shared with another new faculty member and plastered over her carefully prepared course notes like those clutched in this girl's hand. Three years of work, but it had been worth it. "Excuse me, Dr Norton, I just wanted to check the due date for the first assignment. It says April 9th, but that's Easter Monday. Will we need to have it in before Easter, or will the next day be alright?"

She turned to answer the question with a smile.

After leaving the lecture theatre, she called at the cafe for what had already become part of her daily routine. She'd grab a takeaway coffee before making her way home. But today, like every day since that horrible morning, her mind, once freed from the intensity of the lecture, automatically flicked to other pressing matters. Troubling matters. It was impossible to explain her conflicting emotions to Richard. A week had gone by, but she still struggled to put it into words.

Yes, she wanted a child, quite desperately most of the time. From the beginning, she'd been open with Gerald, now head of the faculty. He had no problems with it. Staff taking periods of maternity leave and asking for reduced hours was a common occurrence. The university had a reputation as a supportive employer. It was she that had the problem.

Nagging doubts gnawed at her, undermining her confidence that she could continue to be a top-notch lecturer and a good mother. Each day immersed in her work, interacting with her students, left her feeling more conflicted by the time she headed for home.

She wove her way through the crowded cafe, sipping the excellent take-away coffee, the caffeine hit boosting her low mood. One advantage of living in Wellington: it was impossible to find a bad coffee.

She made her way across campus on the now familiar path to the cable car that would glide quietly down the hill, delivering her right into the centre of the city. From there, it was only a short stroll to the waterfront apartment. But the usually pleasant walk was today spoiled by the turmoil in her mind.

Drawn by the sound of children's voices, she stopped by a tall iron fence. Seeing them playing happily in the grounds of the campus creche, rather than reassuring her, only added to her dilemma. Mel's words echoed in her head, standing in harsh judgement on the working parents of children in her junior classroom:

"I don't know why some people have kids. After the holidays, they can't wait to send them back to school to be rid of them."

"You know some kids in my class are in care or at school from six in the morning till six at night? Poor little mites, all day in the hands of strangers."

Some of those parents had to work. It was necessary to the survival of their families. For her, it would be a deliberate choice to put her own needs ahead of their child, leaving strangers, albeit well-trained and well-meaning ones, to take her place.

A young woman emerged onto the deck, holding a baby in her arms, a little girl with feathery dark curls, a cupid bow mouth and a frilled peach pinafore. The woman murmured to the child before following the direction of its chubby outstretched hand, moving to place it in a bucket swing. She pushed the small girl gently back and forth, continuing to talk to her, and the child babbled back in between giggles of glee. It could be a beautiful mother and child moment.

But it wasn't. The woman: a carer. The child: someone else's. This was what she'd be committing her child to if she continued to work. And the guilt of an action not yet taken still stabbed at her.

Behind her, a car sidled into the kerb with a low rumble, accompanied by the whir of an electric window.

"Sarah."

Her favourite voice in all the world. She turned and in two steps, opened the heavy door of the Jaguar and settled into the seat beside Richard.

"Well, that's a pleasant surprise," he said. "My meeting finished early. I'm heading home. Didn't expect to see you on the way." His smile dampened as he saw her face. Damn him, he was too perceptive. And damn her, she had never learned how to prevent her emotions spilling over for him to see.

"What's wrong?" He reached across to tuck back that stray strand of hair that somehow always escaped its tether, his hand gently brushing her cheek. She could see his mind working, calculating the sum of all the parts and coming up with the perfect answer. "Ah, now I see. You were stopped at the day care there. Thinking about babies."

Tears came. Never in her life, apart from when her mother died, had they lurked like this, bobbing below the surface, aggressively taking every opportunity to spill over and trail down her face. Her emotions were a tangled mess, and she never knew which one was about to assert itself at any given moment.

He pulled her to him and she sobbed against his expensive navy suit, while he stroked her hair and dotted soothing kisses on it.

"Tell me," he said, his voice soft in her ear. "I need to know. My strong, beautiful wife shouldn't be like this. We have to sort this out."

"It's just…" Another small sob escaped her, and she breathed in, counting to three in her head. Feeling steadier, she leaned back to face him and took one last calming breath. "It's just that today I saw a glimpse of my future life—and I didn't like it. I'm loving the work, Richard. Truly loving it. I never imagined standing up there giving a lecture would feel so good, so right. And then when I stood outside the day care, I saw the price I'd pay if I continued to work. Our child, well-cared for, but by strangers."

"Why didn't you say?"

"Because I've been so confused. When you asked me why I was delaying, honestly I couldn't put it into words. The thought of it seemed wrong, but I wasn't able to say why. This is the first time I think I've connected all the dots."

As he studied her face, she could see his mind busy tossing ideas around at lightning speed. And then, incongruous as it was, he smiled.

"Well, there is another option." She looked at him quizzically. Of course, for Richard, teasing apart the knots of a difficult problem was what he did on a daily basis. "We both work and we both look after our child. You don't have a full-time workload, and you know I'm pushing off as much as I can to my underlings. They love it. They're the same as I was, hungry for the chance to prove themselves."

She had never imagined, despite knowing her husband well, that he'd make such a suggestion. But it had possibilities.

"Even with Paul gone now?" she asked.

"Especially with Paul gone. It means I can't fall into the trap of picking up any of his stuff as well as my own. It will force me not to be such a control freak. After all, I need to show some confidence that what we've built is robust enough to survive without either of us. And I think it is." His smile broadened as another thought flickered through his racing mind. "And while I'm daddy day care, I can work from home on things for us. Like the distillery. It's perfect. I don't know why I never thought of it before."

"Oh my god Richard, it's perfect." Happiness flooded her, as the impossible choice she thought was facing her evaporated. In its place, she saw a new vision, a life where they all got what they needed.

He kicked the engine into life. "Let's go home," he said. "Time to work on making that baby."

---

"Only you could make that get-up look sexy. It may well be tradition, but it's frumpy as hell," he said, tweaking her hat playfully.

He was right. The doctoral gown wasn't too bad, especially since she'd purchased one in a length that showed more leg than was probably seemly, but she didn't care. Her dizzying, high patent leather stilettos added to the illusion. They were her present to herself for the years of slog–a genuine pair of Louboutins. Richard told her the flash of their red soles was a perfect match for the scarlet satin stole draped around her shoulders. But there was no way to redeem the floppy black velvet Knox bonnet, perched askew on her curls.

"Now the photos are done, I need to relieve you of that." Richard whisked it off her head. "Giulia, can you pop that somewhere safe? Or maybe not, as I doubt she's going to need it again."

Giulia Silver laughingly took the offending bonnet, and reached for the gown as Sarah let it slip from her shoulders, welcoming her escape from the heavy fabric.

"Well, I will need it," she said. "At next year's graduation. I'll be invited to attend as academic staff, so of course I'll wear it."

It felt good saying that. Academic staff. She mused for a moment, imagined herself sitting there on the stage, watching the new graduates make their way in front of her. Knowing she'd helped them on their journey.

"I feel naughty even having one of these," she said as she raised the champagne glass to her lips. It was her favourite Veuve Clicquot. She'd allowed herself this small indulgence, a brief break from her newly teetotal status in anticipation of becoming pregnant.

"It's only for a while. When our child is born, my love, I'll buy you as much champagne as you want." He looked thoughtful for a moment. "I tell you what—out of solidarity, I'll give up too. I don't have to drink."

"Oh, and how are you going to explain that to the team at MacFarlane's? Of course you'll have to drink. Can't give an opinion on a batch of whisky if you haven't tasted it."

"OK, no drinking except for our whisky. Now Doctor Norton, what do you think you'll order?" he said, scanning the menu. He still had that silly smile on his face. It seemed to have been there permanently this past week. She felt a rush of pleasure that she could give him this. Life was so damn good.

***

In the bathroom, Sarah went through her new morning routine. She'd become adept at peeing on the little stick, following the instructions to the letter. But she hadn't got used to the disappointment when each time the longed-for second line didn't appear.

The doctor said it could take months, even years, for her body to rid itself of the contraceptive pill. She cursed the time she'd wasted, dithering over problems that in the end weren't problems at all. Wasted months in which her body could have discarded the synthetic hormones. But it seemed her body, understanding the urgency of the need to do so, had cooperated. There was a sense of finality in the twin pink vertical lines on the pregnancy test. Those lines marked a decision from which there was no return.

She hesitated in the doorway for a moment, excited anticipation causing a fluttering sensation in her stomach. It had to be that. Too early for the new life inside her to make its presence felt.

Richard sat at the counter drinking coffee and reading the financial pages. Although the internet delivered the numbers and trends to his computer desktop in an instant, he was too attached to this morning habit, despite it being old-fashioned. Every day the same routine: up at six, a run along the bay, and then off to the gym. On the way home grab the newspapers and a coffee from Lola's cafe. They themselves owned a commercial sized coffee machine that almost needed a licence to operate, but Richard was loyal to his favourite barista, who delivered a reliable brew and cheerful gossip to launch the day.

She placed the plastic test down on the counter where Richard perched on a bar stool. Without looking, he reached out one arm, clutching her to him, his hand grazing her hip, finding the gap in her robe, sliding down her stomach to caress her thigh. It wouldn't be the first morning she'd taken him back to bed, while still sweaty from his earlier exertions and given him a second workout of the more pleasurable kind. But not today. Not yet anyway.

She tapped her finger on the plastic tube and his eyes flickered away from the newspaper, following the sound. Recognition dawned on his face, his eyes brimming with love and happiness. He rose to wrap her in his arms so tightly that it squeezed the breath from her, kissed her so deeply that she couldn't inhale the next. And picked her up and carried her back to the bedroom, where they celebrated the creation of their child with the same love that had brought it into existence. There was no going back now.

# Sarah

Five years later, Wakefield, New Zealand – June 2016

SARAH TRUDGED ALONG THE track towards the farmhouse, tired, filthy and with her passionate hatred of sheep even further entrenched. Noel's insistence on running the small flock to keep the house paddocks neat was a long-standing pain point. The stupid, woolly-brained beasts caused more problems than the entire herd of three hundred dairy cattle put together. And somehow those sheep contrived to cause the biggest problems when their lone supporter, Noel, was conveniently off the property.

When the sharemilker's wife reported a sheep in the pond, she'd grabbed her father's overalls, having no other clothing suitable for retrieving the moronic ewe from her dip in the slimy green depths. Today, when he saw the smelly state of his work clothes, evidence of what the little bastards got up to in his absence, she might convince him to call the home-kill butcher to dispatch them. In her mind, the only good sheep was a roast one.

Two identical pairs of startling blue eyes welcomed her at the kitchen door. Her bad mood from wrangling the unruly sheep trickled away at the sight of the two people she loved most in the world.

"Look—it's mama. Doesn't she look pretty?"

Richard grinned at the state of her. She could feel a streak of congealing pond slime on her face. Her hands were smeared with mud after losing her grip on the sheep who'd thrashed around in an attempt to escape, mistrusting her motives, unaware that she was, in fact, its rescuer.

"Pretty mama." Theo echoed his father's compliment.

"Bloody hell, you are a bit of a wreck, darling."

"Bloody hell," Theo mimicked.

She couldn't help but laugh, despite Richard having broken the 'no swearing in front of Theo rule' with the inevitable result. The almost four-year-old had a fast-growing vocabulary. He parroted every word back at you, his enormous eyes seeking approval. It was hard not to be charmed by that cherubic face, and the sweet pink upturned lips even when bad words issued from them. Richard went to pass the boy into her arms that opened wide out of habit and then stopped abruptly, realising that they should spare their clean child the cloying mud that caked her overalls.

"Mama's a dirty girl," he said, then laughed raucously as Theo repeated the words flawlessly back at him.

Sarah saw the wink, coupled with a gleam in his eye and knew he was thinking what she was: put Theo down for his nap and take the opportunity with Noel out of the house for the day to have an afternoon 'nap' themselves. Napping would definitely be secondary to the other plans she had for her husband. Her bed had been empty of him most of the night while he sat on conference calls to the States. At least soon these too would become a thing of the past, as Richard finally extracted himself from

Crombie Norton. The company would bear his name, but not steal him from her and Theo any longer.

She was tired too, up and down continuously to a restless child last night. Tired for sure, but not so exhausted that she would waste the empty house. The old farmhouse was well-maintained, but had the lack of soundproofing common to all houses of its vintage. After three days of surreptitious sexual encounters as if they were furtive teenagers rather than an old married couple, it would be wonderful to throw aside all inhibitions, with no one to hear their noisy passion vibrating through the walls.

"I'll go put him down," Richard offered. "You go strip off those clothes. Theo's going to be a good boy and go for his nap, aren't you, buddy? Come on. Daddy has your blanky."

Theo's comfort blanket was looking rather tatty, but neither of them was prepared to bin it, knowing the distress that would provoke. Not to mention how compliant mention of the blanky made him. Richard headed for the small room adjoining theirs where they'd set up Theo's things. He was so proud of himself sleeping in a 'big boy's bed', his portable cot no longer accompanying them on their travels.

In the farmhouse laundry she stripped down to her underwear, disposing of the mucky sodden overalls and her damp track pants and t-shirt. She met Richard at the door to Theo's room, taking a moment to peek in at her son, nestled under the covers, his blanky scrunched in one chubby hand.

"Night, night, sleep tight," she said.

"Don' let bedbugs bite," the little voice replied, eyes serious as he concentrated on retrieving the rhyme.

God, he was so damn cute. Having a child had taught her it was possible you could love someone so much it hurt. It had also taught her that being a mother to this beautiful child was the most important job she would ever do. After he'd been born, she'd held out at the university for less than a year before giving it away to spend all her days with him.

The only thing that tarnished her decision was that making it had allowed the company to tighten its tentacles around Richard once more. But he'd fought back. Building on the success of his foray outside Crombie Norton by buying the distillery, he'd continue to amass a personal portfolio. He'd found others like the MacFarlanes, good people with good businesses, in need of a more beneficent partner to help them grow without tearing away or squashing all they'd worked for.

They now owned major shares in a stunning tourist lodge on a pristine trout stream, an alpaca farm and three spin-off companies that turned the exquisite fibre into high-value products, and a thoroughbred racing stud. In addition, they'd established a MacFarlane's Southern Hemisphere distillery. That was undoubtedly Richard's favourite, a little corner of Scotland here in New Zealand. Yes, nights like last night would soon be behind them, and Richard could focus on the things he loved: her, Theo, and this bespoke collection of businesses he was passionate about.

"Sleep well buddy." Richard slipped his arms around her waist, leaning his head on her shoulder, sharing the adoration of their perfect little human being. Then, pulling the door closed with a quiet click, he led her to their bed, quickly stripping off his own clothes. She stood admiring his delicious nakedness while he disposed of her lingerie in two deft movements. With a playful shove, she sent him sprawling on the bed, straddling his eager erection, with a satisfied gasp. She was tired, but sleep could come later.

———

The bang of a door woke Sarah from her pleasant doze. Familiar footsteps told her that Noel was home. She dragged on a robe, and padded out to the kitchen, leaving Richard snoring softly. He was exhausted. She'd leave him to grab whatever extra sleep he could.

"You lot been in bed all day? No one stirring when I left, and no one up when I came back."

"I wish," she said. "No, I did quite a lot today, including pulling one of those stupid sheep out of the pond. You have to get rid of them, Dad. They're a bloody menace."

He chuckled to himself. "Never have any problems with them myself. Reckon they spot me heading out and decide it's time to play up."

"Exactly," she said. "Anyway, after wrestling that cranky ewe back to her paddock, I needed a lie down. To be honest, Richard and I didn't have much sleep last night—him working and me running in to deal with Theo every hour."

"Reckon the boy's awake now? Go and get him love. I brought him back a treat—those lollies he likes. I know, I know," he said, seeing her exasperated look, "he shouldn't have too much sugar. But it's not often I see my grandchild. Let me spoil him a little."

"Yeah Dad, it's OK," she said, not able to be annoyed at him for indulging Theo now and then. "I'll go get him. It's been a couple of hours, so he's probably awake. He's such a good boy. Never gets out of bed. Just plays with his toys until I come in." For the child of two strong-minded parents, Theo had proven himself surprisingly respectful of rules. Chances were, it wouldn't last. "Put the kettle on, Dad, and I'll make us a cuppa, and Theo will want a snack, and then you can give him the lollies."

As she headed down the passageway, Richard called out to her. "Sarah, that you?"

She poked her head in the doorway. "Yes, sleeping beauty. Just going to get Theo up. Dad's home. Shall I make you a coffee?"

"Yeah, be there in a minute." He rubbed his hands through his tousled hair, shaking off the shadow of sleep.

At Theo's room, she found the door ajar, and frowned to herself. She was sure Richard had closed it. The bed was empty. It struck her as strange that Theo had escaped the room. She thought the old door with its rattling twisty knob was Theo-proof.

Her next stop was the bathroom. Theo's latest proud accomplishment was toileting himself independently. She smiled to herself–of course, any son of theirs would fight to master new skills by himself. She called his name, but only her voice echoed back off the tiles. The bathroom was empty. Now uneasy thoughts pushed their way in, and she called for Richard.

"Richard, I can't find Theo." A small quaver of concern rippled through her words. A gnawing whisper of worry accompanied a growing nausea in the pit of her stomach.

He appeared, rumpled t-shirt, half buttoned jeans, barefoot, and joined the search as they raced from room to room of the sprawling farmhouse, calling for Theo. But they found only silence and emptiness, sending her rising sense of panic off the scale. Where the hell was he?

The answer lay around the last corner of the hallway, where a door leading to an old back porch was ajar. It had a lock and key, but of course, in the country, old habits remained. No one bothered to lock the house. Only one more of those old-fashioned door knobs had stood between Theo and the dangerous outdoors. And it had obviously not deterred him.

Now she shrieked for Richard, and he was there in an instant. He plunged outside with no thought of footwear, sprinting across the lawn and vaulting the fence. He disappeared from view behind the prickled barberry hedge and she followed, uncaring of her robe flapping in the wind, or the sharp pain of the stony track under her feet. The early evening air was icy, like the fingers of fear that clutched at her mind. She tried to thrust them away, telling herself that he couldn't have gone far, that they'd find him safe. But they came barrelling back at her. A farm held so many dangers for a small child. God, please let her baby be OK.

She found them by the pond. She screamed, not words, just an outpouring of the terror engulfing her. Richard's jeans were wet to the knees, trailing tendrils of green weed wrapped like shackles around his ankles. And in his arms, a small dripping figure.

He lay the boy tenderly on the ground and she flung herself down beside them. She'd done all the right things–gone to the first aid sessions, practised CPR on hard unmoving mannequins, confident that if the worst happened to her child, she would know what to do; she could save him. Part of her hovered above, surveying the scene in horror. Reeling from the relentless waves of shock that broke over her, threatening to crush her. Watching as the Sarah below did what she had been taught to do, summoning the knowledge that could bring her child back.

Beside her, the guttural sound of her husband's despair echoed across the pond. He sobbed beside her as she went through the motions, counting the desperate beat as her hand pumped the tiny chest, willing life into him with all her being as she puffed breaths into the lips she had kissed only hours earlier. Richard knew what she couldn't yet accept. It was too late. Theo was gone.

## CHAPTER 31

Farewells

*Sarah*

Wakefield, New Zealand – June 2016

A BITTER WIND STRAIGHT off the Antarctic chewed at the crowd huddled in the small town cemetery, its savage teeth biting at the exposed hands and sombre faces of those assembled. Sarah might have been in the Antarctic, standing like an Emperor penguin in a huddle, flanked by Richard and her father, with her sisters and their families clustered behind, protecting her from the onslaught of the wind, but unable to protect her from the grief. And Mel, who'd flown in on the gruelling seventeen-hour flight from Dubai, stood at her shoulder, her small reassuring hand simply saying, "I'm here."

For five days she'd gratefully accepted the pills prescribed by the family doctor, a man who'd delivered her into this world. God, he had to be almost seventy, some would say past it, but not past knowing that medicine offered a small reprieve from the crippling pain. But today, she'd shunned the pills, left them sitting on a bathroom shelf, rejecting their offer of numbness. Today she welcomed the agony of her grief, needing to etch each moment of this day in her brain, to forever remember burying her child, not look back on it like some vague bad dream.

Richard's solid bulk supported her on one side, his contorted face a mirror of her own. Her father's smaller wiry figure held her up on the other, the smell of his Old Spice aftershave a familiar comfort. If either walked away, she was sure she would collapse, unable to hold her own weight under the crush of reality.

Chelsea and Hannah stood beside their father, clutching bunches of soggy tissues, their faces streaked with tears. Richard's daughters were distraught. They'd adored their baby brother from the moment he was born, cradling him, cuddling him, delighting in their games. And Theo had found these two beautiful angels enchanting, his big sisters who appeared from time to time bearing gifts and promises of fun.

Their mother's arms rested lightly on their shoulders. Victoria's upbringing in a wealthy family had left her well-equipped to navigate even the most delicate of situations with tact. She had discreetly supported the girls over the last few days, while not intruding on the family's grief. It probably wasn't normal to consider your husband's ex-wife a good person, but Sarah did, and couldn't help but be thankful for her quiet presence.

Just as she was grateful for the young woman who approached them now. Seeing her in the street, no one would pick out attractive thirty-year-old Kelly Foster as a funeral director. They'd assume her a lawyer or a banker from her conservative dark suit, not the heir to her family's business that had delivered most of the former residents of Wakefield to their final resting place. She'd been a quiet, capable guide on this journey, helping Sarah and Richard through the last decisions they would ever make for their son.

Kelly held a wicker basket brimming with flowers. Bright colours, red and orange, sun bursts of yellow, happy colours, exactly as Sarah had asked. Her hand gravitated to a vibrant sunflower, like a smile on this dark day. She clasped it to her as if trying to infuse it with every last ounce of love, crushing the stem with the force of her thoughts. As she stepped forward to let it drift onto the tiny coffin where her child would rest next to the grandmother he'd never known, she had the sensation of falling. Were her unsteady legs failing her?

Her father's grip on her waist loosened at the very moment she needed his steady support more than ever. And then she comprehended it wasn't her falling, but him. Noel Mitchell crumpled to the ground, clutching his chest. Sprawled there, his face pale, drenched with sweat, Sarah froze in horror. Others sprang into action. Her sisters surged forward, falling to their knees, Vivienne clutching his hand, Katrina, a nurse, wrestling with his tie.

"Heart attack, someone call an ambulance!" Katrina barked, before drawing on her training, methodical in her actions as if this wasn't her father's puny chest she pounded on. The steady rhythm of the compressions and her grunts of effort were audible above the hushed murmurs of the crowd. To Sarah, it was as if she had a whole handful of Doctor Gordon's pills on board, observing the scene in front of her through a gauzy curtain. Close enough to see, but not touch.

Within minutes, the ambulance screamed up to the cemetery gates, turning in to cross the manicured lawn at a more sedate pace. The local paramedics leapt out, faces she recognised, drawn with tension as they assessed the scene. What a terrible job, she thought. Most call outs would be to someone they knew. One took over from Katrina, while another produced a defibrillator. The mourners respectfully dropped back, leaving only the family clustered tight, shielding Noel from view, as the woman applied the paddles, the fragile-looking body shuddering at each pulse, but not moving of its own volition.

Sarah caught the solemn glances between the paramedics, saw Katrina's resigned expression. As they loaded him gently into the ambulance, Sarah knew what they knew—her father was dead. Noel had left them, journeying to be with his wife and grandchild, leaving her behind clasped in Richard's strong arms, wondering if she could survive this day.

## CHAPTER 32

## Falling

## Richard

Wellington, New Zealand – August 2016

She was unreachable. Richard's wife had removed herself to a place he could not follow. When he closed his eyes, his dead child was more present to him than this flesh and blood woman. Theo's still babyish laugh, shimmering eyes, tousled curls, the sticky hands clutching his, the comfortable weight in his arms—all of these he could summon at will. But his efforts with Sarah had proved futile. He was unable to retrieve her from the place she now inhabited. It was as if she existed in some desolate parallel universe.

Lowering himself gently onto the bed, he placed the steaming coffee on the cabinet. Her eyes snapped open. The tablets seemed to have this effect on her. She slept deeply, untroubled by restless nightmares like those that plagued him. And then she would lurch back into sudden wakefulness, unlike the way he inched his way slowly and painfully into each new day.

"I'm going soon. There's coffee there for you."

"Thank you." Her voice was flat, a brittle mechanical edge to it. He reached for the curtains. Outside, the wind flung droplets of rain like pebbles at the glass. "Don't," she said. "Too bright."

It wasn't a bright day at all, but he quietly complied. He approached the conversation gently. Other times he'd tried to be strong with her, but she'd simply pushed back in equal measure. It was the only time he'd glimpsed the old Sarah. When she refused to budge even an inch towards dealing with their loss.

"I can call back for you later on if you like. That's if you want to come with me."

This was his fourth appointment with the counsellor. He was grateful for Paul, who'd nudged him in that direction. While Richard had always sought advice, always known it made sense to draw on expertise, in the past he'd only applied it to work. It had taken an enormous leap of faith in his old friend's wisdom to phone the number Paul had slipped into his hand, make the appointment, and then invite a stranger into his own private hell.

Strangely, once sitting in Laura Kerslake's office, it hadn't been so difficult to accept. Paul, Camilla, Josephine—even Gwen—each of them had taught him that sometimes another person had the knowledge and skills that you lacked. It wasn't a weakness to admit that. Smart people used others when they couldn't do it on their own. And this—well, nothing in his life had prepared him for these last three months. This he could not do on his own.

But Sarah couldn't, or wouldn't. Inside her, she raged at the unfair hand dealt to them. That was normal. In his own way, he had done the same. But her anger spilled over, directed towards him at times, as if it was totally unreasonable of him to ask anything of her.

"No, Richard. No."

"Sarah, please, if you won't do it for yourself, please, do it for me. I love you, Sarah, but I can't save both of us. I can't even save myself." He was playing every card he had. She ignored his pleading.

"I said no. I don't need anyone else to make me face up to the facts of my life. Theo's gone. We lost him. You forget, I've been through this before. And I know how to find my way back. I did it with mum, and I can do it now."

"OK, OK," he said, backing off from what could quickly escalate into an argument.

What he couldn't make her see was this was not the same as before. The loss of her mother had been sudden, unexpected, unnecessary. Her father's death sudden too. Losing Theo had been all of those things. But the crucial difference was Sarah had been able to channel her anger and blame for her mother's death towards another. She could blame the carelessness of an American tourist for taking Ellen from her. She could blame an ageing body finally giving up for her father's loss. She placed the blame for Theo's death squarely on herself. She'd sobbed in his arms, her body wracked with the pain that engulfed both of them. But from that first day, she had looked to herself as the one responsible:

"I should have checked that his bedroom door was latched."

"If only I hadn't fallen off to sleep."

"How could I have forgotten about the back door?"

She wouldn't accept his equal culpability in the situation.

"I am his mother, damn you," she'd flung at him. "It was *my* job to protect him."

With Laura's careful guidance, he'd faced it—an undeniable crippling guilt that they shared, blaming themselves, blaming each other. That was what needed to be brought into the open. While painful, taking it out and examining it made it a little more bearable and gave him hope that one day he could move beyond it. He feared Sarah never would. She was determined to shoulder the blame on her own, and had convinced herself that if he didn't already, he would grow to hate her for it—and leave. And he was starting to wonder if she was right.

CHAPTER 33

Apart

# Sarah

Wellington, New Zealand – May 2017

THE FAILURE OF HER marriage caught Sarah by surprise. She'd always assumed that relationships ended in an explosion, like the death throes of a distant sun, burning ever more brightly, violent angry flares increasing in size, until it could no longer bear the instability, going out in a blazing supernova, before imploding leaving only a small black sadness.

She would never have predicted that a relationship between two head-strong people, who'd butted heads regularly, unafraid of conflict, knowing that they'd always work through it, could simply fade away. But their marriage disintegrated in slow, painful steps, ending with a whimper. She realised it was over when all possibility of salvage was gone.

After Theo's death, she had built an emotional wall, higher and more impenetrable than Richard's. If only in this desperate act of self-preservation, she'd thought to create a small hidden door connecting the two of them, leading to a place where they might meet, share their grief and help each other understand it. She didn't blame Richard. He had tried, but it was she who'd shut him out.

And in his own attempt at self-preservation, Richard had thrown himself back into work, jetting off on business trips where normally he would have dispatched others. He'd always hated it when the company took him away from her, from them. Once Theo was gone, it seemed he wanted nothing but to flee.

She understood his reasons. Her dark curls and wide mouth must serve to conjure up images of their lost child, as his blue eyes and smooth olive skin did for her. Once, it had been a wondrous thing to look at the features of her lover and marvel at how they were imprinted on the face of their child. Now, it served only to emphasise that they would never look upon his face again.

In a few short weeks, it would be a year since that morning, when she'd last hugged her sweet baby to her, soothing his grizzles with a kiss on that tousled head. A year since she'd watched him tumbling into sleep, cheeks flushed from the warmth of a blanket cocoon. A year in which her love for Richard had been tested and failed.

Standing and looking back at her marriage from the outside, as she now could, Sarah admitted that in the early days she'd simply been in love with the idea of Richard. He made her feel safe, but able to take risks. He accepted her as she was, but challenged her to be more. She'd always thought that over time, it had grown into a proper, deep love that would withstand anything. Now she wondered if she had been wrong.

These past years, entwined in the love of their child, perhaps they had been lulled into mistaking that for love for each other. Without Theo, their marriage may well have ended, anyway. That's what she tried to tell herself.

The unpalatable alternative was that she'd destroyed it, by the carelessness of losing Theo, the one thing that held them together, and then gone on to neglect her husband, absorbed in her own guilt and grief.

Mel saw it at once, from the moment Sarah swung open the apartment door. Sarah had made a genuine effort too, as she responded to the intercom with a calm voice, but there was no hiding it once face-to-face with someone who knew her so well.

"How did this happen? Why didn't you tell me?" Mel was incredulous.

Sarah had also shut her out, the only other person who might have helped her through. She'd bluffed her way through Mel's weekly phone calls, not hinting that her world was falling apart. She hung her head, not wanting to face her friend, ashamed that she'd locked her out precisely as she'd locked Richard out of the true heart of herself.

The tears fell, and she was grateful for the reassurance of Mel's bony embrace. Still whip-thin and delicate, despite having borne two children in quick succession and now living the indolent life of an ex-pat wife in Dubai. Her familiar hug was welcome. Sarah relaxed a little, sensing forgiveness in her friend's touch. She had killed her marriage with neglect. At least it hadn't had the same impact on their friendship.

"You know me," she said.

"Yes, always too bloody independent. But there are some battles you shouldn't fight on your own."

"Well, this one's lost. Richard moved out a week ago. One of the Crombie Norton companies owns the West Quay Hotel. He's living in the penthouse." Only two blocks away. So close, but it might as well be on the other side of the world, so great was the space between them. "But I'm not going to stay on here. You can help me look for somewhere else."

She couldn't face living in the waterfront apartment on her own. The memories were too raw. They'd turned this luxurious bachelor pad into a family home. But she'd shut the door forever on Theo's room, with its pistachio green walls, shelves of toys, a rainbow floor rug. She couldn't go in there without seeing images of his smile-dimpled face, careful hands building towers of blocks and zooming cars around imaginary racetracks. And the rest of the house was no better. Too many memories. She didn't have to explain that to Mel. Her friend simply accepted her need to recreate her life.

"I can understand that. It must be so hard. How about I give Olivia a call?" Mel suggested gently. "She's bound to have something on her books."

"OK, sounds like a good place to start."

Their university friend Olivia, teacher trained like Mel, had recently reinvented herself as a hotshot real estate agent. And Olivia wouldn't need to be told the details. She knew what Sarah had been through this past year. She'd be perfect.

"Hey but I don't want to take up all of your holiday. Four weeks will go fast."

Mel had already used one of her two paid-for annual airfares to rush to the funeral. Sarah didn't want to commandeer all of her time now.

"Oh god, no, it will be a good excuse. Staying with Mum and Dad is already claustrophobic. And they're more interested in spending time with the kids than me."

She could see Mel carefully scrutinising her face, hoping the mention of her own two beautiful kids hadn't caused Sarah pain. She tried to keep the conversation cheerful.

"What about Tim?"

"Heading to his parents' place as we speak. Going to break the bad news that he's renewed his contract."

Sarah was a little sad at that. But she wouldn't begrudge her friend this opportunity. Tim's lucrative tax-free position as principal of an international school would set them up for life. Two years under their belt, they already had enough saved for a house. Another two and they could return here with a comfortable nest egg. It would be churlish of Sarah, who even now had Richard's millions behind her, to not support her friend's chance to get ahead.

"That's fantastic. Congratulations. So, another two years of maids and nannies."

"Yeah," Mel laughed. "You're not the only kept woman."

Then she stopped, her hand covering her mouth. It had been a running joke between the two of them, ever since Richard's pronouncement at their first meeting that pretty girls like Sarah never had to work. Sarah stretched out her hand, seeking to quell Mel's distress at her faux pas.

"Hey, it's ok. We may have parted ways, but Richard is happy to keep me in the manner to which I'm accustomed. Although I don't plan that to be forever. But the fact is, these last years, I dedicated everything to him and Theo. I have no money of my own. And walking away from the university—well, I have no career to earn any. So I don't feel bad about him helping me out. It won't be forever, only till I manage to get myself sorted."

"Any idea what you'll do?"

"Not really. You know, I always thought academia would be my whole life. I could phone up Gerald and beg for a position if there's any available. But somehow going back there—it's a step back to my old life, but it won't be my old life. No Theo, no Richard. I think it would be too painful."

Mel's lips quivered, holding back her own tears. She'd always been so empathic, feeling others' pain almost as deeply as her own. Sarah tried to move on the conversation, brightening her tone.

"However, I'm pleased to say that as of yesterday, I am employed. Only two days a week, but it takes me out of the house."

"Well, that's a start."

"Yeah and it's fun—I'm helping Ginny Brooking in her antique shop."

'The Time Traveller's Wife' was a mecca for antique hunters. Tucked away in the Aro Valley, it was a destination for anyone seeking a special piece, as long as they had plenty of money to spend. Sarah had been browsing in there, aimlessly filling yet another empty day, when Ginny mentioned she was currently tethered to the shop seven days a week. She was desperate for a new assistant. Sarah took it as a sign that her life wasn't a total disaster and within minutes, had a job.

"That's great, Sarah, a good thing. A step forward."

"Yes, I think so."

"OK, then let's take another one. I'll call Olivia," Mel said, pulling up the real estate agent's number on her phone.

## CHAPTER 34

## Full Stop

# Sarah

Wellington, New Zealand – September 2018

SARAH DALLIED IN THE foyer for a moment, going through the motions. Touched up her lipstick, bright red. At the age of thirty-seven, perhaps it was too young for her, but she didn't care. She liked its cheerful touch. Smoothed her hair a little. On a Hollywood A-lister walking the red carpet, it would suffice for a messy bun. On her, it just looked unruly.

She braced herself, clasped the large chrome handle, and swung open the heavy door. Inside, the room was warm, the hot air spouting from all the movers and shakers gathered. And there he was.

She hadn't been looking for him, but he was the first person she saw. In fact, she had hoped that he would have found an excuse to turn down the Blackwood's invitation. His hand rested casually around the waist of a young blonde-haired woman, the tips of his slender fingers lightly brushing her arse. The blonde was gushing all over him, pouty, filler-enhanced lips spitting out words of enticement. Good god, she had to be a similar age as when she'd met Richard. Younger than his daughters.

He wasn't paying attention to the flirtation, looking bored and preoccupied, his eyes scanning the room, and then meeting hers. And in that moment, she could feel it, the memory of his hand on *her* waist, sliding down in one smooth movement, cupping *her* arse. In her mind, she heard the rustle of a tumbling satin gown as it hit the floor.

A flood of nausea washed over her, and she dashed out of the room, struggling to remember the way to Claire's bathroom. She fell inside, grateful that no one else was present in the chilly marble expanse. Her breaths came heavy and panicky, echoing off the pristine walls. Staring in the mirror, her own wide eyes reflected the pain back at her.

She shouldn't have come. After all, Claire's daughter Abigail was nothing to her really, even though she'd known the girl for most of her life. She shouldn't have succumbed to Mel's subtle persuasion to attend the grand sixteenth birthday bash.

"It will be good for you to get out. Put on a nice dress."

"But he'll be there, won't he?"

"Maybe, maybe not."

"I've lived in this safe cocoon for so long. You know what it's like. I hang out in the sort of places where he wouldn't. Avoid the ones where he might be. To make a conscious choice otherwise frightens me."

It had been an act of self-preservation. To face Richard was to face the life she'd had and lost. The life where her husband loved her. Where he trusted her to care for their child. A life where this crushing guilt didn't exist.

"You're ready, Sarah. You can do this."

But she couldn't do this, even now two years on from the long, slow, painful disintegration of their marriage. She wasn't ready to see him, especially not with someone else. The door burst open. Damn, why hadn't she turned the lock?

Richard surged in, distress in his eyes, distress that only grew when he saw the state of her. Part of her wanted to fend him off, but most of her simply wanted him to hold her, erasing all the bad memories between them and allow her to pretend it was the beginning again. And she let him.

"Sarah, oh god, I'm so sorry that you had to see that."

He murmured in her ear, that same voice, that same touch of his breath on her neck. She was sobbing on his shoulder now, tears for herself, for him, for Theo, falling on the smooth expensive fabric of his jacket.

"It's OK. I know you need to move on. It's not reasonable for me to expect anything else." She fumbled with the words. That's what you were supposed to say when you saw your ex with another woman. She couldn't expect him to do otherwise. After all, she'd pushed him away.

"I don't want to move on." His voice was soft, gentle. "Certainly not with someone like her. You know what they're like. Girls like that. They only see money, power, status. You never saw that. You only ever saw me." He stroked her hair, allowing his fingers to catch in a curl, twirling it gently around a finger. Those old familiar mannerisms reassured her, and the sobs lessened. "How about I take you home?" he offered. "Let's get out of here. You and I have spent enough time with arseholes like this to waste any more."

She lifted her head to meet his eyes, and with a small nod, gratefully accepted his hand. They fled the house, making their escape without anyone intercepting them. In the safety of his car, they were almost at her house, when she realised she'd never told him where she lived. He knew without asking. It made her feel safe, knowing he'd quietly been keeping tabs on her.

# Richard

It would have been too easy. To simply take advantage of her vulnerability and satisfy the instant rush of desire ignited by her familiar body against his. But she deserved better than that. He wasn't a perfect man, but he was a better man than that.

Time gave perspective. And he was at ease with the realisation that while his earlier love for Sarah had borne no resemblance to the relationship he'd had with Victoria, now his second marriage was over, it had reached a similar place as the first.

It had been a wild ride, and an unexpected one, admitting to himself that he could fall so hard and so fast and so undisputedly in love with a woman. But it had flared instantly, blazed brightly, and now he was left with the quietly glowing embers.

What remained wasn't bad. His feelings for her now were warm and comfortable. There was fondness, a nostalgia for the good times of their shared life. There was an immense gratitude for the child she'd given him. There was still an overwhelming need to make sure she was OK. He'd never ever let her want for anything, never deny her anything it was in his power to give. He still wanted to protect her. But his love had been through the furnace and came out the other side, much altered.

He pulled up outside her home, confident that he could simply follow her inside, sit and talk with her like a friend, and walk away with only a touch of sadness that they weren't still together.

# *Sarah*

Sarah made him coffee, an Americano, exactly how he liked it. The aroma of it drifting between them anchored his presence: Richard here, in her house.

They sat and made small talk, as if this comfortable coffee and a chat between friends created a safe buffer between now and their earlier emotionally supercharged meeting. He talked of the girls, Hannah with a successful law career and a partner (but no talk of a wedding) and Chelsea off on her OE, currently backpacking in South America.

She told him how much she loved the antique shop, and the thrill of new finds in the dusty estate sales she frequented. She sensed he knew the depth of her gratitude for his help in making it her own when Ginny had grown bored with the business.

"I'd better go," he said, when the old Victorian clock on her mantelpiece chimed eleven. "Early flight tomorrow—Auckland then Singapore."

"Oh, Richard," she chided.

"Yeah, I know, I know. But I promise, I am close to calling time on it. Give me six months, and the only bit of me in Crombie Norton will be my name on the door. And they can change that too if they like. I'll be beyond caring."

"You know what? I'm going to call you up in six months and check."

He laughed at that. "OK, you do that. The thought of being told off by you is still enough to motivate me in the right direction."

They stood face-to-face, as if unsure how to say goodbye. There had been so many goodbyes over the years, but there had been no final goodbye to their marriage.

"I wasn't going to go to that party tonight," she said, looking into his eyes, "I was terrified of seeing you, of this. How stupid I was. Thank you Richard. It was exactly what I needed."

"Me too," he said. "At first when I looked up and saw you there, well, all I could think of was how much I regretted being too polite to tell Jeffrey Farmer's girlfriend to piss off and leave me alone."

"*His girlfriend?*"

"His girlfriend." Richard's smile was rueful. "Yeah, I know she's young enough to be his daughter. And she seems to think draping herself over all the other men in the room is going to scare him into asking her to marry him before one of them does."

Things hadn't changed much over the years. Same old crowd, same old nonsense.

"Well," she said, "although I could have done without seeing her in action, I have no regret about seeing you."

He took her hand, softly stroking the finger that no longer held a wedding ring. Just as his own hand was bare. His voice was low and gentle.

"Sarah, I know what we had is broken. And I don't know that we could fix it even if we tried. But Sarah, despite how it ended, I will *never* regret you."

He kissed her gently, not with passion but with lips tender and comforting, and she once again felt that sense of safety. That although he wasn't in her life, her life was better for having had him in it.

"And I'll never regret you, Richard."

She probably wouldn't call him in six months. It was best that way. But it was good to see him.

After watching his car glide away below, Sarah grabbed a tumbler and poured herself a whisky for old times' sake. Alone in her Thorndon bungalow, she sipped at it, turning over the complex flavours in her mouth, thinking of the complex man, his great passion for creating this spirit and the passion they had shared, their beautiful boy.

The warmth of the alcohol crept through her body, stretching to the extremities, at the same time bringing with it an unexpected peace. This was what it meant when they talked about closure. Perhaps, in a strange way, this disastrous night was exactly what she'd needed, to put a full stop on her marriage, and be open to what the next sentence of her life story might be.

CHAPTER 35

Her Ladyship

## Sarah

Four years later, Wellington, New Zealand – June, 2022

THE CITRUS YELLOW CAR was a joy to drive. Even on the repetitive daily commute, it lifted Sarah's mood as she wove around the hilly outskirts of the city before dropping down into the centre where the day's work awaited her. To her amusement, the car was a source of interest to groups of young men who she sometimes found clustered around it, disciples of a cult previously unknown to her. Apparently, the wee Mazda's rotary-engine heart was also a thing of joy to them.

And so it was with a feeling of lightness she drove into work, despite it being a grey Wellington Monday morning. Mondays always brought a sense of excited anticipation, as she threaded her way through the city streets, inching steadily towards her little shop, block by block creeping closer to the place that made her happy.

Today, however, being the annual Queen's Birthday public holiday, for once she wasn't buried in a line of cars. She had dithered about opening. But tossing up between a winter day at home alone and the thought of enticing whoever might be out to come and rummage through her treasures, the decision was easy. She loved watching the spark of curiosity that these special things she handpicked brought to others. Even if they didn't buy, she enjoyed seeing visitors engage with the objects and their stories.

Turning onto Cuba Street, the lights ahead turned red, and she used the moment to flick on the radio. As usual, she also used this opportunity to finish her daily makeup routine. She weighed her appearance in the mirror. Eyes more amber than brown reflected back at her. While the colour may have lacked the wow factor, they were still her best feature. They elevated a fairly ordinary face to one that could be considered pretty. Large and well proportioned, fringed with long dark lashes and topped with a natural arch of eyebrow that many women spent hours in the chair at a brow bar to achieve. The quick dash of brown eye pencil, already deftly applied from years of daily practice, magnified them even more. She snatched up a peachy pink lipstick from the selection she kept in the centre console. Katy Perry's Kitten Collection: Miaow Pink. It was her current favourite. So what if the name was a little immature, no doubt reflecting the singer's tween audience. It set off her complexion well and made her full lips stand out without dominating her face.

As she drew the careful outline of her lips, she was half listening to the news on the radio. The first story today was predictably those who had made the Queen's Birthday Honours list. And there he was: Richard Norton, for services to business and philanthropy. Sir Richard Norton. She sat paralysed for a moment, not registering that the light had gone green. A honk from the solitary car behind her jolted her into action and she surged forward through the intersection.

Hearing his name uttered aloud still had the power to catapult her back into the past. They'd set out with so much hope, like a bold, brave, abstract painting, the two of them pushing back against the constricts of the corporate world and the vacuous life of capital city society. But after Theo's death, grief had erased so much of what they'd been, their own withdrawal inwards smudged other parts, while ugly grey layers of emptiness washed over what little was left. Now even six years on, hearing his name, or worse, seeing him, might still take her straight back to the pain, something she struggled to bear.

Still in shock, she pulled into the car park behind her shop. She sat for a moment with a nauseous knot whirling in her stomach. It was as if he could appear at any moment and her life would spiral downward again. Keeping Richard out of her life was an act of self-preservation. Despite the city being small, she moved in different circles, never having to face him and the memories that came with it. Without him, she could simply think of Theo as he was, forever captured in a bubble of blissful love and happiness. With Richard, there was the vicious pain of their shared loss.

As she climbed out of the car, the legendary Wellington wind snatched at her hair. Long brown tendrils wrapped themselves across her face and she caught them up, roughly tucking them behind her ears. She was glad that she had resisted the advice that a woman of her age should succumb to a shorter style. At least she could scoop her wayward hair up and secure it from the windy fingers that clutched at everyone in this seaside city.

Once inside the shop, she snapped into the familiar routine of opening up. Going through the motions of turning on the computer and organising the display at the front door was unfailingly soothing. So much so that by the time she finished, the earlier inner turmoil had ebbed away. In fact, the shock of the news now seemed to unlock something in her. A mood of decisive determination that from here on in things were going to change. As she bustled around the shop adjusting a cushion here and rearranging a rug there, she caught sight of herself in the exquisite Victorian looking glass she had acquired last week. It could have come straight out of Alice In Wonderland. She stopped to return the gaze of the woman in the mirror.

Lady Sarah Norton stared back at her and then broke into a broad grin. His reluctance to divorce her had unexpectedly delivered her a title. The ridiculousness of the situation turned the grin into a giggle, and the giggle spilled over into full on laughter. She collapsed into an antique rattan chair and laughed till the tears trickled down her face and threatened to ruin her makeup.

The shop door swung open. Two women paused in the entrance, gushing over an elaborately carved hall settle. She'd placed it there strategically, hoping to catch her customers' attention the moment they stepped inside. Today, it also bought her just enough time to stifle the laughter and paste on a composed and welcoming face.

She loved Mondays. But this week she had a feeling Tuesday was going to be even better. On Tuesday, she would phone her lawyer friend to make an appointment, and set in motion what she should have done before now. She was happy for Richard; the accolades deserved for his business acumen and generosity. But it was time for her to divest herself of Sir Richard Norton and her unexpected title. And in doing so, her life could take another leap forward into the future.

———

Life was a strange thing. She wondered if it was random coincidence, or was there some grand master plan that brought people to the same place at the same time? These were the thoughts that invaded Sarah's head as she sat at the intersection of Cuba and Vivian Street that Tuesday morning. Almost without fail, each morning, as she drove along this street, the same three people shared this time and space with her. To pass the time, and as an outlet for her overactive imagination, she'd attributed a name and invented a backstory for each of them.

Stationary in the cycle lane beside her was Edith, balancing her heavy step-through bike. Adorned with a large wicker basket and sporting a bell, it looked ancient. She'd chosen the woman's old-fashioned name as a nod to her mode of transport and her dowdy attire, and because she bore a striking resemblance to Lady Edith of 'Downton Abby'. Sarah was a massive fan of the period drama. This Edith had a wardrobe of sedate suits: knee-length skirts in tweed fabrics, matching jackets; not the most suitable outfit for cycling in the city, although she had chosen sensible tan leather brogues for her feet. Sarah had at first imagined Edith as a librarian, but rejected that as too cliché, instead settling for a nanny, a cross between Mary Poppins and Mrs Doubtfire.

Stopped at the lights in front of her was Brock, the thumping of his HSV Holden audible even inside her own car. Brock had named himself. The custom plate on his car proclaimed him as a fan of the legendary Peter Brock, an Australian motor racing idol, and one of her father's heroes. She'd met him once. The real Peter Brock. That first summer after she'd hooked up with Richard. It was a corporate event in Melbourne, and as she shook the great man's hand, she'd wished it had been her father standing there, not Richard. The meeting was wasted on him. Her father had been beyond excited that his daughter had actually spoken to Brockie, making her repeat a blow by blow account of the evening whenever an oppor-tunity arose. The first time she'd glimpsed this Brock, a slightly balding fifty-something, he'd revved the engine a little, and flashed her a smile of pride in his vehicle, while casting an admiring glance at her own.

Then in her side mirror, she caught sight of Hillary striding up the street, his usual purposeful expression on that weather-beaten face, ruddy in the early morning chill, and his breath illuminated by the first rays of sunlight. His arms swung rhythmically, two walking poles in his hands. He wore a Gore Tex jacket, heavy boots, and long woollen socks pulled up over the cuffs of his pants to seal them tight. He'd topped off his outfit with a hand-knitted hat that sported a jaunty pompom. This man appeared to be of a similar vintage to the one she'd named him after—Sir Edmund Hillary, national hero, conqueror of Mount Everest and the man who adorned New Zealand's five-dollar note. Sarah had invented numerous stories why her Hillary should walk the streets of Wellington dressed in mountaineering gear each morning at this time.

These last three weeks, her trio had grown to a quartet. Every morning at this exact time, the newcomer emerged from the coffee shop on the corner, climbed into a jaunty Jeep and sidled into the lane, sometimes beside her, sometimes ahead, other days behind. Each day they shared a part of the journey together, before she peeled off into the sidestreet, while he continued on to places unknown.

She didn't know why she'd been drawn to this man. He had a shock of the darkest auburn hair that hinted at once being a vibrant true red, but was now the colour of the chestnuts she'd gathered in the park in London. Dressed for the outdoors, but not as extreme in his attire as Hillary, he was still an anomaly in this city of suits and ties. She had almost decided on a name for him. Grylls. He had the look of a Bear Grylls about him. She could picture him thrown into the wild, surviving by drinking his own urine and eating deer droppings.

The first time he'd caught her staring at him, he'd flashed a friendly smile and now whenever their eyes met, he always waved in greeting. She was tempted to make a sign that said 'Meet me for coffee tomorrow?' and hold it up to her window. Maybe tomorrow she would.

## CHAPTER 36

8:53 AM

# Sarah

Wellington, New Zealand · June, 2022

WEDNESDAY, AND THERE SHE was again. Same place, same time, same people. Sarah peered at the dashboard clock as if willing it to make the minutes go faster and trigger the green light. The council's recent change to the traffic signal pattern, for some unfathomable reason, created a frustrating, unnecessary extra pause in the cycle at this intersection.

There was a V8 rumble behind, and a glance in her rear-view mirror confirmed that, as suspected, Brock had parked his prize Holden on her bumper.

In the lane beside her, Grylls—yes, she was definitely going to call him that—eased his vehicle to a halt. She peeked across and caught him looking back at her. She smiled and gave a tentative wave, then forced her eyes back onto the road ahead, feeling embarrassed, hoping he didn't think she was some weirdo, smiling and waving at someone she didn't know. That was the problem. When your overactive imagination invented a backstory for someone in sufficient detail, your mind accepted it as fact.

*"And it's 8.53 on a wet, windy Wellington morning. Drive times were looking pretty bad there for a while, but coming back down now. Here's Queen's 'Bohemian Rhapsody' taking us to the news on the hour, and after that, we have Rochelle keeping you company as you get into your workday."*

The announcer's voice was smooth and upbeat. Essential for a drive-time radio host, jollying along the inhabitants of the capital city as they headed to their jobs as bureaucrats and bankers. Hearing the first beats of a favourite song, she turned up the music and smiled, taking it as a sign that today would be a good day.

Hillary strode up to the kerb, gave the pedestrian cross button a cranky thump, and then scanned for approaching traffic. Seeing none, he muttered to himself and, ignoring the flashing red man on the opposite traffic light, resumed his trek.

She glimpsed movement in her wing mirror, as Edith wobbled to a halt in the cycle lane. She didn't look like a rule breaker, but the daily holdup at these lights had obviously worn her down, too. Judging the absence of oncoming traffic to be a convenient opportunity, she pedalled across the intersection.

Sarah weighed up doing the same. After all, although she too had been a stickler for the rules, this was ridiculous. Her fingers dropped to the gear lever, ready to nudge it into first, but the strange small vibration that issued from it caused her to pause.

It began as a gentle, almost imperceptible rocking, like a mother's hand soothing a baby in the cradle. Within seconds, it became a soft rolling motion, enough for her to grasp what was happening. Earthquake.

She'd never become accustomed to their frequency in this part of the country. It wasn't only the unnerving sensation as the floor beneath your feet undulated. Or the imminent threat of danger as bookshelves teetered. No, it was the question that pushed its way to the front of every Wellingtonian's mind: was this the big one? The scientists' warnings echoed in her brain: "It's not if, it's when."

As the rocking transformed into a violent, insistent shaking, she decided that when was now. Another fact leapt to mind: if you can feel the shaking in your car, then it's bad.

The first falling bricks danced on the road in front of her. A few rained on the roof of her car, a slow staccato beat at first, increasing in intensity to a thundering crescendo. A cloud of dust showered onto the windscreen. The ominous rumble, as the earth protested being ripped apart, was drowned out by a roar as the building beside her cascaded in a frightening waterfall of brick and metal.

She instinctively huddled into a ball, her hands thrust protectively over her head. Her world imploded with a deafening scream. The scream of metal intensified as the roof of the car collapsed under the avalanche of rubble. The scream of fear erupted from deep inside her as she grasped she was about to be crushed beneath it.

She struggled to breathe, the cloying dust choking whatever small airspace remained in the car. She squinted her eyes shut against the prickling cloud engulfing her. Sarah descended into darkness and welcome silence. Even the voice in her head that had told her she was about to die now quieted.

Scrabbling sounds and distant muffled voices triggered a faint hope in her newly conscious brain. She registered that the closer, small whimpering sound came from her throat. Through crusty slitted eyes, awareness of her surroundings pushed forward, and with it recollection of how she'd come to be here.

Panic overtook her. She gasped small rapid breaths, even though each one dragged dusty air into her already clogged lungs, and she coughed, trying to clear it. She lay like a discarded puppet, limbs heavy and useless. Now and then, slight tremors wracked her body, as if some unseen hand tugged at her marionette strings.

Her rational mind resurfaced and now, back online, its command centre issued directions:

*Slow your breathing—in for four 1-2-3-4 out for four 5-6-7-8.*

*Keep calm. Help is here.*

*Don't try to move. Keep still or you might do more damage.*

Outside, other voices were in charge. "I've a crowbar in the back there. Might need it once we can uncover the door. Can't see it just swinging open after all that lots been on it." A man's voice, calm, practical.

"Yeah, good idea man, go get it. And you, give us those poles. My hands are buggered already. These bloody bricks are sharp." Another man, not a Kiwi, a different accent. Scottish, she thought.

"There's a first aid kit in my pack. Let me get it out. It could be useful until the ambulance arrives." The voice was thin and reedy, the weariness of age lying across it.

In the background, distant sirens whined. They seemed to move away. They weren't coming for her.

"I can see a hole in the windscreen. Do you think if you gave me a leg up, I might be able to talk to her? See if she answers?" A soft woman's voice.

"Yeah, good idea. Come round, I'll help you. And if she's conscious, keep her talking, try to keep her calm till we get into that door."

With a small thud, Sarah felt, not saw her arrival. An unusual hood ornament, she thought.

"Hello in there. Can you hear me?"

Sarah's voice was small. "Yes," she croaked. "I can hear you."

"Oh, that's good, so good. Well, you don't need to worry now. These guys will have you out soon. What's your name then?"

"Sarah."

"Hi Sarah, I'm Janice. I know your little car. See it every day. Not sure if you've seen me, but I'm riding my bike to work around this time."

"Edith," she replied, allowing herself a small smile.

"Edith? No, I'm Janice. Now I can hear you're having a bit of trouble talking, so let's leave that to me for now. I'll tell you a bit about me, and then when we have you out of here, you can tell me your story. Does that sound OK?"

"OK," she said, as she relaxed and let Janice's sweet storytelling soothe her distress.

"Now, Sarah, I want you to keep looking at me. They're going to break the passenger window." She fixed her eyes on Janice's kind, homely face. Even though she knew it was coming, she jumped as the crash of a heavy object shattered the window, and a light rain of glass splattered her hair. "Good girl. Now sit tight, they're almost through."

A graunching sound drew her attention, and she turned her head away from Janice's voice towards the broken window. The door frame surrounding it buckled. She could see the shapes of people, and as her vision stabilised, she could even discern the expressions on their faces as they strained with the effort of levering the door open. It succumbed with a painful sound, like fingernails on a blackboard. A man climbed into the passenger's seat, and she recognised the face. Grylls. Of course. He would know what to do in an emergency.

"Hi there. Sarah isn't it?"

She'd listened to his Scottish accented voice barking orders, offering encouragement and muttering curses. Now seated shoulder to shoulder inside this damaged tin can, it was calm and friendly, as if they were standing in the coffee shop, making small talk. But his green eyes told a different story, worry written there. She nodded.

"OK Sarah, well, we're going to get you out of here. Now, first of all, a few questions."

She responded mechanically as he assessed her situation. Ruling out bleeding and neck injury, and discovering that she wasn't pinned by any of the damaged car, he unclipped her seatbelt, wrapped strong arms under her and edged backwards, twisting her one way and then the other, gently levering her from the cockpit sized space she'd been wedged inside, dragging her with him. As she emerged, she turned her face skyward. To simply be outside in the open air felt good, even though it was still laden with dust particles, like a brown fog.

Lowering her feet to the ground, it surprised her to find they could still support her, though the safety of his steady arms behind her was still welcome. Sensing she wasn't about to topple, he let them fall, and she turned to face her rescuers.

Hillary's crinkly smile, embedded in a gnarled face, gave the impression of a benign gargoyle. Brock, crowbar in hand, projected modest pride in a job well done. Edith—no, Janice—stood beaming with pleasure at the outcome, her plain face made beautiful by the warmth of her expression.

And of course Grylls, his face concerned, scanning hers, as if not fully convinced she was OK. Only he noticed the slight wobble and reached out, taking her by the hand to steady her. At his touch, she experienced the oddest sensation, a whisper inside her mind, a name.

"Calum," she said, giving voice to the thought.

His eyes widened a little, then lowered to her hand, coming to rest on the ring she wore. His fingers followed his gaze, lightly brushing over it. Although not one of the flashy baubles that Richard had insisted on showering her with, the silver band with its interlaced pattern and tiny thistle motifs was her favourite. Mel called it her Outlander ring, as it resembled the one described in her favourite series of books. She didn't even recall where she'd got it, but she loved that ring. And it was no fan token. From what she knew of antique jewellery, this piece might be as old as Jamie Fraser himself.

His eyes widened in confusion, mouth falling open as if to speak, but the roar of an aftershock swept away any words.

He grabbed her, pulling her close, then threw her to the ground alongside the car. His body curled protectively across hers as a curtain of rubble descended over them.

## Chapter 37

## Ward 6

# Sarah

Wellington, New Zealand – June, 2022

Sarah opened her eyes, still gritty and encrusted with dust, to find a blurry figure sitting beside her. As the person came into focus, from the spiky blonde halo of hair, she knew it was Mel. She tried to speak, but only a rasping croak emerged from her throat. But it was enough to alert Mel that she was awake.

"Hey there, how you feeling?"

Sarah lay for a moment, mentally reaching out to the extremities of her body: arms, hands, fingers, legs, ankles, toes, tentatively testing each in turn for pain. She found far less than she'd expected for someone who'd been practically buried alive.

"Not too bad," she said, her voice still cracked, her mouth dry. "Is there water?"

"Yeah sure, here." Mel held a paper cup of tepid water to Sarah's lips.

"Give it here, I can do it Mel," she said, forcing out more words, and hoping to prove to herself that she could do something as simple as drink.

"Go easy then. Don't gulp it." She obeyed, even though her body was screaming in thirst. "Well," Mel went on, "there's a reporter camped out there waiting for news of you. Do you think I should put him out of his misery? Tell him you're awake and talking, and he can bugger off and leave you alone?"

"That's an excellent idea," she said, sipping the water, grateful for its soothing effect on her throat. Through the window, she noted the daylight slipping away. She'd lost the better part of a day.

Mel ventured into the corridor and returned with a satisfied smile. "Great. That's done. Now they know everyone's safe, they can send their story out."

"The others? They're all OK?" She needed to hear it was true.

"Yeah, all good. You remember what happened?"

Sarah sat grasping at threads of memory. "It's still hazy."

"Well, today Sarah Norton, you were in the wrong place at the wrong time. It was a 4.5 earthquake, fairly shallow, big enough but not so big to cause major damage. Except you happened to be stopped beside the one building in that entire block they hadn't finished strengthening after the last one."

"Not my lucky day, huh? Not a good day to buy a lottery ticket?"

"Maybe it is. You made it out alive. Twice. They'd just pulled you out of the car when the aftershock brought some more of the building down."

"Yeah, I remember," she said, but it was still vague. Who had been there? Brock—yes, he'd been holding a crowbar, looking proud of himself. And Hillary, offering medical advice. And then Edith—no Janice, her name is Janice—was she close by still? And…"Grylls?" she blurted out. "What about Grylls?"

"Who the hell is Grylls?"

"The one who pulled me out of the car. He was right next to me. He made it?"

"He certainly did. If it wasn't for his quick thinking, throwing you and him in against the car, you'd probably both be dead."

"So he's OK?"

"Yeah, he took the brunt of the stuff that came down in that second collapse. He was injured, but I asked a nurse about him. She said he's doing well. His name's not Grylls though," she said, looking puzzled. "Don't know where you got that from."

"It's a long story. So who is he?"

Mel's eyes sparkled as if that was the question she'd been hoping for. "That's the exciting bit. Not every day you're rescued by none other than Calum MacFarlane."

"And who is Calum MacFarlane?" The name MacFarlane was familiar, of course—the mainstay in Richard's love affair with whisky. She searched back in her brain, but had no recollection of a Calum MacFarlane. "I don't know that name. Should I?"

"He only happens to be 'The Kilted Climber'. He has his own show on Netflix. Goes all over the world. Climbing. In a kilt." Mel's dreamy expression suggested she was a little besotted with the man. "If you haven't heard of knee porn, well watch one of his shows and you'll know what I mean."

"Oh," Sarah said, feeling a little pleased with herself. She'd correctly picked him as an outdoors type. But she'd not predicted the kilt. That was a unique concept. Sounded a bit chilly though, mountaineering in a kilt.

An hour later, she'd convinced Mel to go home and sort out her teenagers and husband. Sarah's ability to conduct a rational conversation and her half-decent attempt to eat the hospital dinner of insipid soup had eased Mel's concern. Now she sat propped up in bed, thumbing through the TV channels, seeking something to occupy her time. She avoided those offering news, not feeling ready to face the reality of what had happened to her today. There'd be enough time for that in the days to come. News people loved survival stories.

Instead, she fixed on an old replay of 'Friends'. Already immune to the constant trail of nurses and care assistants passing through her room, she didn't even look up when the door swung open. She wondered how anyone recovered in a hospital, when uninterrupted rest seemed impossible.

As her gaze drifted away from the TV for a moment, she caught sight of the approaching visitor: a man clad in a hospital gown, one arm bandaged up against his chest, the other trailing a drip on a stand. He made his way awkwardly across to her bed, where he dropped into the chair. She recognised the face. It was the last thing she'd seen before he'd flung her to the ground under the avalanche of rubble.

"Hi," he said, looking sheepish. "I'm probably not meant to be here, but I had to talk to you. I'm Calum."

"Yeah, I remember. It sounds like I owe you a massive thank you. Some quick thinking saved us both."

He flushed a little, dropping his head modestly. "Well, self-preservation is a pretty powerful instinct. Your good luck. In saving myself, I saved you."

"If you say so," she said, smiling at her reluctant hero.

"So, what's the verdict on your injuries?"

"Mild concussion, bruising on almost every part of my body." She was acutely aware of it, unable to position herself in the bed without some tender spot making its presence felt. "I'm going to look like one of those aliens in Avatar in a few days, blue from head to toe. And you? I see you've a bag of happy juice attached."

"Yeah, that's for this," he said, jerking his head towards his shoulder, then wincing. "It's OK for now while I'm full of drugs, but they reckon a break like this will cramp my style for a while." His shoulder must have taken the brunt of the avalanche of bricks, as he'd curled himself to protect her. "But for now, one little press of this." He flipped his hand over to show the rubber cone in his palm, a large red button in its centre. "Well, let's just say being here talking to you has a certain dreamlike quality about it."

"Ah, the woman of your dreams." She laughed. His casual expression disappeared. That was odd. But she didn't know this man. For him, there must be some unpleasant connotation attached to those words.

"You might say that," he said, caution in his voice. "Give me your hand."

That was odd, too. But she stretched out her right hand obediently, and he held it in his, rubbing his fingers across the silver ring, those green eyes scrutinising it carefully. She recalled seeing that same look right before the building had collapsed on them.

"Calum?" she asked, breaking him free of the thoughts that had captured him. "What is it?"

"No, you'd think me stupid." He dropped his chin and smiled up at her enigmatically. "It's nothing. Probably the drugs messing with my head. But I'd like to talk to you properly. You know, when they finally let us out of here. How about you and I have dinner?"

"Only if you let me pay. It's the least I could do."

"Only if you let me shout some champagne to toast our lucky escape today."

"Deal," she said.

The door flung open and this time it was a nurse, dismay written on her face. "So there you are, Mr MacFarlane," she said, with an exasperated tone. "Now, you know you shouldn't be out of bed. Let's get you back to your room and give Sarah some rest." And with a look that suggested it would be pointless to argue, she took Calum by his good arm and steered him towards the door.

"I'll be in touch," he called, looking back towards her with a grin, while ignoring the nurse, who was still muttering, clearly unimpressed that he'd strayed from his room.

Sarah lay back and closed her eyes, thinking that she'd been lucky in more ways than one today. The bruises might be a small price to pay for the unexpected good fortune at having Calum MacFarlane drop into her life.

## CHAPTER 38

## The Kilted Climber

# *Sarah*

Wellington, New Zealand – June, 2022

SARAH LOVED THIS GAWKY teenager perched on the side of her bed, stick-like legs protruding from a pleated tartan uniform skirt. Although Sienna lamented the height and lean build she'd inherited from her father, Sarah knew it held promise of the beautiful woman she would be in a few years' time.

Her fine blonde hair, so like Mel's, would be a crowning glory, not an annoying combatant that she struggled to contain in a school-regulation ponytail. The peppering of pimples that erupted without warning would disappear, leaving her with the porcelain doll skin of her mother. But you couldn't tell teenagers that. It was a brutal time for any young girl. Peer pressure seemed out of control these days in this Instagram world.

"You make sure you rest Auntie Sarah. Don't try to do too much. We want you well."

Sarah smiled at this admonishment, the words a replay of Mel's.

"Will do hun. Have a good day at school."

Sienna rolled her eyes. Her scowl at the mention of school conveyed disbelief in the likelihood of that happening. "Oh, yes, school's simply fabulous. I'm sure it will be wonderful," she said, dripping with teenage sarcasm as she flounced out of the room. Sarah tried not to laugh.

Mel and Tim's house, in a quiet Karori street, was ideal for a recovering patient. The tastefully restored bungalow, with polished matai floors clad in colourful rugs, oozed warmth and comfort. Sarah sat at the kitchen table, trying to drum up an appetite for the healthy Greek yoghurt and keto granola, while secretly longing for a bit of toast with butter and Marmite. However, knowing it was good for her, she persevered, spooning it down while checking her phone.

There were a couple of texts from Tandi, one a cheerful report on the shop, the other telling her to take her time and not hurry back. Tandi secretly loved being in charge, and Sarah was grateful that she'd found such an employee who loved the place like her own, and was in her own quirky way a persuasive salesperson.

Then, her healthy breakfast dispatched and with not-so-healthy, strong coffee in hand, she flipped open Mel's laptop and logged into her Gmail account. Nothing much there. Only the usual notices of estate sales, an upcoming auction wanting entries, and a few customer queries that the efficient Tandi would take care of.

Relaxed that all of her work life was under control, she opened a tab and set about a personal task that had been niggling at her for a couple of days. She was certain she'd never met Calum MacFarlane before, but there was still an unsettling familiarity about him. Richard had invested years and significant amounts of money in his Scottish passion project, saving MacFarlane's distillery from ruin and turning it into a business he was proud of. God, she probably still owned shares in it.

She remembered her one visit to Scotland fondly. Hamish was a grumpy old bugger at the best of times but she and Heather had got along well. And there was, of course, the New Zealand operation that he'd set up in Cromwell. She was curious about a possible connection between these MacFarlanes and her Calum MacFarlane. She smiled a little at that. Her Calum MacFarlane. He was certainly an attractive man, and she was looking forward to having dinner with him, not only because of their shared survival story.

Typing 'Calum MacFarlane' into the search bar, the computer proudly announced: 'About 7,510,000 results (0.62 seconds)'. Shit, he even had his own Wikipedia page.

Within an hour, she had a dossier of information on her rescuer. There was a brief mention that he was indeed the forty-three-year-old son of Hamish and Heather MacFarlane of MacFarlane's Distillery. A few articles mentioned his army career, including a medal for bravery in Afghanistan. It seemed he had a history of heroics. But most of the hits extolled his feats as 'The Kilted Climber', one going so far as to describe him as the "Scottish Bear Grylls". Looks like you were spot on Sarah, she congratulated herself.

Scrolling back to the top, she clicked on 'Images' and rows of pictures filled the screen. Head shots, profile shots, casual and formal. Calum Mac-Farlane was a good-looking man, whichever way you looked at him. With one click, a photo of him clad in his kilt exploded to fill the screen. Darn, Mel was right. Knee porn was a thing, perhaps her new favourite thing. She wondered whether he'd be sporting a kilt when they had dinner on Saturday night.

He wasn't. In fact, to onlookers, they would have seemed like any other couple on a dinner date. A dark-haired woman, still attractive even though she must be close to forty. Her hair hung in loose waves past her shoulders. She wore a splash of candy apple-red lipstick, emphasising sensuous lips. The man of a similar vintage opposite her, stood out from his shock of dark auburn-tinged hair, but even more remarkable was the compelling set of mossy green eyes, made all the larger by the dark lashes that fringed them, giving him a boyish wide-eyed expression.

When Sarah searched Calum's chiselled features, the high cheekbones, she could see a look of Heather MacFarlane and she told him so. And how she knew his mother.

"How is she? Although it was a long time ago, I remember she took me out riding. Of course, I disgraced myself and fell off."

"Mam's doing well. Her life took a turn for the better the day Hamish died. And mine. Best news I ever had when she rang to tell me that the bastard departed this world. He made my life hell, and hers."

Sarah hadn't heard that news. But more surprising was the bitterness in Calum's voice, referring to the man only by his name, no recognition as his father. She regretted asking after Heather and what it had unleashed in him. Obviously, that reflected on her face, and he offered reassurance.

"Hey it's OK, I'm good with it. You see, when he died last year, she found it in her to tell me something: Hamish wasn't my real father. The day he'd asked her outright, and she confirmed it, was the day my relationship with him changed. Back then, I was a confused eleven-year-old kid. How could my father switch overnight from loving me to despising me? But now I know."

"God, that must have been terrible," she said, thinking of her own father, unable to imagine what it might be like to lose that love.

"Yeah, he pretty much put me through years of hell for something that wasn't my fault. I could never understand how to please him. Pathetic the ways I tried. But he wrote me off the day she confessed to him. I was fighting a battle I could never win."

"So, is she keeping the business going?"

"For now. Jo Brodie—you probably met him, too?" She nodded, the name stirring a vague recollection of the distillery manager. Dispatched to New Zealand to get the second operation running. "He's been here ten years. Has a hankering for home. So he's going back to Scotland. He'll take charge again. I'm off to Cromwell next week to catch up with him."

There was an unsteadiness to these words, an odd look in his eyes, but she didn't probe. He'd already opened up on a vulnerable subject, and she didn't want to intrude further. She deftly switched the conversation to a less troubling topic, mentioning his Kilted Climber alter ego.

"Oh, you've seen it, have you?" he said, with a flash of pride, while still looking a little embarrassed, as if not totally comfortable with his fame.

"Ah, just a couple of episodes," she admitted. "My friend told me it's a must watch."

"Series 1," he said. "That first one is the best. All my favourite places in Scotland."

"OK," she said. "I didn't see much of Scotland when we visited, so I'll look forward to that."

"And the new one, Series 4, it's going to be right up there with the first. It's here in New Zealand."

"That's why you're here, then?"

"Yeah, filmed over the summer. Been back for a few weeks working with the post-production crew here in Wellington. It looks amazing. Your country is so like home—well, down South, anyway."

After two courses of the meal, most of a bottle of wine and an easy flow of conversation, one important topic lay untouched. It was as if they'd made an unspoken agreement to avoid addressing that which had brought them together. Didn't want to revisit the terrifying moment not much more than a week ago that had threatened to snuff out their lives with so much left unlived. Reluctant to relive the moment that would connect them forever.

"So how *are* you doing?' he asked. "Honestly. Not what you tell your friends and family, but what you feel when you're lying in bed at night, alone with your thoughts."

"Honestly—and I'm only telling you this—I'm still in shock. I've watched the news footage, read the reports. It doesn't feel like it's me. More like I'm observing someone else's near miss. And then I fixate on it, imagining that it wasn't a near miss. That I died there, and this is some weird half-life and at any moment, death's going to show up and whisk me away." Emotion pricked at her eyes. Her chest constricted, gripped by the fear she'd kept at bay. It coursed through her. She'd enjoyed her wine until then. But her hurried sip now tasted sour in her mouth. "And you?"

His face took on a slight tension, his lips a grim set, and he took a deep breath as if to prepare for the telling.

"You know, Sarah, I've nearly died three times. Once in Afghanistan, when our convoy blundered into a mine. Once on a mountain in South America, where my climbing party was caught in an avalanche. And then last week, with the roar of that building coming down upon us, I thought I—we—might die there."

She hung on his words, trying to suppress the nausea they evoked, the sick feeling that took hold every time she thought of that moment. She pushed back the bile rising in her throat, her body's reaction to the reminder that she'd come close to being extinguished.

He looked at her now, his eyes intent, willing her to fix her attention on him, to hear what he had to say.

"You know what they say, that your life flashes before your eyes?" She nodded, having heard it many times over. "It's true. Every one of those times, it was like a movie playing double-speed in my head. Not all of my life, but parts of it." He closed his eyes, recalling those disturbing film reels.

"But there's something more." He paused, as if taking stock of her, judging the impact of his next words.

"Each time it happened, the piece of my life that flashed before my eyes was a part I didn't remember. Like it was some other life. That alone is disturbing. But the thing that I can't comprehend—in every one of them—there was a woman." He stopped for a moment, and she saw his prominent Adam's apple pulse as he took a gulp of air. "And that woman was you. In that long moment, after I dragged you out of the car, when you stood there and looked at me, I thought, my god, here she is. And then the building came down."

"But we'd only just met?"

"Had we?" he said. "The last thing I remember before we were buried alive was you saying my name. How would you know my name if we'd just met?"

"You must have told me inside, in the car? Or I heard someone say it outside? After all, you're kind of famous. Someone there knew who you were. Called you by name."

"No," he said, his voice sure and steady. "No one there knew my name. Except you." His large hand stretched towards her, brushing aside the strands of hair that she always let flop over her forehead. She shivered, as with the lightest touch his fingertip drew a line, tracing the zigzag scar she'd had since she was six. The scar that was hardly noticeable, unless you looked closely. "And I...," he said, his voice almost a whisper. "I knew about this. The woman I saw...she had a scar, just here, just like you."

She reached up and grasped his hand, pulled it away, wanting to break the circuit. But then when he lowered it to the table, she reached for it again, clasping it tightly in hers, a sudden need to once more make tangible the link between them. He eased away from her grip, his fingers gravitating to her ring. A simple band of silver, embellished with interwoven thistles.

"And then there's this," he said, his eyes fixed intently on the ring. "Tell me about it. Where did you get it from?"

"You know—I don't remember."

She genuinely didn't remember buying the ring. But she first remembered having it in those strange days in London. When she'd been so desperate to hide the hole that had opened up in her life. A time where her only memories of over two weeks were those suggested to her by others.

"When you're married to someone who likes to shower you with jewellery, well, you end up with loads. There's hardly any that I could precisely say when and where I got it."

It was embarrassing to admit that she'd been that woman, lavished with expensive jewellery, luxury cars, designer clothes. That woman was a stranger to who she'd been before she met Richard and to who she was now.

"But I know where it didn't come from. Richard would never have bought me something like this. In fact, he teased me about wearing it. Asked why I bothered to put that on my finger when I had my choice of dozens of more expensive ones he'd bought. All I can say is I've had it for a very long time."

"Take it off," he said. She slid the ring off, balancing it on her palm. Was this some kind of trick? "Now, look inside." His voice had dropped to a whisper. "What's inside?"

She'd always focused on the patterned outer, loving the interlaced design created by some long ago silversmith's hand. Not modern and mass-produced, but crafted by someone who cared, took pride in the object. She held it up to the light of the candle that flickered between them, not expecting to see anything highlighted in its warm glow.

"Words," she said. "Unbelievable." How many times had she plunged her finger into the silver circle? How many times had she slid it off into the ruby velvet nest of her jewellery drawer? Curious now, she peered more closely, recognising the script. Not English, but Latin. She read the inscribed words aloud, Calum's voice echoing her own "In perpetuum et unum diem."

She looked up at him and he translated flawlessly, "Forever and a day."

"Forever and a day," she repeated.

"But how did you know? How could you?"

"Because I've seen it before. That ring is my mother's."

She spluttered with indignation now. "Are you calling me a thief? I certainly had no need to steal, not now and not then."

The cheek of the man. Yes, she couldn't remember where the ring came from. But she'd certainly remember if she'd stolen it.

"Look," he said, "I'm not saying that. But Mam inherited that ring—passed down from her grandmother and who knows how many others before her. She gave it to me years ago. Said to keep it. That, as she didn't have any daughters, she'd trust me to give it to someone special. Said I'd know when the right one came along. I presumed I'd put it into storage with all my stuff when the army posted me overseas. Not a good idea to be dragging family keepsakes from one scruffy barracks to another. But when I resigned, went back to civilian life—well, one day I remembered about it, but couldn't find it anywhere. I didn't have the heart to tell Mam I'd lost it."

"And now it's found."

She placed it on the white linen tablecloth between them. No matter how it had come to her, she didn't want to give it up. He may be its rightful owner, but she'd been its caretaker for all these years, and she'd miss the familiar glint on her hand. He picked it up, rolling it in his palm, closing his fingers over it, taking it back into his possession.

"I really like it. It's a favourite." Her voice came out whiny, like a small unhappy child. Well, she was unhappy.

"Liking it doesn't mean it's yours. And I still can't understand, if it is your favourite, that you'd have no idea about where it came from." She was annoyed, the taint of his questioning weighing uneasily upon her. Their pleasant evening had evaporated. "Sarah, you can have it back. I'm just intrigued."

"Take the bloody ring, Calum. I don't want it."

She was a little ashamed of herself, her tone snappish. Her disquiet at parting with the ring seemed disproportionate to its value. She couldn't fathom why handing it over had upset her so much. There was no doubt it was Heather MacFarlane's ring, and it was right to return it. But it had ruined the evening. Now all she wanted was to leave, shut the door on this unpleasant episode in her life and get back to normal. Begging off dessert, she called a cab and headed home alone.

But her brain wasn't prepared to let Calum MacFarlane go yet. Thoughts of him followed her to the house on the hill, invaded the pastel calm of her bedroom, disrupted her comfortable sleep, interrupted her dreams. That she should have his mother's ring was odd, but not beyond rational explanation. That he had wanted it back was not unexpected, although it made her angry simply thinking of it no longer in her possession. That she, a woman who'd entered his life one week ago, should have appeared in his past, occupying the void between life and death—that was the thought that intruded on her peace, stealing any chance of tranquillity.

CHAPTER 39

Spoiled Rich Girl

*Calum*

Cromwell, New Zealand – June, 2022

SUCH A TINY SEAT would inevitably be uncomfortable for a man of his size, but with a slowly healing broken shoulder, its confines were painful. He was relieved when the plane commenced its steep descent into Queenstown, a familiar plunge down between mountains, the runway a small target.

He'd been there several times, climbed some of these mountains and others in the surrounding Southern Alps. This country had echoes of home. No wonder it had attracted those nineteenth century Scots looking for a new place to land.

And the face that met him in the arrivals lounge was familiar too. He'd known Jo Brodie for most of his life, the tall man with an easy smile, and a steady handshake which he'd once offered to a little boy treating him as if he were a man, an equal. What he hadn't known till recently was the reason those green eyes were so like his own.

"Calum, good to see you."

Calum took his father's outstretched hand. But then, as if each recognised the massive shift in the universe that had occurred since their last meeting, the handshake morphed into a solid hug. He winced a little at Jo's arm, heavy on his shoulder. Two weeks on, it was still tender.

They passed the hour-long drive in small talk. There would be plenty of time to deal with the things that needed to be said over the coming days.

Tucked in behind the distillery was a house made unobtrusive by its use of the local stone. Like the distillery buildings, it looked as if they had hewn it from the rocky landscape.

Jo had acquired the Kiwi love of outdoor living in his adopted home. Undeterred by the winter chill, he insisted on cooking at the huge barbecue grill. Wielding an enormous set of tongs, he manhandled two generous chunks of steak, eventually declaring them perfectly done.

Despite the cool evening, he insisted they eat at the outdoor leaner, a giant slab of wood crafted into a rustic table. Perhaps he'd sensed that this big conversation would be more comfortable away from the confrontational seating of a regular dining table. As they sat there side by side, the rubble of their steak meal still strewn in front of them, he chose his moment. He took a gulp of beer and emitted a nervous cough.

"Calum, you know I never wanted to be an absent father. I'd have been proud to publicly own you as my son. Proud to do so now, if that's what you want."

"You can't know how much I wish you had. But you didn't have the guts to stand up to Hamish, did you?"

An irrational anger surged in Calum, colouring his words. He wasn't making this easy for Jo. Some part of him raged at the life this man had forced on him, leaving him with Hamish the only father he'd known.

"It was never about Hamish. Surely you can see that Calum. This was always only about one person, and that was Heather."

"So it's Mam's fault, this bloody disaster?"

"That's not what I'm saying, Calum. It's me that's to blame."

Jo's face showed resignation, as if he'd expected his son to struggle with the truth. Calum wanted to show him more understanding, but the years of bitterness won out, and his own face remained grim. He said nothing, not wanting to offer even the smallest sign of compassion. Jo, not waiting for Calum's forgiveness, went on.

"But in my defence, everything I've done, or didn't do, was only to protect her. Of course I feel regret about what that did to you. You deserved a decent father. You didn't deserve the treatment Hamish dealt out to you. God knows the times I wanted to knock him down. Beat the crap out of him, for the way he spoke to you. But I couldn't. I promised her I wouldn't get involved."

"It sounds like you made a lot of promises to her over the years."

"Calum, I have loved your mother since before Hamish even set eyes on her. From the time I met her when I was eighteen years old, I'd have promised her anything. Even gave her a ring to show it."

"But I thought you met her through Hamish?"

"No, your Mam hasn't quite told you the full story, lad. She and I were dating for a bit when we were youngsters, but I obviously read more into it than she did. It was my own fault. I didn't understand that you have to nurture a relationship if you want it to last. Came back from a stint in the army thinking we would pick up where we left off, to find the girl I loved was about to marry someone else. One of my friends."

"She didn't tell me that." Calum loved his mother, but it seemed even she hadn't given him the full truth.

"Don't be too hard on her, Calum. It was a long time ago. She was young. We all were. I accepted that she'd made her choice. If I'd had any brains, I would have got out of there then. But I didn't. And then when she and Hamish lost their first wee bairn...well he didn't know how to be there for her. And I did." His face was drawn, troubled.

"I'm not ashamed of you Calum, but I'm ashamed of what I did to Hamish. His wife grieving the baby, and him not knowing what to do. She came to me, and I saw my chance to have the woman I loved. It was wrong for me to take advantage of her grief and I regret that. And the pain it's caused you all over the years. But I don't regret you. I loved your mother, and I really thought that she would leave him for me. Especially once you were born."

"Mam said it was her that sent you away."

"Yes, she asked me to go. Because she wanted to try to make a go of it between her and Hamish. You can't imagine how much that hurt. But it was what she wanted. Said it was the right thing to do. She had a husband, a baby, a good life. I couldn't deny her that. So I went back up to the Highlands. Had family up Lochcarron way."

"But you came back."

"Those first ten years, I stayed well away. Never planned to come back. And in those years I was lucky in my work. Had a great opportunity to learn the whisky business. And I was good at it. But then Hamish wanted to grow his business. He needed expertise. And he thought in me there was someone with the knowledge who he could trust. I secretly met with Heather. There was no way I'd have come back otherwise. We thought it would be OK. Never realised that Hamish would work it out. I swear Calum, we never, ever, gave him cause to think otherwise. Not a word, not a look, not a touch. God, it broke me sometimes, seeing her with him, and you. But he was my friend. He asked for my help, and I gave it."

Calum could see the lines of weariness on his father's face, etched deep from a heavy burden, carried for a long time. For every year of his own entire life.

"So, yes, I'm guilty as charged. And my only excuse is that I loved your mother too much to come out with the truth. More than I loved you. I can never make up for that, but I'm hoping that because you love her too, we might retrieve something between us, for her sake."

"You said you gave her a ring," Calum said, thinking of what sat in his pocket. But his Mam had said it was a family ring, passed down. Surely she hadn't lied about that too.

"Yes, sentimental young fella that I was. It was a family ring that my mother passed to me to give to the woman I loved and wanted to marry. Which, when I was eighteen, was your mother. I had it engraved for her specially."

"Forever and a day," Calum said. "In the Latin. Forever and a day."

Jo looked puzzled.

"So she told you about it, did she?"

Calum fumbled in his pocket, finding it there, and letting it fall onto the table beside him. Jo reached for it, a slow dawn of recognition creeping across his face.

"Well, I never thought to see that again."

"Appropriate choice of words you put there, Jo. Seems that's about how long it will take to end up on the right person's hand."

"What do you mean? Did you give it to some lass who let you down?"

"No, but it's spent years on the hand of a spoiled rich girl who shouldn't have had it in the first place."

"You don't say," said Jo, intrigued now. "Sounds like a bit of a story to tell there, lad."

Calum accepted the invitation, sharing the uncanny coincidence that the ring his father had gifted his mother all those years ago should appear on the hand of the very woman he'd saved from death.

What he didn't share was the disturbing fact that she was also the very woman who haunted his memories from times when death had come calling for him and been sent away. He wondered if it was her who'd driven it off, holding him here in the land of the living. In that case, he should be grateful to her.

But that wasn't the emotion he felt towards her at this moment. In fact, he couldn't select one from the whirl of feelings that confronted him every time he thought of Sarah Norton. She'd plagued him in his past and now here she was again, unsettling his present.

## CHAPTER 40

Memory

Sarah

Wellington, New Zealand – July, 2022

WHILE MOST PEOPLE RELISHED escaping routine, Sarah was eager to plunge back into hers. Although she mourned the loss of her sassy yellow car, she was grateful that she had the money to easily replace it without waiting for the insurance to come through. This one was a more sedate blue, but still had the distinctive rotary engine whine that was like a favourite piece of music to her ears.

The digital clock on the dashboard flicked over to 8:50 a.m. as she eased to a stop at the traffic lights behind the V8 Holden. Brock's number plate was a welcome sight, a reminder of the hero that sat at the wheel, who'd been part of her rescue. He'd popped in to see her in the hospital, bringing his wife, who oozed pride in her husband's role in extracting Sarah from the collapse. Lovely people, they'd even suggested lunch some time.

The rest of the team arrived on cue. Hillary strode with the confidence of a far younger man, his walking poles clacking on the pavement, an interruption to their rhythm as he stepped into the cycle lane avoiding the fenced-off area of the fallen building. The screech of bicycle brakes drew her attention. She glanced in her wing mirror in time to see Edith aka Janice also take evasive action. She wobbled to a halt and Sarah punched the button on her electric window and it slid down with a buzz.

"Hi Janice. I'm glad I saw you. Never had the chance to thank you properly."

Janice smiled modestly, a faint blush creeping up her cheeks.

"It was nothing. I'm so pleased it all ended well."

Hillary's gnarled face appeared over Janice's shoulder, like some grotesque tree goblin.

"Good morning, Sarah, good to see you."

"And you. Without all of you, I might not be here."

And without him, she thought, realising that Calum was the only one of the team missing. Part of her wanted Calum's four-wheel-drive to pull up alongside her, to see him flash that smile, dazzle her with those green eyes. But mostly she was glad to be rid of him.

She was still annoyed about losing the ring that had sat so comfortably on her hand all those years. Although she'd reluctantly admitted he had more right to it than her, the thought of how Calum had tricked her into parting with it stuck in her gut. A more charming man would have insisted she take it back. But not bloody Calum MacFarlane.

An impatient toot from the car behind her jerked her back into the present, and she jammed the Mazda into first and surged across the intersection, farewelling her friends with a wave, while cursing Calum for her distracted mood.

Arriving home that evening, she decided there was no doubt about it: Netflix appeared to have taken Calum MacFarlane's side in all this. She'd watched two episodes of his TV series during her recuperation, intrigued to know about her red-haired rescuer. Now thinking of having a pleasant evening with something mindlessly relaxing, she flicked over to find that once again, the streaming service was determined to offer a daily dose of him.

*Continue watching for Sarah: The Kilted Climber*

*Popular on Netflix: The Kilted Climber*

Tiring of this game, she decided to admit defeat and binge watch the whole bloody series. Surely if she made it to the end, it would satisfy Netflix and so put an end to its daily demands.

Five minutes into Episode 3, she found herself hooked. No wonder he'd found fame. The beauty of Scotland and his droll humour were captivating.

Not to mention the attractive sparkle in his eyes, especially when he batted those long lashes at the camera, and spoke to the viewer like you were the only person in the world. Or when he tossed that lazy smile with a come-hither invitation that would be difficult to resist.

And then there was the dreaded knee porn. If it wasn't for Mel, she'd have never considered the possibility that knees could be sexy. How wrong she'd been. They peeped seductively from beneath the swinging kilt, as if begging her to lay her hand on one, beckoning her to follow where that might lead.

Oh well, it didn't hurt to have lascivious thoughts about Calum Mac-Farlane since he wasn't here for her to act on them. Although the more she saw, the more she was tempted to jump on a plane south, make amends for her frostiness when they'd parted and check out those knees in person.

She was feeling a little sad when the introduction for Episode 8 appeared on the screen, announcing it was the series finale. She wasn't sure how she would fill the rest of the weekend once she'd dispatched Calum to the past.

Titled *Coming Home: Beinn Alligin*, she settled in to watch with a glass of whisky. It seemed only fitting to toast his farewell with the family drink. She rarely poured one for herself. The association with Richard was too strong. But tonight it seemed appropriate, and she slugged a large splash of amber MacFarlane's 16-Year-Old into a crystal tumbler, adding a dash of water as Richard had trained her. The aroma of honeysuckle drifted to meet her and lingered on her tongue alongside a pleasant grassiness

She wondered if it was the added sensory hit of the whisky that made her feel drawn into this last episode more than the earlier ones. As the camera followed the sway of Callum's kilted derriere, she had this odd sensation of being there with him, her footsteps falling in the spaces vacated by his booted feet.

It must be the whisky. She had followed the doctor's advice and limited her alcohol since the accident. Perhaps her body was soaking up each droplet, extracting every tingling molecule and pumping it directly into her brain.

In front of her Calum trekked onwards, higher and higher on a steep zigzag path. He paused to survey the view, and as he named the landmarks sprawled before him, the words came to her lips unbidden, the Scottish names rolling forth as if she were speaking in tongues. "Rua Reidh." "Gairloch." "Torridon."

And then they were moving again, higher and higher, the view opening like the pages of a vast book and the liquid tones of his voice, the easy laugh, the dry sense of humour, encouraging her to follow wherever he led, as they climbed to the roof of the world.

Late afternoon sun no longer flooded the lounge, and as dusk descended on her hillside house in Thorndon, the twilight also claimed Beinn Alligin. Calum MacFarlane looked out through the entrance of a small tent he'd erected in the lee of the rocky cairn marking the summit.

As darkness fell in both worlds, Sarah was overwhelmed by an odd sense of dislocation and a warmth that spread from the tip of her right hand ring finger, caressing her arm and coming to rest as a small inner glow. There was a pang of loss as his face faded from view and the credits rolled over a mournful Celtic tune. She sculled the last of the whisky and sat in the darkness pondering her next move.

# Sarah

Cromwell, New Zealand – July, 2022

THE JET SKIMMED ALONG high above the South Island, the teeth of the mountains sitting dangerously close, as if waiting to crush the small white tube in their powerful jaws. But the sky was blue, the engines' drone even, the ride smooth with no threat of random turbulence to jolt the passengers out of their complacency.

Sarah welcomed the calm weather. Her last flight to Queenstown had been like a seat on an unruly rollercoaster, her faith in the bucking plane and its pilot undermined by the white-faced cabin crew sitting strapped in facing her, not daring to whisk out trolleys laden with coffee and cookies.

She'd only brought carry-on, the quicker to escape the claustrophobic plane and dodge the crowd waiting for luggage at the carousels. She made a bee-line for the rental car company's desk and was soon zipping along the road, Cromwell in her sights.

On any other day, she may have taken some time to linger at Lake Hayes, where she had happy memories of tranquil walks. Once, when Theo was small, she'd even taken him in a backpack, his comforting weight on her shoulders and him babbling in her ear as if giving a guided commentary. Even in four short years, he'd given her so many moments of joy that could pop up unexpectedly, reminding her of what she'd had before it was lost.

As she navigated the narrowing curved road, she glanced out at the Kawerau River, its turquoise waters a surreal shade that suggested photo-shopped magazine pictures designed to lure tourists. But here was proof that it existed in real life.

At the turnoff to the bungy jump site, she wondered if Calum had notched up a jump. Leaping from a platform, plummeting towards the water in freefall with only a large stretchy rope around your ankles standing between you and death was certainly not her thing. But she could imagine an outdoors man like Calum thriving on the adrenaline rush.

She smirked as her crazy brain offered up a picture of him in his Kilted Climber garb, poised on the edge, ready to give himself and any onlookers the thrill of their lives. Some things were best not done in kilts.

The stone gateway of the distillery wouldn't have looked out of place on a postcard from Scotland, the homeland of the liquid created within its walls. The MacFarlane name, picked out in bold brass lettering, glinted in the morning sunlight. Easing the car into a park, she paused for a moment to gather her thoughts.

She'd rehearsed the lines over and over on an endless loop. But these conversations in her head made no allowance for the thing she couldn't control: Calum's reaction.

Their parting had been cool, Calum unimpressed with her sulky insistence on him keeping the ring. She'd left no doubt that it was goodbye, the strange circumstances of their first meeting put behind them while they resumed their old lives.

She had no idea how Calum would respond to her now, turning up unannounced, desperate to explore the inexplicable connection that she'd brushed aside in her hot flash of anger. That night she'd turned her back on his curiosity, but when the same questions confronted her, she'd raced down here to demand answers.

Her heart pounded, anxiety about the reception that awaited her sapping her usual confidence, substituting an unsettling doubt.

A quick glance in the mirror showed lipstick still intact, hair reasonably under control, and after a few deep calming breaths, she ventured from the car, stepping towards the entrance to MacFarlane's distillery trying to look relaxed while pushing back the clenching fear in her stomach.

The award-winning architecture of the building inspired the same awe as when she'd stood here on opening day alongside Richard, feeling like the Queen, greeting guests in a receiving line. The roofline soared skyward, echoing the mountains in the backdrop. Rough slabs of local schist contrasted with the towering walls of glass. The tall doors crafted from slabs of earth-toned cedar radiated warmth and welcome, and retained a woody scent that permeated the entrance way.

Stepping into the reception area, she stood paralysed for a moment.

At a desk in the far corner, she caught sight of a man with dark red hair, bent over a computer. His dark brows furrowed as he scribbled figures on a page. She hadn't expected to encounter Calum so soon, and took a deep gulp of air as she desperately searched for the script she held in her head.

But hearing the automatic doors close behind her with a soft hiss, the man's head flicked up. The green eyes that met hers were a twin to Calum's, as was the thatch of curls, although this man's bore a hint of silver. And

Calum's face held softer lines, less angular, the jaw rounded, the mouth wider.

Ten years older than when she'd last seen him, but she recognised Joseph Brodie. And she didn't need to see them standing side by side to know without a doubt that she was looking at Calum's father. There was a flicker of recognition in his eyes as she moved to the desk.

"Sarah Norton," she said, helping him out with her name and extending a hand in greeting. "It's been a while."

"It sure has. Sorry, I had to think for a minute there. I wasn't expecting you." She could see hesitance, as he tried to understand why Richard's estranged wife should have waltzed into the distillery unannounced on a sunny winter morning.

"No, it's OK, I'm not here on business. That was always more Richard's thing than mine, and of course now…"

Jo nodded, his face sympathetic. They hadn't aired their grief at losing Theo in public, and the disintegration of their marriage had fortunately gone unnoticed by most, but the ripples of their private hell of those years had reached those who knew them.

"It's good to see you, Sarah." His beautiful Scottish accented voice radiated kindness, easing the tension that gripped her. "So how can I help?"

"I'm looking for Calum, actually. He said he was coming down for a visit, so I thought I might find him here."

"You thought right."

The voice from behind her was neutral, not overjoyed to see her, but not pissed off with her like when they'd parted. She turned as he walked towards her with those confident strides, crossing the space between them with three of his giant steps.

Her heart leapt at the sight of him. There'd been a nagging fear deep inside of her that he could be gone already, putting thousands of miles between them and already erasing her from his memory.

"So, what are you doing here, Sarah?"

Again, there was nothing combative in his tone, but neither did it suggest he was about to sweep her into his arms and tell her he'd forgiven her for her tantrum over the ring. And he didn't.

"Calum, we need to talk. Things have happened. Things that I don't understand. Things that I think only you can help me with."

"Take her next door lad." Jo nodded towards the empty cafe. The sign on the door said 'Hours 11:00 a.m. - 4:00 p.m.' "No one will bother you in there. Although the staff are already out back in the kitchen. How about I ask Elsa to bring out a coffee?"

"Thanks Jo, that'd be grand." Calum headed for one of the kauri slab tables scattered across the café.

She trailed after him, taking a seat opposite a vast expanse of glass that framed a view of peaks still thick with snow.

"I take it you haven't been doing any climbing?" she said, trying to break the ice with a topic that would put him at ease.

"Nah, not a real fan of the winter stuff anymore, weighed down with axes and crampons and all that guff. No, I think I've become more of a fair weather climber in my old age."

She grinned back at him. "A bit cold around the knees in the kilt, too?"

He laughed. "So you've been watching me and my kilt?"

"Ah, yes, I have," she said, welcoming the convenient segue into the strange conversation that she must have with him. Her rational mind argued that this was ridiculous, and she was about to make a fool of herself. But her heart urged her on, encouraging her to be brave and confront what she must.

"Calum, there's something I need to know." The smile melted away, his eyes fixed on her, his face on alert as if sensing the topic she was nudging them towards. "I need to ask you something, but I don't want you to tell me the answer straight away. Just think about it for a moment."

She took a deep breath, steadying herself, trying not to let the nervousness overwhelm her. Underneath the tablecloth, her hands were gripping the chair so hard that it hurt as she braced herself.

"At dinner last week, you told me you'd seen me before. In your near-death experiences. That I was there. Where were we Calum? Where was it you saw me? Don't tell me, just think." The answer came to him with ease, as his gaze met hers and he gave a slight almost imperceptible nod, indicating he was ready. "We were on Beinn Alligin, weren't we?" she said.

His eyes widened. His face wore the incredulous expression of someone dazzled by a magician, who now struggled to understand the illusion.

She explained in halting sentences, the words still strange even to her own ears. The steep climb, so real that she'd felt the burn in her thighs. The tiny tent in the lee of a stone cairn, wind whipping at the ropes as he banged pegs into the rocky ground. The view to the western sea, the silhouettes of ragged islands clutching at tattered remnants of red sky.

But there were also things she couldn't bring herself to describe. Not yet. Like her hands sliding over skin slick with sweat, his body melded to hers. Or his lips placing delicate kisses on the pale skin of her thigh. She shuddered at the rush of emotions that shadowed those memories.

"Calum, I think we were more than friends."

"We were lovers," he said in a whisper, stretching his hand to rest lightly on hers. There was an awkwardness in the gesture, as if he weighed the risk of overstepping the boundaries of the present based on half-remembered past intimacy.

Sarah, also torn between the then and the now, felt unsure of the way forward. She was acutely aware that this man, who was practically a stranger, had a dormant knowledge of her now awakening in his head. It was unnerving, and she felt an uncharacteristic shyness, as if he'd barged in on her half-dressed.

But in the touch of his hand there was also comfort, a sensation of warm contentment.

It was very different to what she'd felt with Richard, back on that first date, when he'd taken her hand in his. Oh, with him there'd been a spark, hinting at the passion that had soon followed.

But not this comfortable glow that radiated from the simple touch of Calum's hand, sheltering hers.

———

The lakeside restaurant was busy that evening. There was no off-season for tourists in Queenstown. Sarah was pleased that she'd managed to secure a booking. It had been a favourite in the times she and Richard had visited, and as she'd hoped, its familiar ambience helped to quell her discomfort a little. The thought of continuing their earlier conversation frightened her. But she and Calum had so much more they needed to explore. Dinner would give them time to talk.

"As long as you're not going to storm out on me this time," he'd replied at her invitation. Those green eyes flashing with mischief and his teasing voice suggested that he'd forgiven her for the debacle of their last dinner. Although as the minutes ticked by with no sign of him, she wondered if he'd reconsidered. She downed the last drops of the wine, and didn't hesitate when offered another. The warmth of the alcohol had already made its presence felt, a calming warmth settling upon her.

Heads turned as he crossed the room. Calum MacFarlane had a presence about him, the relaxed but confident gait, the unusual intensity of his hair. This man was a natural for television. No wonder he'd been such a success. She savoured a little leap of pleasure when she caught the envious glance of the two women at the next table as he manoeuvred his large frame into the chair opposite her.

"Thought you were going to stand me up," she said. "Written it off as a bad idea."

"No, this was definitely a good idea," he said. "I so need to try and sort this stuff out. When it was only me seeing crazy things, well, I tried to write it off as the result of one too many bumps on the head. But then you turn up and..."

"And you know you're not the only crazy one."

"Yeah, that should make me feel better, but it doesn't."

"Isn't there such a thing as a shared delusion?"

"Yes, but I think you need to be having it at the same time. This—well, this is something else and I have no idea what the hell is going on."

He looked thoughtful for a moment, then reached inside his jacket pocket.

"And then there's this."

He laid the small silver ring on the table between them.

"You know, I've been thinking about that." She twirled it between her fingers, feeling the soft undulations of the Celtic thistle design. "The rest of it is inside of us, in our heads. But the ring is real. Do you remember the last time you saw it? Before you saw it on my hand?"

He looked thoughtful, his hand grazing that square jaw, its dimpled contours all the more attractive for the slight stubble that peppered it. "I think I do. It was when I packed up my stuff when I was heading to the army. I put most of it into a storage locker down in Cluanie."

"When was that?"

"In 2008, late August, early September I suppose."

From her training as a historian, her brain was wired to make the connections, the leaps between dates and events, and at that moment it sprang into overdrive. She still didn't understand *what* had happened, but now she knew *when*. There were possibilities..

"Calum, I'm sure that was about the time when I got the ring. But as I told you, I don't remember where it came from. Something happened to me around that time, that I've never been able to explain. It was scary when it happened, but as you said, I put it down to one too many bumps on the head and tried to forget about it."

"So you'd better tell me."

"In 2008 I went to London with Richard. As well as doing bank business, he was in negotiation to buy a distillery—MacFarlane's distillery. That's when I met your parents." She grimaced a little, thinking she should have been more tactful and so rephrased it. "I met Heather and Hamish in London. And then we came up to Scotland for a weekend to sign off on the deal. I think you were there, but we never met. There was an empty seat at dinner. Your mother had set a place for you, but you didn't come."

His look was dark. "Yes, I was well over playing happy families with Mam and Hamish by then."

"Earlier that day, Heather took me out horse riding. It was lovely, and I enjoyed myself. Up till the point that I took a fall going over a fence and knocked myself out."

"That's horses for you. Been tossed off a few myself as a kid. But Mam's always loved them. She still has them, you know. Think she always will."

"Yes, I remember that was one of the good things about the partnership—that she'd be able to keep her horses. Anyway, I thought nothing of it. Apart from a bit of a headache and a few bruises, I was fine. Brushed it off and wouldn't let anyone make a fuss. I was sure I was OK."

"But you weren't."

"No, I wasn't." She understood it now. "From part way through the dinner that night, till a morning over two weeks later when my friend opened the door of a house in Kensington to find me lying on the steps, unconscious, I have absolutely no memory. It was like I was somewhere else for that time, and someone else took my place."

"Maybe you were somewhere else. Maybe you were with me."

"Maybe I was."

"And maybe *I* gave you this ring. In which case, you should have it back."

"No," she said. "It's yours to give, but not mine to take. Not yet. Not till I'm sure it's meant for me." After so desperately wanting the ring back, now in her heart, she needed to know it was truly hers before claiming it.

"OK," he said slowly, patting his pocket as he slipped it back inside for safekeeping. "So, what do we do now?"

She knew she couldn't walk away from this. But the next steps were unclear. Meeting up with Calum had stirred up more questions than answers.

"I honestly don't know Calum. What do you think?"

His eyes met hers, with a quiet resolve.

"I think you come with me," he said. "To Scotland. Let me take you home. If that's where this all started, perhaps we'll find the answers there."

## CHAPTER 42

Homecoming

Sarah

Stirlingshire, Scotland – July 2022

SARAH BOUNCED AROUND IN the passenger seat of the wagon. Heather sped along the narrow road, humming along to a cheerful song on the radio, her mood buoyant since her son's return.

They'd left Calum at home to ferret out gear for the climb, while they'd taken a trip to the nearby town of Cluanie. McPherson's General Store stocked an astonishing array of goods, including all the items on the list of requirements for their expedition to Beinn Alligin.

"So you've had a bit of a tough time of it, I believe?" Heather's query was gentle.

"Could have been worse if it wasn't for Calum."

"Oh yes, the earthquake. That too." She hesitated a moment, but then went on, her voice low and kind. "But no, I mean, since I saw you last. I heard about your wee boy. I know we sent messages and flowers and such, but it's not the same. You poor love, my heart broke for you. I wanted to tell you myself, as one mother to another, how very sorry I am."

The tears welled in Sarah's eyes. They always lurked there, under the surface of her calm, her getting on with life without Theo.

"You know, I think about him every day." The words squeezed out of her constricted throat in a whisper.

"Of course you do. You're his mother. You'll always be his mother. You know if you ever want someone to talk to, given your own mam's passed on... well, I'm here for you." She laid a hand over Sarah's, a gentle reassuring pat.

"Thanks, Heather."

Heather took a deep breath, as if unsure, but then spoke anyway.

"You see, I do understand a little. Hamish and I, we lost our own wee baby. Before Calum. Oh, he barely took a breath. We never had the chance to know him properly. But he was ours. I loved him for the nine months I carried him. And I still love him now. That's what we mothers do."

"Yes, we do."

Sarah clasped Heather's hand, offering her own comfort. How lucky she was to have had almost four years of Theo's life. She'd never see him dressed in uniform ready for a first day at school, grow to be an unruly teenager, a man, a father. He would forever be that sweet little boy, with her mop of dark curls and Richard's knowing blue eyes.

Poor Heather, to have not even that comfort. Was that where her marriage to Hamish had begun to unravel? Grief could do that, as she well knew.

As if reading her thoughts, Heather added, "Well Hamish and I, it was never the same after that. Even Calum, such a bright sunny lad from the moment he was born, wasn't enough to bring back what we had together."

In its own strange way, Heather's admission was reassuring. There were times she'd agonised over the disastrous end to her marriage. Wondered if they'd found enough common ground, had another child, that she and Richard could have salvaged enough to be happy again. But Heather and Hamish were proof that children didn't mend marriages.

Heather sighed with resignation, the memories of past sadness extinguishing her good mood as they rode in silence for the remaining miles till at last she swung the car into the gates of her home.

Last night, arriving in darkness, Sarah hadn't noticed the bold new signage. But today, next to the unmissable distillery sign, she saw another. It announced 'BUCHANAN HOUSE' in ornate gold capitals, and below in deep burgundy gilt-edged letters 'Boutique Accommodation.'

"You've changed the name. How come?"

Heather smiled. "I've changed mine too. Thought it was about time I reclaimed the Buchanan name for myself, and for the land. Oh, the distillery can keep Hamish's name. It was his love, not mine, and it would be a bit churlish to take it away—as well as bad for business. But yes, I was born a Buchanan and I intend to die a Buchanan."

"Good on you. I'm going to take mine back too. In fact, I started the divorce proceedings last week, although Richard was a little surprised that I'd do it now and give away the title."

"The title?" Heather sounded puzzled.

Sarah explained the odd situation, that for now she was officially Lady Sarah Norton.

Heather turned to her, eyes merry, choking back laughter. "Oh my god, you should have told me. I'd have dipped a curtsey. Perhaps you should ride in the back so I can be the chauffeur."

They pulled up outside Calum's cottage to unload with Heather's laughter pealing from the open car window. He ambled across to meet them, and seeing his mother bent over the steering wheel giggling to herself, shot a confused look at her before registering that Sarah too was in on the joke.

"What's so funny Mam? You're in a good mood."

"Oh lad, you picked a posh one there. Best you whip around and open the door for her ladyship." She collapsed back over the steering wheel, still chortling to herself.

"Sounds like you have some explaining to do," he said, as he acted on his mother's suggestion, opening her door and bowing with a gentlemanly flourish.

"A little," said Sarah, enjoying the firm clasp of his hand as he helped her from the car.

Heather spurned the idea of them having dinner in the big house. "The least I can do is cook my son a proper meal," she declared before disappearing into the kitchen for the rest of the afternoon, with promises of a hearty home-cooked dinner.

Sarah, meanwhile, took a nap in the beautiful guest room in the old mansion that Heather had allocated to her. It wasn't expansive, like the top-floor suite she and Richard had shared all those years ago, when he was tying up the deal to partner with the MacFarlanes. This may have been a deliberate ploy on Heather's part, assuming rightly that Sarah wasn't particularly keen to dredge up those memories of her past visit. However, as she lay staring at the beamed ceiling, positive recollections of that weekend edged their way forward.

She definitely remembered deciding she liked Heather, a feeling that remained with her now. Although old enough to be her mother, even back then, Sarah had sensed a kindred spirit. She was pleased to have the opportunity for them to get reacquainted, although the terms of this engagement differed completely from what she had imagined.

Finally, the last wisps of jet-lag overtook her, and she drifted into a sleep where images of sailing over a hedgerow with a grey horse beneath her whirled alongside memories of Richard, fishing rod in hand, and she and Mel clinking glasses of champagne.

———

Calum leaned back in his chair, resisting his mother's urging to have seconds of the heavy fruit pudding. Anyone seeing the quantity of food that she'd produced would have thought it was Christmas.

"Truly Mam, I couldn't eat another thing." He placed a large tanned hand over the bowl to prevent Heather heaping it with more. She turned to Sarah, serving spoon poised, a query in her eyes.

"No Heather, I couldn't either. I've hardly room to finish the whisky."

"In fact, Mam, I think I might beg off and have an early night." He rose from his chair before she could argue. "After all, it was past midnight when we turned in last night. I think the jet lag is catching up with me."

He downed the last of his whisky, throwing his head back. At the sight of his broad throat, the curve of the Adam's apple, Sarah swallowed herself, as in a flash of imagination, she saw Calum poised above her, lost in another form of pleasure. She reined in the tremor that rippled through her body, trying to suppress the images and the accompanying overwhelming attraction to this man that came unbidden, often at inappropriate moments like now.

"OK, love," Heather said, as he leaned over, planting a kiss on her cheek. "Sleep well. Big day tomorrow. I promise not to keep Sarah up too late."

He headed off to his cottage, leaving the women to clear the last of the dishes, set the dishwasher whirring and take a seat in two large comfy chairs by the fire. Heather topped up the whisky, and they sat in silence for a while, each lost in thought, hypnotised by the darting flames that ate away at a massive log. It sparked with boisterous crackles as the fragrant bubbles of sap ignited.

"I hope you're not going to break his heart." Heather's gaze was beseeching, looking for assurance. "You might not see it yet. But I know. There's something in the way he looks at you. The way he talks about you."

"I don't want to hurt him, either. I'll be careful. This has all happened so fast."

"Sarah, boys tell their mother's things. I know what happened, what there is between you."

"So you don't think we're mad? That this is some kind of shared delusion? After all, what happened in the earthquake... maybe it affected us somehow?"

"I don't think you're deluded. Far from it. I believe what he's told me. It's not in the realms of impossibility. You know, I may seem like a practical person. The type who wouldn't believe such things are possible. But I do. I grew up on the knee of my Granny Beaton, with tales of fairies and monsters, and water horses luring women off to be their wives. She was staunch Methodist, but that generation, they were comfortable with the old ways, happy to keep them alongside the new."

"I'm finding myself in the same situation. A lifetime studying history, looking for evidence, demanding proof. But I've come to accept that there's more to this world, this life than any of us can ever truly know."

"Well, whatever happens up there on the mountain, I hope you're not going to hurt him. He's been hurt too much in his life." She saw Heather's eyes fix on a portrait of Calum on the wall, in full army dress uniform, a blaze of medals on his chest. Seeing Sarah follow her gaze, she shook her head. "No, not that hurt. Oh, for sure Afghanistan scarred him—physically and mentally. He's probably not told you how he earned those medals, but it cost him a lot. But no, Hamish damaged him terribly, and I have to take my share of the blame." Heather sat slumped in her chair, waves of regret drifting across her face. "After we lost the baby, when I needed him most, Hamish shut down. When all I wanted was him to hold me, to tell me it would be all right, he shut me out. Always off on his own. Wouldn't let me talk about it."

"I understand. People all deal with grief differently, in ways we can't fathom." Sarah herself knew how shutting out the person you loved was the way some people coped.

"But I did have someone who understood. Someone who was there for me."

"Jo Brodie."

"Yes, Jo. I know Calum's told you."

"Yes, when we were in Cromwell…"

"So you see why I'm protective of Calum. Once Hamish knew he wasn't his true son, he set out to punish Jo and I. He made us pay for our deceit by taking it out on Calum. The more I tried to defend him, the worse he treated him. He knew Calum would leave, eventually. That was to be my final punishment. To lose my child, driven away by a man who was his father in name only. But it wasn't fair to punish Calum for my sins."

"No," Sarah said softly, understanding the venom in Calum's voice whenever he mentioned Hamish.

She finished the whisky, the warmth lingering on her tongue, and rose to go. Heather stood and wrapped her in a soft embrace. The touch was comforting, the touch of a mother. She'd missed that for so long. But as they parted, Heather's voice was earnest.

"Sarah, I don't know how you feel about Calum. Maybe you love him a little, maybe you don't. But take care of my boy."

"I will," she replied, hoping that she could live up to those words, for all their sakes.

---

Sarah sat on the steps of the towering mansion house, the early sunlight already teasing the edges of a shroud of mist that blanketed the buildings.

Ragged patches of sky appeared and then whirled away. But she knew the blue would not give up until it regained full control, leaving them with a stunning summer day for the drive north. Hopefully, they'd get a second tomorrow for the climb.

A now familiar large energetic figure loomed through the pale gloom as Calum traced the path from his cottage. He handed her a coffee, its wisps of steam rising and merging with the tendrils of mist.

"I haven't known you long, but I know that you'll need this if we have any hope of an early start."

She accepted it gratefully, and with a touch of amusement, seeing how proud he was to be attuned to her needs already. Travelling together on two long flights, through three busy airports and then a lengthy train trip, Calum had learned that strong coffee kept her functioning.

She wrapped her fingers around the proffered mug, enjoying the warmth seeping into her chilled hands. Her gaze drifted downwards from his smiling face. At this height, it was impossible to ignore the view right in front of her: a pair of rather sexy knees protruding from the bottom of a dark plaid.

He'd put on one of his climbing kilts, and she decided it was just as well that she would spend most of today alongside him in a vehicle. It would give her time to damp down the lustful thoughts that circled in her brain. How had she managed to get to over forty without realising the very real attraction of a shapely set of male legs? Or experience the imagined thrill of running her hands the length of them to see where that might lead?

His plaid was a modern iteration of the traditional pattern, a palette of greys: softest dove contrasted with intense charcoal, crisscrossed by threads the colour of a muted winter sea and a slender vein of red. It was a subtle design, not the gaudy tartans of the skirling pipe bands and Highland dancers with flying feet she remembered from her childhood summers.

She had fond memories of the annual Wakefield Agricultural Show, a highlight of the year for the rural residents of the area. Sarah could recall the happy feeling of skipping alongside the parade, she and her sisters following the pipers' measured steps and drummers' flailing rhythms through the streets of the town. And she'd stood mesmerised by the stage, envying not only the dancers' skill, but their vibrant costumes. She'd longed for her own set of tartan stockings encased in soft leather shoes, a swinging bright skirt topped by a velvet waistcoat, its silver buttons glinting in the sun. In those moments, she'd desperately wanted to be Scottish. It was as if that blood ran in her veins, passed down from immigrant ancestors.

Heather wandered over from the family house to sit alongside her on the steps. Her younger self had liked this woman, her down-to-earth manner a refreshing contrast to the company wives she'd had to endure. Last night at dinner, she'd sensed a more relaxed Heather, relieved of Hamish's brooding presence in her life. Freed from her unhappy marriage, she was certainly young enough for a second chance at love. She wondered if it would be with Jo Brodie, rekindling the flame of their youth that had produced a son.

Today, Sarah saw something else in Heather's eyes. While she tried to prevent her eagerness spilling over, there was no doubt that Heather was excited. After dinner she'd made no secret of her hopes that it would be Sarah who stood alongside Calum carrying on the family legacy. Although the distillery bore the MacFarlane name, Heather's ambition was for Calum to embrace her own Buchanan family inheritance, settling here to manage the property rather than travelling the world climbing mountains. But for now, a certain mountain came first.

"All set?" Heather indicated the pile of bags Calum was loading into the back of the Range Rover.

"Yes, I think so. Thanks for the loan of the clothes."

"Well, it's not flash, a bit worn, but plenty of warmth left in the jumpers and tread on the boots. Luckily, we're of a similar size." Heather took a sip of her own mug of dark tea, so thick you could stand a spoon in it. "There's no way Calum would let you go up there unless you had the right gear. It's an easy walk, but this is Scotland. Anything can happen with the weather."

"I'm in good hands, I think."

"That you are." Heather flashed her a smug smile, reading her own meaning into the words. Unbeknown to his mother, Calum had hardly laid a hand on Sarah or she on him, despite the invisible current that arced between them. It was as if they were skirting around the inevitable, setting aside their mutual attraction as they worked through this process. They needed to trace the steps of their strange memories to find what awaited them at the end of the journey. Only then could they decide where this was headed.

Calum slammed the back door of the vehicle and sauntered over.

"We'll be off then?"

Sarah nodded, emptying the last dregs of coffee from her mug.

"Take care, love." Heather stepped into her son's bear hug. Sarah caught the words she said under her breath. "And look after the lassie. She's a good one."

"Will do Mam. A bonnie lassie for sure," he whispered in his mother's ear. His grin was broad as he glanced over to where Sarah pretended to study the weather.

CHAPTER 43

Answers

# Sarah

Beinn Alligin, Scotland – July 2022

"YOU DOING OK?" CALUM called down from a rocky knoll above her.

"Only because you're being kind and keeping the pace slow."

"Number one rule of trekking, always go at the pace of the slowest person in your party. No one left behind."

"Well, I'm grateful for rule number one," she said, slumping down beside him, pleased to take the weight off her feet even though the seat was hard and knobbly, the rough edges of rock pressing into her aching butt. At least Heather's boots were comfortable, the well-worn leather moulding to her feet with no threat of blisters.

A trickle of sweat pricked her spine. The day was warm even though the full flush of summer had yet to come. She dumped her pack on the ground and ferreted inside for water. The cool liquid eased the tightness in her throat, and she allowed her breathing to return to normal after the effort of that last steep climb.

Not that the pain of exertion was unwelcome. It served to keep her mind off the disturbing images that danced on the periphery, like a movie playing in parallel, with the screen just out of sight. She'd seen them first in the carpark, as they loaded up gear, intensifying as they crossed a bridge, where an exuberant cascade of crystal water tumbled beneath their feet.

And on the climb, the film reel had settled in alongside her, as if to say, *I'm here, I'm not going away, I'm part of you.* It wasn't déjà vu, that brief flutter of recognition of an experience lived before.

This wasn't fleeting. No, it was as if another version of herself walked in tandem, at times whispering enticements, at others urging her on. *Retrace these steps, relive that time.* She shuddered as if to flick it off, but to no avail.

As Calum's voice jerked her attention back to the now, she wondered if his own earlier self was nagging him on the journey.

"Here, snack time," he said, throwing her a chocolate-coated muesli bar retrieved from his own huge pack.

"My shoulders ache even from my puny pack. How the hell do you manage that?"

"It's all in the weight distribution. Keep it nice and high and it's easier than you think."

In hers, Sarah had stashed clothes for every possible weather the mountain could throw at them, along with a borrowed sub-zero rated sleeping bag. In addition to his own bed and clothing, Calum was also hefting their shelter for the night, the bulk of their food, and a carefully checked list of emergency items.

Despite her lack of fitness, Sarah was still enjoying the adventure, excited by the thought of conquering the mountain. It was exhilarating to be in the outdoors, rekindling that sense of freedom from her teenage years when she and her friends had roved the bush-clad slopes of Mt Taranaki, a convenient escape from the scrutiny of their parents.

No vegetation hugged these slopes. This was a harsh landscape, dominated by the remains of long-lost glaciers. She recognised the distinctive u-shaped valleys from her high-school geography classes. In all directions, they were surrounded by the debris carried for a time on those rivers of ice and then discarded along the way. It was as if some giant had tossed rocks haphazardly in a prehistoric lolly scramble.

In places, wiry patches of tussock grass pushed their way between huge fissured slabs of rock. The ubiquitous heather was already in full bloom, undeterred by the inhospitable conditions. Seeing one of the woody shrubs within arm's reach, she broke off a piece and closed her eyes to inhale its fresh scent. Although sweet, it had a mossy, masculine undertone. The smell of a Scottish man, she mused.

"You look stuffed? Are you sure you're OK?" His concerned voice dragged her back into the present.

"Yeah, just bloody hot." There was no reprieve from the sun on this rugged expanse of mountainside. In the distance, its light glared off the distant sea. She took another slug of water.

"Well, the bad news is that we have a way to go. But the good news is that the rest is less steep."

"Thank god for that. Let's get at it then," she said, settling the pack onto her weary shoulders with a grimace.

She fixed her eyes on Calum's shapely legs, the hairs on them glistening gold, and followed the hypnotic sway of his kilt as they climbed step by measured step towards the sapphire sky.

Several hours and a few rest stops later, they stood on the sprawling summit of Beinn Alligin. It was more open than she'd expected, wide and flat, offering options for their campsite.

"So, where shall we set up our home for the night? Any likely spots?" he said, hoisting his pack off his shoulders.

She was surprised to be asked, given he was the mountain man, but surveyed the land, pondering her choice. Something drew her eyes to the base of the cairn that marked the summit. She could envisage their little tent there, snug under its shelter, protected from the prevailing wind. She wandered over and stood in the spot as if trying it on for size. Her other self, lurking on the edge of her vision, seemed to nod in approval.

"How about here? It looks sort of cosy."

"That's my pick too. OK, let's see if we can put this up without an argument." He pointed to the jumble of fabric, fibreglass poles and hooked metal pegs he'd upended on the ground, spread like pieces of a puzzle.

She laughed. "I'm not arguing. Happy to let you direct the construction. Tent pitching is not one of my skills."

Once perched in front of the surprisingly sturdy shelter, there was time to sit and simply soak up the sun. It was a magical spot, protected beneath the rocky cairn, with a million dollar view of the Hebridean Isles.

"Isle of Skye out there," he said, pointing to the rugged outline silhouetted against the hazy late afternoon sky. A trick of the light gave the illusion that you might simply reach out and touch it.

"Ever been?"

"No," she said, "But I've been told it's amazing."

"Next adventure perhaps," he said with a grin.

She tried not to think of the strange events that led to her being in this place, at this time, with this man. Relax, enjoy the view.

She attempted to suppress the nagging fear that whispered in her brain, messing with her thoughts, hanging over this trek in search of the truth. What if, now, at the summit, having retraced the steps of their shared past, they felt nothing? Or what if they felt something? This was uncharted territory, no map for where either outcome might lead.

They sat and talked companionably. Once or twice Sarah almost brought up the odd sensations that had dogged her on the walk, and still lingered. But the moment never seemed right. It was as if they were skirting carefully around the reason for their being here.

As the sun dropped a little lower in the west, Calum dived into the tent and she could hear him rummaging in his pack. She found it hard to believe that it could contain any more, given all that had emerged so far. He produced a small gas stove and some non-descript foil packages of dried food.

"Right m'lady, I am now going to cook you dinner."

She cuffed him playfully. "Stop it," she said, sounding forceful, but failing to suppress a smile in the face of his mischievous expression.

"Yes, m'lady," he said with an insolent grin.

"Just get on with the cooking. I'm bloody hungry after all that walking."

"Of course, m'lady," he replied, ducking to avoid another swipe of her hand.

After eating, they faced each other across the rubble of the meal, the deepening twilight rendering his features soft in the dim light. He swept the empty plates aside, and shuffled closer to sit opposite her, his green eyes locked on hers.

Her stomach tensed from the nervousness of knowing that there was nothing left to do but face the reason they were here. To decide if a past they vaguely remembered suggested they had a future.

His warm hands clasped over hers were soothing. A sliver of moon peeked out from behind the rocky overhang, lighting his hair with strands of copper and silver. His handsome face was serious, his eyes flickering across hers as if trying to read her thoughts.

"So what now?" His voice was cautious, as if he sensed any sudden move would spook her.

She knew what came now. This was insane, but her body longed to mirror the inexplicable intense connection she had with this man. She wanted him. And something in his tone suggested he wanted her too. Lost for words, Sarah answered the only way she knew how, reaching for him, her touch tentative.

His stubbled cheek was rough under her trailing hand, but the lips that grazed hers were warm, inviting her in. Strong, insistent arms wrapped around her, and Calum laid her back gently to rest her head on his discarded jacket.

He smiled down at her, his hand stroking her hair, twining his fingers in the tendrils of her springy curls. She closed her eyes, luxuriating in the caress on her cheek, a little gasp escaping as his lips met her hungry mouth once more, and his body pressed against hers.

"You OK with this?" he asked, his murmured words in her ear, his breath taunting at the nape of her neck.

"Oh, I'm more than OK," she said. "God, Calum, I so want this."

She more than wanted him, she needed him, as if this was a missing piece of the puzzle of her life that must be fitted into place. Her hands slipped inside the collar of his shirt, and her fingers rested on a pulsing heartbeat, racing like her own.

Hands fumbled at her shirt, his big fingers struggling with the buttons. Those same fingers traced the curve of her breasts and marked a pathway for his lips to follow as he placed delicate kisses on her skin.

Her shiver was not from the touch of the cool night air, but from the large hand that found its way into the waistband of her pants and explored with an unexpectedly exquisite delicacy.

He stopped for a moment, sliding upward along the length of her exposed body.

"Aww," she groaned, her body strung so tight that the absence of his hand brought almost physical pain.

"Sorry," he said, now resting it against her cheek where she could smell the scent of her, of him, of them. "But I need to ask. Are you sure? Really sure? I don't want to presume that because you were willing to stay the night here with me, that this was the inevitable conclusion."

"Calum, I have never been more sure of anything."

"And if we do this, it's more than tonight. Well, it is for me. If we do this, it's saying, you and me, we are going to try to make a go of this, together, back in the real world."

And now she knew. In that moment, it struck her with blinding clarity. She would not question it. Her analytical mind could go to hell and accept what her heart told her to be true.

"Can't you tell Calum MacFarlane? Somewhere between a crushed car in Wellington and the top of this mountain in Scotland, somehow I fell in love with you."

This was so far from the way she'd ever approached any previous relationship. With Richard, it was he who'd fallen quickly and unreservedly in love with her. And while she'd repeated the words back to him, not wanting to risk her lack of certainty harming their future relationship, she knew that in reality it had taken a long time for her to truly mean them.

But here she was, with no reservations, knowing with absolute certainty that she meant those words.

"Well, not wanting to sound like I'm trying to outdo you." A shy smile flickered around his lips. Such a sweet contrast to his normal gregarious, confident grin. "But somewhere between a wrecked armoured vehicle in Afghanistan, and this, my favourite place in the world, I also found my favourite person in the world. The person it seems I have loved for a very long time."

All her fears drained away, leaving her fully present in this moment, this time, this place. The annoying other version of herself that had persisted all day, whispering in her ear, dancing on the edge of her vision, now merged with this one, as if satisfied at having led her to the journey's end, was now freed from its task and would leave her in the care of the man who had loved her. Who still loved her.

Afterwards, she lay lazily tracing the shape of him as if to make sure he really was there and that this wasn't some strange dream. Her hand ran over broad sloping shoulders, her fingers detecting the faintest dip, the only trace of the injury he'd borne from protecting her.

She stroked the taut abdomen and that tantalising v-shaped groove, like a map directing her hand downward. As she let her touch play over one muscular thigh, she discovered a gnarled ridge of flesh. A jagged scar, etched down the inner length. He felt her pause there and sat up, angling the leg so she could see what her fingers had revealed.

"Looks like it was pretty bad," she said, peering at the raised slash of silver at least six inches long, and the puckered marks of stitches that had anchored his skin.

"Sure was. The only reason I'm still here is a sweet little Welsh medic who was with me when it happened."

"Not the thing they gave you those medals for?"

"No." His face told her he didn't want to talk about how he'd earned those medals. She didn't pry. Her grandfather had been a war veteran. She understood. There were things seen and experienced in war that were best not spoken about. He'd tell her when he was ready, if that time came.

"Well, it seems I should be very thankful to your Welsh medic."

"Yes. I sure am," he said. "Arterial bleeding is often fatal. She was my driver. Our vehicle hit a mine. The explosion threw that great big vehicle through the air like a kid's toy car. And ripped off bloody great bits of it. That there—that was where the gear stick punched into me."

She caressed the scar, her fingers gentle, as if her touch could erase it and the bad memories.

"Yes," he said softly, "I have to be thankful that Erin Davies was beside me." He paused, his green eyes seeking hers in the tent's dimness. "And that you were inside my head. Showing me that one day we'd be here together. Giving me a reason to hang on."

She leaned forward and his kiss was slow and deep, flooding her with a profound sense of gratitude that she and Erin Davies had prevented death from stealing him away, giving them this possibility of a new life together, although they'd had to wait years to find it.

---

"Where are you going?" She had been dozing blissfully when she felt Calum shuffle free of their bedding, followed by the tearing sound of the zipper. She could barely make out his shape silhouetted against the moonlit roof of the tent.

"Just something I need to fetch. Back soon."

A moment later, he returned, and with a flick of a switch, the small lantern burst into life. Its luminous heart drew the tent walls in close, giving it a cosy feel. He was clutching his jacket, the one that had made a rather comfortable blanket. She almost blushed with the memory of what she'd let him do to her sprawled on it earlier. She saw one hand reach into an inner pocket, retrieving a small object that now lay balanced on his outstretched palm. The glow from the lamp picked out the light and shadows of the embellished silver band.

He took her hand in his, guiding the band into place. The ring slid comfortably onto her finger, radiating warmth as if content to be home again.

"Mam was right," he said, rubbing his thumb across the silver but never taking his eyes from hers. "That I'd know when the right one came along."

She woke hours later with a terrible thirst. Next to her Calum slept, one arm sprawled across her as if still claiming her for his own. She lifted it carefully, trying not to wake him, but fearing she had as he stirred, mumbling to himself. She reached out and stroked the tousled hair, smoothing it gently to soothe him back to sleep. As he relaxed into slumber, she wiggled herself clear of the sleeping bag and leaned forward to unzip the tent with a slow, careful motion, and a faint buzz as the nylon teeth parted. Expecting only a star-studded black velvet night, she gasped at the blazing sky.

"Oh my god, Calum look," she said, her voice brimming with excitement, knowing she had to wake him. A magical ribbon of whirling green swirled across the sky, interlaced with slashes of pink and gold. Pulsing ripples of light spanned the horizon, enveloping the distant isles in a spectacular light show.

He snuggled in beside her in the opening, his sleepy eyes at first struggling to focus on the scene.

"The aurora," he said. "And a bloody good one. I've seen a few in my time, but nothing like this. That is spectacular."

Sarah knew the science, how fierce solar storms hurled supercharged particles into Earth's atmosphere. But tonight she put the science aside, letting the magic enfold her as the whirling spectral figures danced only for the two of them, in a blazing celebration of their rediscovered love.

## CHAPTER 44

Reality

Calum

Beinn Alligin, Scotland – July 2022

MOVIES PLAYED IN HIS head, the same features over and over. Afghanistan, the Andes, Wellington. The same images, echoes of his current reality here on Beinn Alligin. Her head on his chest, heavy with the weight of sleep. The tickle of her hair splayed across his shoulder. The rhythmic rise and fall of her breath, peaceful and content. It was exactly as she'd described her own experiences. A past version of himself, alongside this version, with this woman, in this place. Not imagined, real. But not remembered except in those far reaches of his mind. Only remembered when he'd been forced to go there. Remembered in those moments when he'd been sure that soon there would be no more thoughts or memories.

But this wasn't a memory. This was real. Wasn't it? He shifted a little to confirm it. Yes, this was real, a world he had control over, where his brain sent a signal and his body complied. He tested it some more, lifting his free arm, extending a finger, tracing her lips, ever so slightly parted as she delicately exhaled. She stirred at his touch, nuzzling her head against him, pressing the lightest of kisses on his bare skin.

"Can't sleep?" Her drowsy words drifted across his chest.

"No. My brain hasn't got the message."

"Too much thinking?"

"Too much to think about. This. Us. What it is. Why it is."

"And have you found the answers? I know I haven't," she said. "And god knows I've thought about it."

"No, but what you said earlier? About feeling like there's a parallel you, a parallel life? I think that's the key."

"Mmmm," she said, "perhaps it is."

She rolled over and lay on her back with a sigh. He could almost hear the workings of her brain in the darkness. Could almost hear it over his own mind, tossing and turning ideas, mulling over how to put it into words. How to describe this strangeness in some way that made it understandable. After a while, his scrambled ideas straggled into a more orderly line.

"OK," he said slowly. "So what if we were to think of it like climbing a mountain?"

"Of course it would be a mountain." He could hear the amusement in her voice.

"Of course. They say go with what you know." A little giggle bubbled up in the dark. "No, but seriously, Sarah. Think about it like this. On some of these mountains, there are lots of different paths to the top. Many of them are just old animal tracks, so they twist and turn, cross over each other or even merge for a while. So imagine you set out on one path, heading for the top. And then part way along the fog comes down and you're simply looking for the path, any path. You follow whatever trail you can see. And so, without knowing it, you might easily wander onto one of the other paths. They're all heading in the same direction, but each taking a slightly different route. You carry on for a bit, moving forward, following the path. Then when the fog lifts, somehow, you've found your way back to the first path, the one you started on. And you don't think about the other, leave it there in the fog. Move on, onwards and upwards, not looking back."

"Until something happens that makes you look back."

"Yes, like half a building falling on you, or bleeding out on the side of the road in the desert."

"OK," she said. "The analogy works. Perhaps we each blundered onto a different path at some time in our lives and found each other there."

Once again, he could hear that mind whirring with a blur of thoughts. Then she rolled towards him, propped up on one elbow. He could make out the drawn lines of her face in the gloom.

"Calum, the thing that troubles me. The thing that scares me..." There was an unexpected tremor in her voice. "We don't know what brings that fog down. Or drives it away. And if we don't know why, it could happen without warning. We could find ourselves on another path at any moment. And what if the other of us isn't there?"

He hadn't considered that. And when he did, it scared him too. Looking back, he'd had a solitary life. Oh, there'd been women along the way. A few he'd cared for, but not enough to commit. He'd pissed off a couple by letting things go on too long before they'd realised he wasn't going to marry them. Now he wondered if he'd been waiting for Sarah all along. That in some other life they'd found each other, and subconsciously he knew that eventually he'd find her in this one too. This sometimes infuriating woman, catapulted into his life by an act of god, and by god, now she was here, he wasn't going to let her go.

"I won't lose you, Sarah. I promise. If we end up on another path, you will be there somewhere, and I'll find you. I promise."

"You can't promise that. You don't know what will happen. May not even know it *has* happened."

"Well I promise anyway."

He wrapped his arms around her, tried to project reassurance in his tight embrace, but it wasn't enough to reassure himself. There was some weird, unpredictable shit going on here. And they were simply at the mercy of the universe, subject to whatever its current whim might be.

CHAPTER 45

The Divide

*Sarah*

Stirlingshire, Scotland – July 2022

THEY SNUCK IN THROUGH the back door of the cottage like two teenagers, evading his mother's watchful eyes. They'd avoided announcing their arrival. There was an unspoken agreement that for a precious few more hours they would exist inside this little bubble, their love shiny and new, only the two of them, protected within its fragile walls, the outside unable to intrude and spoil it.

On the mountain, their lovemaking had been slow and careful, as they took time to explore each other, testing their memories of each other's body, the remembered nuances of past encounters evoking a unique pleasure. Now, it was fast and frantic, knowing that the world waited for them.

Eventually, they would have to face it. The bubble would burst and these interludes between the demands of real life would become more precious.

"That's more like it," she said with a grin as his hands deftly unbuttoned her shirt. "Improving with practice."

"Just as well," he mumbled, his lips already finding her erect nipple, "otherwise I would have ripped the bloody thing off." His hands remained busy. Unzipping her jeans, he moved them in one rough tug.

"Stop," she said. "My turn."

With her own well-practised skills, in moments Calum too was standing bare in the middle of his lounge. It was the first time she'd seen him like this in daylight, and she couldn't help but let out a small gasp as she took in the sight of him. He was a substantial man, sturdy muscled legs and nicely curved buttocks, no doubt kept that way by his penchant for racing up mountains. The hairs of his pale red fuzz shone copper in the firelight, giving him a glowing aura.

The sickly sun slanting in from the lounge window glanced off his face, reminding her that anyone passing by would easily spot the two of them, unclothed in the middle of the afternoon. She hoped no lurking guests had already spied them.

"I think I'll pull these."

With a flourish, she drew the heavy curtains across, throwing the room into gloom, lit only by the flicker of the unexpected fire burning in the hearth.

"Mam," he said, seeing her questioning glance. "She always does this when she's expecting me home. Summer or winter, doesn't matter."

The dancing fingers of flame not only warmed the room, but added a touch of romance. Not that there was time for that. Calum lowered himself onto the thick dark rug that sprawled in front of the hearth and drew her down beside him. Although made from long tufts of yarn, it resembled a bearskin brought back from one of his mountain expeditions. The luxurious, shaggy pile cushioned her naked butt a little from the hard wooden floor. It had a slight smoky odour, overlaying the fresh pine-sap smell of the logs stacked high on the nearby hearth. Seeing her grimace of discomfort as she lay back, with one sweep of his hands, a tumble of pillows cascaded from the couch.

"Now where were we?" he said, tucking one under her head at the same time as he straddled her, his strong legs pinning her to the floor.

"Right here," she said, stretching out to caress his erection, marvelling at how, despite its firmness under her hand, the skin was soft and malleable. She gripped more tightly, and her rhythmic movements not only left him groaning with the wanting of her, but sparked her own arousal. Her other hand clawed at the broad muscular chest, desperate to connect with him. Then, unable to hold off any longer, she clasped his shoulder, drawing him into her, guiding him home, making her whole.

They lay in drowsy contentment, limbs intertwined, not yet wanting to release the other. The fire sparked merrily, a warm, happy sound.

Sarah thought they should be polite and venture over to the house. Heather was sure to have dinner organised. But she was reluctant to suggest it. Still revelling in the feeling of skin to skin, even if they were both sticky and sweaty, she wasn't yet ready to release her lover. No, not only her lover, the man she loved, she corrected herself. There it was: she loved him.

She smiled, knowing how Mel would tease her about this sudden decision. But maybe this was the way she was wired. After all, she'd plunged into a relationship with Richard almost overnight. Of course, she thought, as she twined her fingers in Calum's tousled curls, this was different. Who knew how long she'd loved him in that other life? Maybe this wasn't impulsive after all.

"You're looking serious," he said, rolling up on one elbow. He trailed one finger down the length of her nose, gently tracing her lips before leaning to place a kiss on them.

"Just thinking."

"About what?"

"About us."

"Me too," he said. He paused for a moment, with a sharp intake of breath. The beat of his heart quickened against her hand. "And what I'm thinking is—Sarah, I can't see a future without you in it. I want to marry you." His green eyes were determined, as if having come to that decision, he wasn't prepared to take no for an answer. She wasn't going to say no.

"Hmmm, there's the slight problem that I'm still married. Although I can probably untangle myself from that arrangement reasonably quickly."

"So you're saying yes, then?"

"Yes," she said, sealing the word with a kiss. "Yes, Calum MacFarlane, I'll marry you."

Although there was no one else to hear, they lay talking in hushed tones, as if keeping a secret, just between the two of them. Making plans.

A wedding. Where? Eilean Donan—a castle would be fun. Do the full romantic Highland wedding complete with a piper. When? Soon, no more time to waste and after all, autumn in Scotland is beautiful. What about the shop back in Wellington? No problem there, Tandi would love nothing better than for Sarah to give her free rein. Should they live here? And that's when things went wrong.

"This is a great wee cottage," he said. "But only the one bedroom. Wouldn't be any room for kids." It was a statement, but she saw the question in his eyes, and could not suppress the shock in her own.

"Kids." She said the word out loud, registering the fear that it held for her. "You want kids?" She tried hard not to let it sound negative, but it still had the hint of an accusation. He didn't seem to notice.

"Well, maybe not a whole tribe, after all, at our age... I'd be happy with one." He paused for a moment, his face thoughtful. "You know, for years I abhorred the thought of children. I was afraid that after what happened with Hamish, I wouldn't know how to be a father. It scared me. Thought I'd turn out like him. That might be why I've shied away from getting serious enough with any woman. But now I know I'm not Hamish. His blood is not in my veins and I'm not doomed to repeat his mistakes. So yes, I'd like a child, a chance to prove I've shaken off the past, that I'm my own person."

His voice trailed away as his eyes met hers, and her face betrayed all the years of suppressed grief that now overwhelmed her. He knew about Theo. She'd told him that first night they'd gone to dinner, but she had glossed over it, shut it down before he could say much, not wanting to talk about a subject so painful with a man she'd only just met. And then other things had overtaken them and somehow it hadn't come up again until now.

The idea of having another child was repellent. Theo was forever her precious boy, a once in a lifetime; a gift that would not come again. But at the same time, beguiling memories pushed their way through. That indescribable sensation, the delicate flutter of life inside her when he'd first made his presence felt. Holding him as a newborn in her arms, Richard so proud and tender, and she overwhelmed with love for them both.

It was so tempting to give in to those remembered memories and say yes. But the other memories of the pain and loss won out, and she looked at Calum and said the words as kindly as she could, knowing the hurt they would unleash.

"Calum, I'm sorry. I can't do that again."

"Surely with time..." He reached for her arm, turned her to face him, and she could see the thoughts tumbling through his mind as he weighed his words. She leapt in before he could speak.

"Calum, time won't change how I feel. I can't go there. And it's not fair of me to leap into a marriage, with you hoping that I'll change my mind... when I won't."

"Sarah, I love you." There was a desperation in his voice that stabbed at her heart. "Please, let's talk about this."

She turned to him, placed a hand against his cheek, her finger gliding down the golden stubble, and summoned the courage to lift her eyes to his. She needed him to see them, to fully understand what had led her to this.

"Calum, I loved Theo more than anyone in this world, more than life itself. If I could have traded my life for his, even traded Richard's life–I would have done it in a heartbeat. But through my actions, he lost his life. I had my chance to be a mother, and I threw it away with a moment's inattention. They said it was an accident. And it was. But it was an accident that shouldn't have happened."

"You can't blame yourself, Sarah–"

"Oh I can, and I do. I grew up on that farm. I knew the dangers. And I didn't protect my child from them."

"OK," he said slowly. "OK. But isn't learning from the past the way we make sure we don't repeat it?" His words made sense to the rational part of her brain. But he couldn't understand the painful emotions that whirled inside it, overriding all common sense. Deep down, some part of herself, when confronted with the idea of a baby, rejected it.

"Calum, it's more than that. I can't really put it into words. I just need you to trust me when I say I *know* I can't go there again."

She couldn't bear to look at him, to see how her words had extinguished the love and hope in his eyes. She pulled away, pushing back the tears of disappointment, but resigned to this future. It had been amazing while it lasted, but it was over. There was a divide between them impossible to bridge.

She headed for the kitchen, her throat tight, desperate for water and needing a moment to clear her head. Standing at the sink, she analysed what had just happened, replaying their words, teasing apart her feelings, but still came up with the same conclusion: she didn't want a child. And then she thought in horror—what if they'd already created one?

She'd been off the pill for years, relying on condoms whenever she'd quenched her need for sex with some casual no-strings encounter. But she and Calum hadn't even thought about that. Too engrossed in the ghosts of their past to think about the consequences of their current passion. Too enthralled in reacquainting themselves with each other's bodies and falling into the remembered rhythms of making love in that other life.

Even now, she could be pregnant. But at her age, maybe not. Oh god, it was such a mess she couldn't think straight.

But honesty was the only basis for a marriage. She needed him to be clear about how she felt and no matter how carefully she chose her words, it would hurt him. As she lowered herself onto a chair opposite him, she hated the way her return kindled a tiny spark of hope in his eyes. And oh, how she regretted that her words were about to snuff it out.

"Calum, I think it's best we face it now." She tried to be gentle but adamant. "Much as you love someone, if you don't want the same things... Well, it's only going to end up with us resenting each other. I can't do that to you. And I can't do that to me."

And now, her mind still reeling from the events of the past hour, the only thing she did know was that she had to get out of here.

She couldn't bear the wounded silence, the slumped head, the broad back turned on her in rejection. She gathered her clothes from the four corners of the room, dressed quickly, and headed for the only place she could think of to seek help, to find a refuge.

Heather opened the door, her smile of welcome turning to an expression of shock at seeing Sarah's swollen red-rimmed eyes and tear-stained face.

"Heather, I think I need my room back." She struggled to push the words out, her voice choked with misery.

Heather sighed and turned to the pegboard, lifting off a set of keys. As she placed them on Sarah's outstretched hand, her own folded over in a gesture of kindness.

"Oh, honey, I thought it was all going well," she said, her eyes filled with concern. Sarah liked to think it wasn't only Calum she was concerned about, that perhaps her own happiness mattered a little too.

"It was going well. Until it wasn't." Despite her best effort at calm, a sob escaped, and tears welled up.

Sarah drank in the warmth of motherly arms around her, a hand stroking her back in comfort. God, how she'd missed that. Even after all these years, she grieved not only the loss of her mother, but the loss of the life they might have shared. It was ironic that a mother's understanding of her pain should come from Heather, whose own son was the source.

Despite the murmured soothing words, her body still shook, wracked with the anguish. She'd found him and now she was going to lose him again.

"You'll work it out, sweetie.' Her voice was calm, offering the reassurance of experience. "Every relationship has its teething troubles."

"It's more than that Heather, I think it's going to destroy us before we've even begun."

Heather stepped back, holding her at arm's length, her eyes still concerned. "OK, so here's what we're going to do. You go over to the big house and upstairs to your room. It's all made up. You run yourself a nice big bath. There's even a lovely bath oil. An aromatherapy one. Can you do that for me?"

Sarah nodded mutely, scared to speak in case the sobs overtook her again. She was grateful for the instructions, needing someone to tell her what to do, with her mind too clouded by this huge, insurmountable problem that threatened to rip away her happiness.

"In about an hour," Heather said, "I'll send one of the girls up with a hot chocolate, and I'm sure they can find something for you to eat. I bet you didn't have lunch, did you?" Sarah shook her head. No, they'd spent the afternoon feeding other needs.

"You need to take some time to relax, calm yourself down. And then later, if you want, come back over. I know it might be hard to talk about it to me, being his mother, but I do care about you, Sarah."

She nodded again, as if the shock of what had happened between her and Calum had robbed her of speech.

"Thank you, Heather." She managed to get those few words out, offering a weak smile, and did as Heather had said.

As they stood on the doorstep, the old Land Rover came hurtling past them. Calum stared straight ahead, and even from this distance Sarah could see the grim, immoveable set of his face.

"It's OK honey," Heather said. "He'll come back."

But Sarah couldn't help but think she might be gone before he did.

## CHAPTER 46

First Husband

# Sarah

Stirlingshire, Scotland – July 2022

THE WARM GLOW FROM luxuriating in a bath overflowing with bubbles still lingered. The smooth mouth-filling hot chocolate and the buttery shortbread cookies filled the pit in her stomach. But no amount of self-care could wrench Sarah back from the edge of the void on which she teetered. A dark, miserable place, a world without Calum in it. Despite her best efforts, the tears kept coming. Outside, the day slipped away, a layer of gloomy cloud covering the late-afternoon sun, as if mirroring the awful argument that blotted out their shining love.

Some fresh air would help. As a child, whenever bitchy girls at school or the inevitable teenage clashes with her parents had overwhelmed her, she'd always sought refuge in the open fields of the family farm. She rummaged in the suitcase that had mysteriously appeared in her room between her leaving Heather's and unlocking the door. The discreet staff knew how to handle any situation, from molly-coddling celebrities to caring for a woman with a broken heart.

Shrugging on a jacket, she caught sight of herself in the mirror. Eyes still bloodshot and face swollen from tears that even now still lurked close to the surface. Hair a wild tumble, knotted in places, but she lacked the energy to untangle it. Never mind, she'd most likely only encounter a few cows or a marauding fox out there in the paddocks and they wouldn't notice her dishevelled state.

Out of habit, she locked the door behind her, and turning to find the stairs, she looked up straight into a pair of incredibly blue and startled eyes.

"My god, Richard. What are you doing here?" She was as surprised as he was.

"Sarah. I didn't expect to see you here. I thought you'd be at the cottage." He knew then. "I've just got here. Flew up from London. Had some business I couldn't put off. And Jo has arrived from Cromwell. Said he needed to sort a few things back here in Scotland. I thought it was a good opportunity to have a meeting of the distillery partners."

She was suspicious. After that awful night at Abigail Blackwood's party, already four years ago, Richard and she had agreed that they'd move on. Now she'd gone and done it, was it possible he was reneging on the deal? Coming to interfere in her new happiness?

"Oh, and so funny how that happened to coincide with me being here, too. I hope you weren't planning to stick your nose into my life?" Her voice sounded snarky, but she was annoyed at being forced to deal with his presence right now when things were going so terribly wrong.

"Sarah, that couldn't be further from the truth. That's why I asked Heather not to say anything. I didn't want you to know I was here until after I'd gone. The last thing I want is to spoil your happiness."

She knew Richard. After all they'd been through together, all those years, she knew he was telling the truth. His guileless face and direct gaze said it all. He had the same advantage. He knew her too, and he knew there was something very wrong. His raised eyebrows and his scrutiny of her miserable face conveyed an unspoken question.

But unable to find her voice, she scrunched her eyes shut, both to avoid his concerned eyes and to prevent the tears coming again. Strong arms reached out, wrapping her in a firm embrace, and the kindness of the gesture overwhelmed her. Wracking sobs burst through once more. She was making a sodden patch on his broad shoulder, as she'd done many times before.

His solid, steady arms held her as she cried until she could cry no more. He released her carefully, wiped away a last stray tear poised on her cheek.

"Sarah." It was good to hear him say her name. Good to know he still cared for her, although in a different way. She hadn't realised how much she liked the thought that they could retrieve a friendship from the wreckage of their past. He placed his arms lightly on her shoulders, and she raised her head to meet his eyes, hoping that it wouldn't set her off again.

"I don't know what's happened, and I don't expect you to tell me unless you want to. But why don't you come with me? I thought I'd head down the pub—you know the one in the village? I planned not to eat in the house tonight—trying to avoid running into my ex-wife." He shot her a crooked smile at his own attempt at levity, and she couldn't help but smile back.

"As long as you don't mind being seen with someone who looks like they've been dragged through a hedge backwards."

"Not at all. Anyway, you could always pull off messy chic better than anyone. Come on, I've a car out back."

As she slid into the passenger seat of Richard's rental wagon, she couldn't help but steal a glance in the direction of Calum's cottage. She thought she saw a slight movement in one of the curtains, but it was only her imagination. Calum was gone. And now she too needed to escape.

God, she needed something to distance herself from this afternoon's awful scene. She was pleased Calum wasn't there to see her leaving with Richard. She couldn't bear him thinking that not only had she betrayed him with a promise of a future she couldn't deliver, but that she'd betrayed him with her ex-husband.

Years of marriage, shared experiences, common friends and acquaintances, meant that it was easy for them to fill an hour over dinner with easy conversation, avoiding anything potentially upsetting. Sarah enjoyed this feeling of a new normal between them. So it wasn't a myth after all. It was completely possible to remain friends with a man on the other side of a painful uncoupling.

That made her think of Calum. If this thing between them tore them apart, would she ever one day be able to sit across from him like this, as friends? She saw with sudden clarity that she didn't want that. Such was her distress at even considering a watered-down version of her and Calum, she didn't realise Richard had stopped speaking. He sat poised, waiting for her response to a question she hadn't heard. As always, he read the troubled thoughts on her face.

"Sarah?"

Why did he have to say her name like that, so kind and understanding? He reached across to take her hand, his fingers brushing the silver ring.

"Not used to seeing it on that hand. So it's gone that far?"

She nodded miserably, and the tears pushed forward again. She decided that not only did she want to tell Richard; it was probably only Richard who would truly understand her dilemma.

"I'm not sure it's going any further, though." Her heart beat erratically, thumping in her chest. She took a deep breath and plunged in.

"You see, he wants a child. And that's not an unreasonable expectation. Ok, we're not that young, but it's not impossible."

"And you don't." It was ironic that it should be the opposite of how it had been with them, all those years ago, with him the reluctant one. Now she knew what it was like to stand on the other side of such a profound decision.

"No. Well, I don't think so. After Theo…" There, she'd said his name. Usually she held it tight inside, wrapped in love and grief in equal measure. But with Richard, she could say it aloud. "Richard, I feel having another child—well, it's like a betrayal. I can't simply replace him."

"Sarah, you were a good mother." The quiet compassion in his voice was almost unbearable. "You loved that little boy so totally, and you know how much I loved you for that. Still do. That child was the greatest gift you could have given me. He is ours, he always will be." His hand squeezed hers, sending messages of reassurance. She took a deep breath, trying to absorb those feelings, but didn't find calm there.

"I'm so scared, Richard."

"You know, Sarah, I think if we could ask him, Theo wouldn't want you to deny yourself that same love again. Just like I don't want to see you alone. Our time has passed, you, me, and Theo. We were a family, a beautiful family. But you're getting another chance. My old Sarah wouldn't hesitate to grab that chance."

"But what if I muck up again? I wasn't a good mother. I failed him. And I failed you. I couldn't bear it, to repeat those mistakes." There it was. The real source of her fear.

"Sarah, it's time you stopped taking all the guilt on yourself. In fact, it's time you let the guilt go. Both of us would have made different choices if we'd known that our choices would lead to such pain. But you can't let that pain and guilt be your whole life. You have another life to live. You have love to give to another child. And to another man."

In that moment, immense gratitude welled up inside her—that she had chosen such a man as Richard to be her first husband. Someone who still cared enough about her to value her happiness, even after all she'd put him through. His hand tightened on hers, as if willing her the strength to do this. He was right. She could do this.

"So you are going to try and salvage this." Not a question. Not a command. Just an observation, as if he sensed a shift in her, saw her new resolve.

"I am." Saying it out loud to him made her feel brave enough that she could actually do it. She leaned across and kissed him softly on the cheek. "Thank you, Richard." The words were inadequate, but he knew how grateful she was that he'd done this for her.

"Another round, love?"

A lilting Scottish voice interrupted. Sarah looked up to see the attentive pub owner, who'd been looking after them all evening. There were few customers on a Tuesday night, and she was making sure Sarah and Richard were well supplied with food and drink. Even in a crowd, she suspected the handsome blue-eyed George Clooney lookalike would have drawn the woman's attention. The dark hair now threaded with silver sat well with his olive complexion. He was one of those men that would be attractive at any age, drawing women like a magnet.

"Why not?" he said, flashing the woman a friendly smile. Sarah could almost see her knees tremble under his gaze. "But how about a whisky each?"

Sarah nodded. It wouldn't be dinner in Scotland without whisky.

"So, enough about me," she said. "What about you? How are you doing?"

"Me?" He seemed deliberately vague.

"Yes, come on, Richard, you're not old enough to be taking a vow of celibacy." A slow, shy smile spread across his face. Not Richard at all. "There is! Is it anyone I know?" It filled her with glee that she'd been able to worm an admission out of him. She hadn't lost her touch, still able to extract secrets.

"Sort of."

"Tell all please." She wasn't letting him off the hook now.

"Well, you know I said Chelsea's getting married? She and her fiancé, Jack, haven't two cents to rub together. Not surprising after travelling the world for five years. But good on them, they had a great time." Sarah had seen the Instagram posts, some in places that she'd dreamed of seeing, but remained on her bucket list. "They both have jobs in Queenstown. Well paid, but rent there is horrendous and buying a home is near impossible, especially for them with no savings. So Victoria and I have been working on buying them a house." Sarah couldn't help the look of surprise at that. Richard had always been careful not to spoil the girls. A self-made man, he believed kids needed to struggle a bit. "No, not a handout. Just a hand up. Seems the only way kids can get on the property ladder these days."

"So? You and Victoria?" There it was, that sheepish look again.

"Yeah, well, between that and the wedding planning, Victoria and I have seen quite a lot of each other. You know the relationship's always been amicable, but, well, it's become a bit more."

"Richard, I think that's wonderful," she said, and genuinely meant it.

"Yeah, how's that for strange? We even talked about marrying again. Who knows? It wouldn't be unheard of. Look at Liz Taylor and Richard Burton."

She smiled, thinking that still handsome Richard and the still attractive Victoria would make rather fetching older newly-weds.

"About time we sorted that paperwork, then?" she said. They had lawyers trundling through the messy task of dividing up their shared past. In the early days, their crippling grief hadn't only been for Theo. They'd also mourned the demise of their love, making talk of a formal separation too painful. Both had avoided it. But with time's healing hand, their recent conversations via email had been amicable. Much of Richard's substantial assets were tied up in convoluted structures of companies, trusts and off-shore accounts. But he was generous and his offer was far more than she was entitled to, way beyond that old prenup they'd signed. She didn't want or need his money, but his insistence meant she was financially free for life.

"Yes," he said. "Not only for me, but for you, too. Bigamy's still a crime, I think." He took her hand again, pressing it in gentle reassurance. "Trust me Sarah, you can work through this. Work it out with him. You need to go for it. Come on, where's my go-getter?"

It was her turn to offer a shy smile. She was so lucky to have him and their years spent together. She certainly held no regrets for her life having intertwined with Richard's, and now he was giving her the strength to go into the future.

"OK," he said, tossing back his whisky. "Drink up. I'm taking you back now. And you'll get over to that cottage and sort it out."

## CHAPTER 47

## Happy Families

# Calum

Northumberland, England – July 2022

CALUM SLUMPED BACK IN the wooden pew. It wasn't designed to accommodate a man of his size. And it was hard and unyielding beneath him. Perhaps that was the point, ensuring the parishioners didn't relax into a daze during a boring sermon or overlong service. When he ran his hand along the gleaming wood, a fresh smell of furniture polish wafted towards him.

Along one side of the church, bright summer afternoon sun set the stained glass windows on fire, a blaze of saints and heavenly deities beaming their light down onto him. It was still pleasantly cool in here, though; the stonework insulating the interior from the heat of the day.

At intervals, colourful flags and coats of arms adorned the walls, providing a splash of colour against the grey. These Anglican churches seemed positively festive compared to the rather dour interiors of those his mother had dragged him into for the occasional family event. Methodists didn't favour anything too flashy.

Despite the thick patterned carpet in the centre aisle muffling the sound, he was aware of approaching footsteps. He turned to see the Reverend Malcolm Harrop ambling towards him. The lanky figure was the same, the angular face sporting that same wide grin as last time he'd seen him. The only difference was that now the title 'Reverend' was more than a nickname bestowed by his workmates. And that Malcolm was entitled to wear the sombre black uniform of his office, the white clerical dog collar fitting neatly around his still scrawny neck. Calum rose to greet him, finding also the same strong handshake.

"Calum," he said, pulling him into a hug. "It's been too long, mate. Given there's only a border between us when you're not gallivanting around the world, you should have come sooner."

"Rev, it's bloody good to see you too. But the road runs both ways. You haven't been up to see me either, you slack bastard." Then, realising where he was, pulled himself up. "Ah, shit, sorry mate, I suppose swearing is off limits in a church?"

Rev roared with laughter, his braying tones echoing off the high vaulted ceiling. "No worries, mate. No one here to hear it but me, anyway. And even I have a hard job keeping a lid on it. Not easy to lose the habits of a lifetime."

At the age of thirty-nine, Rev had made a life-changing decision. After years of finding himself unofficial chaplain on every construction site he'd worked on, ministering to the rough men in his own quiet way, he'd decided to formalise his calling. Now an ordained Anglican minister, this small parish in the far north of England was his, with his own flock to tend.

"OK," said Calum. "I'll do my best. And trust I won't be struck by lightning if I slip up."

Seeing Rev, he was grateful for the sudden impulse to head south that had led him here. Fleeing from yesterday's disastrous conversation with Sarah, he'd driven blindly, not really caring where the road took him. In the past, when he needed to get away, he'd set himself on a northward course, heading for the Highlands or the islands. They'd always been his place of refuge. But this time, he'd given no thought to the destination, simply needing to put distance between the two of them.

Last night, as the sun was setting, he'd found himself on the outskirts of Carlisle and checked into the first small hotel he saw. Over dinner of a sad, cardboard tasting pizza he'd got to thinking that he wasn't too far away from where Rev was living. So he'd made the phone call. And today, after meandering through the northern English countryside, here he was, set to spend a couple of days with the local vicar who just happened to be his friend.

"Anyway, now you've seen my office, come on over to the house," said Rev. "The girls are beyond excited. It must be two years, but Isla and Sadie haven't forgotten the last time."

Calum hadn't forgotten either. Back then Rev and his wife Annie had been living in Clapham. Calum had made a point of stopping in London to see them on the way back from his first trip to New Zealand. Rev's seven-year-old twins, two delightful little girls with sparkling eyes and mischievous grins, had monopolised 'Uncle Calum', engaging him in backyard cricket, building forts in the lounge and bedtime stories.

"Neither have I," he said. "They're great kids. Bet they've grown." Even then, they'd been tall like their father. "And how's wee Ella?"

"She's three now. Full of herself. She swears she remembers you too. Got really cranky when the twins insisted she was too little last time and couldn't possibly."

The white-washed nineteenth century vicarage was of far newer vintage than the church. With ivy climbing up the stippled walls and a cottage garden out front, it projected an air of idyllic village life. As they approached, the door flew open, and a whirlwind of little people poured out onto the path, racing towards him in a flurry of laughter. Wrapped around Calum's legs, so he could hardly walk, Rev eventually had to peel them off.

"Get inside and wash up for lunch." Rev shooed his unruly offspring towards the door. "Annie's been busy," he said. "You know she loves any excuse to cook."

"And you both know how much I love to eat," said Calum, following him into a rustic kitchen.

"Well, Calum MacFarlane, it's a surprise to see you, but a good one," said Annie, wiping flour-covered hands on a cloth, before wrapping him in a welcoming hug. She was one of those wonder woman types who seemed to juggle career and family with an ease that others would envy. She continued to run her own law practice, specialising in employment cases. Alongside that, she was a nurturing mother who still found time to indulge in her passions: food and marathon running. The guys had always joked that it was a mystery how Rev had ever managed to catch her. And now she'd added vicar's wife to her CV. He must bring Sarah to meet her. They'd get on well. And then he remembered. The way things were at the moment, Sarah and Annie might never meet.

"Rev, get Calum a beer," she ordered. "I'm sorry, lunch will still be half-an-hour. Bloody oven is on the blink."

"See what I mean about the swearing?" Rev gave Calum a knowing wink.

"What's that?" said Annie, returning to rolling out pastry.

"Nothing, love," he said as the two men headed for the deck.

After two of Annie's generous home-cooked meals and an afternoon entertaining lively kids, by nightfall Calum felt as exhausted as the small girl sleeping in his lap. He'd long ago accepted that playing happy families would never be his lot in life. But then Sarah had come along and for a brief moment he'd dared to consider the possibility only to have that small hope dashed. He gazed down at Ella, sprawled across his knees, thinking how she was similar age to Sarah's little Theo when he'd died. And when Annie reached down to pluck the child from him with gentle arms, a mother's tender love written on her face, he thought of Sarah, who'd had her child ripped away from her.

"So, what's troubling you, Cal?" Rev tossed the question at him casually while pouring out a whisky. Calum knew there was no point trying to fob him off, but sat in silence wondering where to start. "This is your friend talking now," Rev said. "Not me practising my minister patter on you."

Rev handed him the glass and Calum paused some more, trying to summon the words while taking a mouthful of the whisky.

"Jesus, Rev. That's a bit rough, mate." The rawness of the alcohol burned his throat. "Remind me to send down a bottle of ours."

Rev laughed. "Sorry, can't afford the good stuff on a vicar's pay." The light moment passed and his eyes met Calum's. "Look, I knew from the moment you called last night that there was something up. It's great to see you, but I know there's more to this than a catch-up with old friends."

Calum took a slow, deep breath. "I've met someone. Someone special. Someone that I thought I could have all of this with—marriage, a family."

"And?"

"And now I have to choose. If I choose her, then the family bit is out of the question. If I want a family, I'm going to lose her."

"She doesn't want children?"

"It's not quite that simple Rev."

"Tell me about it. We've got as long as it takes."

If there really was a God, Calum had to thank him for giving him friends like these. But after two days wrapped in their bustling family, it was time to go home and face his life once more. He had a carefully wrapped batch of Annie's famous Eccles cakes on the seat beside him. She stood in the gateway, hands resting on the shoulders of the dark-haired twins, so like their mother except for the matching toothy smiles that were all Rev. Ella giggled in her father's arms, waving a chubby hand at him. The sight of their beautiful family emphasised further the sorrow he felt, knowing this experience might never be his. However, spending time with them had also heightened his appreciation of Sarah's grief. She'd had this. And she'd lost this. And perhaps it had broken something inside of her that no amount of love could fix.

Rev swivelled the wriggling child under one arm and stepped forward to lean in the open window. "Just take it slowly, mate. Be gentle with her. If you love each other, you'll work it out."

He could be patient. Give her the gift of time. But as Calum drove north, the chorus of farewells ringing in his ears, he wasn't sure Rev's usual wisdom would be enough to get him through. Not this time.

## CHAPTER 48

Journey's End

Sarah

Stirlingshire, Scotland – July 2022

THE TWO DAYS OF waiting were the hardest two days Sarah had experienced in a long time.

But now Calum was back, it didn't feel like she'd had anywhere near the time she needed to prepare for this conversation. Her emotions were in turmoil, lurching her from despair to hope within seconds.

She allowed him a couple of hours to himself after she saw the Land Rover pull back into the driveway. It gave her time to rehearse the words, even though she doubted they'd come out in that order when the time came.

She tried to hold on to the brave feelings Richard had encouraged in her. On Tuesday night he'd literally shoved her from his car, urging her to go and lay herself bare in front of Calum, to believe that she could be the wife he needed, a mother to his child, their child.

But Calum wasn't there. And again, when Richard had left yesterday, the confidence he'd projected in his last kiss on her cheek, that it would all be all right, had carried her through till now.

The cottage was dark, and she fumbled in the still unfamiliar gloom, feeling her way through to the lounge.

Calum sat in the exact same place as where she'd left him: hunched on the couch, beneath his feet the rug on which only days earlier they'd lain basking in the afterglow of their love.

He'd let the fire go out, only a few still smouldering embers remaining, enough to light the uncertainty on his face as he lifted his eyes in recognition. The bleakness within them stabbed at her heart. A stab of guilt that it was she who'd robbed them of their spark.

"You've been with Richard?" To her surprise, there was an undercurrent of jealousy in his voice when she tried to explain.

"He was here to meet with your mother and Jo. Distillery business."

"I didn't ask what he was doing here. I asked if you've been with him."

He delivered the words through gritted teeth. The waves of emotion he wrestled with were visible on his face even in the dimly lit room.

She sat beside him, maintaining a careful space between them, sensing that he might not be ready to accept her touch. She kept her voice calm and gentle, despite wanting to project that dark anger back at him. But no, this man loved her and she owed him an explanation.

"Richard and I had dinner at the pub. It was only dinner. Our marriage is long over, Calum. You have nothing to worry about there. We talked."

"So you've made him privy to our problems. I thought, ex-husband or not, in fact, especially *because* he's your ex-husband, he's the last person you should be talking to about this. It's not as if he's going to have an objective viewpoint."

There was a cold edge to his voice she hadn't anticipated.

She risked placing her hand over his, hoping to channel her sincerity with a physical connection. He didn't shrug it off, which she took as a good sign.

"Calum, I ran into him by accident—at the big house. Heather told him we were here. He wasn't expecting to see me—thought I was in the cottage with you. He was trying to avoid me, avoid us. And he didn't ask. He saw I was upset, but he didn't say a word."

"And what did you tell him?"

"Only what I'm going to say to you now. If you'll hear me out."

Her voice shook, as did her hands, and he turned at that, instinctively responding to her distress, even though things between them were still tense. God, this man is special, she thought. Despite all the inner turmoil, the hurt she'd caused, he knew she needed him.

"Calum, I've had a child, been a mother. And I've lost a child. Losing Theo damaged me in ways I didn't even realise until the other day. Talking to Richard helped me understand that it's not that I don't want another child, but I'm scared. Scared that it will diminish the memories of the child I've lost, replace those memories with new ones, send Theo even further away. And I'm scared that I'll be a bad mother. I couldn't protect my first child. What right do I have to think I'll be any better the second time around?"

He reached for her then, his fingers caressing her face, tracing the damp line that edged down her cheek.

Her voice came out in a whisper. "And you see, Richard understands those fears. He lived that time with me."

"If you give me the chance I'd understand them too, help you, be there for you."

"I know that now. But Richard's not your enemy, Calum. He's the one who told me that's what I have to do. Let you in. And I want to."

He drew her to him, his embrace so tight it almost crushed her, his relief palpable. She was sure he must feel hers, too. It was a surreal feeling; that she may have just pulled their relationship back from a precipice by simply opening herself to him. She'd learned that from her past failures.

"I love you Calum." She met his green eyes, transformed from an angry glare, now bright with hope. "And I want us to have a child. I've done a lot of soul-searching these last two days. And I think that with you by my side, I can overcome my fears. You were right, given time, I can do this. With you, I can do this."

"God, you don't know how much that means to me," he said, leaning to press his lips to her forehead. They sat like that for a moment, bathing in the bliss of that simple connection.

"And I'm sorry I let the old green-eyed monster rear its head when you mentioned Richard. I let my insecurity do the talking, and it was wrong of me. It was good that you had someone to talk to. That Richard could help you. Unfair of me to expect otherwise. Especially as I've had help with some soul-searching too." He could see her curiosity and went on. "I've got an old friend who's a minister. Yeah, I know," he said, at her raised eyebrows. "Not what you'd expect. But then he's not your average minister. You'd like him."

"Perhaps you should phone him up and ask him to marry us? That's if you still want to..."

They needed to get onto that soon. And she already liked the sound of this minister. After all, he'd been part of this new understanding they'd brokered between them.

"Later," he said. "Great idea, but right now there's something else I'd rather do."

He swept her up in one effortless motion, his strong arms rendering her as light as a feather, and carried her through to his bedroom.

"I think making love on the rug once is more than enough for one week," he said, laying her carefully on his sprawling bed.

And in their coming together, there was both passion and forgiveness. And the still faintly frightening but thrilling idea that out of their love might come a baby, joining them together in an unbroken bond.

----

It had been a long time since Heather had a gathered a family at her table. Food was her language of love and she showered it generously on them the next night as they gathered in her modest dining room.

Freed from poor Hamish's glowering presence, Jo took his place at the head of the table, Heather beside him, her hand under the table often resting on his knee as if checking that he was actually there. Calum sat at the other end, facing his father. No one could deny their relationship seeing the two of them together, those green eyes a mirror of the other, that same mouth, both sporting a grin of delight at having a second chance with the women they loved.

"So how did the meeting go?" Calum asked, obviously curious about his parents' plans.

"Pretty good, I think, wouldn't you say Heather?"

Jo still hadn't lost the habit of deferring to her as the major partner in the distillery alongside Richard. His own modest shareholding, earned as part of his remuneration package, along with bonuses for the success of the New Zealand operation, didn't give him much say. But that would soon change.

"Yes, it went well. Richard agreed it made sense for Jo to return here permanently. He's built up a good team in Cromwell, and young Nathan's more than capable of taking over the reins. Richard will keep an eye on things."

"Which means…" Jo had a twinkle in his eye and the look of love on his face shone for them all to see. "Well," he said a little shyly, "Heather and I have some news. We're getting married."

"That's bloody marvellous," said Calum, leaping to his feet, shaking his father's hand and embracing his mother in one of those huge bear hugs.

Sarah smiled at Heather across the table, filled with happiness for her future in-laws, and for Calum, seeing his parents reunited. With Richard's parents never being part of her life, she'd not had to navigate the role of daughter-in-law before. But she had a good feeling about this family's future.

"So," said Jo, again a little hesitant. "Well, your mother and I want to know if you might be doing the same?"

"No might about it." Calum looked at her with a flush of excitement. "Just as soon as her ladyship here dispenses with her previous husband."

To hear him joking about Richard like this told her he'd accepted her assurance that there was no more than a mutually respectful friendship between them.

"After all, we intend to make you two grandparents soon enough, so it would be nice to have some wedding photos without a giant baby bump intruding." Seeing the look of delight on Heather's and Jo's faces, Sarah was pleased he'd shared their decision.

"You know," she said, a sudden impulsive thought leaping into her head, "we could have a double wedding. You men in your kilts and we ladies in the tartan too—after all, we've both done the white wedding before. What do you think, Heather?"

"Ach, no," Jo interrupted. "We wouldn't want to intrude, would we love?"

Heather nodded, although Sarah could sense her reluctance to shelve the idea.

"Don't be silly. I think it would be wonderful. We could have a piper and a reception over at the big house." Sarah's mind was running away with images.

"We could get married at the castle," Calum suggested, joining in with the plan. "Rev will expect to come up and do the honours. I know three little girls who'd love to be flower girls."

"Oh well," said Jo, "you women sort it out. We'll just make sure our kilts are clean and turn up, won't we, son?"

It was the first time she'd heard him say it, and Sarah's heart swelled with happiness for Calum, knowing how he'd craved the love of a father, a man who was proud to call him son.

———

They stepped out of Heather's cosy house, into the chill of an autumn night. The Milky Way sprawled over their heads, dominating the moonless sky. Hand-in-hand, they followed the trail of glowing solar lights out to the driveway, weaving their way around the neat gardens alongside the big house. Sarah had the sudden urge to stop, as if the rough stone beckoned her.

"I have the strangest feeling, just here," she said, her palm flat against the wall, as a small current tingled through her. She closed her eyes to better take it in. "It's like an echo. Of you. Back then."

"It's the me in the here and now that you need to worry about,' he said, drawing her away and into his arms. His kiss grounded her in the present, the familiar smell of him, the taste of his lips, the slight smokiness of that last whisky lingering there.

"Look." His voice in her ear was a whisper, as if any loud noise might chase away the sight. "They're putting on an encore performance."

Off to the west, it was as if someone had drawn a curtain of light across the sky. The aurora leapt into action. Pulsating colours billowed before their eyes, like gauzy technicolour fabric, sheer as a dragonfly's wing. They stood in awe, hands entwined and hearts singing, as once again the universe rejoiced in the love they'd found on a lonely mountaintop.

# Sarah

Edinburgh, Scotland – December 2023

"THANKS FOR DOING THIS," he said, ever the gentleman as he held the cab door open.

"I should thank you," she said. "Dinner with Alex MacLeod. Lots of women would kill to be in my shoes. After all, he's one hot Scot."

"You already have one hot Scot. So keep your greedy eyes off him. Spare some for the rest of the girls out there," he admonished with mock seriousness. "Anyway, he already has a Kiwi wife, and from what I know about you women from down under, one is more than enough."

She laughed. "Oh, yes, I know I'm more than enough for you," she said, shooting him a knowing look. "You still look like you're recovering."

He grinned, his face flushed with the memory. "An afternoon tumble in the sheets with you—well, let's say I think I used up more calories than bagging a Munro."

"But I'm more fun to bag."

"God, you're wicked. So much so that I'd like to aim for a second summit later on, if you're keen?"

She glanced up to see the cab driver observing them in the rear-view mirror with a smile. The Perspex barrier was obviously not soundproof. She imagined theirs wasn't the first suggestive conversation he'd been privy to.

Calum's face became serious again as he turned back to the topic of their dinner. "I do appreciate you coming along. You know this project means a lot to me. My career's been good so far, but with Alex on board—well, the power of two hot Scots, it's going to be huge. And the potential spin-offs. merchandising, brand ambassador stuff, outdoor wear and the like. And Alex already has an idea for us to write a book. Said some other guys did a similar thing, and it's still earning them good money years later."

Alex MacLeod was every bit as mesmerising in real life as on screen. He had the charming Scottish accent that seemed to lend a suggestive note to even the most innocent comment. She wondered if the accent had always appealed, or only since Calum had come into her life, with his voice soft as velvet, rolling 'rs' like a cat purring in her ear, as he whispered "I love you Sarah MacFarlane" in the night.

Alex's wife, Kate, was best described as a Kiwi Cameron Diaz, huge soft eyes and a wide smile, blonde silky hair loose over a casual shirt and jeans. Sarah felt an immediate affinity with this woman that went beyond their shared country of birth. They fell into an easy conversation like old friends reunited. Given that Calum and Alex seemed to have developed a full-on bromance, it boded well that she and Kate bonded over dinner.

"So, how did you two meet?" Sarah asked Alex, curious to know how a girl from Auckland had ended up married to a Scottish film star.

"We first met on Barra, an island in the Outer Hebrides." Alex paused, casting a questioning look at his wife, and Sarah was sure she saw a slight, almost imperceptible shake of her head, as if to say "Not here," before he went on. "But unfortunately, we lost each other. For a very long time."

Sarah was listening to him but watching Kate. Her grey-blue eyes held sadness, like some unspoken sorrow lurked beneath the perfect life she projected to the world. Perhaps they were more alike than she'd thought. She knew what it was like to struggle to push back the past, keep one step ahead of the black dog of depression, stop it using grief to trip you up and snatch you into its jaws.

"But we've been making up for it these last few years," Kate said. "It's been a whirlwind, especially since Sorcha was born." They had a nine-month-old and the moment her name fell into the conversation, their faces became animated. "All those years as a teacher, I had no idea what parents went through. Let's say I've found a new appreciation of the work that goes into a child before it walks into the classroom."

Kate's laughter suggested she was in the throes of the typical exhilarating highs and exhausting lows of motherhood.

It was Sarah's turn to hold back the sadness as Calum quietly reached across his hand under the table, blanketing hers softly, knowing the smile on her face masked the hurt of a woman who had experienced nurturing a child, only to have him taken from her. Her little Theo, forever three. She held him close in her heart, and she knew Richard did the same.

But her other hand rested lightly on her stomach, protective of the new life swelling there. At four months along, it was still unseen, but definitely there. She and Calum exchanged a smile, not yet ready to share this knowledge with the world.

Seeing Kate and Alex MacLeod also allayed some of her fears of them becoming parents at this age. She'd brushed aside the risks of an older mother giving birth, knowing that Calum deserved this. He would be an amazing father, having vowed to make up for the flawed relationship he'd had with his own. There would no doubt be challenges, but they'd make a good go of it, perhaps with new friends like these to offer advice.

"So, Sarah, you trust me to look out for your husband on this wild expedition?" Alex was teasing her. They both knew that it was Calum, the outdoorsman, who'd most likely be hauling Alex the last few feet up the Munros they intended to bag in their TV series.

"Alex, as long as you have a flask in your pack, I'm sure he'll follow you anywhere," she said.

"Only if it's filled with MacFarlane's," said Calum. "None of the cheap stuff."

"Speaking of which, how about we have one now to seal the deal?" Alex waved over one of the wait staff.

The four of them clinked glasses with a resounding, "Slainte mhath!"

Sarah thought about how the universe threw certain people across your path at the point you needed them. A warmth grew inside her, not the effect of the whisky since she'd opted for sparkling water, hoping that the MacLeods wouldn't associate her avoidance of alcohol with the secret of her pregnancy. No, she had a sense that this was the first day of a long and happy future friendship with this couple, with whom they shared so much common ground.

---

"I wonder what he meant?" she said as the taxi wound back through the cobbled streets of the Old Town. "That they lost each other?"

"Hmmm, not sure," said Calum, sounding preoccupied, his mind no doubt still tangled in visions of striding up mountain pathways alongside Alex, a camera crew swarming around them, recording their adventures.

She sat in silence. The dark thoughts that circled her from time to time grew emboldened, thrusting themselves closer, cloying fingers stretching towards the gossamer veil of her happiness, trying to rip it away. Life, love, loss. It was all so tenuous, and there was no way to control it. You were a victim to the whims of time and fate, unable to battle against them.

In panic, she looked across at Calum, as if expecting to find him missing. But he was there, and she snuggled closer, to feel his comfortable warmth. She hesitated a moment, reluctant to give voice to her thoughts and erase that hint of a smile that played around his mouth. But knew that this was the key to their relationship—bringing things into the open, not harbouring secret doubts and fears. That was the only thing that could undermine them. She wouldn't let it.

"Does it still frighten you?" she said. "All of this? Our life?"

He pulled her head to lie against his chest, understanding her need to be cradled, his hand stroking her hair, but saying nothing.

"Calum, I'm scared. Sometimes, like today, I have this horrible sense that one day, in the blink of an eye, I'll turn around and find you gone. And maybe worse still, I won't even know what I've lost. Isn't that part of loving someone? That you feel their loss in every part of you? And a bit of the pain never goes away, to remind you, always. When Theo died..." She shuddered at the memory, eyes closed as if trying to block it out, at the same time treasuring its existence. "The possibility that I might lose you and not feel the pain of it. It frightens me."

"Yes, it frightens me, too," he said. "But I've learned something that gives me peace of mind. In this life, and that other strange half-remembered one, we are together. Two out of two, we've found each other. And so I believe that in a world full of limitless lives, of endless possibilities, I will always find you."

She clung to him, trusting in his love, and wanting to believe as well, willing the silver band on her finger to act as a talisman, a compass, always drawing her back to her true North, guiding her footsteps on the path to him.

If you loved this book, I'd appreciate it if you have time to leave a review on your favourite retailer, review site, or social media.

And if why not grab *Sydney Streets* a bonus chapter for this book available on my website.

### Sydney Streets

Richard Norton's mind should be on business, but here in Sydney all he can think of is Sarah Mitchell. Has he got what it takes to make this acquisition?

www.carolinecorvin.com

For details on all books in the series, turn over a few pages to see more from Caroline.

# Acknowledgments

Oops, I DID IT again! Wrote a book... If only it was that easy. But just because it isn't easy doesn't mean it's not a wonderful experience. And it's an even better experience when you share it with those who care about you. I am forever grateful for the universe that gave me a husband who loves books, who shares my obsession with reading, who understands the joy I gain from writing, and above all, doesn't begrudge the time it takes to bring a book into existence. David, you're my true North.

Once again, I've had a brilliant team supporting me. Jacqueline Cangro, my editor, you are such a gem. I am in awe both of your knowledge and the way you share it. Working with you is a pleasure. My Grenwyvern Publishing support team; you know how much it means that you have my back. And finally, a sincere thanks to my fellow writers. To quote one of the many writers' groups I belong to: "Writing is a solitary practice, but it doesn't have to be a lonely one." And it's not when you have these people cheering you on. We all rise together.

*Caroline*

Caroline Corvin

WHEN NOT WRITING, YOU can usually find Caroline with her nose in a book from any one of an eclectic mix of favourite genres. While officially a resident of Auckland, New Zealand's stunning City of Sails, she has become adept at juggling her love of writing alongside her other magnificent obsession of travelling the world. Caroline didn't set out to write romance, but her characters took control the moment she let them loose on the page, reminding her that finding happy ever afters are the reason she's one of those people who sometimes reads the last page first, just to be safe.

Follow Caroline Corvin on all your favourite
social media or review sites!
Visit her website: www.carolinecorvin.com

# More From Caroline

Caroline's Tangled In Time Series takes time travel romance and twists it in a new direction. Each book can be read as a satisfying standalone, so if you haven't already, check out the other titles.

Find the links to purchase on her website.

The prequel novel, Tangled In Time is available free!

www.carolinecorvin.com

# Tangled In Time

**A free-spirited artist, a wandering astronomer,
and an instant connection.
Is their future painted in the stars?**

Landscape painter Blair Silvestri hasn't time for stargazing —or love. It's her immediate, more precarious situation that she needs to focus on for now. Daniel Tremayne spends his life looking skyward. Maybe that's why he's made such a mess of all his relationships so far. A trick of time throws them together, but also threatens to tear them apart.

# *Tangled Threads*

**What if her future lies
in a time tangled past?**

Now the last of those who loved her are gone, there's nothing left for young teacher Kate Moreton in New Zealand. It's time for her to forge a new life. Pinning her hopes of finding friends, family—and maybe even love—elsewhere, she heads for the bright lights of London. What Kate doesn't know is this journey will lead her to two men, two loves, and two lives. And offer a future lifeline when her world falls apart.

# Tangled Hearts

**Two loves, two lives. One heart shattered.**
**Can a love from another time heal the pain of the present?**

Young emergency room doctor, Layla Angell, is living the dream: in the perfect job, surrounded by friends who are like family—including the man she's always wanted to be more than a friend. Life is full of potential. But the future is never promised. Caught in a time-twisted love triangle, Layla's connection to two men, across two parallel lives, offers a second chance at happiness beyond tragedy—if she can learn to accept the impossible.

# *Tangled Past*

**When the past holds you in its power,
is love enough to set you free?**

Cassiopeia Tremayne isn't looking back at her sleepy hometown. Facing the future, all she can see is her dream of being a writer, just there on the other side of her final high school year. But Cassie's future also includes navigating the turbulent waters of two parallel but intertwined lives, forcing her to confront truths about herself, her family and the men she loves in two separate worlds. And when those worlds collide, will love give her strength enough to rewrite the past and become the hero of her own story?

www.ingramcontent.com/pod-product-compliance
Lightning Source LLC
Chambersburg PA
CBHW030826110726
47900CB00006B/1767